The Day of
Small
Beginnings

As always, if we can help you in any way,
please contact the church here at:
P.O. Box 68309, Indianapolis, IN 46268
(317) 335-4340

©1996 Kingdom Publishing

Cover photograph © Dennis Mosner

ISBN 0-9627202-1-6

A Note From the Author(s)

When pressed to take responsibility for this book, we were in a bit of a dilemma. Unlike most other novels and books which are written by one person, this book really was a corporate effort. What follows below (in no particular order) is a list of the saints who, as God enabled, participated in the authoring process of this book. Beyond these, dozens of others were involved through editing, reviewing, offering suggestions and investing their hearts.

Preparing this gift from the Church here to the Body of Christ as a whole has been a privilege and a lot of fun. Proceed prayerfully with the intent to be permanently altered — not just entertained or informed. This is about the stuff for which the Universe was built and for which Jesus died. Our hope is that this book will kindle the desire among God's people to understand, fight for, and experience the true meaning of the Body of Christ.

Mike A., Debbie W., Anthony L., Andy R.,
Sharon R., Sheri C., Nick B., Chris Z., Tim C., David W.,
David W. (this is not a typo), Laurel S., Russ J., Bryan B.,
Kevin M., Molly K., Mike P., David M., Kathy P.

Preface

This novel is about Christianity as you have probably never experienced it but have always known, deep in your heart, it should be. Be like the Pearl merchant that Jesus commended and treasure this Dream — His Dream — in your heart. Let it fill your soul and alter your destiny forever!

God is building something that is made of His Son Jesus, worthy of His Abiding Presence for all Eternity. It is being forged at this very moment in the hearts of those who care. He is enlisting men and women with the vision, courage, and a willingness to pay the price of bringing to a conclusion the Ancient Task. As weak and foolish as we are, that's what we must be pursuing, with all of our hearts.

While it may seem like the Church has a long, long way to go in order to fulfill her calling...don't be disheartened. It will happen! As our brother Zechariah encouraged some builders of God's House long ago — in a time when things looked bleak: "Do not despise the day of small beginnings." (Zecheriah 4:10)

MAIN CHARACTERS

Hampton Street
Wayne Davidson — Pastor
Emily Davidson — Wayne's wife
Blake, Amanda, Ashley — Wayne's children
Hal Ramsey — Elder
Virginia Ramsey — Hal's wife
Tom Hartley — Elder

The Campus
Rick Adams — Student
Eric — Rick's roommate
Amy — Rick's girlfriend
George Archer — Bible professor

Pine Ridge
Ted and Carolyn Stone
Alan and Marsha Hart
Brian and Susan Stephens
Don Chambers

Metro Chapel
Nelson Reynolds — Senior Pastor
Phil Malone — Associate Pastor
Steve and Teresa Parker — Home group leaders

Others
Tony Veneziano — Local waiter
Mark Wallace — Friend from out of town
Luis Rodriguez — Friend from out of town

This is what the Sovereign Lord says:

I Myself

Will search for My sheep

And look after them.

Ezekiel 34:11

The Awakening

1

DUSK PRESSED IN around Wayne Davidson's car as he drove his family to Hampton Street Bible Church. It was almost 7:30, as best he could tell, and a black satin blanket studded with diamonds was quickly replacing the soft pastels spreading out across the western horizon.

Wayne hardly noticed the colors reflecting in his rearview mirror as he drove toward the building. His mind was busy sorting the points he hoped to cover in his Bible class.

Four more days 'til Sunday, Wayne thought. Wednesday signaled the midweek count down. *Need to get that outline done for Sunday's sermon.* He turned on to Hampton Street as he'd done a hundred times before. *Check Smith's Anecdotes and Illustrations,* he reminded himself.

Street lights now illuminated familiar trees and other landmarks as he ascended the last hill before reaching the church driveway. As the vehicle quickly passed the church sign, it occurred to Wayne that the sign had an almost neon glow to it, reminding him of pictures he'd seen of Las Vegas. *Was that blue and pink? Silly thought.*

The car was parked now, and Emily and their three children were already out of the car. Tonight the building looked different to Wayne, though he wasn't quite sure why. He exited his car and slowly made his way toward the entrance twenty yards or so behind the rest of his family. He noticed that the parking lot was full. *Everyone's on time,* reflected Wayne. But something seemed odd. For a brief second the thought crossed his mind that he was about to become the victim of a surprise birthday party. *But it's not my birthday.*

Loud music escaped through the open doors as Wayne traversed the broad sidewalk up to the entrance. *Huh? That's not a praise tape.* Sometimes their audio technician would play music over the P.A. until things got started, but this music sounded more like something from a night club. *Strange.*

Wayne moved into the foyer, where several folks were conversing and holding refreshments. *Refreshments? Maybe it's a party.* The music seemed much quieter now, and Wayne scanned the room looking for Hal or one of the other elders so he could ask what was going on. *Why wasn't I told about this? Odd!*

Just as Wayne spotted Hal on the other side of the foyer, a burst of laughter spilled out of the open auditorium doors. As Wayne glanced into the auditorium, a troubled feeling twisted his gut. He took a second look.

An array of small round tables occupied by various members of the congregation filled the open room. *What's going on?* A single candle sat shimmering in the center of each table, betraying appetizers and assorted beverages. *Where are the pews?* Wayne noticed a smoky haze hanging over the auditorium that gave the room a disturbing, bar-like appearance. Two more waves of laughter escaped through the double doors.

Cautiously, Wayne moved closer to investigate. What had been a muffled voice over the sound system now became clear to him. A man Wayne didn't recognize stood on the platform in a leisure suit holding a microphone just below his chin. "...and the man says, 'Is the Pope Catholic?' And the waiter says to him, 'Yeah, but when he sees this, he might change his mind.'" Another pounding wave of laughter erupted from the crowd.

Wayne quickly turned around and found Hal staring at him from across the room. Wayne wanted to shout, "What is going on?" But he felt paralyzed. Why couldn't he speak? Why couldn't he move? *Must talk to Hal!* His feet felt like lead. *Something's wrong!* Each step took a lifetime. *Why is Hal grinning? Lord, what's happening?*

Finally, Wayne was in front of Hal. He wanted to pull Hal aside to emphasize the urgency of his confusion. He reached out to put his hand on Hal's shoulder. *I'm falling!* Clumsily he grasped for Hal, who only stared at him with a sinister grin. *Hal, help me!*

Every movement took place in slow motion. Wayne grabbed Hal's sweater with both hands as he tottered backward. His fingers sank deep into Hal's chest and turned cold. *Ice!* The sweater peeled easily from Hal's torso as Wayne hit the ground. *That smell! Ahhhh! Dead animal.* Wayne looked at Hal in horror. *Bones!*

Hal's torso opened. Hundreds of rotting bones spilled from his chest, instantly burying Wayne. *Death!* Panic seized Wayne. He couldn't breathe. *That smell! Sickening.* He kicked and pushed, closing his eyes in a silent scream.

Emily Davidson gripped her husband's arm firmly. "Wayne! Sweetheart, wake up!"

Wayne's eyes opened wide. Beads of sweat glistened digital-clock red on his forehead. He sighed deeply, then began to relax.

"Are you all right?"

"Yeah...yeah...I'm okay." Wayne didn't feel like talking. This was the third time he'd had the same dream and he wanted to dissect it in his mind before it evaporated. "Just a bad dream, thanks. Why don't you go back to sleep, Honey," Wayne whispered.

Emily hesitated. "If you're really okay..." She kissed him on the cheek, turned over and was soon fast asleep. Wayne didn't sleep again that night.

2

AT THE GAS STATION the next morning, Wayne sat with his head pressed against the steering wheel. His mind was still captured by last night's dream. He jumped as he heard a sharp rap on his passenger window. Looking up, he saw a long–haired, teenage boy dressed completely in black. Wayne reached across and cranked down the window.

"Yeah...uh, Sir?" The young man, who couldn't have been over sixteen, placed both half–gloved hands over the top edge of the window and talked through the gap. "Could you help me?"

Wayne regained his composure. "What's up?"

"Oh, I missed my ride. Just need a lift home. I only live a couple miles from here." The young man pointed in the direction Wayne's car was facing. "I was walkin' by here, saw your car at the pump and...thought I'd ask. What d'ya say, man?"

"Um..." Wayne paused, evaluating the implications of the request. "Sure...I guess. Hop in." Wayne smiled slightly as he gave in to the tug of compassion.

As the young man climbed in, Wayne rolled down his window in an attempt to dilute the pungency of his passenger's love for cigarettes.

"Where do you live?" Wayne asked, taken aback by the silver cross dangling from the young man's ear.

"216 Edgewood Avenue. It's in Prestwick. Do you know it?"

"You live in Prestwick?" Wayne asked skeptically.

"Yeah, just off 7th."

"Right...I know where it is." He put the car into drive and headed toward the street. "You just don't seem like the Prestwick type."

"My name's Philip." He stuck his hand out to Wayne as they sat waiting for traffic to clear. "But my friends call me Loner. It's a nickname, you know."

Wayne took the hand and grasped it firmly, "Wayne...Wayne Davidson."

Spotting a gap in the tight morning traffic, Wayne lunged the car onto the busy street.

"What do you do, Wayne?" Philip fingered the lapel of Wayne's suit jacket in mock inspection. "Sell insurance? Play the market? What?"

"Actually," Wayne admitted, "I'm a pastor."

"Really? Hmmm. That's what my grandma wants me to be. My dad's a pastor."

Wayne looked again at Philip as they turned the corner, raised an eyebrow at the ink dragon on his arm and kept his sarcasm to himself. *Right!* He eased the car in front of 216 Edgewood. "So...your dad's a pastor?" He craned his neck to look at the three–car garage and impressive house, half–hidden behind two towering oaks.

"Yep. Sure is. Hey, thanks for the ride." Philip slid out of the car and started up the lawn. He turned and gave a loud, "God bless you, man," then disappeared, laughing.

Wayne grimaced as he watched after Philip. *So, that's a pastor's kid at age sixteen?* He turned the car around, fretting the future of his seven–year–old son, Blake. *But I suppose a pastor's kid is the same as any other kid in the youth group. Scary thought!*

As he drove toward the office, Wayne took a mental inventory of the teens at Hampton Street Bible Church. *Wow, what a mess!* He struggled inwardly to find a significant difference between the teens in his own youth group and those of the world. It bugged him that the bulk of the teenagers in his congregation had a look in their eye that said, "Yeah, I'm worldly...so what?" And a few seemed more than worldly. Their hearts seemed dark.

HAL RAMSEY LEANED against the door frame of Wayne's office. "You look terrible, Wayne. Are you feeling all right?"

"Ah, I had a rough night last night, Hal," Wayne answered. He shuffled papers on his desk, waiting to see if Hal planned to probe deeper.

"Is, uh..." Hal hesitated, trying to be tactful. "Is...everything okay at home?" He looked down, shifted to the opposite side of the door and looked up again.

Wayne debated frantically in his mind. *He'll think I'm crazy. So what? It's the truth.* "Yeah, everything's fine," he answered unconvincingly.

"Emily and the kids?"

"Oh no, they're fine. I just—"

"What is it, Wayne?" Hal interrupted.

"Well...I know this is going to sound kind of crazy, but...I had a pretty intense dream last night. I couldn't get back to sleep."

"Oh, is that all? I thought it was something serious," Hal chuckled lightly.

"Well, it is," started Wayne defensively. "I mean..." He sighed. "It's the third time I've had this dream."

"You've had the *same* dream three times?" exclaimed Hal, now not sure how seriously he should approach this.

"Well, not exactly the same. I mean...it changes." Wayne struggled for words and wondered if he really wanted to say more. "Each time it kind of gets longer and…and more detailed."

Hal Ramsey was clearly uncomfortable and scrambled for the perfect thing to say. "Sounds pretty strange," he said lightly. He took a deep breath and stood up straight. His countenance took on an aura of seriousness. With all candor, he looked Wayne in the eye and cautioned, "Wayne, you know what my advice to you is?" He paused and took another deep breath. "Lay off the lasagna." Then he released an exaggerated laugh and repeated, "Get it? Lay off the lasagna!?"

Wayne didn't laugh. His heart sank. For Hal's sake he conceded a smile. *That's fine. He doesn't understand. That's fine.*

Eager to change the subject, Hal said, "Hey, you and Em still comin' over for dinner tonight? Ginny's fixing up some of those pizzas you like so much!"

"Yeah, sure." Wayne sat up straight and again shuffled the things on his desk. "We'll be there."

"Good, good. Then I'll see you 'round 6:00." Hal looked at his watch. "Well, I gotta run. I'll see you tonight."

3

THE AIR WAS THICK at the Davidsons' Saturday night.

"I told you to hold my calls!" The curt phrase echoed around the hallway and into the kitchen as Emily Davidson felt a familiar knot rising in her stomach. Rounding the corner, a quick glance at her husband's countenance confirmed it — he was angry.

"For crying out loud, Emily, how in the world will I ever get this sermon ready for tomorrow morning if I can't get some peace and quiet?" Wayne's gaze was stern as he held her eyes in silence for added effect. It wasn't rage. It was just that constant underlying tension that pervades most families.

"I'm really sorry. I must have misunderstood you." Emily replied guardedly. "I did tell most people you were tied up." She forced a smile and searched Wayne's face for some sign of reassurance. "I didn't know you couldn't have *any* calls. It's Ed Lowry. He said it would just take a minute."

"Oh, never mind," Wayne resigned, sighing. "I'll take it. He

14

probably just wants to tell me about the schedule he's prepared for this fall."

"What schedule?" Emily wondered, relieved at the change of topic.

"The football schedule — nothing important. You remember, last year when the men got together once a week to watch football?"

"Oh, football fellowships." Emily smirked, playfully putting her hands on her hips.

"Yeah, Ed likes to make sure he has the whole season mapped out in advance. He tries to rotate through all of the homes that are willing," Wayne explained. "I'll take the call. It shouldn't take very long, I hope. But remember, I don't want any more interruptions."

"Okay. I'll try harder." Emily knew her husband cared about the Church and wanted to do a good job, but she hated the tension that periodically invaded their otherwise peaceful home.

Wayne gave a slight nod and turned toward the bedroom to field the waiting call. The call was soon over and Wayne once again immersed himself in his work.

It was already Saturday night and, though it was uncommon, he still did not have his message prepared for the morning. Wayne found it very hard to prepare for a sermon whose topic had been chosen months in advance. The elders and deacons had decided it would be easier to coordinate the material for Sunday school if Wayne would provide a quarterly schedule of his sermons.

He tried praying for direction, but felt dry and empty. It seemed hypocritical to ask the Lord for direction with his sermon since neither he *nor* Jesus were allowed to choose the topic.

There was a small prick in his conscience that told him he ought to apologize to his wife for the incident in the hallway. He quickly suppressed the thought and turned once again to the draining task at hand.

"AMANDA," EMILY CALLED, holding little Ashley and chasing their escaping four–year–old. The Davidsons' oldest daughter ran past her dad in the foyer. Emily slowed a little to catch Wayne's eye. "Sorry. She's just anxious to get outside. It is nice, you know?"

Wayne smiled at his wife from his post near the rear doors of the auditorium and turned again to Mrs. Rugger. "What was that, Sister Rugger?"

"Well, I was just saying how much I appreciated your words. Ever since my health started going downhill, I just haven't been able to be here as much as I'd like. It's good to know that..."

Wayne let his mind drift to another conversation within earshot. Hal Ramsey and Tom Hartley, two of the longtime elders, were engaged in a lively discussion with a couple visiting for the first time.

"I think you'll find Hampton Street to be a friendly Church," Tom began. "We're kind of like a big family; small enough for you to know everyone and feel a part, but big enough to be able to meet all your needs."

"And our youth group," Hal interrupted, noting their teenage daughter, "is very active! Both of my children really enjoy their involvement."

Hampton Street was a closeknit group — by most standards. They had frequent cookouts, ladies' Bible classes, and all the teenagers went to Bible camp together each summer. Visitors, like those this day, were often struck by the warm, friendly atmosphere.

Wayne shook free from the distraction and refocused his attention on Mrs. Rugger. "I sure hope you're feeling well enough to be here next Sunday for the monthly potluck. I'd hate to miss out on your chicken and dumplings."

Mrs. Rugger blushed, releasing an embarrassed smile, and continued slowly toward the inviting sunshine.

Wayne stood staring after her, unsettled by the conversation he had overheard in the foyer. He reviewed in his mind his eight years at Hampton Street. True, the people were closer, more family–like than the suburban mega-church he previously worked for. Still, something was missing — something beyond the flaws of the youth group.

Wayne had actually come here, attracted by the openness, excited by the chance to share his heart, unhindered. Over the past several years he had done that, covering every major theme he had learned in seminary. He hadn't been afraid to say things that might even be considered "radical." And while most seemed touched by what he said, it still seemed to him that nothing was really changing. Month after month drifted by without any clear sense that progress was being made. That bothered him.

I've gotten to know a lot of people since I've been here, but who knows God any better than they did before I arrived? Are the sheep growing? Are the lost being saved? Do the members have a real relationship with God?...I know some do, but shouldn't that be the norm for every Christian if Jesus really lives inside of us?...

"Daddy...up pwees?" His thoughts were interrupted by a tug on his pant leg and the sweet voice of his little Ashley.

He stooped down and swept her up into his arms. "Daddy loves you, Sweetie!"

We loved you so much

that we were delighted

to share with you

not only the gospel of God

but our lives as well,

because you had become

so dear to us.

I Thessalonians 2:8

The Campus

4

SOME TWENTY MINUTES southeast of Hampton Street, in an older part of town, Rick Adams watched with interest as a small pickup truck pulled up beside Haskall Hall.

As the pickup rolled to a stop, Rick walked out the double doors, quickly descended the concrete steps and poked his head into the open window of the pickup. "Can I give you a hand unloading?"

"Uh, sure." The owner of the vehicle, a lean redhead with faint traces of a moustache, squinted into Rick's face. "Rick Adams!"

Rick smiled. "Hello, Eric. Did you have a good summer?"

"Yep!" With that, the energetic youth climbed out the window of his pickup while Rick watched in bewilderment.

"Why did you do that?" Rick asked as he grabbed a guitar and basketball from the truck bed.

"Just following Robert Frost's advice."

"Robert Frost...the poet?"

"Precisely." Eric cleared his throat and drew a clenched fist to his chest. "Two paths converged in a wood and I chose the one less traveled by. And that has made all the difference."

Rick raised his eyebrows suspiciously. "You're kidding. That's why you climbed out your window?"

"No." Eric shrugged and bent over the back of the pickup. "The door's broken. But I thought you'd like the poem." Eric smiled, grabbed a taped up brown suitcase and waved for Rick to follow as he led the way up the steps.

"By the way, you're looking pretty tan," Eric commented over his shoulder as they trekked down the long, narrow hallway. "There must have been a lot of sun in New Guinea."

"How'd you know I went to New Guinea?" Rick asked with amazement.

"Well, there are two reasons." Eric stopped to make his point. "One, I am a genius. And, two," Eric shrugged, "I saw your picture in the school's summer newsletter."

Rick rolled his eyes at Eric's playful arrogance and watched as he continued down the hallway. *What a goofball!* Rick shook his head. Although he didn't know his new roommate well, he suspected there was depth behind his quirky personality. Smiling to himself, he followed Eric through the brown metal door into their room.

IT WAS SATURDAY morning, and for Rick, the first week of classes had flown by. The first week of his senior year was over. *Only thirty-five more to go.* His mind filled with anticipation as he made his way, sports bag in hand, down the street from his dorm. Finally he reached the large wooden building and stepped inside. As the wood and glass doors closed behind him, he stood and took a long, reminiscent breath through his nose.

The "Old Gym," as it had come to be called, still had the musty, sweaty smell Rick remembered from before the summer. It had always seemed the temperature inside this stuffy building was more extreme than it ever was outside. Today was no different.

"Hey, Rick, wanna play a game? We need a good outside shooter," a sweaty player asked with a bounce pass to Rick.

Rick stooped over, bounced the ball twice, and went up for a ten–foot jumper. "Uhhh!" The ball hit the front of the rim and bounced off to the left. "I thought you needed a good player," Rick teased, chasing the loose ball. "Thanks for the offer, but I'm actually here for intramural practice. We're starting early this year, so we'll be good and ready to take you out way before the championship." He had the ball in his hands again and went in for an easy lay-up.

"Yeah, we'll see!" the other student taunted. "Maybe you can play next time. Looks like the summer's made you rusty, anyway."

Rick laughed and made his way to the other side of the gym, where the rest of the team was already gathered. He knew most of these guys, having played with some of them for three years. There were a few new faces, mostly freshmen, hoping to make the A team.

"Hi, my name's Rick Adams." Rick shoved his hand toward one of the newcomers.

"Eddie." The young man nervously accepted Rick's hand and gave but a quick look up.

"Today, let's do some warm–up drills." The announcement came from their intramural coach. "I want a chance to see how some of you new guys look and see how many of you old guys were slacking off this summer."

The young men began a series of dribbling, lay–up, passing and one–on–one drills. Some of the freshmen found it hard to keep up, though one or two showed promise. One of those was Eddie. Though a timid 5 foot 7, he demonstrated exceptional ball–handling skill.

During the one–on–one drill, Eddie tried defending a 6 foot 5 junior who burned him to the goal.

"Ah, give the short guy a chance, Moose," one of the onlookers rebuked playfully.

"I figure if a guy's that short," Moose retorted, "he's gotta prove himself to play on this team. So far, he ain't done it." He gestured with his head toward Eddie, who was making his way to the back of the line, head down.

Rick placed himself strategically in the opposite line, cutting in front of Moose. When it was their turn for the one–on–one drill, the ball came to Rick. He passed it to Eddie. "I think you can do it, man. Let's see." Eddie hesitated — then, noting the warm confidence on Rick's face, looked up and started toward the goal.

Rick was all over him, guarding him with all he had — but Eddie was quick. Every time Rick tried to steal the ball, Eddie bounced it between his legs and maneuvered away. As they approached the goal, Eddie head–faked right, then went in for a left–handed lay–up.

"I guess he's proven himself now," the coach retorted with a chuckle. "Welcome to the team!"

21

THE AGING WOODEN floor of the stately Bible building creaked under the weight of the pacing professor. Classes were over for the day and George Archer, twenty–two–year veteran professor of Old Testament, listened attentively to the summer missionary ventures of his prize pupil.

"It certainly sounds like you had an exciting summer, Rick," Professor Archer concluded. "It's great to see you back on campus. The break was refreshing, but this can be a lonely place during the summer. There are no headhunters here to break up the monotony."

Rick laughed, "You know...actually, there was one man in the Church we worked with who was a former cannibal. Can you imagine that?!" Rick shook his head.

Professor Archer returned a smile and continued thoughtfully studying the face of the young man seated in front of him. Hope tugged at the corners of his mind. *I wonder?*

The recent years had been bleak. True, church growth figures in their denomination did not reflect the alarming decrease in attendance, conversions, missions and benevolence that many denominations were experiencing. Nevertheless, the professor had long since resigned himself to the facts. The bulk of the student body, even at this Christian college, cared little about spiritual matters. Faith was sentiment — not devotion to the person of Jesus.

What was the point of lecturing students who cared more about their GPA than about God or His Word? Professor Archer wasn't sure.

It wasn't that no one cared. There was a core group of students who were very involved in spiritual activities. But even many of them seemed motivated by fleshly adrenalin for their own "ministry" or ambition for a religious career. Surely, that wasn't the case with everyone. The glimmer of hope the professor sensed that day spawned an idea: *Invest in those with potential — they are the future.*

Professor Archer broke the silence. "Do you plan to return?"

"To New Guinea?" Rick shook his head thoughtfully. "I don't think so. The thing on my mind right now is finding some way to wake up the students here."

"That's quite a task," Professor Archer acknowledged. "Many appear to be sound asleep."

"True enough." Rick wrinkled his brow. "But I really think it's because they haven't had a chance to see something different. There's been very little demonstrated that would inspire them. They need to see the life of Jesus walked out — not talked out."

5

"NA EM I TOKIM olgeta disapel, Sapos wanpela man i laik beihainim mi, em i mas daunim em yet," Rick smiled broadly as he held the small leather book in one hand and waved his other hand in the air as if telling a story. "...na i mas karim diwai kros bilong en long olgeta de, na em i mas beihainim mi."

"What was that?" A voice braved from the back of the crowd.

Rick laughed heartily, then addressed those gathered on the campus lawn before him. "Well, that was the verse of Scripture I want to talk about tonight...in Pigeon."

"Bird talk?" the same voice ventured, evoking laughter from the few who heard.

"No, not bird talk. In fact, those are the words of Jesus in the language of the people of New Guinea. Let's read it again in English." Rick grabbed another Bible off the grass. "Turn to Luke 9:23."

It was a beautiful night to be outside. Very few clouds were visible, and a myriad of stars adorned the sky. The moon, nearly full, illuminated the faces of the gathered students.

"Then Jesus said to them all: 'If anyone would come after me, he must deny himself and take up his cross daily and follow me. For whoever wants to save his life will lose it, but whoever loses his life for me will save it. What good is it for a man to gain the whole world, and yet lose or forfeit his very self?'"

This particular Friday night tradition was older than any of the students gathered there. This was the first devotional of the year, and many were eager to listen to Rick. During the previous year, he had become one of the more frequent and popular speakers at these events.

"In case you couldn't tell, I spent some time in New Guinea this summer. Our time with the people there was eye–opening.

And as costly as it was for them, some of the natives gave their lives to God. That passage in Luke really means something when they become Christians. Many of them really do lose membership in their families. The costs are real. The costs are high."

Looking around the circle of familiar faces, Rick spotted Amy. He had met this tenderhearted girl last semester in an advanced Bible class. Sensing something special about her, Rick had begun to look for ways to get to know her, and it wasn't long before they began spending a lot of time together. While he was overseas, they wrote back and forth as often as the slow mail delivery allowed. Rick smiled at the thought of being around her again. He laid aside the fond memories as the call of the moment pulled him onward.

"As I flew back to the States, I thought about how easy we have it here. Then I read these words of Jesus: 'Deny yourself.' I see how they would apply to me if I was a New Guinea native. But how does this apply right here on a Christian college campus? What does it mean to take up my cross when the biggest challenge I face is a term paper? How do I lose my life when the choices I face each day — my degree, my goals, my future — are all about *me*? Obviously, I have a lot of questions and not many answers — yet. Mostly, I want to challenge us all with the things that have challenged and convicted me lately.

"In view of what Jesus has said, here are some questions you can ask yourself that are a little more practical: Why are you pursuing the degree you are pursuing? Is it so you can have a high–paying job and live comfortably after retirement?" Rick paused and scanned the faces closest to him. "Or, is it so you can use your talents and money to serve others? When you're deciding how to spend a Friday night, is your decision based on how much fun it will be…or is it based on how you can make a difference in someone's life?"

The words sounded direct because they were. But those gathered knew they came without accusation. They were rooted in sincerity and concern.

Rick's new roommate, Eric, candidly weighed the night's thoughts. He had not known Rick long, but had already caught glimpses of his gentle, sober insistence that the words of Jesus be followed, even when they hurt. Eric was beginning to learn, with Rick's help, that caring about people and eternal things could be part of his everyday life.

Drifting clouds now veiled the light from the moon, and only the faces nearest Rick were distinguishable. He softly finished the words he'd begun only minutes before.

"You get the idea, don't you? And if you pursue these thoughts — and I hope you will — you'll begin to realize like I did...it's not that we have it easier than a native in New Guinea. We just need to open our eyes more to the opportunities we have to deny ourselves, take up our crosses and follow Him. After all, isn't that what it's all about? Why don't you look for opportunities, even tonight, to serve someone...to serve Him."

6

THE HILLS BLAZED with fiery colors, as fall announced its triumphant arrival into the valley. The semester was well under way, and the campus bustled with activity. Hearing the 1:00 bell, stragglers quickened their pace and darted into various rooms of the old Victorian mansion which housed the Bible department.

In Professor Archer's classroom, it was quiz time. The students strained and sweated over the tough questions staring back at them from their test papers.

As his students finished their quizes, Professor Archer stroked his graying beard, musing the question he was preparing to ask. "Did the Christians in the first century study the Scriptures?"

"Of course!" came the immediate response.

"Oh, really. Now what do you suppose they read?" Professor Archer loved forcing his students to think.

A senior Bible major in the front row shot back an answer. "I imagine they studied the earliest Gospel."

"Well, the first Gospel, the Gospel of Mark, isn't thought to have been written until after the year 65. So, did that leave the first thirty years of Church history with nothing to read?" The wrinkles next to his eyes, evidence of decades of smiles, clearly marked the professor's enjoyment of this game called education.

"Let me put it another way." Professor Archer didn't let the silence settle too heavily before he prodded again. "In the book of Acts it says that Paul reasoned from the Scriptures, proving that Jesus was the Christ. Now, consider this: If what we commonly call the New Testament was not even written until at least the sixties,…then what was Paul using to convince people about Jesus?"

"I guess…the Old Testament," came a hesitant reply.

"That's right!" The professor paused long enough to get the attention of the drowsier students. "For a Christian in the first century, what is called the Old Testament was the Bible." He quickly scanned the room, noticing looks of surprise. "Most people in our generation don't read the Old Testament with the sense of awe and respect it was intended to engender. These aren't just quaint Bible stories, but the unfolding of the divine plan of a Just and Sovereign God.

"Let's look at it through the eyes of a first–century Christian, shall we? Open to Acts 3:17." He turned the pages of his well–worn leather Bible and began reading:

"Now, brothers, I know that you acted in ignorance, as did your leaders. But this is how God fulfilled what he had foretold through all the prophets, saying that his Christ would suffer. Repent, then, and turn to God, so that your sins may be wiped out, that times of refreshing may come from the Lord, and that he may send the Christ, who has been appointed for you — even Jesus. He must remain in heaven until the time comes for God to restore everything, as he promised long ago through his holy prophets. For Moses said, 'The Lord your God will raise up for you a prophet like me from among your own people; you must listen to everything he tells you. Anyone who does not listen to him will be completely cut off from among his people.' "Indeed, all the prophets from Samuel on, as many as have spoken, have foretold these days. And you are heirs of the prophets and of the covenant God made with your fathers. He said to Abraham, 'Through your offspring all peoples on earth will be blessed.' When God raised up his servant, he sent him first to you to bless you by turning each of you from your wicked ways."

"Do you notice," the Professor peered over his reading glasses directly into the face of a front row student, "how Peter used the

Old Testament to reason about Jesus? And notice, also, that he declares that Abraham, Moses, Samuel and all the prophets were pointing to the Kingdom that would come through God's Son, Jesus."

Out of the corner of his eye, the professor saw a hand go up. "Is there a question?"

"Yes, Professor Archer," Rick answered. "This may be off the subject, but I'm very perplexed about something in verse 21 of the passage you just read."

"No, please, go ahead. If you have questions, that means you're awake. That's good!"

"It says Jesus — *must* — stay in heaven until the time comes for God to restore everything. 'Must' sounds like a strong word. What needs to be restored? I always thought the second coming was an arbitrary time that only God knew, and that Jesus might come back at any minute. But verses 19 and 20 make it almost sound like it's something we actually have a *part* in. See...Peter encourages them to repent so that God could send Jesus back."

The professor was caught off guard by Rick's question. This one certainly had no pat answer. "Boy, trying to throw me a tough one, huh? That sounds like a topic for a research paper," he responded playfully.

"I honestly don't know. That's a very good question." Professor Archer glanced at his watch, closed his Bible and walked out among his students as they prepared to leave. "Oh, remember your term papers, guys. I know it seems far off, but the semester will be over in only eight weeks. Don't let it sneak up on you."

RICK SPOTTED AMY across the campus lawn. Gathering his things, he ran to catch up with her.

"Hey, Ames, wait up."

She stopped just short of the forty–step ascent to the entrance of the Welton Memorial Library.

"Whew! I'm glad I didn't have to sprint up those," Rick gasped, out of breath.

"Hi, Rick," Amy smiled. "Where did you come from?"

Rick motioned across the lawn. "I thought you'd be heading to the mail room after History. So, how was the dreaded exam?"

Amy laughed as she pulled her hair to one side to maneuver it in the late afternoon breeze. Rick reached over to relieve Amy of her backpack.

"Thanks, Rick. The 'dreaded' exam was tough but I think it went okay."

She smiled again as she rolled her eyes a little. "I can't believe I was so uptight about the whole thing last night. It seems so ridiculous after the fact! Thanks again for praying with me about it. I'm glad I called you. I appreciate you pointing me back to sanity and reminding me to trust God, even with the small details of a history test."

"LET'S GO BIG BLUE, LET'S GO! Whew–whew! C'mon, Rick, score a three pointer for Amy! Let's go! Whew!" A large–boned young woman with long, blond hair spilling onto her thick, fire–engine red sweater yelled at the top of her lungs. She stood in the middle of an old set of bleachers peppered with a handful of intramural basketball fans.

"Diane, sit down! He's not even in!" Amy's cheeks were painted with embarrassment as she tugged on her roommate's sweater. Her comrade acknowledged her request but insisted on bellowing one more encouragement before relenting, not satisfied yet that she'd accomplished her motivational mission. "No excuses, Rick Adams! Go for it!"

Rick heard his name and looked up from his rest on the sidelines. His squinting eyes relaxed as he spotted the source of the outbursts. Amy saw a broad smile breach Rick's face as he marvelled at her animated friend. He then looked at Amy and appreciated her quiet spirit.

"Time out!" bellowed the balding man in the black and white stripes.

"Adams!" the coach barked as Rick snapped to attention. "Keep your head in the game. She'll be there when it's over."

Rick shook his head and chuckled at his coach.

A whistle blew and the coach slapped Rick on the back. "You gotta get back out there, man! You're in at point guard. Dobrekowski can't handle the full–court press."

"Full blast, Rick. Full blast." Rick could hear the encouragements from the bench as he ran onto the floor.

"Full blast," Rick answered to himself. He found his opponent and caught Amy's eye for an instant before the whistle blew, then focused on the game.

"Rick's back in, Amy! Aren't you excited?" Diane wiggled on the bench, longing for permission to cheer. It seemed to Amy that perhaps some people were born to cheer and get excited. *The gift of excitedness?*

"Yeah, I'm excited." Amy smiled, her dimples sinking deep into her rosy cheeks. "But it's in here." She bit her bottom lip and tapped on her heart with her finger.

"Well you've gotta let it come out, Amy. You'll go crazy," Diane implored.

Amy smiled and tried to think of something kind to say. "Maybe I like being crazy."

"Well, if you don't let Rick know you love him and start cheering for him, I'd say you're already crazy."

"Diane!" Amy turned red again and looked around, relieved no one she knew was in earshot. "Who said anything about loving Rick?"

"So??" Diane said playfully. "Are you telling me you've never practiced signing your name as 'Amy Adams?'"

Now Amy's face became serious. "No, I haven't."

Diane recognized Amy was not enjoying her teasing and became sober. "I'm sorry, Amy."

"No. That's okay. I know you were just playing. I guess you just took me a little bit off guard." Amy rubbed her hands together as she composed her next sentence. "I'll tell you, Diane. I really do like Rick a lot. He's kind. He's gentle. He loves Jesus."

"He's cute!" Diane volunteered with a smile.

Amy conceded with a nod. "Yes, he's cute. And that's nice, but cute can be ugly if the inside is rotten. And not–so–cute can be beautiful, if the inside is right." Diane took particular comfort in these words. Amy continued, "I guess I'm hoping that if Rick is the one God wants me to go through life with, I will see that, and so will Rick. And if it isn't God's will, I hope I'm not so blind with emotion that I miss it."

"Whoa, that sounds deep!" Diane said in a deep tone, mocking playfully.

Amy hid her disappointment with Diane's immaturity. It was

a pretty serious statement, more serious, perhaps, than most people were used to. Amy hoped she could live it out at the time of testing.

She answered with a gentle smile. "It's the truth."

THE GENTLE BREEZE sent red and brown leaves dancing across the sidewalk under the students' feet. Clinging tightly to their jackets, they responded to the 9:15 bell in a rush to make their compulsory devotional attendance timely. Caught in the crowd, Professor Archer and Rick talked casually while they made their way across campus. The professor, clad in a tweed jacket and hat, appeared oblivious to the cold air and the occasional bump from a student. He turned to Rick and surprised him by saying, "You and Amy seem to be hitting it off well."

"I..." Rick's stomach tightened as his guilty conscience twinged. "I suppose so."

"Good, good. She seems to be a sweet girl."

They joined the converging crowd ascending the steps into the large auditorium.

"You ought to really enjoy chapel today." The professor spoke above the chattering crowd.

"Oh? How so?"

"There's a missionary from Irian Jaya who's speaking. Who knows, you might even know him."

Rick laughed politely at the professor's humor. "Not likely."

They followed the crowd into the carpeted foyer and went their separate ways.

But admonish one another daily,

as long as it is called Today,

so that none of you may be hardened

by the deceitfulness of sin.

Hebrews 3:13

The Community

7

THAT EVENING, forty miles west of the city in the small community of Pine Ridge, a bonfire blazed. The air was crisp, and there was just enough bite in the northeast wind to force the donning of warmer clothes. The sun was disappearing over the horizon as an old pickup loaded with rakes and bags of leaves pulled into the Stones' driveway. Several of the men had spent the afternoon raking leaves for some widows in the neighborhood. The truck was quickly surrounded by a mob of children, wives, and friends of the tired, hungry men.

At first glance, one might have thought it was a family reunion. The fifty people gathered in the Stones' backyard had been playing volleyball and preparing dinner. After the new arrivals washed up, the family of believers gathered together to offer a word of thanksgiving.

This was a rare group of Christians. They had come to this city from many places throughout the country, desiring closer fellowship with believers who were serious about putting New Testament Christianity into practice. They gathered together continually and sought to share all things in common — not in an external or legal way, but case–by–case, from the heart.

Times like these were frequent. As they enjoyed the evening together, people milled around in small circles, talking about the day's events. The children played together while several women finished clearing the picnic tables.

As the last bit of sunlight faded away, everyone began gathering around the glow of the campfire. Worship filled the air as the firelight inspired a voice to begin singing.

It wasn't unusual for these people to sing and pray together. It happened often and spontaneously, not limited to certain places or pre–arranged services.

This community of saints had been together for seven years. They had long since given up on "Sunday–morning Christianity" and had decided together to plunge into the adventure of "Body life." Those who were able had moved into a lower middle–class neighborhood, filled mostly with elderly retirees or lower income families. By living close to each other, it was their desire to learn how to love each other in the practical, daily circumstances of life, and to serve their community. Those content to be an audience listening to moral sermonettes each weekend found this kind of commitment radical and unnecessary. This group of believers found it exhilarating. To them it was not optional — Jesus had commanded it.

By the time the fire died down, a few tears had been shed and all agreed it had been a peaceful time together. Since many young eyes were noticeably droopy, they decided to call it a night. Some loaded strollers for the walk home, while others firmed up last minute plans for tomorrow's various activities. The hum of quiet conversation continued until all were inside their modest homes. That is, almost all — two brothers engaged in an exciting new topic hardly noticed that the once–crowded lawn was now empty.

"...and you're not going to believe this either...the old Turner place just went up for sale."

LATER THAT WEEK, a steady flow of believers filed into Alan and Marsha Hart's large living room. People sat wall–to–wall, up the stairs, spilling into the kitchen.

"Good morning, everybody! Sorry to drag you all out of your homes so early this Saturday morning. Anybody a little curious as to why we're all here?" Alan paused for effect.

"C'mon. Don't torture us any longer. Just what are you guys up to?"

Alan Hart flashed a mischievous look toward his cohorts Brian Stephens and Ted Stone. "Are you sure I can't get anyone some coffee? Ted, what about you?"

Ted Stone shot back another teasing look and Brian cleared

his throat as if he would give the whole thing away.

"Okay, okay." Alan finally dropped the show and started talking in his more professional tone to which everyone was accustomed. "I wanted to fill you in on a pretty exciting opportunity in front of us. Do you all remember Aaron and Kathy Richardson from out east? Most of you realize they share in our desire to be a part of a Biblical functioning Church." Alan sat down. "As you know, they've been wanting to move here for some time now, but they've been unable because of financial difficulties. Well, it seems that God may be making it possible for them to come to Pine Ridge now — but perhaps in a way we hadn't expected."

"But Aaron has a broken leg."

"Yeah, and he's a construction worker."

"Besides, there aren't any houses available close by. Even if there were, it wouldn't be big enough for all seven of them."

Ted gave a light whistle, trying to calm the objections.

"It *would* be big enough…if we *built* it big enough." This time, Alan's comment was answered with silence. The whole room seemed to hold its breath in anticipation of the explanation.

It was Brian Stephens who unveiled the secret at last. "Well, I got a call this week asking if we knew anyone interested in the old Turner house." He waited for the eager nods to subside before he continued. "It's up for sale. It's no mystery that the house hasn't been lived in for years and is in really bad shape. It would need to be completely renovated." He took a deep breath. "I'll just be real honest with you — the Richardsons are in no place, financially, to do this. But they are only going to get into more debt where they are. So if we really believe God wants them in Pine Ridge, we're going to have to be the ones to make it happen. Do we all agree God wants them here? If not, please speak up."

Brian waited several moments before continuing. "Okay, if that's the case, then, realistically speaking, this is going to require a lot of sacrifice on our part. Time, money and energy from each individual here will be needed to pull this whole thing off. Alan's been able to push some things through, and it looks like he could purchase the house at a good price. However, that won't cover the cost of fixing it all up."

Alan Hart took over. "Now, nothing has been said to the Richardsons about all this. We felt like we'd better ask all of you if you are really interested in doing this. We're talking about a big commitment that will keep us busy for the next two or three months. We need to know up front if this is something you *really* want to do.

Alan's wife, Marsha, called out enthusiastically from the kitchen, "I say let's do it!"

Carolyn Stone eyed her husband, Ted, and added, "In some way or another, each of us has paid a price to be here together in Pine Ridge — whether it's jobs, money or relationships. I like the idea of making the way a little easier for someone else."

"So does that mean this is a go?" Alan scanned the excited faces.

"GO!"

"NAILS, HAMMERS, power drill, drywall…okay. That seems like enough to get started. Hey, Ted, can you give one of your famous country–boy whistles to let everyone know we're ready to get started?"

The last part of Alan's question was drowned out by the deafening call. Everyone within earshot came running, recognizing the sound with warm familiarity. Those nearby stood with heads tilted, rubbing their ears, trying to recover. People came out from all corners of the old house, and a couple of boys jumped through a broken window.

"Hey, we're going to have enough things to do without you guys tearing down that window sill. But we do have a wall upstairs that needs to come down, so wait around and we'll give you some work to do soon enough." Brian smiled at the boys.

Once the laughter subsided, Alan spoke up. "It looks like we're all ready to get started. As you can see, we were not exaggerating when we talked about the amount of work we'll need to do over the next three months. We have organized a list of jobs into three different categories according to skill level. So at this point, there isn't a lot to talk about. Just refer to that list over on the east wall. Talk to Brian, the Assistant Renovations Director, if you have any questions."

A few chuckles ensued, and Brian rolled his eyes. The list was mobbed instantly. After several minutes, Alan noticed his wife standing next to Carolyn Stone at the front of the line. Alan smiled, confident that whatever job Marsha tackled would undergo a miraculous transformation.

"I guess you know which category *we* fall under?" Carolyn taunted playfully.

"Yep," Marsha replied.

"UNSKILLED," they said in emphasized unison, now laughing.

"I'm surprised they didn't create a special category just for you, Marsha," Carolyn teased. "Disaster Control Specialist."

"Very funny," Marsha grinned.

"Well, what shall it be...scraping wallpaper or trash detail?"

"What about this," Marsha pointed enthusiastically at the last item on the list. "Clean out upstairs closet."

"Sure. Sounds like it's right up our alley."

Marsha grabbed a broom and a roll of trash bags. "We'll have this house ready in no time."

"And then the Richardsons can move in," Carolyn added. "I want to work hard, as a gift to them."

The two women mounted the creaky staircase and found their assignment. It was a large, walk–in closet at the end of a long hallway, filled with mildewed rags and moth–eaten sweaters. Marsha bounded into the closet, scouring the wall for a light switch. She let out a piercing scream and emerged back into the hallway, visibly shaken.

"What's wrong?" Carolyn was alarmed.

"Something ran across my foot," Marsha replied a bit sheepishly.

Carolyn found a light switch and swept the cobwebs out of the way with Marsha's broom. Then the women began to fill trash bag after trash bag with old dresses, crumpled scarves and rotting shoe leather.

"I wonder what Mrs. Turner was like," Carolyn mused, holding up a slipper. "Does anyone know how long she lived alone before she moved into the nursing home?"

"I don't think so," Marsha said absently. "Look at all this dirt!" she exclaimed. "This whole place needs to be hosed down."

Carolyn was looking at a torn photograph she found lying in a corner. "I wonder if she had any friends."

Marsha looked up, puzzled. "Who?"

"Mrs. Turner."

"Oh. Well, if she did, they sure didn't clean for her."

"And now she's gone. Life is so short, Marsha." Carolyn was still gazing at the old photograph. "I really want to make it count."

A nearby wall came crashing down with the help of several strong men. Carolyn excused herself and went across the street to check on her daughter. She found Marie napping soundly in her travel crib, while several of the sisters prepared lunch for the other children they were watching.

8

FFFFFFFTTT! The broadhead arrow sailed over an unsuspecting doe. Its brief flight terminated abruptly as it sank deep into the bark of an ancient oak. The doe lifted her head from her foraging, motionless and wide-eyed.

Not even daring to breathe, Ted Stone waited in silence for the doe to again lower her head. When she did, Ted quickly prepared another arrow and drew back the cable until the cams in the compound bow were poised. He leveled the sight, aiming for the tuft of hair behind her forequarter.

"Ted," Alan whispered. "Look." Ted's arrow left the bow prematurely and buried itself at the feet of the startled doe. She leapt fluidly into the brush and was gone.

Ted spun around, flush with frustration. Now crouching, Alan held up three fingers on his left hand and pointed over his shoulder at three bucks directly behind their tree stand. His eyes confessed his shame at blowing the opportunity. Ted flashed a forgiving expression accompanied by a quick nod.

Ted moved quietly and deliberately as he prepared to dispatch another arrow. He slowly retrieved an arrow from the floor of the stand, careful to keep an eye on his new target. For a split second he allowed his eyes to dart to his bow. A rustle of leaves and his prey bounded back down the trail. Gone.

"YOU SEE, YOU HOLD THE KNIFE this way. Don't force it, Alan, let the blade do the work." Don Chambers, one of the first members of the community, stood with Alan Hart in front of the makeshift rack that held Don's kill for the day. He was giving Alan his first lesson in cleaning a deer. Don was thorough, covering every detail and obviously enjoying every minute of his lecture.

"I showed Ted how to do this last year. Too bad he won't be able to get some practice in this season."

Good–natured chuckles percolated from the circle of men that finished dinner around the camp fire. Ted rolled his eyes at Brian as if to say, "Oh no, here it comes…"

"Funny, don't you think — one of the best athletes in the whole Church can't get the hang of a little thing like shooting an arrow straight?"

Ted was used to Don's ribbing. He shook his head in mock regret. "I thought for sure I would get one this year. Especially after buying all that expensive equipment you talked me into, Don! From the way you made it sound, all I had to do was bring that bow out here and it would track and kill the deer for me."

"That way, I get to borrow it when he gets too frustrated to use it." Don whispered to Alan with a sly wink.

"It was my fault," Alan finally apologized. "I startled a doe that would have been a sure kill."

"Oh, don't you worry about it," Brian cut in. "They're just sparring with each other. Ted's not upset. He's made it quite clear he doesn't care for hunting. If we weren't here, he wouldn't be here."

"I'll do anything to get some time with these guys," Ted confirmed. "Even if it means wandering around these *frigid* woods for a day or two."

In reality, Ted was glad to be out there. He was a sportsman and a competitor. He just didn't like to lose, and last year's hunting adventure had left him with a bad taste in his mouth. Not only had he failed to bring home any meat, as Don frequently reminded him, but he had never even seen anything, except Don's catch.

Now football was a completely different matter. As the assistant coach of a winning and prominent high school football team, Ted had enjoyed his share of winning. His down–to–earth, big–hearted personality made him a favorite with the boys he coached.

Ted smiled to himself as he thought about the times he had

enjoyed with these brothers. He watched the shivering Alan make his way to the fire to get warm as the circle of brothers broke up and began cleaning the few pans and utensils they had brought for meals. The shadows were low, and the last bit of daylight was noticeably fading. They each began laying out their bedroll for the night, as close to the fire as caution would allow.

Alan thought out loud, addressing anyone who would listen. "I love being out here like this. Everything is still and quiet. As you look up through the trees, the branches make the oddest patterns against the sky. They play with your imagination. There's no sense of rushing or schedules. Everything is free to live as God intended."

"That's how God has made us to live, Alan. Free and unhindered," Don added.

"He sure is generous to let us live that way together." Alan let the reality of his own words sink in. "I'm really glad I let you guys talk me in to coming out here."

"Yep. It just doesn't get any better than this."

"C'mon, Don, you sound like a beer commercial," Ted said. "You've been watching too many football games."

As Alan slipped eagerly into the inviting warmth of his sleeping bag, he yelped when he felt something like a water balloon next to him in his bag.

"Looks like Alan is this year's victim of Don's deer liver joke." They tossed the organ from one guy to the other as Brian shouted, "Hot liver, hot liver, who's got the hot liver." After a few minutes of raucous laughter, the men decided it was time to settle down and get some sleep.

"Can you imagine the women doing this?" Laughter followed.

"Guys, it just doesn't get any better than this!"

The night became colder, but the fire's embers would burn for several more hours. One at a time the men drifted off to sleep.

9

IT WAS ALMOST 9:45 on Tuesday morning. "I can't believe it!" Carolyn mumbled to herself. "I'm already fifteen minutes late, and now the phone!" Juggling a fussy, little Marie in one arm,

Carolyn debated whether to just let it ring. Finally, she grabbed the phone.

"Hello, Carolyn...this is Teresa."

Carolyn heaved a sigh. "Shhh, shhh, Marie...Teresa?...Teresa who?" Her thoughts were scrambling. She heard the name but wrestled momentarily to place the voice. She brightened as she realized it was Teresa, her college roommate. "Teresa Parker! I can't believe it. How are you? How's Steve? It's so good to hear your voice!"

It *was* good to hear her voice. Carolyn relaxed a little as affection flooded her mind. The warmth flowed from two years of college memories — sharing a suite, all–night study sessions, and late nights of just talking and praying together. Though Carolyn didn't realize it, there was a longing in her for the closeness of those days — sharing everything from heartaches to dirty laundry. However, as with many college relationships, it didn't last. Carolyn and Teresa had both since married and drifted apart. They had little regular contact, though they had settled less than an hour apart.

"Oh, Carolyn, it's good to hear your voice, too. I can't believe it's been so long since we last talked. Is that...Marie I hear? How old is she now?"

"Yeah, that's my Marie. She's almost a year old, although today she's acting like she's hit the terrible two's!"

Remembering the women waiting next door, Carolyn almost offered to call Teresa back later. She changed her mind after hearing Teresa's unexpected question.

"Anyway, I know there's a lot to catch up on, but I was actually wondering if I could ask a few questions about your Church."

Carolyn was pleasantly surprised. "Really, like what?" She always enjoyed talking about their life together in Pine Ridge.

"Here at Metro Chapel," Teresa continued, "we're doing things a little differently these days, and it reminded me of you guys. I don't know if you're familiar with home groups, but Metro has gotten so large, and this new home group idea really seems to be the answer to Steve's and my prayers for closer fellowship. Have you ever heard of home groups?"

"Yes." Carolyn wasn't quite sure where this was heading. "I

have heard of them…but I don't know a whole lot about them."

"I don't either, to tell the truth. But, the leadership here at Metro is considering breaking the whole congregation into smaller groups. Maybe seven families each, based on where we live and our age brackets. You know, putting us in touch with people who go to Metro and live right in our own neighborhood…kind of like you guys. That's why I called you. I'm on the Research Committee. We're investigating ideas and are going to present our findings to the leadership. We're probably still six to nine months away from actually starting anything. Steve and I can't wait. We're excited about the possibility of building deeper relationships at Metro." Carolyn lodged the phone between her shoulder and ear. She leaned down, set Marie on the carpet and found herself a seat as Teresa continued, "Like I said, it really seems like an answer to prayer. Metro has grown so much in the last three years, it has been hard to keep up with all the new faces. And since we moved into our new house, it's such a long drive across town to be with the folks we know well. Isn't that neat? We might even be able to link up with people right here on our own street."

Marie, unwilling to play on her own, was crying, pulling at her mom's pant leg. Carolyn picked up her little princess. She had long since given up on getting to the reading next door on time and was actually delighted to hear Teresa's excitement.

"Wow. It certainly sounds like a step in the right direction, Teresa. But I'm not sure exactly how I can help. You already know Ted and I moved into our neighborhood to be with the people in the Church here. God has shown us how important it is to be 'joined and knit' to people — like the Bible says. To walk daily, in close fellowship with his people…you know we're together every day—"

"Yep," Teresa interrupted, "I remember you telling me something about all that! That's what I'm talking about. It's so hard with our busy schedules. How will we find the time?"

"Yes," Carolyn laughed, "I know what you mean. It can be hard with busy schedules. But the time is there if you know where to find it. It's a matter of priorities. It depends on what is most important for everyone. Around here, for example, the men gather together one morning a week before work for breakfast and to spend time in prayer together. The women meet together, too, although it is a little more difficult with the children. Often, we moms like to plan special time in the week just for the children."

She was interrupted by a sharp rap on her kitchen window. It was Marsha Hart. "Should we wait?" Carolyn heard Marsha's voice filtered by the glass.

Carolyn shook her head, waved Marsha on and continued, "Sometimes we go to a park or McDonald's, or sometimes we take the older children to a matinee. We try to set aside Monday nights for concentrated family time, but most nights we're all together somewhere around here. Sunday is automatically family day for the whole Church. We usually get together in the morning for worship and then have a big lunch together. The rest of the day is spent together somehow. I don't know if that helps much but, you know, finding the time really does work out if you're committed to each other."

"I see what you mean," Teresa said thoughtfully. "We know it's going to take more sacrifice on our part if we really want to care about these new people. We believe God is calling us to a new level of commitment. I just know this home group idea is the answer. I hope the people we're grouped with are hungry for fellowship like Steve and I."

"Me too, Teresa. But if they aren't, you will know soon enough."

"You're right."

"Was there something else on your mind?" Carolyn asked, sensing the conversation was already tapering off.

"No, not right now. If I think of some more, do you mind if I call back?"

"No. Please do. I'll be praying for you."

"I knew you would. Goodbye for now."

This is the verdict:

Light has come into the world,

but men loved darkness

instead of light

because their deeds were evil.

Everyone who does evil

hates the light,

and will not come into the light

for fear that his deeds

will be exposed.

John 3:19–20

Skeletons

10

WALKING AWAY FROM Amy's dorm, Rick ached inside. His conscience told him he was treading on dangerous ground, while his mind tried desperately to justify the feelings he was struggling with. His heart and body were engaged in a dreadful battle. He feared the outcome.

"Who can I talk to?" he wondered aloud.

Rounding the corner, Rick passed the administration building and quickened his pace as his thoughts again retraced the evening's events. It's not that they were doing anything wrong...or were they? He wished he could know for sure. The one thing he did know: every time he and Amy were together, he felt like a freight train heading for certain disaster. He knew he couldn't trust himself when he was alone with her. In fact, something inside told him a line had already been crossed. And that hurt. She was special.

How do you tell somebody you're afraid something might happen without making them think it already has? How does a Christian send out an SOS without taking the risk of losing everything? He passed the psychology building for the third time and only then realized he was walking in circles.

At that moment, Rick thought he saw a familiar face coming up the sidewalk. He lowered his gaze and took off across the lawn to avoid interaction. Finding a dark, private place beneath a tree, he tried to reel in his tangled thoughts. He wasn't far from the grassy area where the student body held their Friday night devotionals.

There are a lot of people with fragile faith looking up to me. Rick winced as he recalled a freshman who came to him in tears after the last devotional. So many looked to Rick as a spiritual leader on campus, solid as a rock, and somehow untouched by the *normal* struggles of life. What would they think if they could see into his heart now? Would they be surprised to find he felt more like a confused child than a mighty warrior? Some might be relieved by his weakness, but most would surely be disappointed. The last thing he wanted was to shipwreck someone's faith.

Rick glanced at his watch and quickly scrambled to his feet. As he jogged toward the dorm, the tragic irony of the whole thing began to dawn on him. He wished people could see inside him and really know *him* — not just the things he said! Deep inside this paragon of a college student lived a real person with real fears, real hurts and real temptations.

Nearing the dorm, he passed a little too close to a parked car with a couple inside. A few months ago, he might have looked at them with disdain. Now he realized that unless something changed, he would end up in the same place. Or worse.

As he mounted the steps in front of the dorm, he pounded the rail in determination. "I've gotta get help!"

"GOOD AFTERNOON, Campus Ministries. How can I help you?"

"I was wondering, uh...if I could make an appointment." Rick gripped the phone tightly in his moist palm. Pacing over to the door of his dorm room, he locked it just in case Eric returned from class early.

"Certainly. Can I have your name and phone number?"

Rick nervously provided the various details necessary to establish an appointment. *Why does it seem so hard just to reveal my name?* he wondered. *What am I going to do when I have to explain the whole situation to a total stranger?*

The secretary paused for a moment to flip through her calendar. "Would this Friday or early next week be better for you?"

Rick's heart fell. "Four days from now? This is important! Isn't there anything earlier than that?"

"I'm sorry, sir. The Campus Minister is terribly busy this week." She sounded sympathetic, but it was clear to Rick she had missed the urgency of his need. After all, this was his *life* they were talking about.

"Well, let's see," she said accommodatingly. "I think I can work you in as early as 1:30 Friday. Would that be all right?"

"Friday?" Rick sighed as he sank to his chair.

"I could call you if anyone cancels."

"No, that's okay…it's not necessary. I'm probably just making too much out of it." Rick began to run through a mental list of people he knew. *Who else…?*

RICK STROLLED NERVOUSLY through the cafeteria toward the lone corner table he had eyed when he first walked in. As he walked, he didn't want to avoid people, but somehow the knot in his stomach wouldn't allow him to face any of them with more than a painted smile. *This isn't easy*, he thought, fiddling with the straw poking from the lid of his Coke.

He saw two girls heading toward the table he had placed mental "dibs" on. His heart jumped — *no!* He felt a surge of relief when they chose another table, and the privacy of his rendezvous was secured. He threw himself into one of the two chairs and, fumbling with his cup, mentally rehearsed his opening line. Inside he felt silly. Why all the fuss, all the anxiety? It was just going to be a conversation with someone he knew he could trust. *This is serious! This isn't about whether or not I should take Greek. What's he going to think? Can he really help me, anyway?* Although Rick was experienced in giving help, he was not accustomed to needing it. Despite the hesitations, he knew this was what he had to do.

Just then Professor Archer walked in. He looked around, obviously feeling out of place. He saw Rick sitting in the back corner of the cafeteria and quickly walked to the table.

"Rick, good to see you. Sorry I'm a bit late. One of my other students had a question after class."

"That's all right. I just got here myself," Rick said, staring at his cup.

Professor Archer looked around and commented, "Is this place always this crowded?"

Rick didn't seem to notice. The professor sensed Rick was preoccupied and asked, "So, what's on your mind?"

"Uh...something's been bothering me lately. It's not much. Umm..." Rick slurped the remaining liquid from his cup. "It's about Amy and me."

"Are things getting serious?" Professor Archer smiled.

Rick's eyes widened as the empty cup threatened to fall from his trembling hand.

"You wouldn't be the first of my students to get married before graduation."

Rick breathed a sigh of relief, knowing how close the professor had come to the bull's-eye. Rick still wasn't sure he wanted to bare his heart. The struggle inside began to heat up.

"No...not exactly. I was just wondering...about the relationship between a man and a woman. You see, I just don't know...we've been seeing each other a lot lately and it's been pretty good. I mean, Amy and I feel strongly about each other and we've been holding hands and, you know, I kiss her good night, and I'm just not sure about—"

"Rick." A knowing smile came to Professor Archer's face. "I'm sure you and Amy will do just fine. Remember, an attraction between a man and a woman is a natural thing that God created. It's beautiful and proper in the right situation — marriage. I've known you for a little over two years and have confidence you will make the right decisions concerning your future."

I don't think he's seeing my problem. Rick let out a long, low breath and sat back in his chair.

"If you're wanting to know my opinion..." The professor leaned forward on his elbows and looked from side to side in mock preparation for revealing a secret. "I think Amy is an excellent choice."

Rick tossed the mangled straw on the table in confused disappointment. His mind, his heart and his body were at war. *I know I'll get married one day. I'm worried about NOW!*

11

WAYNE DAVIDSON'S FAVORITE danish awaited him on the breakfast table. Next to it was a glass of orange juice and a folded cloth napkin — the kind reserved for guests. Had he not already decided to apologize, his wife's kindness would have compelled him.

He looked at her from across the room, nervous but determined. "Emily…I'm so sorry…There is absolutely no excuse for the way I spoke to you in the van last night. I know it's not your fault Blake needs new shoes. Can you forgive me?"

Emily blinked back the tears and gave her husband a big hug. She didn't quite know how to act. Apologies were a new thing. "I…I forgive you." She smiled and then ended the awkwardness by inviting him to the table.

"Ohhh…I'm sorry, honey, I forgot to tell you. I'm supposed to meet John Carley for breakfast." He glanced at the clock on the kitchen wall. "And, I'm almost late now…" He cut himself short as he remembered what a heel he'd been the night before. "But, I can stay for one danish. They smell delicious." He sat down to eat, convinced by Emily's demeanor that he had made the right choice.

WAYNE'S DOUR MOOD made his little office at Hampton Street seem darker than normal. He wanted to sink into his swivel chair and disappear.

His breakfast with John Carley had been a flop.

John, converted by Wayne three months before, was a construction worker with a rough history. His mother was an alcoholic and his father…who knows? So, he had been raised with his mother's maiden name. Although only twenty–four, his skin had a brazen, leather–like appearance, and his arms were a menagerie of tattoos. Despite his rugged appearance, he had earned respect through his quiet manner and relentless labor.

As Wayne mindlessly fidgeted with a paper clip, he recalled their first meeting. It was back in June. A summer thunderstorm had downed one of the large oak trees in the Davidsons' backyard, collapsing the roof of their screened porch. When John had first come out to begin the rebuilding, he had seemed cold and hard — never a smile, only a stern, sweaty brow that kept about his work. The only thing that had ever slowed his pace was an occasional break to light a quick cigarette.

While playing in the backyard, little Ashley Davidson inadvertently had revealed that John wasn't as hard and tough as he appeared. Unintimidated by his six–foot–one, 210–pound frame, she had offered a small rubber ball to him during his lunch break. Watching this brief game of catch, Wayne had found a way into John's heart, and from there, his life.

Wayne was brought back to the present by the sound of footsteps on the tiled hallway outside his office. Relieved to see Tom's familiar pin–striped suit move on past his doorway, he once again retreated into his dispirited reminiscence.

John had a small daughter of his own, born out of wedlock. His voice quivered when he spoke of her, wondering where she even lived.

For most men, the pain of life only makes them harder and more resistant to the truth. But for John it was different. God had drawn him with cords of human kindness, and Wayne was never more grateful for a damaged porch.

It seemed like a genuine conversion...how rare. It was refreshing to see God open a man's heart and watch him leap for the Gospel as if it were a hidden treasure he had always wanted. He was so alive, so on fire...

Recently though, things had begun to sour. John seemed more distant, less open. Wayne tossed the paper clip onto his desk and slid deeper into his chair. *I think we're losing him.*

It was no mystery. The young men in the Church had taken an immediate liking to John. They were "good ol' boys." They liked to hunt and fish, enjoy a rough game of football and — if Wayne's hunch was right — drink a little on the weekends. Their effect on John was obvious.

In the beginning, there was a certain fresh quality to John's prayers. They weren't sterile, raised–in–the–church kinds of prayers. They came from the heart.

But lately, he sat in the back of the assembly with the rest of the "boys" — though they were legally men by age. He hung out with them on evenings and weekends, and it had taken its toll. Now, when he prayed, he merely sheepishly parroted religious clichés. Such an obvious difference! Where had the life gone?

Wayne slid from his chair onto his knees and let out a long sigh. *Oh, God, You've rescued this lamb from the WORLD...now how do I protect him from the leavening in the Church?*

A QUICK KNOCK at the partially open door brought Wayne, fumbling, back up into his chair.

"Can...I come in?" asked Tom Hartley from just outside the doorway.

"Uh...sure, come on in."

"You seemed kind of out of it when I walked by earlier. To be honest, you're not looking much better now. Do you have a lot on your mind?"

Wayne instinctively straightened his tie, quickly composing his thoughts. "Yeah...I'm just kinda worried about John Carley. That's all."

"Something up with John? He's not in any kind of trouble, is he?" the elder asked with exaggerated concern.

"Well, not physical trouble...it's spiritual. I had a lot of hope for him. He seemed so alive, so serious about following God. Now he's fallen back into a lot of old habits." Wayne lowered his gaze. "I think he's drinking again. His attitude and perspective seem more worldly than ever."

Tom made his way further into the room, stroking his chin as he carefully selected the next words from his storehouse of fatherly advice. "Well, you've got to keep in mind, not even Jesus saved everybody. He told us to just scatter the seed. And remember, He said that some spring up with great joy, but later wither because they have no root. Maybe this is what's happening with John." Tom leaned forward, placing a hand on Wayne's shoulder. "You shouldn't take it so personally, Wayne."

"I...don't think that's the case this time." Wayne eyed him nervously, gathered his resolve and continued. "This time I think it's a matter of bad company corrupting good morals."

"Bad company?" Tom peered more intently at Wayne and asked, "Any idea who?"

"Tom...I wish I could say it's old influences from the past. But I can't." Wayne shook his head. "Unfortunately, it's some of the young men in this Church."

"This Church? You've got to be kidding." Tom folded his arms across his chest, reflexively protecting. "I think, for the most part, we've got a fine group of young people here. I know things aren't perfect, but they're better than average."

Wayne dropped his head, frustrating Tom with his silent rebuttal.

Tom abdicated. "All right...who here at Hampton Street do you think has been a bad influence on Mr. Carley?"

Wayne stared past the tenured elder, avoiding eye contact. He didn't want to hurt Tom's feelings. He forced himself to meet Tom's questioning gaze. "I don't know how to say this...it's your son, Tom. The main negative influence on John is your son."

Tom's face flushed. "Is that an accusation?"

"No, Tom, it's not an accusation. Just an answer to your question. You initiated this conversation. Remember?"

Tom clenched his jaw, controlling his initial impulse. "Let me give you some advice. You worry about John. I'll worry about my son. You've got to understand, Wayne, these young men don't have to meet your rigid expectations. They need space to sow their wild oats. If you push stuff down their throats, they'll leave. That wouldn't solve anything, now would it?"

12

IT WAS THURSDAY NIGHT and Wayne was working late at the church building. As he was about to leave, he spotted Hal in the eastern wing. "Hey, Hal, you got a minute?"

Hal Ramsey lifted his lean, six–foot frame from the water fountain. "Sure, Wayne...hey, before I forget — great message last Sunday." He lowered his voice a fraction as Wayne drew closer. "I know some people may not be as ready to hear that as I am, but...be patient. Like I've told you before, it takes time to turn big ships."

Hal allowed a generous smile to overtake his ruddy face as he shook Wayne's hand firmly. He enjoyed this role as his pastor's confidant.

"Are you sure the ship is really turning?" Wayne made no effort to conceal his uncertainty. He led the way into a vacant classroom and began unloading his burdened heart. The situation with Tom's son and John Carley was tying Wayne in knots and he longed to get to the bottom of it.

Hal intercepted Wayne's consternation. "Relax, Wayne. I

already know about Tom Hartley. I've talked with him. He'll cool off in a few days."

"I'm not worried about Tom, Hal. I'm worried about John. Why is it that a young man like John can be so on fire and then have the wind knocked out of his sails? And not by the world, but by other so–called 'Christian' peers. Like Hartley's son, for instance?"

"Let's not overreact. Let's think this through…slowly. Here, grab a chair."

Wayne chuckled involuntarily.

"What's so funny?"

"We're in the second grade classroom, Hal. Do you want the little red chair…or the little blue one?"

Both men laughed as Hal congratulated himself for inadvertently disarming Wayne. As he leaned against the cinder–block wall, Hal regained a sober composure. "Wayne, there's one thing you've got to realize. Even in the Church, some people are good and some people are bad. There's nothing you can do about it. It's like Jesus said in the parable of the wheat and the tares." He picked up a piece of chalk and, almost without thinking, drew a rough picture of a field on the chalkboard. "Some of the crop is good." He pointed to one part of the drawing. "And some of it is bad. But you don't know for sure which is which, and there's really nothing you can do about it. Besides, Jesus said the harvesting angels would separate…" he drew a line through the middle of the field, "…the good from the bad at the end of the age.

"Relax! Don't have a messiah complex. You can't save everybody, and you'll only wear yourself out if you try." Hal picked up the eraser and cleared the board. "I know you're worried about Carley and you care a lot about him. But you can rest easy. If he has a good heart, then God will take care of him." Hal punctuated his conclusion, brushing the chalk from his hands.

Something in Wayne recoiled at Hal's logic. *But how can I dispute a parable of Jesus? If Jesus said it, it must be true. Right? So what do I do in the meantime? Just watch people's lives get trashed? Sickening! Why even care about people if you can't really help them or keep the "members" from being a bad influence on them? And what could Paul have meant when he commanded us to remove the leaven from the batch?* Wayne was sure the Scriptures did not contradict each other, though this apparent paradox between the words of Paul and the words of Jesus was perplexing.

"Thanks, Hal," Wayne responded. "I'll think about what you said."

"Sure," Hal replied. "Why don't you take some time to look over the parable of the wheat and the tares? Read it tonight. It'll help you see things more clearly."

The conversation was over. Hal knew Wayne was still unconvinced — but at least temporarily defused. *He's got to learn that he can't change the whole world by himself.*

AS WAYNE DROVE HOME, his mind was still tangled in confusion. *I just don't get it. Why is this so hard to understand? Maybe Hal is right? But...*

He hit the brakes suddenly. He was so deep in thought ,he had missed the entrance to his subdivision. As he turned the car around he concluded, *I guess head knowledge doesn't automatically equal discernment.*

He coasted into the driveway and prayed, *Lord, please give me wisdom. I don't want all my scholarship to get in the way of knowing You, like it did for Nicodemus. Help me to SEE the Kingdom. Give me a childlike heart.*

Wayne walked in the door and laid his briefcase and coat on the table in the hallway. He kissed Emily, who was in the kitchen peeling potatoes, and made his way to the bedroom. He plopped down at his desk and opened his Bible.

This parable will drive me crazy until I read it again for myself.

He started to read Matthew 13 aloud to himself:

"The kingdom of heaven is like a man who sowed good seed in his field. But while everyone was sleeping, his enemy came and sowed weeds among the wheat, and went away. When the wheat sprouted and formed heads, then the weeds also appeared. The owner's servants came to him and said, 'Sir, didn't you sow good seed in your field? Where then did the weeds come from?'

'An enemy did this,' he replied.

The servants asked him, 'Do you want us to go and pull them up?'

'No,' *he answered,* 'because while you are pulling the weeds, you may root up the wheat with them. Let both grow together until the* *harvest. At that time I will tell the harvesters: First collect the weeds and tie them in bundles to be burned; then gather the wheat and bring it into my barn.'"*

Hal was right, he conceded. *I guess even Jesus accepted that there would be pretenders and hypocrites in the Church. If He wants to wait until the end to pull them up so as to protect the good plants...I have to, too.*

But a wave of despair began to crash over Wayne as he thought about John and the life he had seen in John's eyes. That life was so precious in a new believer, yet it had been choked out because of the "weeds" he'd met in the very house of God! *Lord, I just don't get it! I am only a servant. This is Your Church, and I will do as You say! But I must confess I cannot see how leaving these bad influences in Your Church is less harmful than uprooting them. Some show little or no evidence that they know You or love You or wish to obey You! Would You leave Your body diseased instead of expelling a harmful virus?*

His eyes moistened with regret, but he read on — compelled. He noticed, a few verses later, the disciples' question: "Explain to us the parable of the weeds in the field."

Yes, Master, Wayne agreed.

"He answered, 'The one who sowed the good seed is the Son of Man. The field is the world, and the good seed stands for the sons of the kingdom.'"

Wait just a minute! his mind shouted. A sensation like wind blowing on the back of his neck hit Wayne as he read the words. *What did He say?!* His eyebrows raised as he reread the verse to make sure he wasn't mistaken. "The field is the WORLD!" he shouted.

He heard Emily in the kitchen turn the faucet off and respond, "Wayne, did you call me?"

"I said, the field is the WORLD!"

"Are you reading the African Missions Newsletter?" she queried.

Wayne jumped up from his chair and ran into the kitchen. Emily was chopping carrots at the counter as he rushed up and shoved the Bible between her and the cutting board.

"No, no, Honey," he blurted out. "Don't you understand? The field in the parable of the weeds is the *world*, not the Church! The good seeds are Christians! The bad seeds are sons of the devil!"

Emily stared blankly at her husband, perplexed by his enthusiasm.

Wayne tried again. "In the world, but not of it — get it? The enemy mixed the bad seeds in the *world*, not the Church. Paul's command to 'expel them from your midst' when they won't repent doesn't contradict Jesus at all!"

Wayne continued, even more excited, "Honey, you don't know how happy this makes me! I don't have to stand by and watch people die! There must be some way Jesus has provided for us to deal with leaven...but how? I've got to figure this out. I know legalism isn't the answer, but what is?" He strained for a solution.

"Does this have something to do with John Carley?"

"It sure does! John Carley and every other vulnerable lamb."

He picked up his Bible, speaking aloud to himself as he walked back toward the study. "The only thing I can't figure out is why Hal hasn't seen it. He seemed to think this meant we shouldn't deal with sin to protect God's lambs. Why hasn't this verse ever jumped out at him?"

"Wayne, dinner will be ready in about half an hour."

"Great. Just call me when it's ready."

13

IT WAS A NIGHT like many others in the community of believers in Pine Ridge. Some women worked side–by–side in the kitchen preparing some of Marsha's famous chili. Rain continued to beat steadily down, as it had for hours. The children were settling down in a back room where some of the older ones were planning to read to the toddlers. Though the wind and rain tormented all those outdoors, those gathered at the Harts' that evening found it quite soothing. The sounds of the heavy rain and full gutters transformed the rolling thunder into a beautiful bass in tonight's environmental symphony. The men, poised on the edge of their chairs, discussed the day's events, strategizing what to do about the emptiness in their workplaces.

"It's getting worse every day. I can't even go into a meeting or ride the elevator without facing a slew of vulgar language, gossip and darkness. It is especially heartbreaking because I know several of them claim to be Christians."

"Yes, I know God wants us to be a light shining out of darkness—"

The front door burst open, bringing in a rush of chilling autumn wind, rain and two saturated, desperate men.

"The old Turner house..." Brian paused to catch his breath. "The tarp...it's blown off. We tried to get it back in place. But with just the two of us..."

Some of the men were already out the door. Others, realizing what had happened, began grabbing raincoats and hats and entered the tempest.

The women and children watched from the front porch as the men scattered down the street toward the distressed property. Wives could barely identify their husbands through the silver sheets of rain blowing under the blackened sky. They tried to calm the questioning children who had been roused by the sudden uproar. The thunder, which had seemed almost playful from indoors, exploded from the darkness, terrifying the children.

Marsha tried to soothe them. "I don't think we have anything to worry about. I'm sure the tarp hasn't been off for that long. I'll bet everything will be just fine." She was trying to encourage herself as well as the others in the sullen crowd.

The women went on to feed the fussing, hungry children, periodically moving back curtains to peek out the windows and door.

After forty–five minutes, the dripping men returned with red, downcast faces.

Alan spoke up to answer the huddle of questioning looks. "Hard to tell for sure how much we'll lose. We'll know more in the morning when it's light. We all knew it would be risky trying to fix that roof after we were so far along, but at the time it didn't seem like we had a choice. We had to do it."

"What does the damage look like?"

Ted spoke up. "It doesn't look good. We only had the flashlights, but water is dripping from the first floor ceiling and the second story floor is buckling. That whole floor could be ruined. The big stack of drywall at the top of the stairs is saturated, and it looks like we'll lose most of the drywall we hung last weekend."

"What are we going to do?"

"We can't possibly come up with the money to replace all that."

"Is there any use in going on?"

"Even if we had the money, we were already working double time to be done by the end of the year. Now there is no way we could finish by then."

There was a hush over the room as everyone considered the ramifications. They all knew it was true.

Carolyn spoke up. "I have to think that if this was my own house and my own situation, I would be forced to find a way to make it work. It seems to me, if the Richardson's are coming here to be a part of our lives, then we might as well be completely committed to them...starting right now."

THE NEXT NIGHT, Carolyn sat on the couch, surrounded by stacks of laundry. It had been a long day, and after several nights of being up with the baby, her body craved sleep. It was 10:30 p.m., but the luxury of sleep must wait because three loads of laundry and caring for a one–year–old took precedence.

Despite fatigue, her mind was restless. Carolyn could not stop thinking about their early days at Pine Ridge. She remembered the things that made them want to move there — the warmth, the level of commitment, the possibility of close, daily relationships. It had all seemed so exciting.

Carolyn's collage of memories was interrupted as her husband came through the front door.

"Hi, Ted. How did it go at the old Turner place tonight?"

"Actually, it went okay. It looks as though the damage may not be as bad as we thought. Now that the floor is dry, the buckling doesn't seem that bad. I think it can be salvaged." Ted left the living room to go to the kitchen, and Carolyn returned to her laundry.

He returned minutes later with two corn dogs and a root beer and plopped down beside Carolyn. "You look thoughtful, Honey. What are you thinking about?"

"Do you know what day today is?"

Ted hesitated, smearing one of his corn dogs in a large puddle of mustard and running through his mental list of important dates. "For a minute I thought I had forgotten your birthday or our anniversary. But today is November 15th. Is there anything special about November 15th?"

"It was four years ago today, Ted, that we moved to Pine Ridge."

"No kidding. Boy, how time flies."

"Do you remember that day?"

"How could I ever forget it! I'll never forget the look on your face when I dropped the fish bowl on the driveway and Marsha's cat ate them." Ted grinned. "I told you we should have flushed those fish before we left."

"That's enough, Dear." She laughed softly. "It *was* a fun day. Remember how crazy our parents and friends thought we were."

"They just couldn't understand us moving out of state without jobs. I remember your dad." Ted shook his finger as he imitated Carolyn's father, "'Now, Ted, this is a very irresponsible thing you are doing...'" Ted let out a deep sigh, then became more serious. "But God sure came through for us, didn't He? I got a job. And look — He's given us a beautiful daughter, a nice home and a wonderful group of brothers and sisters to share our lives with. God has been very good to us."

"Those were some good days," Carolyn agreed. "Remember how excited we were? It was such a time of growth. We seemed to see God answer our prayers on a daily basis. God was so real, so alive to us."

Carolyn placed the last stack of laundry into the basket and started upstairs. Ted rinsed his dishes and shut off the downstairs lights for the night. When he walked into the bedroom, Carolyn looked up from the dresser. "Do you think we're the same?"

"The same? What do you mean?"

"My relationship with God seems different now — not as fresh, not as exciting. Does it seem that way to you?"

"I guess so. That's the way it is with anything, isn't it? When things are new, there is always something exciting about it. But it's nothing to get upset about. I think we're both doing okay. You've been so busy lately, and Marie has been up for the last four nights in a row. You just need to get some rest."

14

WAYNE WAS NOT PREPARED for his next discovery.

It was the Saturday after Thanksgiving. A half–dozen families had gathered at Hal and Virginia Ramsey's house to take in the local college football rivalry. Ed Lowrey, another one of the elders at Hampton Street, was sitting in front of the TV with a mason jar full of sweet tea, prepared to rib the opposition. He didn't plan on missing a single play.

The smell of fresh–baked bread still lingered in the air, with faint traces of cinnamon from the homemade cider and just a scent now and then of turkey and dressing. Most of the men sat huddled around the screen, each giving his synopsis of the last play and his opinion of the coaching. The ladies stood idle in the kitchen, struggling to make conversation. They defaulted to discussing the latest capers with the children and their favorite recipes.

Cheers erupted from the living room. It was a touchdown play. During the commotion, Ashley, the Davidsons' eighteen–month–old daughter, wandered down the hall and into the master bedroom, whose door was slightly ajar.

When Wayne realized she was missing, he began looking for her. He had seen the messes this little one could make in a matter of seconds — a few loose crayons, a fragile lamp, a box of laundry detergent left a little too low…Wayne's memories dictated that he had better find this little culprit, before she struck again.

A brief journey down the hall revealed a now fully–opened door to the master bedroom, the only clue Wayne needed.

It looked like the room was safe, at least from any major damage. Just a few seconds of cleaning and stacking and everything would be back to normal. She had waddled her way over to the mini–entertainment center in the bedroom, and several rows of VCR tapes now lay scattered across the floor.

Most were the usual, worldly videos Wayne knew most of his congregation watched — *Back to the Future, Terminator, An Officer and a Gentleman, Die Hard* and a few other blockbusters. He was still wondering how to address this subject with the congregation, but he never expected to find one of his elders watching this sort of thing.

As he reached to straighten the tapes in the back row, he felt his stomach knotting. They were plain black cases without pictures, but the words on the sides sent a shriek of terror through his soul. Triple–X movies, at least a dozen, with names too perverse to repeat. He hastily shoved everything back into the cabinet, grabbed Ashley and headed for the door.

He could feel the surge of tears about to explode through his face. He was hoping to make it through the living room and into the yard without being noticed. He quickly handed Ashley to Emily and bolted out the back door.

He sat and wept for what seemed like hours in the open field outside the now distant home. Waves of emotions swept over him as he heaved and prayed and sobbed. The dreams were beginning to make sense — too much sense.

Wayne recalled Hal's compromising counsel about the tares. It was all making sense now...except what to do next.

15

THAT SAME NIGHT, on the college campus, Rick Adams sat alone in the corner of the vacant cafeteria, at the same table where he and Professor Archer had talked a month earlier. On the table lay an open theology book — the kind normally found only in the reference section of a library — an untouched tray of food and a closed Bible. He stared out into the dark night, watching the light mist fall onto the holiday–emptied sidewalks.

The sound of approaching steps brought him back into the room. "Hey, Rick. I've been looking for you." It was the campus minister.

Rick acknowledged his beaming visitor with a nod and gestured toward an empty chair across the table.

"Listen. I know it's late, but I'm in a tight spot," the campus minister began, sliding into the chair. "Here's the deal." He leaned forward onto his elbows. "The pastor at the college Church came down with bronchitis, and we need somebody to fill in for tomorrow morning's sermon. I recommended you, and the elders concurred. We've definitely appreciated the times you've helped out in the past."

Rick was quiet. "I'm sorry. I'd rather not."

The campus minister cleared his throat uncomfortably. "You know it really wouldn't have to be a big thing. Not like you'd have to prepare ten hours for it. Just something simple."

"It's not the time factor," Rick countered softly. "It's just…it's just I don't feel like I have anything to say right now. That's all."

16

AS WAYNE DAVIDSON STOOD in the pulpit of Hampton Street Bible Church the next morning, the gravity of the moment began to close in on him. All night long he had wrestled for a solution, finally concluding that his only course of action was to address this problem through the pulpit.

As he stood there looking out on his congregation, Wayne spotted Hal Ramsey seated in the middle of the crowd. He thought for a moment he would lose his balance when Hal offered him a warm smile. Wayne grasped the sides of the pulpit, took a deep breath and looked down at his notes. He knew what he needed to do. After arranging his notes and taking a drink of water, Wayne looked at his congregation and greeted them. "Good morning."

"Good morning," answered the majority of those present.

"Well, I trust the Lord has blessed you this week. If we—"

"Our team won!" volunteered Ed Lowrey in support of Wayne's statement. Many of the younger members laughed, while most of the elderly sat stone-faced, still not completely comfortable with such modern informality in the worship. Wayne was startled only by the poignant reminder of the discovery made the preceding day.

"Yes, well, thank you for sharing that, Ed. I'm sure each of us has reasons to be thankful." Wayne cleared his throat as a small chuckle in the auditorium concluded the matter.

"If we could, I'd like to ask God to bless our time together here this morning." Wayne allowed a few seconds for folks to shift into a more comfortable position, then petitioned, "Our Heavenly Father, we ask that You would be with us here this morning as we study Your Word. We ask that You would give me wisdom as I teach from the Scriptures, and that You would show each one of us how to apply Your truth to our lives, individually, starting today. Amen."

"Amen," the congregation echoed. They shuffled Bibles, notebooks, pens and pencils as they prepared to study together. Wayne looked out on those entrusted to his care. Things were not as pure as they looked, and he knew it.

He saw Hal slip on a pair of reading glasses, legs crossed, note pad on his knee, pen in hand. *Hypocrite!* Wayne charged in his mind. *Wait! I can't react that way. Jesus never compromises, but He is always redemptive. God, please give me wisdom. Please reach my brother with this message.*

Wayne realized he had lost track of time when Hal's eyes narrowed in unison with the smile on his face. He quickly snapped to attention and addressed his congregation. "This morning, I'd like to deviate a little bit from our exposition of Matthew and share with you a message I feel is more...urgent right now." There was some shifting in the auditorium, including some whispered conversation. Wayne could see anxiety on his wife's face. She was looking across the aisle at Ron Beuford and his wife Katie, seated in the second row.

Ron and Katie were a middle–aged couple who had been unable to have children. Ron poured himself into his work at a mortgage company, and his wife found solace in volunteering at the Church. She was a meticulous woman who had overseen the Sunday school curriculum for the last eight years. She planned the classes months ahead of time to match the sermons, and then fretted as she waited for things to come off as planned. Wayne sometimes wondered why she tortured herself.

Wayne noticed Emily taking a second look at Katie. He knew Katie was taking this personally, imagining she had let everyone down because he was departing from the preprinted schedule. Wayne also knew what Emily was thinking. Ron, a generous contributor to the needs of Hampton Street, was determined to keep Katie happy. Wayne recognized this as the source of the anxiety that flashed across Emily's face. He was not entirely unsympathetic. *But I have to do this.*

Wayne continued, "We'll pick up with our study in Matthew next week. I know this is a bit unusual — but as your pastor, I feel the message I'm planning to share this morning is more needed at this point." Wayne took note of Ron and Katie's expressions as he scanned the faces of those in front of him.

"I'm calling today's message 'The Corinthian Excuse.'" Wayne waited a few seconds while papers shuffled. "The Corinthian Excuse. What is the Corinthian Excuse? Well, I'm sure you've heard it. We've all heard it in one form or another at some point in our lives as Christians." Wayne paused dramatically, then continued in a probing tone. "*You* may have even used the Corinthian Excuse. What is it?" Wayne gestured with a shrug. "Well, it comes in many styles and forms. Please open your Bibles to First Corinthians.

"What do we usually think of when we think of the Corinthian believers?" Wayne scanned the room for a response. "Ed, what are some things we usually think of when we consider the Church in Corinth?"

"Carnality. Sin," Ed Lowrey answered in a loud voice.

"Good, good. Carnality and sin." Wayne proceeded to write these words on the left side of a large white board behind him. "What kind of sin?"

Several others volunteered details. "Divisions. Selfishness. Pride..."

Wayne wrote hurriedly as descriptions were offered. Encouraged by the response so far, he capped the marker and faced the audience again. "Okay, we've got divisions, selfishness, pride, drunkenness, gluttony, boasting. Anything else you can think of?"

Wayne froze as Hal's hand went up. He looked him in the eye and nodded involuntarily. Wayne thought he was going to be sick when Hal suggested, "How about immorality?" Wayne couldn't move. Hal continued, somewhat uncomfortable with his pastor's delayed acknowledgment. "It certainly was a problem there." That was the answer Wayne was soliciting, but he never envisioned it coming from Hal.

Wayne spun around to add it to the list. "Yes, it certainly was." He gathered himself as he wrote on the board. "Okay, now I'd like to know some things you think of when you consider the Corinthian Church that are more positive in nature. What are some of the good things?" Wayne recognized a hand on the front row. "Yes?"

"Paul said they had every spiritual gift."

"Every spiritual gift," Wayne repeated as he wrote on the white board. "What else?"

After others offered positive attributes of Corinth, Wayne began to make his point. "Now—" Wayne paused to make sure everyone was following him, "what do people say when someone challenges the sin in their lives or the level of worldliness in their congregation? What is their reply if someone suggests that God isn't amused at sin — that He will bring judgment if there is no repentance?"

Wayne paused again to let the full weight of the questions sink in.

"They say, 'What about Corinth?'" Ed Lowrey offered. "'There was a lot of sin there and they were still God's Church.'"

"Exactly!" commended Wayne. "And what is the motive for bringing up the sin in Corinth after someone offers a challenge?"

"It keeps the heat off you, it's a smoke screen," another member retorted.

"And it makes it seem like sin's not that bad," volunteered someone else.

"Now, before I expose that myth," Wayne began, "let me ask one more side question. Tell me why any true follower of Jesus would want to pick the weakest Church in all of the Bible as a role model? Have we really slid that far to where the heroes of the faith are no longer the role models? Do we now, instead, search through our Bibles trying — on purpose — to find the weakest acceptable standard?" The rhetorical questions left silence in the air.

After enough silence had passed to convince Wayne the point was made, he began again. "It is true that Paul still addresses these folks as 'a Church' despite the corruption that had slipped in. But keep in mind that he had made some pretty bold statements. He also said in the same letter that 'their meetings did more harm than good' and that what they thought was the Lord's Supper was, in fact, a cup of demons instead.

"Whew! Some pretty tough language, don't you think?" Wayne began to pace the rostrum. "It's always puzzled me — this Church is in such a mess and Paul speaks so harshly to them. Yet, at the same time, he still seemed to have a confidence that things would be all right. It puzzled me — that is, until I found a few other verses that complete this story. Turn in your Bibles to Second Corinthians chapter seven.

"In this passage, Paul unlocks the mystery of his confidence in this weak, infant Church. In fact, in this same passage he goes on to say that he had already bragged to Titus that he knew they would repent of the sins he had brought to their attention in his previous letter. Where does he get the confidence that would cause him to brag about how they would respond to his first letter?" Wayne returned to the podium and flipped the pages of his Bible. "What clues does the text give us about how they responded to his first letter? Let's look."

He lifted his Bible from the podium and began to read:

"See what this Godly sorrow has produced in you: what earnestness, what eagerness to clear yourselves, what indignation, what alarm, what longing, what concern, what readiness to see justice done. AT EVERY POINT YOU HAVE PROVED YOUR-SELVES TO BE INNOCENT IN THIS MATTER..."

Wayne returned his Bible to its resting place and began pacing again. "Now, stay with me," he pled. "His confidence in them was *not* based on their condition! It was based on his knowledge of how they would respond! He knew things were a mess! A big mess! But, and you've got to see this, he also knew that 'the — sheep — know — the — shepherd's — voice.' He knew in his heart of hearts that they would respond with repentance. And what a massive repentance it was!

"They didn't say, 'What about Ephesus — they're not so hot.' They didn't try to blame–shift or to hide behind the Galatians, who were also in a bit of a mess, if you remember. What did they do? They were cut to the heart and they repented!

"I got excited the other day — someone brought up Corinth." His voice was raised, but it wasn't theatrics. "That used to make me nervous. Not any more. I said, Yep, Corinth was a weak Church. Maybe the weakest Church in the whole Bible. But let this be a commentary on us today: We don't even measure up to the weakest Church in the Bible. Here's why." Wayne held up two fingers. "Number one, when their sins were exposed they responded with violent, sweeping repentance. And two, when the Corinthian Church withdrew from the immoral brother, the text implies in chapter two, that not eating with him almost killed the man!

"What do you think of that? To be 'disfellowshiped' in the weakest Church in the Bible was more painful than going through a divorce. An intense, painful separation. Oh, that we were as weak as they…"

Wayne finished out the hour by admonishing his congregation to turn from sin. He pleaded with them to not let the leaven of private sin destroy their whole lives and work its way into the lives of the whole Church as Paul had warned. Many in the congregation were moved emotionally by the passion Wayne displayed as he begged them to be honest with themselves about their lives.

Wayne could usually tell if his message had been delivered and received successfully. This morning, he was confident it had. It occurred to him there was a healthy sobriety when the service ended, and he was fairly certain Hal had taken his message to heart. He knew he would see him when the service was over and was eager to find out how he was taking it. As the congregation sang the concluding hymn, Wayne noticed Hal wasn't singing. *God, I knew You'd come through. Help him to turn to You.* Wayne prayed silently.

As was his custom, Wayne went to stand at the front doors and exchange pleasantries with families as they poured into the parking lot. Occasionally, he scanned the sea of faces, hoping to find Hal. *I hope he's not avoiding me.*

"That was a wonderful sermon, young man," an elderly woman greeted him.

Wayne looked down and smiled. "Thank you, Mrs. Rugger." *There he is!* Wayne now saw Hal talking jovially with Ed Lowrey. Mrs. Rugger released Wayne's hand and surrendered to the tide of the vacating crowd.

Slowly the throng dissipated, and Hal approached Wayne with a placid expression on his face. They were relatively alone, as those remaining were turning out lights and locking doors. Wayne breathed another prayer for wisdom and placed his hand on Hal's shoulder. "Are you doing okay, Hal?" Wayne asked cautiously.

Hal cocked his head and donned a confused grin, "Sure. What do you mean?"

Wayne stumbled for words, "Well, I mean with…with what was said this morning. I just thought that maybe…"

"Oh, that," Hal interrupted.

Wayne lit up, seeing the realization on Hal's face.

Hal continued, "Hey, listen. I'm sorry if what I said this morning was…um…if what I said was inappropriate."

Now Wayne was confused. "Inappropriate? What do you mean?"

"You know, the comment about there being a lot of immorality in Corinth. I wondered after I said it if maybe I shouldn't have."

"No. I mean…" Wayne wasn't sure what to make of this. He could see Emily walking with Hal's wife, Virginia, down the hall toward the exit. He quickly steered Hal out the front door and walked slowly toward the parking lot. The fresh air cleared his mind and he again groped for Hal's inner thoughts. "So what did you think of the…message this morning?" Wayne searched Hal's face for a sign of conviction.

Hal looked up with a comfortable smile, "It was good, Wayne. Real good." Hal sensed that perhaps he hadn't said exactly what Wayne wanted to hear. He tried again. "I think your delivery was very effective. You were really able to solicit a lot of participation."

Wayne stared at Hal incredulously. *He didn't get it.*

Hal wasn't sure why Wayne looked so stoic. "Hey, Wayne, if you're worried about Katie Beuford and her Sunday School curriculum getting side-tracked," he continued consolingly, "I really wouldn't let it bother you. She'll get over it."

Emily and Virginia were rapidly approaching with their children. The knot in Wayne's stomach confirmed that the issue was still unresolved. "Listen, Wayne, I promised Virginia I'd take her to the mall today and get the kids some new clothes." Wayne still stood like a monument. "Are you going to be all right?"

Wayne yielded to reality. "Yeah." He sighed. "Yeah, I'll be fine."

Hal moved across the parking lot toward his car, where his wife and children were buckling in. "You need to relax, Wayne," Hal advised loudly. "You seem stressed. Hey, why don't you and Emily take a couple of days off this week. The children can stay at our house."

Wayne felt nauseous.

Do not merely listen to the word,

and so deceive yourselves.

Do what it says.

James 1:22

Resolve

17

THE BELIEVERS IN Pine Ridge were gathered to share the highlights and concerns of their day. They did not gather for "services" or "sermons" but to renew their affirmation and commitment to each other. This particular night's discussion had centered around First John and a challenging chapter about the cross by T. Austin–Sparks. After the discussion came to a close, they all held hands and spent some time worshiping together.

As the touching evening came to a close, everyone began bundling children and gathering belongings. They still managed to make it out the door by eleven o'clock.

It appeared no different than any other night they were together — except Carolyn felt strangely stirred. A peculiar dissatisfaction. Normally, she was encouraged by a night with the saints. *What's wrong? Why do I feel this way?* Carolyn reflected on the time together, trying to find the source of her discomfort. No tension. Normal conversations. She recalled the familiar faces of her sisters. *Why did I feel like a stranger...?*

"Carolyn." Ted placed his hand on his wife's knee in an effort to get her attention. "Carolyn, we're home." It was a short drive and her thoughts were abruptly interrupted.

The evening routine of feeding Marie and preparing her for bed passed in silence as Carolyn continued sorting through her thoughts. Ted broke the silence as they climbed into bed. "You're awfully quiet tonight, Honey. Are you feeling all right?"

"Oh, I feel fine. I just have some things on my mind. That's all." Carolyn was still desperately trying to make sense of her thoughts and emotions and wasn't sure what to share.

After a light kiss, they said good night, and Ted soon drifted off to sleep. Carolyn lay awake, trying to squelch the questions still spinning in her head. Unable to find peace, she quietly got out of bed and made her way to the living room floor.

"Father, help me understand. What is going on?" She pressed her face against the carpet, trying to communicate the dull ache in her heart — finding no words, only painful silence and inward groans. Several minutes later, she pushed herself up to her knees and struck the floor decisively. "There *is* something missing!

"There has to be more than teaching the children how to read and share their toys, cleaning homes, preparing meals together, reading a lot about being led by the Spirit...God, I'm not content with my life."

She closed her eyes and sat quietly for a minute. Her life suddenly struck her as empty. Nowhere did she see anything from Heaven breaking through. It seemed so normal, so human. *That's it — it's of the earth in every way. Nothing life-changing, nothing heart–wrenching, nothing freeing. I want to get past the earthliness and share the inside of my life with Susan, Marsha and the others! The pleasant, spiritual meetings and organic lifestyle are not enough! We've got to get inside of each other's hearts! We've got to help each other walk with God and obey Him — not just have a 'granola lifestyle' about Him.*

Carolyn began asking God what to do and how she could open up the curtain of her own heart with the people around her. And she meant it.

THERE WAS A FRESH BLANKET OF SNOW when Carolyn awoke the next morning. To her, the snow was a testimony that God was doing a new thing. With an energy she hadn't felt in a long time, she set off for the Harts. Sisters regularly gathered there for coffee and some time together in the Scriptures. Carolyn was eager to be with everyone.

As people were piling in, Marsha was in the kitchen getting mugs, coffee, tea, doughnuts, cream and sugar all in line — just right for everyone. All the women were anxious to get to the hot coffee this cold morning. As everyone stood around talking about the latest household happenings, Carolyn tried to look each person in the eyes and really care about what they were saying.

While she was a little uncomfortable, she could sense the renewing of her spirit. *This is right. Something about this is right.*

Carolyn wasn't the only one excited about the day. This was the first big snow and the children did not want to miss it. After the last little hand was squeezed into its mitten, the ladies all smiled and let out a "Whew!" in unison as the door slammed shut.

"Does anyone know of a prayer need this morning?" Traditionally, this time together consisted of an hour of just simple prayer and intercession, some reading from the Scriptures, and a few songs. Even though they had been reading through Esther, Carolyn was hoping they could talk about the chapter that had been read the night before.

Carolyn tried hard to contain her excitement. "Did anyone look back over or think more about that chapter Brian read last night?"

"Not me," Marsha explained. "I haven't had a chance. I was busy cleaning and getting everything ready for this morning."

"I thought what Brian read was really encouraging," chimed in a sister leaning against the back wall. "Why, did something specific stick out to you, Carolyn?"

"Yes, very much so. I would describe it...more as challenging than encouraging. The part about truth–centered relationships rather than friendship-centered relationships, I found very convicting."

"Yes," Brian's wife, Susan, spoke up. "Just think. All we used to do is sit in pews near each other once a week. I can't imagine having to live like that again." She took a careful sip of her hot coffee. "Once again, I am just in awe of how good God is to have delivered us from shallow relationships and brought us here to have real fellowship with one another."

Carolyn's heart sank deep within her. All the previous energy from the morning had evaporated, swallowed in confusion. She could hardly think, much less respond. As the others went on to read in Esther, Carolyn was stuck in that moment, trying to make sense of the last twenty–four hours.

Surely, we didn't just exchange pews for living rooms. Is this all that there is? God, am I just making all this up in my head?...No, there's just got to be more!

18

HIS HANDS FELT uncomfortably sticky against the leather steering wheel. Wayne wiped them on his pants and took a deep breath. He was absolutely positive he had never attempted anything this difficult in his entire life. He had been fasting all day, though unintentionally.

He pulled into the Ramseys' driveway and was disappointed to see Hal's car. It would have been fine with him to try another day. This kind of thing wasn't covered in seminary. What pastor in his right mind wants to confront one of his own elders, one of the few that still likes him, about serious sin? He was well aware that this could blow up in his face. What about Hal's marriage? Did his wife know? Was this just the tip of the iceberg?

He had stalled long enough. If he stayed in the car any longer, they would know something was up. He took a last deep breath, very slowly, and opened the car door. The trek across the yard to the front door passed more quickly than he had hoped. He wrung his hands one last time, trying to keep his sweaty palms from being too obvious. He rang the doorbell.

"Hey, Wayne, what brings you by on a Tuesday evening?" Hal's voice sounded from the open doorway. "What a pleasant surprise."

"Well, I need to talk to you before you leave town...It's kinda serious."

Hal noted Wayne's demeanor. "We could go to my study. It's private."

They quickly made their way through the living room and down the short hallway to the den. Virginia gave a quick glance toward Wayne and could tell he was not himself. As the door clicked shut, she went quickly back to the kitchen to finish preparing dinner.

"Well, hurry and tell me what's on your mind before you pass out, boy," Hal started.

"Hal, remember the football game Saturday?"

Hal gave a consenting nod.

"I'll try to get right to the point. During the game, Ashley accidentally wandered into the back of your bedroom and got into

74

your VCR tapes...Hal, I had no idea you had a problem with pornography. Why haven't you said something? If it really is a stronghold for you, I want to help."

For a split second, a strange tension hovered in the room. Hal blushed slightly, but quickly composed himself. An instant later, he let out a hearty but somewhat spurious laugh that caught Wayne completely off guard. Wayne was about to caution Hal that this was no laughing matter when Hal continued.

"What do you...Oh! I know what you're referring to. Those weren't pornographic tapes."

"Huh, they weren't?" Confusion clouded Wayne's relief.

"No," Hal reassured, "those were some cases I picked up at a flea market. I guess I should have removed the liners, but...I never really thought about it."

Hal seemed so genuine. *Could I have misjudged him? But those covers — could anyone be that naïve?*

Wayne prayerfully considered his next move. "Hey, Hal, I'd like to believe you. I mean, I do believe you. But it would really help me to sleep better if I could just, maybe, look inside those cases." His boldness surprised even himself.

"What would be the point? I told you, they're just cases." As Virginia quietly approached the door to see if she could offer some beverages, Hal continued. "Wayne, I know what it must look like to you." His reddened face betrayed his true emotions. "But you're just going to have to take my word for it — friend."

Wayne paused and internally asked God for the courage to push one more time. "Hal, I'm not trying to be obnoxious. I really do care about you. And I really want to be wrong about this thing. If you could just show me..."

Now Hal stood up, glaring at the still–seated Wayne. His intimidating voice blared. "Wayne, are you calling me a liar? This is my house! I don't have to put up with this kind of harassment!" Hal put his finger in Wayne's face. "You may be the pastor, but that doesn't give you the right to go flinging accusations around."

Wayne tried to soothe Hal's temper. "I just thought..."

"You think too much! You need to get your imagination under control, Wayne. What have you been feeding your mind that you would assume I am involved in pornography? Maybe *you're* the one with the pornography problem and you're just pushing it off on me! Well, I don't have to put up with this!"

Virginia slipped quietly away from the door.

Wayne sat in stunned silence, wishing he were anywhere but there. He wished he knew what to say to make everything right again. This was not what he had envisioned.

Hal opened the door and gestured, "Wayne, perhaps you ought to leave now, while we're still friends."

Wayne looked up, bruised, wanting to apologize, but not sure why or if he should. He walked slowly out of the den and down the hall to the front door. The air around him felt thick, and the noise echoed as if he were in a tunnel. As Wayne opened the front door, the sound of traffic seemed dream–like. Everything seemed to move in slow motion. As he stepped out of Hal's house, he thought he heard the sound of a woman crying.

EMILY BEGAN QUICKLY changing the sweat–dampened linens, hoping they could still salvage the rest of their night's sleep.

The dream had come again. This was the seventh and most vivid time. Wayne still trembled as he relayed to Emily this episode's most recent details. With the wet sheets in the hamper, she paused from her work and sat down by Wayne as he continued.

"Em, this time the dream ended at Judgment Day. I had to give an account for Hal, for Tom, for John Carley. And Jesus was just standing there...standing right in front of me." Wayne suffered as he nervously related the details to his wife. "I always knew I would give an account for everything I taught, and I've tried to be faithful and accurate with the Word of God...But I had no idea I would have to give an account for the spiritual condition of everyone at Hampton Street!"

Emily wasn't sure what to say. "Just be glad it was only a dream," she consoled. But as the words left her lips, they felt empty and hollow. *Was it really just a dream?* Seven times he'd been assailed by vivid images challenging his work at Hampton. She wondered if she'd been so dull that she hadn't recognized God's thumbprint.

As she tucked in new sheets, she recalled how fresh her walk with God seemed before she married Wayne. Every day seemed to be an adventure in faith. "What will God do today?" she would wonder.

When did things change? She and Wayne had intended to change the world, to do great things for God. At one time they had seriously considered joining a mission team going to Africa. Maybe she'd let herself become too distracted by the children, by the mundane responsibilities of motherhood. Or maybe she hadn't understood God very well. Who knows?

RRRRING!

What's that? Already morning? Wayne hit the top of the alarm clock. The ringing persisted. *Telephone.* He reached for the receiver.

"Hello." Wayne's froggy voice revealed his slow morning start.

"Oh, hello, Wayne. This is Virginia Ramsey. I'm sorry I woke you."

"No, no. That's okay. I was going to get up." Wayne looked at the clock. *8:38.*

"Um…" Virginia stammered for words. "Oh, you left your jacket here yesterday. And I thought I'd…let you know that."

"Are you okay, Virginia?"

"Yes. I just wanted to thank you for coming over yesterday."

Wayne's mind raced wildly. *Why would she…Did she hear…But why?…Oh, the crying!* "Virginia, when I left yesterday, were you crying?" His heart burned as he waited for Virginia to break the silence.

"Uh–huh."

"You heard us talking?"

"Yes."

"Then, you know what we were talking about?"

"I think I do." She paused for a moment, then conceded with a sigh, "About the videos."

"Then it's true?"

"Yes," she said softly, the pain now coming through her voice. She proceeded to tell Wayne the whole sordid history through muffled sobs. It was worse than Wayne had imagined, and he felt incensed as he recalled how Hal had so sincerely defended himself.

"I want you to know we're with you. We want both you and Hal to make it, with each other and with Jesus. We really do."

"Oh, Wayne," she tearfully interrupted, "maybe it's too late for us. Maybe I should just give up. What about the children?" She was sobbing again and losing her coherency.

"Virginia, get a hold of yourself," Wayne calmed. "I know it's painful and, honestly, I don't know how everything will turn out. But I can promise you this: if you will commit to doing things Jesus' way, and trust Him, He will honor that and bless you."

"I'll try. But I may need help."

"We'll help you, Virginia. We'll help you all the way."

19

BACK ON CAMPUS, the students were packing up their books as Professor Archer gathered the remaining test papers.

"One down, three to go," the professor said under his breath. "Monday's finals are always the most difficult." Professor Archer noticed a familiar ache in his heart. He longed for the truths he shared with his students to penetrate past their minds and into their hearts.

His thoughts were interrupted when another professor stuck his head into the room and cleared his throat. "George, have you seen Rick today?"

"Wasn't he just taking a Greek final?"

"He never showed up."

"That's odd. Maybe he's sick."

"I would have thought he would have at least called me." The Greek professor shrugged. "Maybe he overslept."

LOUD SCREAMS echoed from behind a door plastered with posters. The entire building seemed to rock on its foundation. The deafening blast from the speakers, left-over fragments of fire crackers and empty shaving cream cans left no doubt — this was either the scene of some major disaster or finals week had arrived.

Has dorm life changed so much...or have I? Professor Archer walked around a stack of pizza boxes.

"Professor Archer! Uh...hi! Didn't expect to see you here." One of his students passed by, obviously hiding something in his hand.

"I'm looking for Rick," the professor shot back.

"I haven't seen him lately, Professor. But that's his room down there. Last one on the left."

Professor Archer swallowed hard as he approached the open door. It was odd for Rick to miss his Greek final, and the professor had been puzzled. But when he also missed his Old Testament final on Tuesday, it was time to find out what was going on.

He knocked lightly on the open door, scanning the room for signs of life. The two beds had been stacked in an effort to make the small room livable. The bottom bunk revealed a bare mattress, though the bookshelves nearest it bulged with Greek lexicons and Bible commentaries — evidence of Rick. A large poster of a lion and a lamb hung on the wall beside the bed.

"Professor Archer!" Eric was startled as he looked up from the sink.

"I was hoping I might find Rick here," the professor began.

Eric rinsed the remaining toothpaste from his mouth. "No, Sir, he's been gone for three days."

"Three days?!"

"Yes, Sir. I came back to the room Saturday afternoon and all of his clothes were gone. I don't know what happened."

"Have you called his house?"

"Yeah. I tried three times...no answer."

"Did you notify the school?" Professor Archer raised his voice.

Eric was taken aback by the professor's tone. He hung his head. "You know Rick. He's real strong. I figured he knew what he was doing. He'll be okay."

"Maybe," the professor said calmly. "But strong or not, he might need our help."

"How about Amy?" Eric asked. "Maybe she knows something."

"She wasn't in. I left a message." The professor studied the room, thoughtfully. "Eric, can I have Rick's home number?"

SEVERAL STATES AWAY, the aroma of roast beef mingled with pumpkin pie filled the Adams residence. White linen covered the long dining room table that was normally reserved for company. Home-baked bread and tossed salad were plentiful. Tall, white candles adorned the centerpiece and cast a warm glow on the room. Sarge, the family collie, barely managed to restrain himself as he waited for precious morsels to fall from the table.

Long after the family had finished offering thanks, Mrs. Adams' head was still bowed.

"He's going to be fine." Mr. Adams took his wife's hand and held it gently. His words were sincere, but she didn't feel like being comforted.

"I thought surely his favorite meal would have lured him out of that room." Rick's mom glanced toward the empty chair. "He's hardly come out at all in the four days he's been home."

"I know. It's just not like our son to keep secrets from us," Mr. Adams replied. "Tell you what — I'm planning on talking to him this evening. Maybe he'll open up a bit when it's just the two of us." He looked up and smiled. "But for now, I think I'll have some of those wonderful mashed potatoes that you worked so hard on. Could you pass them this way, Sweetheart?"

Everyone was a little startled when the telephone rang. "It's for me!" Rick's younger sister called out behind her as she rescued the phone from a second ring. She reappeared a few moments later, disappointed. "It's for you, Dad."

Mr. Adams lifted the receiver, half expecting to hear a sales pitch for storm doors and windows. "Hello," he said cautiously.

"Hello, Mr. Adams." Professor Archer's heart was pounding with anticipation. "My name is George Archer. I'm one of Rick's professors. I believe we met briefly during homecoming."

"Professor Archer! Why, yes. Rick has always spoken very highly of you."

"I hope I'm not interrupting anything. Is this a bad time?"

"No, I can't tell you how glad I am that you called! You've had a tremendous impact on Rick's life, and I know he has a great deal of respect for you."

"I've been rather concerned about Rick." The professor proceeded cautiously. "Is everything all right?"

"I'm not sure I know the answer to that." Rick's father sighed as the weight of their dilemma pressed him. "Professor Archer, to be honest, I'm very worried. Would you speak with him? He trusts you, and I think he might listen to you."

"Sure. I'd like to do that."

Without waiting for the answer, Mr. Adams had already sent his wife upstairs to get Rick. As Professor Archer waited, he carefully considered his next words. He was uncertain how to approach this.

Rick's mom returned, visibly shaken.

"Honey! Are you all right?" Dropping the phone, Mr. Adams moved quickly to meet her. After several moments, he returned. "I'm sorry, Professor. I don't know what to say. Rick's never been like this."

"Is something wrong, Mr. Adams?"

"I'm sorry. He refuses to speak to you. In fact, he said he never wants to see or hear from you again. Forgive me, I..."

"Perhaps I should call back later?"

"Well, I think you might want to give him some time. He's pretty upset. But would you pray for him?"

20

AS WAYNE PARKED at Hampton Street Bible Church, the night sky bore an eerie resemblance to the one he'd been witnessing in his haunting dream.

He had felt this coming for three weeks, ever since the incident with Hal. Only two days earlier, he had warned Emily, bracing her for their uncertain future. And now, that morning's phone call. No surprise. *"The elders would like to meet with you tonight, Wayne. 8:00 sharp."*

Hal's car was in the lot, along with everyone else's. It was now ten minutes before eight and everyone was early. As he opened the door, he could hear deep voices in the first classroom to the right. The closing door announced his arrival with a hollow boom, and the conversation subsided.

As he entered the room, some eyes darted nervously as if ashamed of participating in the proceedings. Others looked stone-faced, seeking to make eye contact with Wayne. Among the latter group was Tom, who broke the silence.

"Hi, Wayne," he said pleasantly. "Please have a seat," he invited with a gesture of his hand. "Thanks for coming on such short notice."

Wayne sat in the chair that was prepared for him.

"Wayne," Tom sighed heavily, "we felt that it was in the congregation's best interest that we get together and have a talk."

"Have I done something wrong?"

Tom was surprised by Wayne's frankness and snickered

nervously. "Well, no, not exactly, Wayne. We just need to discuss some…concerns that we have — and that others in the congregation have, too."

"What kind of concerns?" Wayne asked soberly. His directness was setting the tone for the meeting.

As two or three of the elders shifted nervously, Tom pulled his trump card. "Wayne, as you're aware, your annual review is in eight weeks. We've appreciated the fine preaching you've provided for our congregation over the past eight years. However, the tone of your messages, of late, has taken a direction that we feel may not be right for Hampton. Wayne, there's a hardness to them, an edge that we feel isn't really…healthy."

"I'm not sure what you mean. My messages come straight from the Bible. Now I realize that I have deviated some from the syllabus, and I may have upset Katie Beuford. However—"

"Wayne, its not Katie. We just feel—"

"We think you're coming across too harsh," another elder clarified.

"Can you give me some examples?" Wayne challenged.

There was a long silence with glances electing who would answer Wayne's challenge. Finally, Tom spoke again. "Wayne, it's kind of difficult for us to put our finger on some specific statement you've made in your sermons. It's more of an attitude that comes across."

"An attitude," Wayne said dryly. "But you can't give me an example."

Tom had his prey. "Well, Wayne," he began with feigned cautiousness, "you came across pretty judgmentally concerning my son, practically implying he isn't a Christian."

"Tom, that's not really—"

Now Hal interrupted, "You know, something very similar happened to me before my business trip. Wayne barged into my home and made some pretty bold accusations before getting his facts straight."

Wayne was shocked at Hal's arrogant audacity. He wanted to scream, yet somehow he managed to address Hal with composure. "Hal, before we continue, could I speak with you outside for a few minutes?"

"No," Hal said boldly, "you're not going to corner me again.

This time if you've got something to say, I want some witnesses."

Witnesses. Now, there's an idea. Jesus did say if you spoke with someone about their sin and they wouldn't hear you that you should bring in other witnesses. Maybe Hal was right. Maybe he should say everything in front of all of these men. Because Wayne still hoped to speak with Hal one on one, he decided to try once more.

"Hal, I really think it would be better if we could speak alone in the hall, just for a moment."

"NO WAY!" Hal shouted. "I'll tell you guys what he is driving at. Our nosey pastor accused me of having pornography in my house. Well, I'll not be bullied! I'm not afraid of these men knowing what you have to say. They've all known me for years, and my character speaks for itself. So if you have anything to say, say it here and now."

"Hal," Wayne began slowly, "your wife called me in tears and confirmed everything. You've been living a lie for quite some time, and she can't handle it anymore. She was so relieved for someone to know."

Hal looked like a punctured inner tube. His jaw hung frozen open, and his face flushed. Everyone stared at the table in silence.

Finally, Hal slid his chair back and briskly left the room.

After sorting through some difficult details, the meeting ended as uncomfortably as it had begun. Gil was assigned to advise Hal to step down from the eldership and to keep things as quiet as possible.

The elders concluded that none of this was to leave the room. They would deal with their problems like they always had — secretly.

Things were still awkward with Wayne. He was right about Hal. It was undeniable. Still, in their minds, Wayne was the "bad guy." They wanted a church that was inspiring, yet comfortable. A place with close friends, but where people had the good sense to not meddle where they didn't belong.

Wayne could read the handwriting on the wall tonight as clearly as Daniel had centuries earlier. He knew his days were numbered. It's fine to hold up a theoretical standard, but the direct application of that standard to individual lives was, in reality, unwelcome.

Wayne knew a line had been crossed. He wasn't just playing church anymore. Either Jesus was Lord of the lives of the members, or it was a sham. And Wayne was more committed than ever to ending the charade — life by life — and calling men to honest reality before God.

If he was going to answer to God for their souls, then he was going to have to get personal with the Word of God and use it for exhortation, rebuke, correction, and training in righteousness — exactly as God commanded him. No longer was he just content to preach sermons and to teach men *about* God, he was now committed to call everyone that wore the name of Jesus to **obey Him!**

"HELLO." Virginia Ramsey grabbed the telephone as she wiped flour on her apron.

"Hi, Virginia. This is Wayne. I just wanted to check and see how you're doing today." Wayne paused before continuing carefully. "So...how did it go last night?"

"Well, it was sort of strange," she answered, wrinkling her brow. "I would have expected Hal to be very angry with me. But, instead, he was withdrawn and quiet. Like all the life and energy had been drained out of him. The house was very still all night."

"So, he didn't seem angry at all?" Wayne asked, puzzled.

"He wasn't happy, that's for sure. But he said so little, it was hard to tell exactly what he was thinking." She hesitated. Swallowing hard, she guarded her fragile emotions. "It's obvious he's bitter...but I'm not sure he cares anymore. I'm worried about him."

"I've been hoping and praying you wouldn't have to take the brunt of all this," Wayne explained. "I'm sorry—"

"Oh no, Wayne," Virginia cried out. "I'm grateful! For years I've been miserable. Just hiding his sin was destroying me. Maybe I never should have hidden it. Jesus commanded us to bring in other brothers and sisters when necessary. I see now that marriage isn't an excuse to disobey Him. I'm *so* thankful things are out in the open. I don't feel like I'm living in Achan's tent anymore. Things may seem messy on the outside, but I haven't felt this free on the inside in a long, long time."

21

THE UPSTAIRS CLASSROOM was quiet. The window blinds were opened high and the bright mid–afternoon sun masked the December coolness outside. Professor Archer sat behind the large oak desk at the front of the room, grading the exams he had given two hours earlier. Finals were now over. For students and faculty alike, relief had come. Most of the students had scattered for home to recuperate. In three weeks, it would be business as usual once again — for most.

The professor let his pencil drop as he breathed a long sigh.

"Why?!!" It was more of a groan than a word. He sat with his face buried in his hands for a few moments. Quietly, he drifted, lost in his own questions.

Finally, he shook his head with vigor, as if to clear cobwebs. He gathered his scattered emotions and set back to the work before him.

Six more to go. The task had been tedious. Twenty–one students in the last class. Seventy–five short essay questions. Not easy work! He'd often mused that the hieroglyphics course he had passed up would have helped him with some of the hand-writing. As he mulled over the answer to question 37, a familiar face passed his open door.

"Amy!...Wait!" Professor Archer rose and moved briskly toward the hallway. By the time he reached the door, she was already to the top of the stairs with her hand on the banister, ready to disappear.

"Amy!" His voice stopped her. "I'd really like to talk to you — just for a minute."

She froze in indecision.

He walked toward her. "I tried to call Rick last night. He wouldn't come to the phone. Amy, what's going on?"

Her head dropped. She fought the urge to run down the stairs, afraid to face the consequences of turning around.

The silence was awkward. Finally, she relented and turned slowly to face Professor Archer. "Sorry I've avoided your calls, Mr. Archer." She lifted her gaze slightly. "It's been a rough week...Rick won't talk to me, either."

He offered a forgiving smile. "I understand. I'm sure this has been hard. Could we talk?" He motioned toward the classroom with his head.

Amy took a deep breath, then resigned. "Sure."

Once inside the classroom, she found a student desk, rested her chin on the backpack she had been hugging, and closed her eyes.

Professor Archer pulled his chair out and sat down beside his desk. He leaned forward. Both were stuck for a moment in their own pain, their own feelings of rejection. This hadn't been easy for either of them. The professor broke the silence. Slowly. Sensitively. "Do you know...surely you must know...what happened?"

"Yes, I do know," she started softly, holding tightly the purse strings of her heart. "He...kind of gave up." She looked up at the professor. "He feels like a failure, like he's let everyone down."

"Let everyone down? Why would he feel that way? I've never known him to be like that."

She sighed. "Something...happened. He felt all responsible and left." Amy closed her eyes again.

"What happened?"

She closed her eyes tighter, battling between the pressure to say more and the urge to run out the door in tears.

The professor noticed her pain and offered gently, "I'm sorry. I know it must hurt. But maybe I can help. Can you tell me what happened?"

Her heart began racing wildly. She knew what she needed to say, but the secrets of the pain she held had not been heard by human ears...other than Rick's.

She opened her mouth. A stutter, then silence. She breathed a determined sigh and continued almost inaudibly. The professor leaned toward her as she whispered, "I'm...I'm pregnant." She was almost in tears. She didn't look at the professor, afraid of what his expression would do to her.

Finding strength, she continued. "I found out last Thursday. Then I told Rick. It didn't go well. He got angry and then depressed. We talked, but he was confused and upset."

Her confidence faltered, the pain obvious. She stared at the floor in silence. Regaining some of her strength, she continued through trembling lips. "The next morning, he called me and said he was leaving. He said he couldn't face the failure. He kept saying he was ashamed. He told me he was sorry, but that he just couldn't face it all. I know a lot of it had to do with feeling he'd let everyone down. He believed his career and all he'd dreamed of were gone."

She let out a long breath. There! She'd done it. Somehow it really did feel better for someone else to know. She wished Rick could know the same solace.

The professor closed his eyes as he allowed Amy's words to sink in. He was shocked Rick had given in to sin, but something else was still bugging him, something he couldn't quite identify. He'd had other students make poor choices, even costly ones. But this seemed different.

Finally, he formed the one question he couldn't help but ask. "Why didn't he come talk to me?" As he asked, the professor was torn between self–pity and genuine confusion.

"He did try," she said gently. "He talked to you one day in the cafeteria. He told me about it. He tried to get in to see the campus minister, too. That didn't work out either."

Professor Archer remembered. *How did I miss it?* He tried to remember Rick's words. *Why was I so naïve?* At that moment, he felt the bite of his own failure.

He shook free from his introspection, remembering that Amy was in the room. He could deal with himself later. Right now, there was a troubled girl, an abandoned mother, in need of answers.

"Amy…I realize this may not sound particularly helpful right now. But I do believe it's absolutely important that you let your parents know about this very soon." The words were slow and deliberate. "Or have you already told them?"

Amy wasn't shocked by his words. The fact that she'd wrestled with that imminent conversation seemed apparent as she answered. "I know…but I can't." Her answer wasn't flippant. She calculated again in her mind the conversation she envisioned. She shuddered. Hadn't her parents always told her to come to them for help? Weren't they Christians? Why did she feel so un-comfortable at the thought?

"It won't be easy. I'm not sure how to even recommend you go about it. But I do think it's really important that they find out, soon, from you."

Amy nodded assent, though it was more an acknowledgment of fate than a commitment to action.

"Please let me know if I can help." The words sounded hollow. They rang of the trained professor and not the broken man he was becoming.

She thanked him quietly and left the classroom.

He put his head in his hands and let go the reins of his heart.

GEORGE ARCHER LIVED in a two–bedroom ranch home within walking distance of the campus. It had seemed pointless to stay in his northside home after leukemia had taken his wife seven years earlier. Too many painful memories. So, after moving, he buried himself in his studies. To George, those studies were meant to be an investment in his students. Instead, they had served to shelter him from vulnerability. But that was changing.

Today, he sat crumpled in the floor of his study. It had been three hours since he and Amy had talked. He replayed in his mind the conversations he'd had with Rick, words he could have spoken, help he could have offered.

God, how could I have been so blind? he prayed. *Was I so caught up in my own agenda for his life that I didn't notice the war going on inside his heart?* George was feeling a kind of pain he'd never known. Yes, Rick's leaving had hurt. But the greater pain was knowing he could have prevented it.

Father, it wasn't the campus minister's fault. It was my fault. Tears began to slowly trickle down his face. *Father...please forgive me. I have been careless and unfaithful with a precious child of yours.* "I'm so sorry." He stayed there with his face in his hands, saying nothing.

Spent, George lifted himself off the floor and sank wearily into his desk chair. He still had more questions than answers as he turned to face his Bible, still open from that morning.

His eyes caught a phrase in Hebrews 3: "Sin's deceitfulness."

Boy, if that doesn't describe what happened to Rick, I don't know what does.

As George thought about the whole situation with Rick, he felt a surge of anger in his heart. He was angry, knowing the deceiver had maimed yet another one of God's lambs through his lying tactics. *Lord, does it have to be this way? Surely, there must be a way to keep this from happening.* He looked again at the worn page, hoping for an answer.

"Encourage one another daily, as long as it is called Today, so that none of you may be hardened by sin's deceitfulness." *What?!* He read it again, hoping he hadn't missed something. *That's what it says! Sin's deceitfulness can be prevented!* Truth illuminated his heart.

Could obedience to one simple command really help keep people — people he loved — from being deceived and hardened by sin? *It says it right here.* He answered his own question, thumping the page. *The Holy Spirit did write that verse,* he reasoned. George's heart began to surge with excitement and hope — hope that his efforts to care didn't have to be forever subject to arbitrary failure.

As he sat and thanked God for opening up the Scripture to him, a torrent of other verses poured into his mind: "Be devoted to one another in brotherly love...Let us encourage one another...admonish one another DAILY...From Him the whole body, joined and held together by every supporting ligament, grows and builds itself up in love, as each part does its work...Therefore confess your sins to each other and pray for each other so that you may be healed...Carry each other's burdens, and in this way you will fulfill the law of Christ."

He wondered if he had ever seen these verses before as he flipped from passage to passage, just to make sure they were really there. He had seen them. Many times. Today, though, circumstances brought them to life.

George winced at the implications. *If we fulfill the law of Christ by carrying each other's burdens, and if true fellowship one with another has to do with "walking in the light" together and "confessing sins"...what in the world have we been doing all this time? Worship services, potluck meals, and Bible classes haven't done the job.* Confused, George stood up and slowly paced the room. He'd always thought the Church needed revival. Now, he was beginning to wonder if the whole foundation was wrong. Had it been built on knowing about a historic Jesus and doctrines, rather than on obeying a living Jesus?

"Yes!" He slapped his palm against the desktop. "Perhaps it can't be fixed by new and improved programs. The problem is foundational. A house built on sand needs more than a paint job. It needs to be rebuilt!"

With this in mind,

we constantly pray for you,

that our God may

count you worthy of his calling,

and that by his power

he may fulfill

every good purpose of yours

and every act

prompted by your faith.

II Thessalonians 1:11

Stepping Out

22

THE RICHARDSONS' NEW HOUSE in Pine Ridge was finally complete. As the last box made its way down the long ramp from the moving truck into the house, Alan Hart wiped the sweat off his forehead. "I think that's it. Is the pizza here yet?"

"It should be here any minute," came the reply from a distant voice. "Everyone's meeting at your place in ten minutes."

"Sounds great! I'm famished, and it's too cold out here to just stand still." Alan jumped from the back of the truck.

"I can't believe how easy this move was! We unloaded that whole twenty–four–foot truck in less than one hour." Aaron Richardson shook his head emphatically. "It took us a whole day to load it with the help of a co–worker of mine."

"Well," replied Alan, "that's because you're part of a family now. I can't imagine what it would be like to try to move all by myself."

Within minutes, the Harts' home was teeming with its familiar host of children, adults, and hot pizza boxes. The room was filled with the kind of warmth that most people only *taste* during the holidays. It felt good to be alive.

As Carolyn was getting acquainted with Kathy Richardson, a familiar face entered the front door. Carolyn felt her spirit lift as she saw Marsha's daughter for the first time since she had left for college in August. As politely as possible, she finished her conversation with the newcomer and headed for the door.

"So, how did it go this semester?" Carolyn asked. The excitement in her voice was obvious. She was very fond of Amy and made no attempt to hide it. "Marsha told me her 'little girl' was coming home this week, but it still took me by surprise to see you stroll through the door." By the time she had finished her sentence, she had made a mock pigtail from a ringlet of Amy's hair.

Amy's silent response was awkward, and Carolyn flushed with embarrassment. *Maybe I shouldn't have grabbed her hair that way? She is in college now. I hope I haven't offended her.* Carolyn paused and carefully considered her next question. "Amy, is everything okay? Did I offend you?"

Amy interjected abruptly, ending the silence, "Oh no, you haven't done anything wrong at all. It's just..." Amy turned her head as emotion gave way to tears.

Carolyn wasn't sure what to say. "Um...would you like to go for a walk?"

Amy answered with a nod. Carolyn grabbed her coat and followed Amy out the door.

They walked in silence for several blocks until, finally, Amy spoke. "Carolyn..." Her words were slow and painstaking. "I'm in real trouble. I...don't know how to say this, but...I'm pregnant." The last two words were barely a whisper as Amy let out a silent cry, and tears began to stream down her face.

"Oh, Amy," Carolyn sighed as she turned to embrace her. "I don't know what to say." The painful awkwardness was no longer a mystery. Carolyn struggled for words. The recent turmoil in her own heart climaxed at that moment. *How could this happen?* She felt unprepared and unqualified to help. All of the responses in her mind seemed canned. She quickly breathed a silent prayer for wisdom as she searched for the words to sustain the weary — words of comfort and hope. That was God's promise for all who walk with Him.

"Carolyn, I knew it was wrong. I didn't intend...I didn't mean..." Amy shook her head, crying. "What can I say? It's all my fault. I have no one to blame but myself. Oh, Carolyn, I would give anything, anything to go back in time and change this." Amy stopped walking and put her face into her hands as she wept bitterly.

Inside Carolyn, a battle raged as she felt the weight of her own guilt. She had watched Amy grow up and had always assumed Amy was growing spiritually — becoming a true woman of God. She realized now that she had never taken the time to find out for sure.

Carolyn had taken it for granted that their informal Church environment would automatically produce a relationship with God. Amy was a warm person who had always shown more interest in spiritual things than her peers. Her quiet, gentle spirit made her likeable. But these characteristics, though commendable, were not enough. There was something deeper God was looking for. This was now painfully obvious.

Carolyn placed her hand gently on Amy's shoulder. She was torn. She wanted to comfort her, to give her a big hug and promise her it would all be okay, but she hated the thought of being a source of false comfort. Amy *had* sinned against Jesus. If she was ever going to find true healing, she must come to terms with that.

"Amy, I'm proud of you for being honest and taking responsibility for your actions. But regret isn't enough." Carolyn again breathed a prayer, not wanting Amy to misunderstand. "To find true freedom and true healing, there must be true repentance. You can't view this as just a mistake you've made. You've got to see it as sin — something that really has hurt Jesus. But it doesn't have to end there." Carolyn lifted Amy's chin and looked into her eyes. "Your Father in Heaven knew this day would come even before you were born. This whole thing can be used as a tool that brings you into a deeper, personal relationship with God."

Amy looked down.

"Do you want that, Amy?"

Amy nodded.

"Then you should tell Him. Tell Jesus you're sorry. Ask Him to forgive you, not as a religious act to make yourself feel better, but because He's a real Person and He wants you to talk with Him."

Amy began walking again and Carolyn followed in silence, giving Amy the room she seemed to need. After a few minutes, Amy slowed, allowing Carolyn to walk alongside her again.

"Carolyn, thanks a lot for talking honestly with me. If this really can be a tool for me to know God better, then I don't want to miss it."

Carolyn smiled and gave Amy a hug. "I don't want you to, either."

They turned and began walking back up the block. Once the house was in sight, Amy looked to Carolyn. "I haven't told Mom yet."

"You know you're going to need to. Right?"

"I know," Amy sighed. "But I'm afraid." She bit her bottom lip.

Carolyn weighed the possibilities, then offered, "Would you like me to go with you?"

"Would you?!" Amy brightened at the thought.

"Yes!" Carolyn's voice rang with resolve. "I want to help any way I can."

"I know," Amy replied with relief. "I think it would help a lot if you came."

"I'd be glad to."

LATER THAT NIGHT, after the furniture was in place and the pictures were hung, the sound of rattling dishes could still be heard in the Richardsons' new home. Marsha was hard at work serving her new neighbor. She and Kathy were putting the kitchen together, making sure everything was in its proper place.

"Now, Kathy, you may have a better idea, but I always like to keep my spices right next to my stove," Marsha commented as she wiped the cupboard again.

"Well...Marsha." Kathy hesitated, still not familiar with all of the new names. "We really don't have many spices."

"Oh, I'll take care of that. You just reserve enough space there."

"That'd be great." Kathy looked again at the empty boxes scattered across the floor. "You've all been so kind. I didn't think people could care so much."

"You know, Kathy, this kitchen is almost perfect." Marsha looked around, tapping her mouth with her finger. "But I think it still needs a nice floral valance over that window."

"Oh, we have one of those. I think it's upstairs. Let me go check." With that, Kathy was off, and Marsha turned to make her final inspection.

As she opened one of the lower cabinets and looked inside, she heard footsteps behind her.

"Mom."

Marsha turned to see Amy and Carolyn walk into the kitchen. "Hi, Sweetie! Where have you been hiding yourself?"

"Oh, I took a walk with Carolyn." She paused, took a deep breath and continued, "In fact, Mom,…that's why I'm here. Can we talk?"

"Well, not right now, Dear." Marsha stooped down to scrub a spot she had noticed on the floor. "Kathy's coming back with a curtain. I promised I would help her. She really does need me, you know?"

"Mom…it's important." Tears began to force their way down Amy's cheeks.

The quiver in Amy's voice caught Marsha's attention. She looked up from her scrubbing chore. "Amy, what's the matter?"

"Marsha—" Carolyn put her hand on Amy's shoulder. "Maybe we should go over to your house and talk. It's important. I'll find someone else to help Kathy hang the curtain."

Marsha's face showed noticeable worry. "Oh…okay…anything for my baby girl."

AMY, CAROLYN AND MARSHA sat around the small glass table that was the centerpiece of the Harts' breakfast nook. The air was thick with anticipation and awkwardness. Marsha almost unconsciously rearranged the contents of the fruit basket as she looked from Amy to Carolyn and back to her own hands. The worried expression on her face temporarily lifted as she spoke. "Can I get either of you something to drink?"

Amy looked at Carolyn. Carolyn nodded reassuringly. Amy swallowed hard, took a deep breath and began. "No…Mom. I need to get this out."

"Get what out, Dear? If there's something on your mind, you know you can talk to me."

"Mom…I'm…" Amy wiped her cheeks with her sleeve. "I'm pregnant." She caught a glimpse into her mother's eyes, then broke down with tears of shame.

Carolyn placed her hand on Amy's back while Marsha stared in stunned silence through her daughter, out into the cold night beyond.

Several minutes passed before Amy finally pulled herself

together enough to look up. "Mom...I am so sorry!"

Marsha fought to slow her racing thoughts. She looked through wet eyes at her brown–eyed little girl, who had suddenly become a stranger. Trying to understand her own feelings, she spoke aloud, though to no one in particular. "How could this have happened?" Marsha crumpled a napkin in her hand. "I tried to protect you from the world. I home–schooled you for twelve years. I sent you to a Bible college. I...I don't understand. Why?" She paused, put her face in her hands and shook her head. "Ever since you were little, we always taught you about the Bible. We've been having daily devotionals for years." She looked at Amy. "Don't you remember? You even memorized the whole sermon on the mount when you were eleven." Tears came to Marsha's eyes at the memory. She sat dazed. "I just can't believe this. My daughter, pregnant. At a Bible college. How could it be? We had so much hope for you. Where could I have gone wrong?" The tears became heavier, and she buried her face in her hands.

Amy found herself crying again as well. She battled inside, not wanting to let her mother take the blame. "Mom..." Amy steadied her voice. "It's not your fault. It's mine. I must...I do take responsibility for my own choices. It's my fault."

"Your fault? Oh, Honey, you've always been the sweetest girl, such a servant, always eager to help with the house or other people's children. I remember the time that Mrs—"

"Mom!" Amy interrupted, more composed. "This isn't about me watching people's children. I did all that stuff, but that didn't stop me from getting pregnant. I don't understand exactly what happened. I mean...I know it's wrong. You did teach me that, and I believe it. But, when it came down to making choices...I didn't have inside of me whatever I needed to be able to really obey God."

Marsha and Amy both looked down in silence. Amy soaked in the reality of what she had just said while Marsha sat lost in a world of scattered thoughts and confusion.

"But you were at a Bible college. Don't they have rules to prevent these kinds of things? Aren't there curfews and things like that?"

Amy closed her eyes and shook her head slowly. She sighed. "Mom, I went to school believing the Bible college was a safe place to be, that I would be protected, and it would be easy to do the right things. But I found out that it's not that way at all. You wouldn't believe some of the things I saw there." Amy closed her eyes and stopped. "But I can't blame the college or anyone. *I* made the choice. It's not that I went looking for ways around the rules. But I met Rick, fell in love…and I gave in to my own emotions and desires." Amy paused again. "I wasn't strong inside, Mom. No matter how much I studied about it, and no matter how many safeguards were in place, it wasn't inside me. I knew what it looked like to obey God, but somehow that wasn't enough."

23

THIS WAS EXCITING! George Archer felt clearer and more alive, as though much of the recent fog had lifted. Two hours earlier, when he first set foot in the restaurant meeting room, he had not imagined the time would actually have any impact on him.

He started the car, threw it into gear and began an energetic drive home. The tires squealed slightly as he pulled out of the parking lot and onto the main street. Driving by instinct, his mind was flooded with the implications of what he'd just experienced.

He had been dubious when he first saw the flyer advertising, "Weekly, City–wide Interdenominational Pastors and Leaders Prayer Breakfast." Who among his colleagues wouldn't have been? He had even cringed at the word *interdenominational*. Yet, something about it all had still sparked an interest, a…hunger.

What was it he went looking for? He wasn't shopping for a new denomination. Perish the thought! He certainly wasn't looking for new ideas to implement. No. Somehow, it was simpler than that. He was just looking for…hope? For an answer? But what was the question?

He sat pondering. The blast of a car horn behind him alerted him that the light had changed to green. George waved a quick apology and was once again on his way.

So, why this searching? There was no doubt that George Archer was committed to his heritage. The beliefs and traditions he'd been taught by his father and grandfather had long been a source of identity and strength. But his recent inner turmoil had driven him to look deeper than ever before, to ask questions he'd never thought to ask. In the process, he had discovered in himself something new. For the first time, he had seen the embryo of a commitment to something other than the denomination of his heritage. It wasn't to another group or another belief structure. No. It was to the Church universal — the one Jesus bled for, worldwide, across all man–made barriers. To unity without regard to sectarian denominationalism. One large brotherhood — those truly sold out to Him alone — advancing the cause of Christ.

The meeting had gone well. Oddly, he couldn't remember much of what they talked about. And at the moment it didn't seem to matter. He was floored by the care he'd seen in many of the people at the meeting. That much he knew. All of his life, he'd been led to believe that only those of his denominational heritage were truly favored by God. Yet, he'd witnessed today people who *did* seem to genuinely care about what God was doing and about each other. He'd never thought it possible that men of different backgrounds, with different doctrines, could hug each other, call each other brother, and even pray for each other. Impressive!

24

IT HAD BEEN A FULL DAY and Carolyn lay flat on her back, wide–eyed. The gravity of last night's conversation with Marsha and Amy still lingered. As she stared at the ceiling, memories from the last four years inundated her mind.

Ted glanced over at Carolyn. She looked unsettled. He made a mental note and returned to his reading. He'd seen her this way before and wasn't eager to get into one of *those* conversations. Her sobriety made Ted uneasy.

He was still staring at the first paragraph when Carolyn turned toward him and propped her head on her hand. She sighed heavily, and he knew a serious conversation was imminent. He read the same sentence four times before finally relenting to her eyes.

"Something on your mind?" he resigned softly, placing his book on the nightstand. He turned to his wife and assumed a mirrored posture.

She looked him in the eyes. "How do you think things are going in the community lately?"

"Fine, I guess. Why? What do you mean?"

"Well, do you remember what we were talking about a few weeks back?" She sat up, facing Ted. "I guess I'm still feeling troubled that there is some realness that seems to be lacking." She looked for a reaction on Ted's face, then continued, "Recently I've been kind of taking a look around and wondering if we're walking in all God has for us."

"What do you mean? What more do you want?" Ted asked incredulously. "I mean, compared to where we were before..." He didn't finish his sentence, feeling it spoke for itself. "Not that things are perfect. But, man, we've come a long way from Sunday morning Christianity, from sermons and time–stamped praise and worship."

"Yeah, I know. But—"

"But what?" Ted snapped.

A hurt look flashed across her face. "You're right, we have come a long way. But I just want to see us go all the way, to walk in all that Jesus desires for us. That's all."

"And you're saying I don't want that!" Now Ted sat up and faced Carolyn.

"I'm not saying that."

"Then what are you saying?"

The impatient tension in Ted's voice temporarily paralyzed Carolyn. What had started as a simple question suddenly had all the energy of a courtroom trial. Reluctantly, Carolyn responded.

"What I'm saying is, maybe we've stopped short. I think what happened with Amy has made it obvious we've gone wrong somewhere. Can't we at least consider it?"

"Oh, come on! I know Amy's situation took everyone by surprise, but let's not overreact. One sin isn't a reason to question our whole existence here. We've got a pretty special thing going, and I would hate to see it spoiled by oversensitivity and paranoia."

That stung. Carolyn took a deep breath and proceeded calmly. "It's not just Amy, Ted. Even before Amy, I started noticing a shallowness in my own heart. You *know* that. Remember?"

Ted surrendered a conceding nod.

Carolyn continued, "It's easy to just kind of meander from one informal gathering to another with no real passion for Jesus. Does Jesus really have full reign in our lives just because we no longer have scheduled meetings and programs? I know Jesus wants a Church, not just scattered individuals. But how is that being expressed in practical ways, every day? Are we becoming less carnal and selfish? Are we going anywhere, or are we just content to *not* be a part of the religious system? I don't know for sure. I'm just disturbed with the lack of vision in my own heart and life and what appears to me to be a lack in the lives of the others."

"Carolyn!" Ted said curtly. "I'm glad God is showing you some things about yourself. But don't project those things on everybody else." He calmed himself to make his point. "Sometimes when God is convicting us of something, we tend to assume everyone else is guilty of the same thing. I'm not sure everyone else feels the shallowness and lack of purpose and direction you're speaking of."

"So, are you saying that you're satisfied with your life?"

Ted's face tightened. He was tempted to lash out but could see her question was sincere and not intended as a dig. "Well, there's always room for improvement."

Silence suspended the next few moments until Ted continued, "But…I don't feel like I, or anyone else here for that matter, am as shallow as you're describing." He held her eyes. "I'm sure if we happen to fall short in some area and God brought it to our attention, we would all respond to what God was showing us." Ted rested his case, hoping she would see the logic of his argument.

Carolyn seemed to accept his answer, but she was actually more disturbed than when she began. They said good night and lay back down, each now facing opposite walls. It would be another hour before either of them fell asleep.

25

THE NEXT AFTERNOON, Carolyn sat on the floor with Marie, helping her play with her favorite wooden blocks. Ted usually finished weight training with the boys around 5:00. It was 5:35 and Carolyn expected him any minute.

Her pulse quickened, anxious about Ted's arrival. He'd left for work before she woke up that morning and hadn't called her all day. After the exchange of strong words the night before, she wondered what she would say. She handed Marie the last block, which the child placed roughly on top of the teetering block tower. Crash! Down it came and Marie let out a delighted giggle. Just then, Carolyn heard a car door shut. Ted was home.

She took a breath as his jingling keys opened the front door.

"Carolyn, I'm home," he called, poking his head into the house.

"I'm in here with Marie."

His eyes momentarily found hers in the living room and she noted his sheepish expression. He didn't stop to take off his coat. He just walked toward her, one hand behind his back. He then revealed a large bouquet of white and yellow daisies.

Her apprehensive expression melted into a smile when she saw the apologetic look on his face.

"Sweetheart," Ted began, "I've been thinking and praying all day about last night's conversation. And I want you to know that I..." He tried to find words. "I spoke hastily a few times and I want to apologize for my attitude. I'm *not* satisfied with my life, and I *do* think I'm missing some of the reality of knowing Jesus and the strength of being in the middle of His will." As he spoke, she could see his eyes beginning to well up. "This morning I was reading a verse where Paul said he was in the 'pains of childbirth,' wanting Christ to be formed in his brothers. That whole idea seems so foreign to me. I've never known the pain of spending myself to see my brothers grow. I've always just assumed that by being around each other a lot, we'd grow by...osmosis.

"I am sorry for being defensive." Ted looked his wife in the eyes. "I don't want to live like a spiritual vegetable. I *do* want to be a true man of God!"

"I forgive you, Ted," Carolyn answered with joy in her voice. Ted was relieved as she jumped up and gave him a hug.

"In all honesty, Carolyn, I still don't know if I fully understand all of this. I know we need to be more involved in each others lives, but shouldn't we let the Holy Spirit work on people's hearts, just like He worked on mine today?"

She consoled with her eyes and pleaded tenderly, "Ted, I'm not trying to take any credit away from the Spirit's work, but do you think you would have wrestled with God today if we hadn't talked last night? Hasn't God almost always used human vessels to help others see the blind spots that they are ignorant of? Nathan with David, Samuel with Saul, Paul with Peter…"

She paused, placing her hands in his. "Truthfully, my concerns aren't about anything that I have not also fallen short in. I'm not pointing any fingers. But the ability to do what you and I have just been doing — opening our lives up, being lovingly honest with shortcomings we see in each other…even these simple things haven't been the way of life among us as a whole. I don't know why, but I believe that is part of the solution. Do you know what I mean?"

"Uh, I think so. But it's definitely uncharted waters for me." Ted took his coat off and walked toward the closet.

"Well," she decided, "I think I'll find a vase for these lovely flowers." She walked into the kitchen, thanking God.

26

IT WAS THE FIRST DAY of the spring semester. As the 8:00 hour drew to a close, George examined the classroom full of students. *This semester is going to be different.* If a lack of relationship had been part of Rick's undoing, George was determined to see that others didn't fall prey.

After making foreboding references to term papers and the grading scale, George dismissed the class. On his way out the door, a lanky, red–haired student approached the professor. "Mr. Archer," he asked, facing his professor with a serious eye, "what did you mean when you said God's Kingdom was bigger than any of our tiny perspectives or backgrounds?"

George smiled and laughed softly. "Well, Eric…how about if you come with me to a meeting tomorrow morning?"

THE NEXT MORNING, after the city–wide prayer breakfast, George Archer and Eric walked across the restaurant parking lot. George's stride was slow. His eyes were on the pebble he sent periodically skipping off the end of his shoe. He wasn't sure what was tugging soberly at his insides.

As they pulled away from the restaurant parking lot, Eric broke the silence. "Professor, you seem troubled. Did something happen?"

George shook his head slowly, without emotion. "I'm...I'm not sure."

Eric was confused. There was something about his new professor that intrigued him and drew his respect. However, this morning's behavior had him puzzled. He tried to change the subject, hoping to engage the professor in conversation and ease the awkwardness they both felt.

"I was really fascinated by the discussion at the end of the meeting today. I'd never..."

"Well, I wasn't fascinated!" Professor Archer shot back, interrupting with sudden energy. He surprised himself with his abrupt behavior. "I'm...I'm sorry."

Eric quickly recovered from his initial shock. "What bothered you, Professor — the unity discussion?"

The professor shook his head. "No, not exactly. I'm all for unity." He turned on his blinker and made a quick left onto College Avenue. "I'm not really sure why I'm so disappointed. Perhaps it's nothing."

"Did you disagree with something that was taught?"

"Maybe." George furrowed his brow. "I've been trying to not get hung up on doctrinal differences. But this bothers me in a different way. It didn't just violate my intellect."

"What do you mean?"

"I don't know...yet. If I could tell you, I would." At that moment, they pulled into the faculty parking lot. As they got out of the car, George promised, "When I come up with something, I'll get back with you. Okay?"

They parted ways and George headed toward his office.

THREE HOURS LATER, Amy and her roommate, Diane, strolled in silence across the lawn toward the student center.

Diane broke the silence with a chuckle. "For the first time in history, I don't know what to say." She laughed again, uncomfortably. Tasting her own shallowness, she tried to recover. "Amy,

I really do want to know if there's any way I can help."

Amy smiled back. "Thanks. Sorry again for not letting you know sooner and for worrying you."

As they entered the student center, Diane gave her a hug. She then turned and started back toward the dorm with Amy staring after her. *Carolyn was right.* She thoughtfully rubbed her cold hands together. *That wasn't easy. But I know it was the right thing to do.* Though it had been awkward, there was something very freeing about being honest and facing the truth.

With her roommate almost out of sight, Amy looked down and pulled a piece of scrap paper out of her purse. She studied it. "I guess it's on to the mail room."

She swung open the door and saw a familiar face. "Hi, Professor Archer." George perked up a bit and broke into a smile. "Well, hello, Amy. It's good to see you. How are you?"

Amy's voice was chipper. "I'm doing better. Really, I am. I talked to my parents."

"Oh, you did? Good. It must have gone well."

"As well as I could hope." Amy smiled slightly. "I've had a lot of help from a special friend through it all. It's been difficult, but good."

Despite the risk of disappointment, George ventured, "Have you heard anything from Rick?"

Amy looked past George and stared out the mail room windows. Hadn't this been her daily expectation and hope? Regretfully, she answered, "No, Mr. Archer. I haven't heard from him...I'm not sure I ever will."

That final admission shocked her, but Amy knew it was the truth. Somehow, George knew also.

They stood in silence for a moment. Then George, eager to change the subject, asked, "Are...are you in classes this semester?"

"Oh, no. I just had some things to take care of. Forwarding my mail back home and stuff like that. Mostly I came to see my roommate."

George glanced at his watch. "Well, I'm off to the student cafeteria. Would you like some lunch?"

"The student cafeteria?"

He smiled and chuckled, "Yes. I'm planning to eat my lunch there this semester."

"Wow, that sounds neat. I'll bet you'll get some funny looks."
She laughed. "I don't think I'll go. It's still not real easy even being here." She looked around.

"I understand. It's great to see you, Amy. Take care."

27

"EMILY, DO YOU remember making withdrawals of fifty dollars and thirty dollars on December fifth and seventh?" Wayne asked as his eyes darted from his bank statement to his small pile of receipts.

Emily looked up from her ironing and glanced at her husband who was at the kitchen table trying to balance the checkbook.

"Oh, yeah, that was the week that we ran out of checks and I had to use my bank card. Um...I think the seventh is when I took Virginia to lunch."

"Well, why didn't you get the receipts to me, Emily? This is at least the third time in the last six months! How many times do I have to tell you — you've got to get the receipts to me right away." Wayne closed his eyes and ran his hands through his hair.

"I'm sorry," his wife replied as tears began to well up in her eyes. "I try very hard to remember to get them to you, but one thing or another..." She cut herself short as she ducked into the bathroom for a tissue.

Why can't she just do the simple things I ask her? Wayne slumped in his chair, his conscience informing him he had crossed a line. He stared out the window, arms crossed. Hearing Emily blow her nose in the bathroom, he got up from his chair. He needed to apologize to his wife.

"Honey, I'm sorry. Can I talk with you?" Wayne asked as he shook his head in disgust with himself. Emily gently pulled the door open a few inches so her husband could enter. As he pushed open the door and saw his wife looking at the floor, he felt like a heel. He placed his finger under her chin to lift her gaze.

"Emily, I am really sorry. I was out of line a few minutes ago. Please forgive me."

Emily blinked her eyes slowly and nodded her head. Her

husband continued, "This isn't an excuse, Em, but I am beginning to feel a lot of financial pressure as I finish up my last few weeks at Hampton Street."

"But why? You have seemed so strong and full of faith through all of this. The way you snapped at me seemed to come out of nowhere."

"You're right, Em. Two things are going on inside of me. On one hand, I feel like I'm gaining more understanding of God's heart for His Church and for my life than ever before. On the other hand, I'm faced with the reality that I won't have an income in a few weeks, and it scares me to death."

"But that elder from the church in Florida called and said he was very interested in your becoming the minister there. You are going to call him back, aren't you?"

"I thought I was, but I'm not sure if God really wants me to be a minister — the way people usually think of ministers."

"What do you mean?"

"Something seems very wrong to me about the whole process. That elder from Stony Creek wants a copy of my resume. He wants a videotape of one of my sermons. He wants to interview me."

"But you know that's the way things are always done."

"That's the way things are done today, but that's not the way it was in the New Testament. Can you imagine the Church in Thessalonica asking the apostle Paul for his resume and a sermon on tape? Would they schedule a job interview with him so that they could possibly 'hire' him? It's absolute craziness! When he asked me for a video of one of my sermons, I wanted to scream."

"Now, Wayne, you have preached some wonderful sermons that have helped a lot of people. You should be glad that God has given you the ability to communicate well. There's no reason to feel bad about sending him a tape that shows how God can use you."

"It's not the teaching, Honey. There's something wrong with the whole system when it requires sending tapes, dressing up in suits, and trying to impress people — so you can receive money for making speeches and planning programs. The more I read the New Testament, the more absurd a lot of the religious world

106

seems. That's just not how the Church functioned in the days of Jesus and the apostles."

"But you have so much to offer people. And if you are going to be in a position where God can use you, there is no choice but to go through the interview process."

"But, Em, it's flat out not in the Bible! In fact, according to the teachings of Jesus and Paul, the whole idea of hirelings and clergy/laity makes God sick!"

"But how will you support our family if you don't get a job as a minister?"

"I don't know, Emily."

"You're not saying that you won't go to that interview, are you, Wayne?"

"I don't know, Em. I just don't know."

28

THE USUAL DIN of studying, eating and chatter filled the air of the student center. Ten o'clock classes were out, and many of the students were trying to squeeze in a snack during the short break before their next class. George grabbed a cup of coffee and scanned the room, looking for someone willing to share a table. He noticed Eric over in the corner, entombed in stacks of books and notes.

"Eric!" George raised his voice, moving toward a corner table.

"Oh, hi, Mr. Archer."

"What are you doing in here with all those books?" George asked. "Shouldn't you be in the library?"

"Well, actually," he smiled slyly, "I was hoping I might run into you. I heard you hang out here sometimes."

George laughed softly. He was growing fond of this student's unique personality. "Then it's a good thing I saw you over here in your fortress. What's with all the books?"

"Oh, I'm just finishing some research for my one o'clock communications class. I'm giving a speech about the Scottish wars for independence during the early fourteenth century. It's pretty interesting stuff. I started checking out books and...I got a little carried away."

"I see you did." George smiled broadly. "I'm glad I caught you. I was hoping to find you, too. I wanted to clear up any confusion I may have caused you after the city–wide prayer breakfast the other day. I had a lot going on inside and didn't want to just blurt out everything I was feeling. I wanted a chance to think about it."

Eric nodded slowly. "Yeah, after chewing on it for a few days, that analogy about different tribes seemed like quite a leap to justify denominationalism."

"And it was," George cut in. "Comparing the twelve tribes of Israel to the denominations of today, as if God really wanted denominational boundaries in His Church, is ridiculous. It whitewashes our divisions. It doesn't resolve them."

"So," Eric joined, "instead of dealing with our lack of unity, we redefine it."

"Exactly!" George's eyes and voice were now animated. "Instead of repenting for building walls of division between brothers — we revise it and pretend it was God's idea all along. Do you follow me?"

"Oh, I follow you all right! So, what's the motive?"

George shifted a little in the booth. "That's simple. Instead of working to bring about actual unity, now we can just agree to get along — and chalk all our differences up to different giftings." George shook his head in disbelief. "It gives pastors the freedom to preach about unity without having to jeopardize their position. It doesn't disrupt the *control* of their flocks or their tithing base."

29

"WAYNE DAVIDSON, good to meet you at last. I feel like I practically know you from your sermon tapes and your resume." Bob Weston, Chairman of Stony Creek's search committee, pumped Wayne's hand energetically as he invited him into his office.

"Good to meet you, too, Bob," Wayne replied, forcing a smile. *What am I doing here? I'm not sure I'm cut out for this anymore.*

"I'm glad you were able to fly down here to be with us. All the elders on the search committee have been very impressed with your qualifications and we're all excited to meet you. We hope you enjoyed that little extra surprise of the first class seat assignment. I always like to do that when I'm flying. The extra legroom and the television are worth the price, I think."

As Wayne sat down across from Bob's desk, he felt a sinking feeling inside. Memories of previous job interviews came to mind, and he recalled the energy and enthusiasm he had projected in them. That energy and enthusiasm seemed completely lacking now.

"Stony Creek is a special Church, Wayne. There are wonderful families here — good, decent people. We have folks of all ages. Our youth group is strong. We have a great singles ministry. And, as you would expect in a Florida Church, we have our share of retirees."

"What are some of the challenges you are facing, Bob?" Wayne surprised himself as he asked the question without intending to.

"That's a good question, Wayne," Bob replied, somewhat taken aback. "I can see that you're a man who likes to get right to the point. I like that." Bob paused for a moment as he loosened the tie around his plump neck.

"I'll tell it to you straight, Wayne. Two years ago, a new Church opened up about a mile down the road. It was started by a guy who had been a professional musician. He's a nice enough guy and he puts a big emphasis on music. From what I hear, he's got a regular concert going every Sunday morning. Anyway, a couple of leading families left us to go there, and there's been a steady trickle in that direction ever since."

This sounds like two entertainment companies competing with each other. What's this have to do with the Kingdom of God? Wayne looked intently at the elder across the desk from him.

"Now, I think we have the music thing fixed," Bob continued. "Two months ago, we hired a music minister, a young man with a lot of talent. And attendance has been creeping back up ever since. Now we need to put the icing on the cake, which is why we brought you down here." Bob sat forward in his chair and clasped his thick hands together.

"What we need is a dynamic, energetic, take–charge kind of a pastor. We need the kind of pastor who can take this Church back to where it was a couple of years ago and even beyond. We need a pastor who can preach great sermons, launch several programs at once, and get everyone involved and excited about Stony Creek again. There is so much potential here, Wayne. We just need the right person to tap it. Does this sound like something you would be interested in?"

Wayne felt sickened by Bob's business mindset. "Before I answer your question, let me ask one or two more of my own, if I can." Wayne waited for Bob to nod before proceeding. "In your view, what is the quality of the spiritual life in the average member here? Is there an eager pursuit of holiness? Is there true consecration to Jesus Himself? Is there a deep desire on the part of everyone, I mean *everyone*, to put God first in their lives?"

Bob pulled a handkerchief from his shirt pocket and patted his brow with a puzzled look on his face. "I think I told you what a great group of people we have here, Wayne. That's what I mean when I say this place has so much potential." Bob paused, then began again with renewed eagerness. "Something I haven't mentioned to you are some of the benefits that we offer the pastor here: a generous salary, health and dental insurance, retirement program, a Church-supplied car, a library allowance, two weeks vacation the first year and time off to travel to workshops and conferences — all expenses paid. We expect a lot from our pastor, but we also intend to take good care of him."

For an instant, Wayne felt like an observer, as if he were watching this interview from a distance. *This is exactly how the world functions. How can God be in this?!* Still, the talk of medical insurance stirred up a fear inside of him as he remembered Emily and the children.

"So, I think you have an understanding of the challenge — and the opportunity — that we have here at Stony Creek, Wayne. What do you think? Does this sound like the kind of challenge that a man of your abilities would be interested in?"

Wayne hesitated, thoughts of his financial responsibilities still gnawing at him. He also felt twinges of guilt as he thought about the expenses these people had taken to fly him down here. *No, I must be true to You, God, and let the chips fall where they may.*

"Bob, I came down here in good faith, thinking Stony Creek might be the place God wanted me to be. But I just don't think I'm the man you're looking for." Wayne stood up and extended

110

his hand to Bob. "Thank you for your interest in me and for covering the expense to bring me down, but I think you're going to have to find someone else. I'm sorry."

WAYNE SETTLED into his rental car in Stony Creek's parking lot, glad to be by himself and to have the interview behind him. *Now what? Two days in Miami with nothing to do. Maybe I could get my flight changed?...Oh, yeah! How about that guy I met on the plane...*

He pulled his wallet out of his back pocket, removed a card and read it again:

Mark Wallace, Marine Biologist.

Hmmm. Maybe I'll give this guy a call.

30

CAROLYN LET OUT A SIGH and knocked on Amy's bedroom door.

"Come in."

Carolyn opened the door just as Amy tossed an armload of clothes onto the bed. Without looking up, Amy returned to the closet and continued tossing empty hangers over her shoulder. "I'm not going to be needing most of these anymore."

Carolyn spoke loudly in an attempt to be heard over the clanging hangers. "Hi, Amy...I just came over to see how you're doing. Looks like you're going through your stuff from school." Carolyn stepped over a stack of books.

Amy said nothing and turned to face her closet.

"Are you all right?" Carolyn sat on the edge of the bed.

"I don't really want to talk about it."

"Is there some way I can help you?" Carolyn picked up some pictures scattered on the floor. Recognizing Rick's face, as well as some of Amy's other college friends, Carolyn shuffled the pictures into a stack. The Amy smiling back at her in the photographs was much different from the troubled young woman Carolyn now observed.

"I don't think so. I just want this stuff out of here!" Amy hastily took the stack of pictures from Carolyn, tossed them into a box, and returned to the closet.

"Amy…"

By now, Amy was sorting through a pile of papers and letters, crumpling most of them and cramming them in a nearby wastebasket. "Carolyn, I told you I just really don't want to talk about it. I know you want to help, but I'm not sure you can help me. I'm not sure if anybody around here can help me."

Amy abandoned her sorting, flinging all the papers toward the trash can. "So much for my eight years here. I tried to do what was right. I tried to be a 'good little girl'…look where that's gotten me — everyone's talking about me behind my back, everyone is giving me those patronizing looks. So much for school and my so-called friends there…and so much for Rick. He's gone and I'm left to deal with this all by myself. ALONE!"

That word jolted Carolyn. "Wait, Amy! You are *not* alone!"

Amy raised her eyes to meet Carolyn's for the first time.

"Amy, I know this is difficult for you. It may seem like you're alone, but you're not. There really is a God who loves you, the God who gives beauty for ashes. He can make each of our lives precious to Him if we'll believe in Him and not look on our own failures."

Carolyn paused, searching for clues in the pained expression on Amy's face. "And in addition to all of that, God's given us each other. I want to help you walk through this. I am here for you. Please let me help you."

Carolyn tenderly placed her hand on Amy's, waiting for a response. Moments passed. Amy's breathing seemed measured. "I need to go for a drive…I'll have to talk to you later." Carolyn's hand dropped abruptly as Amy rose to her feet, grabbed her keys and was gone.

Carolyn sat in stunned silence. *Something is terribly wrong…Father, how could one of Your children refuse Your hand like that?*

Marsha poked her head into the room. "Carolyn? What happened?…Amy just stormed past me and didn't say a word. Do you know where she was going?"

"No…we were just talking…."

Marsha nodded knowingly. "Oh, I remember those emotional days of early pregnancy. Amy seems to have had her share lately, but it's so much worse in her situation. I just haven't known what to do. She's so irrational sometimes...and so sensitive to the awkward glances and the comments she overhears."

"I'm not sure that's all she's...."

Marsha didn't seem to hear. "I just wish it wasn't so hard for her here."

31

"WE NEVER ANTICIPATE a drop in cabin pressure. But should that happen, an oxygen mask will drop from the compartment above you."

Wayne wasn't listening. He'd heard this speech too many times before. Besides, he had more important things on his mind today than airplane safety.

"And remember, in the unlikely event of a water landing, every seat cushion is also a flotation device."

The questions kept nagging at him, tugging at his mind and refusing to let go.

"Please notice that the captain has turned on the fasten seat belts sign in preparation for takeoff. It is important that you remain in your seats, with your seat belts securely fastened and your tray tables and seat backs in their fully upright and locked position until we have made our ascent and the captain has turned off the fasten seat belts sign. On behalf of the entire crew, I'd like to thank you for flying with us."

Miami International Airport fell deeper and deeper into the distance, until it was swallowed up entirely by the city itself. As the 727 carved a homeward trail through the clouds, Wayne tried again to unravel the mystery.

Maybe it was God's will for me to come to this interview, but for different reasons than I had originally thought. Is it possible He would lead me all the way out here just so I would end up meeting Mark and those precious believers he's with?

The countryside lay before him like a green and brown quilt. Toy cars crawled along narrow streets between rows of identical doll houses. An occasional blue sparkle revealed the backyards of those who could afford swimming pools. Everything was so predictable from up here, so manageable.

After awhile, the plane leveled out and the fasten seat belts sign clicked off.

"Excuse me, sir, would you like something to drink?" The flight attendant handed Wayne a small bag of dry–roasted peanuts.

"Uh, yes. I'll take a Diet Coke."

Wayne unfastened the lap tray in front of him and absently deposited the snacks on top. He reviewed the weekend's events once more, trying to capture every detail before it all started to fade. He had seen something about what "Church" could be.

This isn't just a pipe dream. It's really possible!

WAYNE WALKED BRISKLY through the automatic glass doors, duffle bag swinging like a quirky pendulum from the shoulder strap. Spotting Emily and the children parked a few yards from the door, he made a beeline for the mini-van. Wayne threw his luggage in the back and hopped into the passenger seat. After exchanging hugs and kisses, they began their journey toward home.

"Well, Wayne, you told me on Friday how the interview went. What about the rest of the weekend with those people you met on the airplane?"

"It was tremendous!" Wayne replied. "I've never seen anything quite like it. The people I met were like a family. It wasn't a typical Church."

"Really?" Emily responded, surprised at her husband's up-beat attitude. "Are they looking for a pastor to hire?"

"Emily!" Wayne shot a disapproving glance. "After that interview with Stony Creek, I'm completely convinced that neither the interview system, nor the pastoral system is pleasing to God! In the one, men of God are hired and fired like employees, and in the other, a pastor owns and runs the church like a family business. Neither of these is what God intends for His people!"

"Besides—" he relaxed his gaze, realizing he was talking to his wife, "I don't think that this other group of people I met would be interested in hiring anyone."

"I'm sorry...I just keep wondering how we're going to pay our bills next month."

"Emily, I know God loves us more than the birds of the air and has promised to take care of our needs. Let's just trust in

Him." After a brief pause, he affirmed, "I know that sounds theoretical, but let's try it anyway!"

"Okay. I was thinking that maybe I could get a job as a secretary someplace, at least for a little while...if that would help things."

"I don't think that will be necessary, Honey. God will come up with something for us. Besides, you need to take care of these guys." He winked and pointed at the back seat. Then he reached back and tickled the three members of his fan club.

When the giggling subsided, Emily started again. "Please tell me about your weekend. What was the name of the group in Miami?"

"They don't have a name. They said that the early Church, for the sixty years recorded in the Bible, didn't really have a name. And they, too, have been able to get along fine for years without one."

"That's odd," she said with a quizzical look. "Did you meet many people?"

"Yes, I was with hundreds of them and got to talk to close to two dozen."

"You must have been to one of their services, then."

"No...not exactly. It was more of a get–together in a park, not really anything you could call a *service*. Some families were planning a picnic, and they made a few phone calls. Before I knew it, the whole Church showed up."

"You mean the whole Church showed up on the spur of the moment for a picnic? They don't do that once a month or anything?"

"Nope. It was amazing to me, too, Em. It all seemed so natural. The people of God wanted to be with the people of God. When you think about it, what could be more natural?"

"I've just never heard of anything like that before. Most Churches can only get a fraction of their members involved in services that *are* planned."

"I hadn't experienced anything like it before, either. It was amazing."

"Hmmm."

"Something else that was special was the way the children and the teenagers behaved. They weren't stifled and they knew how to have fun, but they were obedient and respectful — definitely head and shoulders above the children and teens here at Hampton Street."

"Boy, I wonder what their secret is? What about the pastor? Did you get a chance to speak with him?"

"Well, they don't exactly have a pastor the way we usually think about pastors. I mean, everything doesn't center around one main person. They do have a number of leading brothers, though. I guess some parts of the body are more visible than others. One man that I really enjoyed speaking with was named Luis Rodriguez. He seemed to have insight into God's heart for what the Church is meant to be. When I was talking to him, he confirmed many of the things that have been stirring inside me over the past few months. It made me feel like I wasn't crazy after all."

"Now, Wayne, you know you aren't crazy."

"Well, I'm not so sure, Emily." Wayne grinned. "But anyway, these folks in Miami are really special. They seem to have learned practical ways to walk out the corporate life together. Up until now, all I've seen is what the Church is *not* supposed to be. But seeing, firsthand, a group of people functioning as a body gave me a taste for what the Church is meant to be. It was awesome!"

"I'm glad you're encouraged. It certainly sounds different. If these people have something to show us, then make sure you don't lose their phone number. We may need their help."

"Oh, I definitely intend to stay in touch with them. Everything about the weekend seemed Sovereign. I went down to Miami to interview for a job that I didn't really want, and I met one of the members of this Church on the airplane. Now I've started some valuable relationships that could last a long time. Isn't God something! Just when things are looking down, He gives us rays of hope."

EMILY LINGERED IN THE DEN as Wayne played with their children in the other room. Her eyes scanned back and forth across the shelves of books her husband had collected, recalling the years of energy Wayne had poured into trying to obey God.

Her eyes blurred. *Father, Wayne's right. You will take care of us.* She closed her eyes. *Why do I worry so much about bills instead of caring about things that matter?*

At that moment, she felt the pain of her own shallowness. *God, I want to become the partner You meant me to be for my husband...not just a Betty Crocker homemaker who feeds the children and keeps the house clean.*

Sinking to her knees, she turned the eyes of her heart heavenward to meet the inviting gaze of the King of the Universe — a gaze she had unconsciously dodged for years. *Father, I will learn to trust You! Please help me.*

32

"OPEN WIDE, PUMPKIN. These peas are good for you." Carolyn's mouth instinctively dropped open in an attempt to coax Marie to take one more bite.

"Carolyn, Amy's here to see you." Ted peered around the corner. "I'll take care of Marie from here."

Amy stood sheepishly by the front door. "Can we talk, Carolyn? There's something I need to say." Moving toward the couch, she sat down beside Carolyn and carefully considered her next words. "Carolyn, I'm very sorry. I don't know what happened. I don't know what came over me. I don't think I've ever been that angry before." Pulling her coat tighter around her, Amy lowered her eyes in shame. "I really wasn't mad at you, or anybody else for that matter. I know everyone is just trying to do the best they can, given my situation. I'm sure it's hard for everyone." Her eyes were pleading now. "I'm sorry I refused your help the other day. Carolyn, I do need help...I need your help."

"I forgive you, Amy, and I do still want to help." Without thinking, Carolyn had extended her hand to Amy's. "What can I do for you?"

"I'm not even sure exactly what I need yet...but stick around."

From the days of

John the Baptist until now,

the kingdom of heaven

has been forcefully advancing,

and forceful men lay hold of it.

Matthew 11:12

Deepening Convictions

33

GEORGE ARCHER SAT ALONE with his muffin and orange juice at one of the many tables in the hotel banquet room. He squirmed in his chair as he listened to the morning's keynote address. *Maybe I shouldn't be here.*

"And so this ties in well with our discussion about the twelve tribes of Israel. It's a beautiful prophetic picture of the church today." George bit his tongue as the speaker continued. "God is not calling us to drop our denominational names, close our buildings and become one big, happy church." George scanned the room, feeling like a wet blanket in this eager atmosphere.

"On the contrary! Our individuality is an integral part of His grand scheme—"

"Brothers, if I might be bold for a second," a voice challenged, "that is not what the Bible teaches!"

George snapped to attention, craning his neck to locate the lone voice of dissent.

"First Corinthians chapter one appears to be in direct opposition to the tribe teaching which is circulating today." It was a young man, early thirties, with thick, light brown hair. "'I'm of Paul,' 'I'm of Peter,' and 'I'm a Methodist' is *still* sin — despite how much it's in vogue today!"

"Sir, I'm going to have to ask you to refrain from further comments until the session is over." A nervous voice reverberated over the PA system as the meeting's moderator stood up beside the keynote speaker. "We would be happy to answer any questions you might have...in person, when the meeting is over."

"Could that be a group discussion?" George called out, surprising himself with his forwardness. "Like my brother, I also have some questions about these issues."

The moderator froze, trying to stay composed and maintain order. A lone voice of dissent is easy to politically outmaneuver, but this...He shot a glance at the speaker standing next to him, imploring his help.

"Go on, brother, continue," the speaker cut in, rescuing his host.

"Well," George began slowly, "I'm all for unity, and I'm glad there are people who want to do something about it. But let's be realistic. A monthly pastors prayer breakfast or an 'open' weekly, city-wide morning prayer meeting is not the answer to Jesus' prayer in John 17. Our barriers aren't doctrinal — they're heart issues. It's our competitiveness and ambition that keep us separated from each other. It's our pride, our self-centeredness, our unwillingness to deal with things that separate us from God and one another — in other words, *sin*."

George's eyes teared up and his voice began to crack. "If we would only learn to walk with each other every day, *not* as pastors, professors, and 'leaders', but as *brothers*, like Jesus said in Matthew 23, then we will have started to answer Jesus' prayer in John 17." His voice broke again. "A prayer that's gone unanswered for nearly two thousand years. If we could only learn to lay aside our own agendas and walk in the light of exposure and vulnerability with one another, then unity would take care of itself. The parachurch substitutes which center on prayer or evangelism or missions or social welfare or 'male bonding' will never be the answer to Jesus' heart cry for the Church!"

AS THE MEETING broke up, people milled around.

"I really appreciated what you had to say." It was the man who had spoken up earlier.

George returned his smile. "Thanks. I was beginning to think I was the only one in here who didn't agree with all of that."

"Yeah, me too." He studied George's face thoughtfully. "Do you think it was okay for me to speak out like that? I mean...I wasn't trying to be rude. I just didn't know what else to do."

"I don't know if it was the *right* thing to do," George began tentatively, "but I'm sure glad you did it. I'd been biting my lip all morning, not knowing what to do either."

"Hey, do you have time to grab a cup of coffee? I'd like to talk some more."

"Sure. I can do that. My first class isn't until one o'clock today." George took a quick glance at his watch and then extended his hand. "By the way, my name's George Archer."

The young man shook George's hand firmly. "Good to meet you, George. I'm Wayne. Wayne Davidson."

BZZZZZZ. THE SOUND OF THE DRYER startled her. Amy jumped up and ran into the laundry room. As she pulled the last of the crackling, static–laden clothes into the basket, the telephone rang.

"Hello."

"Hello, Amy? This is Carolyn. What are you up to?" she said cheerfully.

"Just finishing up some laundry. Why? What's up?"

"Well, I was getting ready to go to the grocery store and wanted to see if you'd like to join me?"

"Sure! I'd like that. I don't need anything, but I would love to be with you."

"Can I pick you up in about fifteen minutes?"

"That'd be perfect. See you then."

34

WAYNE LOOKED UP from the water fountain, a little worried his partner might pass out. Sitting down on the bench next to him, Wayne initiated cautiously, "You gonna be okay?"

"Oh, yeah. Just a little bit out of shape. Give me a second to catch my breath." George caught Wayne's eyes and laughed in spite of himself.

"Actually," he admitted, "I think the last time I got this much exercise was back in my freshman gym class." He noticed Wayne's face. "I know, I know, that's terrible."

"Now wait. Don't be too hard on yourself. Paul did say 'bodily exercise profiteth little,'" Wayne teased. He stood up, wiped the sweat from his own neck and began stretching.

Fearing Wayne might suggest they return to the racquetball court, George asked, "So how's the job hunt going?"

"Oh, slow."

"You never did tell me why you're leaving the ministry."

"I'm not exactly leaving God's work. I could never do that! I'm just trying to redefine my role in God's work in a more Biblical way."

"But you are leaving Hampton Street. Did something happen?"

Wayne nodded slowly, closing his eyes. "It was probably happening all along...but I never knew it."

George waited for Wayne to continue. When he didn't, George ventured, "Knew what? What was happening?"

Wayne rested his foot on the bench and leaned forward onto his knee. "God has made some things very clear to me. I found that a lot of the religious world draws near to Him only with their lips, but their hearts are far from Him — just as Jesus said would be true." He looked into the face of his focused partner. "George, I had no idea of the extent to which worldliness and filth had filled the lives of members and even leaders!" He watched George for a reaction. "It's almost unbelievable."

"I think I understand. I've had my share of surprises recently," George acknowledged with regret. "How people's lives look on the outside can be very deceiving. But I still don't understand why you're leaving. How will that help? It's the sick that need the physician, remember?"

"I've been asked to leave, George." Wayne rolled his towel into a tube and looped it around his neck. "The rest of the leadership didn't like what I was trying to do. They wanted a happy church, not a truth–centered one. I promise you, I don't say this out of bitterness or sour grapes. My heart is as broken over the state of the Church as it would be if my wife were in a serious accident. But the truth is, when some of the evil among us was uncovered by God's hand, and sin began to be challenged, the elders asked me to leave."

George looked away. "I'm...I'm sorry that happened, Wayne."

"No, no, don't be. I believe it was God's will. I'm finally beginning to see that there's something wrong, something fundamentally wrong, with how the Church today functions — including the whole clergy/laity system."

"I know what you're saying, but that doesn't mean you should leave the ministry altogether. There are a lot of problems, that's true, but I think they're due to a lack of deep relationship with each other. I mean, look at the Corinthians. These guys, as messed up as they were, at least had enough relationship among themselves that when they refused to eat with a certain brother, it nearly killed him." George stood up, his energy returned. "See, it was their relationships that held them together and brought cleansing. Not quitting or over–reacting with legalism...but *relationships!*"

Wayne remembered the sermon he'd preached about the "Corinthian excuse." He had emphasized that the Corinthians were committed enough to God and His Word to actually deal with the sin in that Church. However, it hadn't occurred to him until now that their deep relationships gave them the very context they needed in order to bring about that kind of heart change in a terribly difficult situation. Something began to click in Wayne's mind, and he gestured in excitement, "George, that's it! That's the difference I saw in Miami."

"What's it? What's the difference? And what's that got to do with Miami?"

"Until now, the main thing I've seen wrong with the Church today is that there's no standard of righteousness being upheld. But that's not the whole problem. Don't you see?" He gestured with his palms. "There's no vehicle. We can't get there from here!"

"To Miami?"

"No, no. I'll tell you about Miami later. It's like you said, Church as a family provides the necessary relationships to live a life committed to Jesus. God never intended for us to do this by ourselves. Jesus said, 'I will build my Church and the gates of hell will not prevail against it.'"

"I believe that, Wayne, which is why I think you should work from within the system, as an agent of change."

"George, look at the current model of Christianity. Basically, it consists of a weekly worship service and a midweek Bible study. That's about it, apart from some rare special events and perhaps some innovative small group program. All I can do is throw sermons at people. The Church needs a change of environment, not good messages. Our lives are scattered and individualistic. Let's face it. 'Church' today is something you attend. It's a place you hear a speech. It's not a family. Not really."

"Couldn't you encourage Church members to pursue deeper relationships and not be just attenders?" George looked puzzled.

"I wrestled with that, but let me ask you this: How could I take a job as a speechmaker and hired leader, and then teach that Christianity which revolves around listening to speeches and being 'laity' is wrong? I just couldn't reconcile those things." He slapped the brick wall in front of him. "No. I don't think I could teach the right things while modeling the wrong things. I don't want to perpetuate a fraud — regardless of how many *good things* I might have to say."

35

THEY CAME FOR DIFFERENT REASONS. Some came to say goodbye. Others came to see that things were done "decently and in order." Some came out of respect. Some because it was Sunday. But all knew something sad was going to occur this day. Today the members of Hampton Street Church were here to observe the farewell sermon of Wayne Davidson.

After ten minutes of singing, whispers trickled through the auditorium as the congregation awaited the appearing of their pastor. As Wayne approached the podium to address the throng before him, his skin tingled. He felt a hundred eyes piercing like needles.

He carried with him a stool, which he positioned to the side of the pulpit. He sat down, attached a lapel microphone, took a deep breath and spoke. "Good morning." The echoed reply helped Wayne to relax. *This is it, Lord. Please help me.* "If you were here last week, you've already heard my *final sermon*, because today I'm not planning to *preach* to you." As Wayne enunciated "final sermon" and "preach," he held his hands up and indicated quotation marks with his fingers. "This morning I'd like to do something a little bit different."

At this, Tom Hartley spoke nervously. "Not anything too radical, Wayne, okay?" Tom's half serious tone could be detected only by those who knew him best. Other's, however, snickered at his pseudo–alarm. "We don't want any trouble."

Wayne felt compassion for Tom and, at the same time, sorrow that this would even have to be said. He was sorry about the whole sickening situation, but he saw it as a chance to share some of the vision he was catching.

"Don't worry, Tom. No funny business. I promise." Everyone laughed, relieved no toes were broken.

"What I'd like to do, instead, is just talk to you all. Somehow I want to express what our Master is doing in my heart and the direction I think He may be taking my life. If I could just plant a seed of some of the exciting things I've been seeing, then I think I can leave here with a lot more peace in my heart." Wayne could see mixed expressions on the faces in front of him but he focused on the inviting smiles of the few soft hearts he knew were listening.

"I'm not going to give you an opening passage because, like I said, this isn't a sermon. Mostly, I just want to share with you all, from the bottom of my heart, some of the core issues for all of our futures.

"There are certain things about following Jesus that are non-negotiable." Wayne scanned the sea of familiar faces. "Most of you got out of bed this morning, got dressed up, and came down to this building to *worship* with the notion that it was somehow related to serving the God that created you. Right?

"Many of you, I expect, if the truth were known, would sometimes rather be fishing, or golfing, or hunting, or sleeping or…name your thing." Ed Lowrey risked a grin. "But somewhere inside of you, there is a sense of duty, or guilt, or something…that compels you to be a church–goer instead. Otherwise, why don't we come together on Saturday mornings, also? And many other weeknights? I think it's partly because we've turned the adventure of getting to *know* God into a lifeless liturgy. And, also, because it's much easier to commit to a set of pre–established, predictable meetings than to live a totally devoted life.

"I'd like to leave you today with two clear thoughts to chew on for the rest of your lives." He pronounced clearly the last words and waited for the silence to regather any wandering ears.

"First, Jesus called all of us, me and you, not to be church-goers but to surrender our entire lives into His hands. If Jesus is not the real–time Lord of our lives every day, then, by His definition we are not Christians. Christianity is not about attending church. It's not about doing good deeds. It's not even about living a strict moral life. It's about giving your insides, your heart, away to the Person of Jesus of Nazareth and letting Him *own* your life. There really is no other kind of Christian life."

Tom shuffled uncomfortably in his pew, looking discreetly for the others' reactions as Wayne continued. "Anything less is only a religious mirage, like parsley on your plate in a restaurant — only there for decoration. It's not really a part of the meal.

"Trust me, I'm not picking on anyone. I know how boring 'church' can be. I've been bored myself at times — even while I was talking." A small chuckle erupted from the congregation. "But hear me out, please. None of us will ever really know the adventure of following Jesus for real, versus the boredom of religion, unless we surrender our own paths and follow Him on His Path. It's like Jesus Himself said, we've got to lose our lives to find them."

Wayne loosened his tie and stood up, one hand on the pulpit. "Now, the second thing I want to leave you with is something I've only recently glimpsed myself. But I'm becoming convinced that without this piece of the puzzle, we will never fully be able to walk out life with Jesus as Lord in anything other than a pledge of momentary commitment. A pledge that we never quite find the strength to live up to. It's amazing but also very simple at the same time.

"Christianity—" he smiled and stepped down to the level of the audience, "is brotherhood and sisterhood and family; not meetings, and services and acts of worship. It's none of those compartmentalized things. It's about our lives *belonging* to each other on the grass roots level, day in and day out, seven days a week. Jesus promised a hundred mothers, sisters and brothers — deep, mutually dependent, daily relationships! Not second cousins and next–door neighbors!

"If that word 'belonging' scares you, it should! It's a big commitment and it's risky. But it is the way Paul described our level of involvement with each other.

"If we don't have each other to laugh with, pray with, sing with, cry with; to shop with, work with, eat with; to share our faith with others with, serve with — day in and day out; then we've hardly begun the adventure of real New Testament Christianity.

"We are not a true Church unless Jesus is the core of our existence together. If every single member isn't cultivating a deep, personal relationship with Jesus as a Person, then we are a department store mannequin, rather than a *body*. The Body of Christ lives in intimate friendship with the Living Jesus in vulnerable, walking–in–the light, confessing–sins–to–one–another relationships!"

He reached up and grabbed his Bible off the elevated pulpit. "Read the book of Acts which describes daily, consecrated, sermon–on–the–mount kind of living, and compare it with a typical week in your own experience of Church life. Will you do that?" He paused, looking into the eyes of those he knew best. "Take an honest look. Is there any resemblance?

"I've just started this journey myself, but the blinders are beginning to fall off and I'm starting to see a much bigger and better way of life. Let me beg each of you — not as a pastor, because I'm not one anymore in the professional sort of way — but as your brother and as your friend. Look Jesus in the eye from the bottom of your heart and give Him your whole life. It's worth it!

"And please, let me also challenge you to search through your Bibles with an honest passion for reality and beg our kind Father to reestablish His Church on Earth — built His way and bearing His Fruit.

"Look through your New Testaments. You won't find broken marriages, drug abuse, teenage pregnancies, gossip, slander, greed and out–and–out worldliness as an unchallenged, unchanging way of life. I know, I know, they weren't perfect. There was sin, and problems did arise from time to time. But when it did come up, they didn't sweep it under the rug. They looked it in the eye and dealt with it, *as a family!* To the Glory of God and His Son Jesus Christ to whom their lives belonged — lock, stock and barrel.

"Please, consider these things before our God. Don't ever allow anyone to convince you to accept lukewarmness as normal, and holy devotion and death to the world system as radical. It's Jesus' only way for His entire Church. The gates of hell will not prevail if it's *His* Church built *His* way."

36

CAROLYN HEARD THE DOOR SHUT harder than usual and peered around the dining room wall to see who had just entered the house. Ted, breathing heavily, took his jacket off and tossed it on the sofa.

Carolyn went to greet him, but, noting his disposition, thought better of it. Ted broke the brief silence. "I think it's finally starting to sink into my thick skull!"

"What's wrong?"

"Oh, I'm starting to think you're right."

"What do you mean?"

"And I've been too dull to see it because my heart has been hard."

"See what? What happened?"

Ted collapsed onto the sofa. "I was with a group of men over at Brian Stephen's house and overheard a flippant remark about Amy. One of the men was joking with Brian and asked him, 'Are you getting fat or are you the second unexpected pregnancy in the neighborhood?'" Ted sat up. "What really burns me up is all the chuckles that followed."

"That's awful!" Carolyn sat on the edge of the sofa beside him. After a few seconds of silence, she asked hopefully, "Did you talk about it?"

"Yeah, I did. It ended up leading into a long discussion. By the time it was over, I was more upset." Ted looked up and assured her, "I don't mean more angry, just disheartened."

"What did you say?"

Ted let out a sigh. "I asked them to be honest about what's happened with Amy and to make sure we were sharing our portion of the blame. I suggested that what happened with Amy might be an indicator of a bigger problem. Maybe we need to consider our relationships and the overall quality of life we share. You know, a tree is known by its fruit."

"Yeah, or maybe even closer to home," Carolyn cut in, "as Jesus said, 'Wisdom is proved right by her children.'"

"Exactly. And that maybe if we'd all been doing our job better, this would never have happened to begin with."

"Did they disagree with you?"

"Disagree?! They thought I was crazy and idealistic to think that way! You know: 'She's young. It's a college campus. Things like this happen and there's nothing we can do about it. Why would you hold us responsible if Amy's not wise enough to be careful who she falls in love with?'"

"You have got to be kidding!"

"It didn't even seem to bother anybody that our own children are just as subject to the laws of probability and statistics as the rest of the world. Don't we have any kind of edge at all over the world or the religious system? I mean, if daily Christianity doesn't have any practical fruit, nothing more to offer than warm fuzzies around a bonfire...what's the point?!"

A tangle of emotions battled within Carolyn's heart. This shallow, worldly reasoning bothered her also. But she was overjoyed to see a fire burning in Ted's bones and a light in his eyes. She felt both despair and elation.

37

MANY THOUGHTS coursed through Wayne's mind. *What am I going to do now? I've gotta get more resumes made.* Both job interviews that Monday morning had gone terribly. He definitely wasn't a car salesman. And his theology degree gave him no advantage toward a mortgage company job. *Nice try.*

Equipped with a red pen and a copy of yesterday's classifieds under his arm, Wayne decided to sample Vito's Italian Kitchen — looking for both a refuge to continue his hunt and a bite to eat. After being seated in a large wooden booth, he folded the paper into a more manageable size and began poring over the tiny ads, hoping to discover a new calling. The garlic and oregano seasoning the air were an almost unconquerable distraction. Wayne's stomach contracted with each breath, sending an array of pangs through his torso. *I'm starving.* He scanned the restaurant, hoping relief would not be delayed long.

The dining room was large and open. Ceiling fans slowly churned the air over the checkered red and white tablecloths that covered the dozen or so round tables peppering the gray linoleum floor. The walls were protected by large wooden booths in which Wayne felt especially alone. The place was only half full, but it was beginning to receive more patrons as the noon hour approached. Wayne hoped the Italian food was as authentic as the accents he heard being bantered around in the kitchen. *I like this place. I'll have to bring Emily or George here sometime.*

Knowing he would be helped soon, Wayne resumed combing the classifieds. *Accounting. CAD. Carpentry. Carpet Cleaning. Customer Service. Hmmm.* Wayne was soon in his own world, circling leads and weighing possibilities.

"Hi. I'm Tony. I'll be ya waita' today. Kin I tell ya 'bout today's lunch special? Today we gotta ham 'n cheese stromboli witda vega'ble o' the day ana bottomless soda o' ya choice witta big piece o' New York style cheesecake. Mm-mm. An' itta only set ya back seven dolla's. Pretty sweet deal in my book."

The waiter stood ready to transcribe his patron's order, but Wayne was held hostage by the classified ads he was combing, unaware of the request. Tony, realizing the customer had missed his introduction tried again. "So, you lookin' for a ca' or somethin'?"

Wayne looked up suddenly, realizing he was being addressed, as Tony continued, "I gotta great one outside. It's a '71 Chevy Impala. Great ca'. Clean as a whistle, runs like a cha'm. It's gotta V8 witta..."

Wayne broke into a smile, enamored by his host's enthusiasm. He was tall and solid, with a square, chiseled jaw, jet–black hair and a pearl–white smile. His appearance, combined with his stereotypical accent, made Wayne feel for a second that he might have taken a wrong exit and ended up in New York City's Little Italy. "No. No, I'm not looking for a car."

"Oh, I saw you lookin' at the ads an' thought maybe you might be need'n a ca' or somethin'. Like my fadda always said, 'Tony, strike while the iron is hot,' see. Meanin' you gotta take advantage of an opportunity when it's dare, 'cus it might not be dare tomorrow. Know whut I mean, uh..." Tony now held out his hand, gesturing for Wayne to reveal his name. Wayne was surprised at this young man's overt friendliness.

"Wayne Davidson."

"Hi. I'm Tony. Tony Veneziano. It's nice to meet you, Mr. Davidson."

"You can call me Wayne, Tony. I don't think I'm that much older than you."

"Okay, Wayne. What can I getcha fa lunch?"

Wayne ordered with a smile, encouraged by the warm disposition of his new friend. As Tony returned to the kitchen barking instructions in his thick Italian accent, Wayne forced himself to resume the job search, intently combing the newspaper before him.

Ah, Lord, he sighed to himself. *I really need a job. I've tried my best to be faithful to your voice. Now please help me support my family. I know it's tough on Em and the children. Please teach us to trust you. Please open a door.*

Wayne had hardly finished one column when Tony returned with a heaping plate full of pasta and meat sauce. Wayne could feel his mouth begin to water as his mind pre–tasted the food in front of him. "Well, ya betta put that paper down long enough to dig in while it's hot," Tony interrupted. "Like my fadda used to say, 'Wasting a hot meal is stupid — but wasting a hot Italian meal is a capital offense.'"

Wayne let out a light chuckle, unable to conceal the effect of his waiter's gregarious personality. "Are you having a good day or are you always this friendly?" Wayne asked, letting his guard down and joining in the spirit of Tony's conversation.

"Ya mood's up to you, right?" Tony retorted. "Well, why not have one that people enjoy? And ya find that you end up enjoying ya'self a lot betta as well."

"I guess that's a decent outlook. Let me guess. You learned it from your father?"

Tony's eyes lit at the mention of his father. "Hey, you catch on pretty quick."

In a few seconds, Tony was beckoned to the other corner of the room to aid another patron, and Wayne was left to enjoy his meal. The whole encounter was pleasant. *It's funny how your mood can change so quickly. It was only a few minutes ago that the weight*

*of the world was on my shoulders. Now things don't seem like such a
big deal after all…An Italian angel, unawares? Naahh!*

38

CAROLYN SAT PEACEFULLY enjoying the spring afternoon sun
on the Harts' front porch. As she gently glided on the family–
sized swing, she watched a robin pecking in the dirt. The storms
from earlier in the week had passed, and a cool breeze ruffled
the pages of her book. She was admiring the large elm, scattered
with fresh leaves, when suddenly the Harts' station wagon roared
into the driveway.

"Sorry I'm so late," Marsha called over the half–open car
door. She flew to the back of the vehicle and hastily loaded her
arms with bags of groceries.

"Let me help you with those," Carolyn offered as she got up
from the swing. "Did you already drop off the milk for the
Richardsons'?"

Marsha unlocked the kitchen door. "Yeah, and I couldn't just
leave her sink full of dishes…"

"How is Kathy?" Carolyn inquired, setting her bags on the table.

Marsha looked up from the refrigerator. "Well, you know
how it is with five children around. I'm amazed at how productive she manages to be. Whew." Her eyes caught the clock on the
wall. "Already four o' clock. I'd better get this roast in the oven.
I don't know how I'll ever get things ready in time for dinner
with the Stephens."

Before Carolyn could say anything, Marsha was stacking
plates into the dishwasher and pulling frozen vegetables out of
the freezer.

"Marsha," Carolyn said at last, "could we sit down for a
minute? I really think you need a break."

"Oh, Carolyn, I'm sorry!" Marsha said as she closed the dishwasher. "You're right. We were going to sit down and read a
chapter from that book, and I forgot all about it."

Marsha dried her hands and followed Carolyn into the den.
Plopping onto the sofa, she let out a long sigh. "Okay, what chapter were we on?"

Carolyn hesitated. "Marsha, slow down a minute. It makes me dizzy just to watch you." She eyed the book in her hand, closed it and placed it on the coffee table. "It looks like you've had a really full day — we don't have to read this chapter right now. Maybe we could just sit and talk."

"Sure, about what?"

"Oh...about how you're doing, maybe?"

"Me, oh, I'm fine." She looked down, uncomfortable with Carolyn's gaze.

"But what's going on inside of you? There's been so much happening lately — with Amy and everything. How are you doing with all that? You live at such a breakneck pace, but is there peace inside?"

"Oh...I don't know. I don't think about that much." Marsha stopped rearranging the pillows on the sofa and thought back over her day. "I guess I am feeling a little frazzled. But there's just so much to do, and I'm running behind."

"It doesn't have to be that way."

"You're right," Marsha conceded. "I probably should plan things out a little better. Get an earlier start on my day." She smoothed her apron, never looking up. "But it seems like there's always something that comes up. Like today, if I hadn't needed to stop for gas...Oh, well. It's always something."

"But, you know, Marsha," Carolyn offered, "I was thinking more of how Jesus said that his food was to do the will of his Father. If we're really busy with the Father's will, it should be food to us. Not something that leaves us feeling empty." Carolyn moved close to Marsha. "I don't know, it just seems like you run yourself ragged trying to serve other people. And I appreciate your heart and desire to help, but I just wonder what it's based on. Are you finding out God's specific will for that moment out of relationship with Him...or doing good just because it is theoretically God's will?"

Carolyn eyed Marsha cautiously, trying to guess her response. *Lord, did I say too much? Am I spouting off about things that aren't even real in me?*

Slowly fingering the fringe of an afghan now draped on her lap, Marsha groped for words. "I don't know what to say, Carolyn. I can kind of see what you're saying, but it's not like I just go around thinking up good things to do." She collected the lint from the afghan into her hand. "I guess I've always been this way. I've been told it's my gift. Besides, what's wrong with doing good things?"

"It's not that doing good things is wrong," Carolyn began slowly. "What I'm talking about is walking the way Jesus walked. He said that even He could do nothing on His own. He only did what He saw His Father doing." She paused a moment to collect her thoughts. "Marsha, I know that in God's mind, nothing — absolutely nothing — is 'good' unless He is initiating it. I know that may sound deep, but it's *real*."

"But I just can't imagine myself living any other way." Marsha was beginning to regain her composure. "Carolyn, I really do appreciate you bringing this up and I will pray about what you said."

At that moment, the phone rang. Marsha hurried to pick it up and was soon caught up in a whirlwind of preparations for dinner. By the time she returned to the den, she was her chipper self again.

"Sorry, Carolyn. Were we finished? I really should get dinner going now."

Carolyn tried to hide her disappointment. "I guess so. Marsha, will you please pray about the things we talked about?"

"Of course," Marsha answered, glancing at her watch. "Oh, no. I better call Susan Stephens. I haven't told her what to bring."

On the way home, Carolyn tried to make sense out of what had just happened. *She's my closest friend, yet it seems like we're living in two different worlds.*

39

"WAYNE, I DON'T UNDERSTAND. I have so many students. They study hard. They do well. Then I give them an 'A' and they move on."

"So what's the problem, George?"

"It's just that…they know more *about* Abraham, Isaac, and Jacob, but they're really not any more *like* them than the day they entered my classroom." George stared again at the long list of

names in his grade book. "I want to see them change inside —
so that they care about God and each other, not just their grades."

Wayne nodded. Their eyes met, and George continued, "I
can't stand the thought of another semester drifting by while I
only impart answers and information. I want there to be more.
I want my classes to be more than another rung on someone's
educational ladder. It's a deception."

"I know, I know," Wayne agreed. "I remember getting my theology degree. It made me think I was close to God and spiritual
when, looking back on it, I don't think I knew God, except su-
perficially. And I was supposed to be qualified to lead others to
know Him!"

Commotion in the hallway reminded George it was almost
class time. He quickly shoved a few papers and a grade book into
his briefcase and rose to tell Wayne goodbye.

Wayne headed out of George's office with the professor right
behind him. George started to hit the light switch when something on the wall caught his eye. He stopped and stared at the
wall for a few seconds. Finally, he grabbed the framed document,
tucked it under his arm and clicked off the lights.

"I AM NOT going to ride that elephant!"

"Come on, Carolyn. Are you going to let one bad experience
ruin your daughter's whole day? So, he sneezed on you last time.
What's the big deal?" Amy smiled playfully as they watched the
passengers loading into the large wicker basket atop the feeding
elephant.

"If you're so concerned about Marie, why don't you take her
on the ride?" Carolyn held the baby toward Amy.

Amy patted her rounding belly and smiled slyly. "I would,
but..."

Just then, Susan Stephens and Kathy Richardson returned
with their toddlers from a bathroom search. "We're back," Susan announced. "Ready to move on to the dolphin show? It starts
in fifteen minutes."

"Saved by the bell." Carolyn grinned. "We wouldn't want to
be late for the dolphin show."

As they walked in the direction of the dolphin pavilion,
Carolyn ventured a question, nodding toward Amy's stomach.

"So how are you feeling today?"

"Pretty good." Amy leaned on Marie's stroller as they passed the monkeys. "I'm definitely starting to notice the extra weight."

"Look! Look! Monkeys! Monkeys!" Justin Stephens stopped the caravan of ladies and strollers to point out the antics in the monkey display.

Kathy and Susan moved toward the rail, while Amy stood back. "But the hardest thing is that it seems like everyone's always looking at me."

Reaching over, Carolyn gave her a hug from the side, gently pulling Amy's head to her own.

"You know, Amy…" Carolyn leaned back and looked her in the eye. "One of the neat things about walking with God is He gives us opportunities to care about other people — in the middle of our own pain." She winked and pointed with her eyes toward Kathy, Susan, and the children. "Wanna show Marie a monkey?"

Amy surrendered an understanding nod. Reaching to take Marie up into her arms, she answered, "I'd love to!"

CRASH!

The sound of breaking glass and a hollow thud stunned the wide–eyed students. Silence.

"What's the value of a diploma?" George paced the front of the classroom, studying his bewildered students. "This isn't an anthropology class. God isn't an ancient relic we become 'experts' in!" Although he wasn't angry, the terseness of his voice revealed an energy he'd rarely shown.

He sat on the corner of his desk. "If we aren't brothers, if we aren't devoted to each other, loving each other and helping each other find a real relationship with Jesus…this piece of paper is useless."

Silence.

40

IT WAS A WARM THURSDAY evening and the saints had decided to gather at the Richardsons'. After spending the afternoon helping Carolyn with laundry, Amy had joined the Stones for dinner. The three now strolled with Marie toward the Richardsons' place. Ted was sure he could hear "A Mighty Fortress" echoing from the open windows of the old house.

"Hi, guys." Kathy greeted them quietly. "Amy, the younger folks are back in the den watching a video."

Amy quickly caught Carolyn's eyes to plead for a rescue. She hoped to avoid the awkwardness she felt around her peers.

"I think Amy was hoping to join *us* tonight, Kathy." Carolyn smiled at Amy's silent, wide-eyed thank you.

Carolyn headed upstairs to drop off Marie, where some of the younger children were being watched. Then she joined her husband and the loose, concentric circles of believers in the large living room.

They worshiped together for at least half an hour, then Brian spoke up. "Does anyone have anything on your heart to share with the saints tonight?"

Ted moved to the edge of his seat and waited, anxiously, to see if anyone would speak up before he began. "Well...if no one else has anything more pressing, I have a verse and some thoughts I'd like to share."

"Go ahead, Ted," the room invited.

"Well, it's just a verse that Carolyn and I were reading and talking about a few days ago. It's in Hebrews chapter three, verses 12 and 13." He paused, allowing everyone time to find the passage.

See to it, brothers, that none of you has a sinful, unbelieving heart that turns away from the living God. But admonish one another daily, as long as it is called Today, so that none of you may be hardened by sin's deceitfulness.

"I'll explain why I read that verse in a moment." Ted looked around, encouraged by the receptive faces. "Carolyn and I have done a lot of talking recently. During the last four years here, God has taught us some very precious things. It's been great, and I wouldn't change it for the world." He took a deep breath. "But it seems like we spend a lot of time dwelling on our strengths, which is okay and can be encouraging. Yet, I wonder..." He looked over at Carolyn. "I wonder if we don't need to spend at least some time considering our weaknesses. This particular thing has been a real difficulty for me...and others as well, I think."

Brian shot Don Chambers a concerned look as Ted continued. "It has to do with true fellowship. Is our fellowship based on applying the Word of God with one another in vulnerability? Or is it just based on friendship? Do we care enough about each other to penetrate each other's lives in personal and practical ways? I know for myself, I haven't wanted to be vulnerable with other people." Carolyn fought to conceal the smile emerging from her heart as Ted continued. "I've also fallen short in helping you. I'm very sorry for that. I've not been involved in your lives deeply enough to even be able to help if I'd wanted to. I couldn't see your lives past my infatuation with my own life."

The room was still and quiet.

"I think it's possible to deceive ourselves into thinking we're building Jesus' Church...without really building on the rock of hearing and obeying the Word of God, as Jesus said. It's not enough to have cookouts, spend a lot of time with each other, have heart–warming devotionals...yet still lose our teenagers to the world because we didn't care enough to get involved or because we allowed the fear of confrontation to keep us from compassionately speaking up when we saw things that weren't like Jesus."

Ted breathed a heavy sigh of release and looked around the room. Brian seemed uncomfortable. But seeing Carolyn's nod, and then Amy, gave Ted the energy to continue.

"You guys have known me for four years. I'm not mad at anyone. I've got no axe to grind. It's just that I've seen the lack in my own life, and I'm sick of it. I want to care enough about you guys to speak up. I want to get out of my own life long enough to notice when you may have lost some fellowship with Jesus and to try to help." He looked into the faces of those he knew best. "One of the things Hebrews three commands us to do is to admonish one another daily so sin won't deceive us and harden our hearts. It doesn't say that if we hang out with each other daily, we won't be hardened and deceived by sin. Admonishing requires deep relationships, buried in loving and finding Jesus together. Not just friendships."

Don, one of the community veterans, spoke up. "Ted, would it be okay if I interjected a thought here?"

"Sure, Don."

"I think I know where you're going with this, and believe me,

I appreciate your heart. Over the years you've shared some very encouraging devotionals with us. I know things have been a little rough the last several weeks."

Marsha gave a protective glance toward Amy, hoping Don wouldn't say anything to hurt her.

Don continued. "Ted, when we talked the other day, I could tell you were in some turmoil."

Carolyn's heart sank.

"Let me give some Biblical examples that might help you see the point I was trying to make then. David was a man after God's own heart, yet his children weren't shielded from sin by his influence. Samuel was a man who was also close to God and his children were still susceptible to the world." Don locked eyes with Ted. "So, what I'm trying to say is that sin is in the world and people are going to fall into sin because of choices they make individually. It's a sovereign issue. Even Jesus lost Judas."

Ted felt deflated by the airtight logic. Confusion swam on his face as Brian broke in. "Ted, if you remember, I was also there the other day, and I think one point that's important to remember in all of this is that we can't be each other's Holy Spirit." Brian sensed Ted waning. "Jesus has given each of us the Holy Spirit to convict us in regard to sin and help shape our character. When we try to usurp the Holy Spirit's role, the result is legalism and nitpicky, sour relationships. It robs God's people of their joy and stifles the freedom we have in Christ."

An uncomfortable chorus of dissonant "amens" echoed from around the room. Carolyn fought discouragement as she looked into her husband's eyes and noticed an absence of resolve. She felt a twinge of panic, and a barrage of accusations assailed her as the implications of what had just been said sank in. She quickly cleared her head, scattering the enemy's attack on her mind, and listened intently to the rising fire within her.

"Um...would it be okay if I said something?" Carolyn raised her hand, still uncertain as to what she was going to say. She only knew she *had* to say something, and she hoped the flame burning within her was evidence of God's supply.

"There's a lot of truth in some of the things you are saying. Yes, it is true that Jesus lost Judas. A good environment alone won't help a bad heart." Carolyn looked right at Brian, who relinquished a reserved nod, then continued. "However, a bad environment can ruin a good heart. Paul said, 'A little leaven leavens the whole lump' and 'Bad company corrupts good character.' While it's nobody's intention to badger anyone, the legitimate danger of legalism doesn't give us a license to ignore the clear commandment of Jesus in Matthew eighteen, the apostolic command of Paul in First Corinthians five, the command my husband read to us in Hebrews, and about fifty other passages that command us to take a proactive role in each other's lives. We are commanded to deal with the enemy's attacks on each other's lives. Do we dare justify disobedience because of the difficulties of obeying — or because of our own guilty consciences?"

Carolyn could feel the heat on the back of her neck as she realized the eyes giving full attention weren't all consenting. She swallowed hard and continued, returning their gazes one at a time. "The doctrine of not being one another's Holy Spirit is popular but not Biblical." She forced herself to look again at Brian, and the concern on his face only compelled her to continue. "It is true that the Holy Spirit does convict us of sin and helps us to grow, but that does not imply that we as believers don't *share* that same role. Even the verse Ted read uses the same Greek word Jesus used to name the *Holy Spirit* when He told us to *admonish* one another daily. That's what *Church* is — the Body of Christ 'Holy Spiriting' one another! Of course, we shouldn't police or judge each other. But we must get involved as God Himself commanded, helping each other walk with God and remove the obstacles. Daily!

"As for David and Samuel..." She now turned to face Don. "I have no doubt that their families could have been entirely different had they grown up in a truth–filled, Jesus–centered Church. Surely, no one here believes that the New Covenant — the one Jesus died to give us — offers us *no* advantage over David and Samuel. If it doesn't, then what is the point? Jeremiah, Ezekiel, Jesus and the Hebrews writer were all very clear that the New Covenant gives us an immeasurable advantage over those in the Old Covenant." Don lowered his eyes, and Carolyn earnestly looked at the others. "No one in here would support the idea that the Church isn't a better place to grow up in than Old Testament Israel! If so, then we've all just wasted the last several

140

years of our lives and we might as well have stayed in pews!"

"Brian—" Carolyn was taken pleasantly off guard when Ted spoke up again. "You mentioned joy being lost by legalism. That's a valid concern. Nothing stifles true, divine joy like living by the law. However, the only thing that is produced by living detached from each other — by not digging in and caring for each other — is a false, shallow joy. And that is a mirage! As the apostle Peter said, 'Times of refreshing come from repentance.' Not from superficiality!"

Brian's eyes showed more than discomfort. He opened his mouth to intervene, but Ted persisted. "If we can live worldly lives, and still be 'joyful,' then that joy needs to be taken away because it's not founded on reality. That's what Jesus meant when He said, 'I did not come to bring peace, but a sword, and to divide.' That is not always fun on a superficial level." Brian and Don shared disconcerted looks, each wanting the other to do something.

Ted continued climactically, "On the other hand, nothing brings more joy to the heart than seeing someone free from something that's held them in bondage for years. Even the angels celebrate, the Scriptures say, when someone is rescued from sin's chains."

"Brother, brother, please," another community old–timer broke in. "I think we all may just need to call it a night." Brian and Don both relaxed as the older brother continued. "I'm not sure anything else can be accomplished in this format. These are foundational issues. It seems clear to me we are looking at two very divergent visions of the Church. One thing is for sure: we must decide which vision we're pursuing. We can't go in two directions. Let's commit to resolving this at a later date."

Relief filled the room as the idea to call it a night was readily embraced by most of those present.

For some, reality is an uncomfortable schoolmaster and honesty an uncomfortable companion.

41

WALKING DOWN THE HALL toward the faculty lounge, George noticed that the walls were now blue. He went inside and looked around the room. *Hmmm. New furniture. When did they...*

Just then, he noticed an odd heaviness in the air. It was quiet. *Why is everyone looking at me?* His eyes darted around the room. Spotting the professor of New Testament, he walked hurriedly toward him. "Bill, I've been meaning to get these books back to you."

"Well!" He was stopped short by a boisterous British voice. "If it isn't our beloved Professor, back from the hallowed halls of the student center to mingle with his peers!"

"What?" George stared in bewilderment as several other teachers joined in laughter.

"Why, George," said one, smiling and searching his peers for support, "what made you decide to grace us with your presence today?"

"The student cafeteria must be closed," answered a sparsely-haired history professor seated across the room.

George looked around in disbelief. These were his friends — he had thought. Unsure how much of this was in fun, he just stood there. *Maybe I'm being too sensitive.* Noting his discomfort, most returned to the food in front of them.

Bill broke George's silence. "You know, we have missed seeing you in here."

"Things have changed, Bill." George smiled, feeling a warm tug at the memory of years of camaraderie with Bill and others. "I've been trying to invest more in the students. That is why we have this job, you know. I think that's what they pay us for."

Bill was four years younger than George, though his tenure with the college was almost as long. "I appreciate your care for the students, George. It's commendable. I'm just concerned with how you are going about it."

"What do you mean?"

Bill clasped his hands together and stared over George's head. "There is a generation gap I think you're going to have to learn to cope with. Students gain stability by learning to function in a world with structure. You're the teacher. They're the students. By changing those roles, you don't help them. You only confuse them more." He lowered his gaze to George's face. "A student shouldn't have to decide, when he sees you, whether to call you George or Professor Archer. By compromising your position of authority and replacing it with familiarity, you lower *our* position of authority as well."

George's puzzled look prompted Bill to try again. "I know you feel bad about the Adams boy. We all do. But demeaning the role of professor because you feel guilty about a student isn't going to solve anything. Exceptions don't change the need for a stable norm. Do you understand my point?"

George's puzzlement became resolve. "I think I follow your reasoning." His voice was calm, but firm. "Now, what if Jesus would have operated under that same premise? Let's think about it. Wouldn't His purposes on Earth have been better served if He had spent his time collaborating with the Pharisees and teachers of the law or simply emerging to offer an eloquent oracle on a regular basis." George raised his voice a notch. "Rather than violating 'order' and *living* with fishermen." Conversations in the room stopped. "Who knows, he might have even saved himself a crucifixion."

42

TWO WEEKS HAD PASSED since the difficult meeting at the Richardsons', and life in Pine Ridge had become noticeably stilted. Alan and Marsha Hart were distressed about Amy. Marsha was a nervous wreck, fretting about Amy's future there, and Alan had grown weary of the whole ordeal.

Meanwhile, the tension with the Stones continued to mount. Ted and Carolyn tried to keep things simple and clear, but their honest attempts to care and clear up misunderstandings were only making matters worse.

Some of the leading families in the community were discussing these problems. As a group, they typically reveled in their diversity — wanting each person to live by his own, Spirit-led convictions — provided, of course, they stayed within the framework of traditional orthodoxy. But this situation was different. Ted and Carolyn were not content to "agree to disagree." To them, Truth was not relative, and obedience was not the enemy of freedom.

The conversations that had filled the past days were going nowhere. Something more needed to happen. In fact, Brian

Stephens and Don Chambers had an idea they thought just might make everyone happy...

"CAROLYN, THEY'RE HERE!" Ted flung open the door and beckoned his guests inside. Eagerly leaving the spring wind behind them, Don and Brian bustled into the hallway.

They exchanged awkward pleasantries as Carolyn collected their jackets. Once they had settled into the living room, Brian started the ball rolling.

"Thanks again for agreeing to talk on such short notice."

Ted succumbed to a nervous grin. "Well, it was plenty of notice. But you didn't tell me what was on your mind. I must confess my imagination's been working overtime all day."

Ted looked over at Carolyn and caught her knowing glance. Brian, not sure how to respond, looked to Don for help.

"Well...we don't want you to feel like this is some sort of disciplinary thing," Don reassured. "We just wanted to follow up on our recent conversations."

Ted nodded.

"Now I realize that the last couple of weeks have been intense, and I don't want to put you on the defensive," Don pursued slowly. "But we've been thinking a lot about our future together and what would be best for the community and for you." He scooted forward on the couch. "We've got an idea that's evolved for several reasons. It may sound kinda crazy, but at least hear us out."

Brian picked up where Don left off. "Alan and Marsha Hart are worried about their daughter, and we've been trying to help them find a solution. I guess it's been sort of hard on her living at home, with the older teens around. Awkward glances, whisperings, that sort of thing. You know how kids are."

Carolyn shot a pleading eye at her husband. *They don't get it, do they?*

Ted opened his mouth to protest Brian's last statement but was cut short as Brian continued. "Anyway, they've been wondering if there was some place Amy could go, you know...to sort of get away from things for awhile."

"So what does that have to do with us?" Carolyn's face betrayed her discomfort with the direction things were headed.

Don used his most diplomatic tone. "Well, a couple things.

For starters, we know you and Amy have become pretty close recently, and it just seems like…" Don stuttered as the controversial thought reached his tongue.

Brian finished for him. "It seems like you guys are embracing a different vision for the Church. One that we're not sure we're going to be able to meet for you." He rubbed the back of his neck. "I guess we have a sort of sinking feeling you're just not going to be happy here." His voice faltered as he continued slowly. "What would you guys think about moving out of Pine Ridge?"

Tension, the kind Don dreaded most, squeezed the individuals in the room. Carolyn slipped into the kitchen to find a tissue. She then stood in the doorway, leaning against the jamb.

Ted looked up after staring past his shoes for a long sixty seconds. The two men in his living room wished they were elsewhere.

Finally, Don made an effort to console the Stones. "I'd like you both to know that this is just a suggestion. It's entirely up to you."

"And the Lord," Brian chimed in.

"Right. After praying about it, you might decide to stay. And that will be fine as long as you can stay with a spirit of unity, understanding the direction of the community. But we do think you guys should consider this as a possibility. It might be helpful for Amy and the Harts." Don longed for the perfect thing to say.

"Ted, Carolyn," Brian ventured, pausing until he had looked them both in the eye. "We want you to know we love you. And we're committed to you unconditionally."

Ted nodded soberly. "You've certainly given us plenty to think about."

"Well, take your time. You don't have to decide anything right now. And again, it's completely up to you. I hope we haven't upset you too much, Carolyn."

"I think we'll be fine," Ted said.

The two men left in silence. Ted and Carolyn felt awful.

43

ERIC WATCHED IN AMUSEMENT as George's old Continental pulled into a parking spot at the end of the lot. Gathering up his backpack, he hurried over to meet the professor.

145

"Welcome ashore!" he quipped as George locked the doors.

George looked puzzled. "What?" Then, following Eric's gaze to his large automobile, he laughed. "Oh, if you think she looks big now, you ought to see her with the sails up."

George followed Eric into the tiny diner. As the screen door slammed behind them, the aroma of greasy hamburgers assaulted the professor. The ceaseless drone of the shake mixer reminded him of his last trip to the dentist.

"I wasn't sure I had the right place," George said as Eric perused the menu by the cash register. "I thought you said the Ice Rabbit."

Eric looked up. "This is the Ice Rabbit. Only place in town with seventy–five different flavors of shakes."

"Then why does the sign say Frozen Harry's?"

"Because," Eric replied with a sly grin, "The Ice Rabbit *is* Frozen Harry's. Get it? Frozen Hare...Rabbit?"

An older woman with her hair wound into a painfully tight bun closed the carry–out window and sauntered over to the register.

"You boys ready to order?"

Eric pulled out his wallet. "My treat this time," he winked. "I'll have the three–piece chicken basket and a large shake."

The woman reached into her hair–bun and produced a pen. After several sharp dabs onto her tongue, she scribbled his order on the pad. "What kind of shake will that be?"

"Make it a chocolate strawberry malt with mint and pineapple."

George grimaced.

"And you, Sir?" She looked at George.

"Oh...uh...I'll have the same. Only make mine a vanilla shake."

The two friends found a booth in the back corner, next to the video games. George consoled himself with the thought that they could move if someone came in and started playing.

"So, how are classes coming along?" Of all the students George had tried to invest in this semester, Eric was the only one who returned the investment.

"Pretty good," came the jaunty reply. "My political science professor made us download an article off the Internet this

146

morning. I got on and back off as fast as I could. Big Brother really is watching, you know. They don't call it 'the web' for nothing. You know, like a spider's web? Serious danger!"

George smirked. "You're really serious about this government conspiracy thing, aren't you?"

Eric tossed his head to the side, "Oh, it's not the government that scares me the most." His face grew sober. "It just seems like every time I'm on line, there's a claw reaching out of my monitor, trying to pull me in to that web of filth and perversity."

The woman called from behind the counter, "Your order's ready!"

Eric sprung to his feet and went to get the food, returning with two colorful plastic trays balanced one on top of the other. He hurled himself into the booth, carefully eyeing the packet of margarine in George's hand.

"You know that stuff's plastic, right?"

George looked up in disbelief. "What?"

"Yeah, it's a petroleum product. They take vegetable oil and blast it with hydrogen molecules until all the nutrients are stripped off. That's why those packets aren't refrigerated. No nutrients, no spoiling."

Eric brushed a hand across his ruddy bangs, then rested his chin on his palm, smiling up at George.

"I never thought much about it," George returned.

"Just an observation," Eric spouted as he opened his own packet and spread the contents on his roll. George folded his hands and waited. For him, this was the awkward part of every meal.

Eric, noting George's discomfort, folded his hands in like manner. "Are you thankful?" he asked.

"Yes, I am."

"Me, too." With that, Eric seized a big piece of fried chicken and bit into it with enthusiasm.

George chuckled quietly. "So, Eric, how are things going with your new roommate?"

"Oh, a lot better. I think we're getting used to each other by now." Eric wiped his mouth on a paper napkin. "Besides, those ear plugs I've been wearing to bed are terrific! I can't even hear his stereo at all."

George swallowed hard to keep from spewing his shake.

Clearing his throat, he managed to say, "I'm glad you're getting along."

"Yeah, hey, thanks for the prayers. For a while there, I really thought one of us was going to have to move out." Eric tossed a chicken bone into a nearby trash can. "Say, is there anything I can be talking to Father about for you?"

George's face took on a serious demeanor. "Actually, there is. I just mailed another letter to Rick."

Eric's eyes narrowed. "Did he write you back last time?"

George shook his head. "No. I'm not even sure he read it. But I just wanted to try again."

Eric was convicted by the pain he saw in George's eyes. "Do you want to talk to Jesus about that now?"

44

"NIGHT, NIGHT. Daddy loves you."

Ted kissed his little Marie on the cheek and softly closed the door. Carolyn was waiting for him in the den, a stolid figure perched on the sofa like a cat waiting for some rodent to scurry by. He looked at her and laughed.

"You look about as sober as the losing team at a homecoming game."

Carolyn smirked, pretending not to be amused. "Could you sit down for a minute, Honey? I'd like to talk if we could."

"What about?" Ted invited as he sank into the cushions next to her. He thought he heard the faint rumblings of thunder off in the distance.

"I just...I'm just not sure about leaving the community. Maybe Don and Brian are right about Amy. Maybe it would be better for her to get away somewhere, at least for awhile. But, I just can't imagine being anywhere else but here. Who would we talk to? Where would we go? It scares me!"

Ted placed his arm around her shoulders. "I know, Honey. All our friends are here; the people we've spent the last four years of our lives with. I can't imagine just leaving them behind like all this never happened." He turned her face toward his. "But you know what's even harder for me to imagine?"

"What's that?"

"It's even harder for me to imagine staying here and just pretending everything's okay when it's not. It wouldn't be real." His voice became animated. "And we wouldn't be able to grow any further if we had to live under this unwritten rule that says you don't touch my life and I won't touch yours."

It was beginning to rain. The two sat in silence, enjoying the euphony of wind and droplets, before Ted continued. "At the same time, though, I don't really want to go, either. I love these guys. Besides, where would we go? And what would we do? Place membership at some church building? I'm open to that, but I just can't see it happening. Why would God want us to go into an even *more* mixed and diluted environment?"

They sat quietly for several moments, listening to the rumbling storm. Carolyn looked out the window. "Would it be okay if we talked about it with the Creator of that thunder?"

"Sure." Ted sat up and placed his head in his hands.

"Please, God," Carolyn began, "show us what to do. We'll follow You anywhere, no matter what it costs. But we can't bear the thought of striking out on our own, apart from You. To whom shall we go? You have the words of eternal life. Please make it clear. Make it obvious. We're so dull — we need help to hear Your voice."

THE NEXT DAY at Washington High School, Ted headed back to his little office in the East Gym. The last health class of the day was over, and his duffel bag held a stack of tests expecting to be graded. *Why grade today what you can put off until tomorrow?* This was the part of the year that Ted endured, for the most part, until football practices started up in the summer.

He pulled open the gym door, shivering a bit at a cold blast from the vent overhead, and charted a course to his office. *What did Carolyn want me to get at the store? Was it milk or juice?* A little note was taped to the outside of his office door. He fumbled absently with his keys as he read it:

CALL MR. REED AS SOON AS YOU GET IN.

He tossed his keys onto the desk. *Reed…do I know anybody by that name?* He pecked out the phone number that was scratched on the paper.

149

"Hello, Northeastern High School, front office. This is Betty. Can I help you?"

Ted was caught off guard. *Northeastern High School?* "Uh...yes, you can. This is Ted Stone from Washington High School. May I speak to Mr. Reed, please?"

"One moment while I ring his office."

Strange that a school from the city would be calling me. Wait a minute, this couldn't be Logan Reed, the principal, could it? I wonder what he wants? A voice brought Ted to attention.

"Hello, Ted, this is Logan Reed. Ted, I'm glad I caught you before the day was out. Thanks for returning my call."

"Sure, Logan. I'm a little surprised by your call." Ted scratched his head.

"Certainly, I understand. I'll get right to the point." He cleared his throat. "I watched your season with Washington High this year, and I must say you gave the rest of us in the conference a good scare."

"Thanks." Ted beamed. "We had a good bunch of boys."

"Yes. And you've done a fine job with them. Your efforts as assistant coach have especially shined through. That defensive line of yours is a WALL!"

Ted enjoyed a smile to himself. "Thanks for the compliment. It was hard work, but it's been worth it."

"I can tell you work very hard, Ted. As a matter of fact, that's why I'd like you to consider coming to coach at Northeastern next year."

Ted was stunned.

"We have put together a good program with a strong coaching staff. We just need the right person to steer the ship."

"Excuse me, are you offering me the position of Head Coach?" Ted hoped his excitement was not too obvious.

"Now, I know it's a big decision. I don't expect you to accept right now. Go home, have dinner, talk it over with your wife. But get back to me in a couple of days."

Ted grabbed his keys and headed out the door, duffle bag and papers forgotten. His thoughts were racing ahead of his feet. By the time he reached the car, his mind was at home breaking the news to Carolyn.

So we just ask Him a question and He answers it? Just like that!

Do you really think this is God's way of showing us what to do?

In his mind, Carolyn nodded her assent.

This is great!! God's alive! Does anybody else know about this?

45

WHY AM I SO NERVOUS? Lord, please grant me peace. George's thoughts became clearer. The anxiety began to dissipate. He breathed a sigh of gratitude. *Thanks.*

The silence was startling as his echoing footsteps ended in front of a closed wooden door. "Arthur J. Kincaid, D.Div., Dean — School of Religion and Missions."

The door swung open, revealing a spacious, red-carpeted reception area. The gray-haired secretary, busily transcribing a letter, looked up just long enough to point in the direction of the dean's open door.

The dean looked up from his Bible as the creaking floor signaled George's arrival. "Well...hello, George. Good to see you." He pointed to a high-backed, red velvet chair against the wall. "Please, have a seat. What can I do for you today?"

"Well..." George calmed the butterflies in his stomach, "there's something I've been thinking and praying about for several weeks, and I want to ask for your support."

"What is it, George? Sounds important." Dr. Kincaid leaned forward in his chair, stirring the sound of Naugahyde.

"I've decided to leave the Bible department."

"George!" The Dean took off his glasses. "Are you resigning?"

"No, no." George shook his head. "I've applied for an opening in the history department." George moved his chair closer to Dr. Kincaid's. "They've agreed to accept the transfer if you are willing to release me."

Dr. Kincaid arose and turned to gaze out the window. After a moment, he turned to face George. "Can I ask why you want to leave?"

"I...don't want you to take this the wrong way."

"George, we've known each other for over twenty years. Be frank with me."

"Arthur, my conscience just won't allow me to continue in

my position." George chose his words carefully, not wanting to hurt his colleague and friend. "God's Word is not a *subject* I can teach and test on anymore. God is a Living Being, not an essay topic." George turned his gaze away from his superior. "For all these years, I've tried to serve God the best I know how. Well, now this doesn't seem like the best way to change lives anymore."

"George, you have served God well, and I believe you've had more of an impact on students than you realize. In fact, if you really want to help them, I can't imagine a better situation than here in the Bible department teaching them God's Word." Dr. Kincaid sighed. "Please don't abandon the students. They need men who care about them like you do."

"I'm not abandoning the students. I'm just trying to change my role in their lives. I want to be able to walk with them as a brother, to seek the Living God *with* them, not just be an expert on things about God. As a Bible teacher, I can tantalize their brains and challenge their reasoning, but that doesn't help them purify their hearts and become friends of God."

The dean walked over to George's chair. "George, I know what you mean. Teaching them facts about God won't, by itself, help them know God better. But these facts serve as a foundation. How can they know God if they don't know facts about Him. Bible knowledge *is* important and it shouldn't be trivialized."

George watched as the dean made his way back to his own chair. "I know it seems crazy." George took a deep breath, realizing the communication gap between them was more than word choice could remedy. "But can you see that treating God like a subject — on the same level as history or trigonometry — is immoral? Bible knowledge is not the enemy. Jesus, Peter, Paul...they all knew the Scriptures well. But Jesus didn't teach classes. He called men to follow Him, to walk by His side."

Dr. Kincaid clasped his hands together. "Now, that's a strong statement. Be careful not to condemn the profession that has carried you all these years." He put his glasses on. "I believe I know some of what you're feeling, George. And I believe this is a decision you'll come to regret. But, because I care about you and because you seem convinced, I will release you."

With that, Dr. Kincaid pulled out a piece of department letterhead and began to pen a letter. After two lines, he looked up. "Are you sure this is what you want?"

"I have no choice. I must obey God."

46

SEVERAL WEEKS LATER, in another part of the city, the Stones settled into their new home.

"I think I'll head on up to bed," Amy called over her shoulder as she awkwardly ascended the stairs, not yet accustomed to her growing frame.

Carolyn smiled inwardly, grateful that Amy seemed to be adjusting to their new life together under one roof. "I'll be heading up there myself in a few minutes," she answered, reaching to lock the front door. Out of habit, she reached with the other hand to flip off a light switch that didn't exist. *I keep forgetting this isn't our house in Pine Ridge.* She surveyed the room and considered unpacking one more of the boxes still lingering since the move. *Just one box,* she told herself, *five minutes.*

Twenty minutes later, Carolyn climbed the stairs. Thinking she heard Marie crying, Carolyn headed for her daughter's room. *Wait, that's Amy!* She paused at the door for a moment, then decided to knock. "Amy? Are you okay ?"

Hearing no answer, she slowly opened the door. Light from the hallway streamed in to reveal Amy, sobbing with her face buried in her pillow. Kneeling beside the bed, Carolyn gently placed her hand on Amy's arm. "Amy..."

Amy composed herself, then lifted her head, shielding her eyes from the light. "I feel like a banished woman, sent away because everyone's embarrassed or ashamed of me." She caught Carolyn's concerned look. "Not that I don't like being here with you and Ted. I do." Amy shifted around, struggling to sit up, "And I don't like being fat!"

Carolyn listened patiently to Amy, simultaneously lifting her own thoughts. *Lord, show her Your mercy.*

"It's more than all that," Amy went on. "Carolyn, ever since I got pregnant, it's become more and more clear that something is missing, something is wrong." Amy shifted again, trying to get comfortable. "It's not just tonight. This is something I've been thinking about for a long time. I see something in you and Ted, the way you talk to God, the way you talk with each other...God just seems so real to you."

The strain and anxiety on Amy's face were evidence of the turmoil raging inside. "What's wrong with me?...My parents treated me great. We studied the Bible all the time. They tried to protect me from the world..." Tears were streaming down Amy's cheeks now. "Carolyn, I want to be on the inside what my parents taught me to look like on the outside. Getting pregnant wasn't just a mistake...something was missing inside me. If it was missing six months ago, then it's still missing now."

Jesus, Carolyn's heart cried, *You are the Answer for all our needs. Please give Amy the answers she needs tonight.* "Amy, talk to God. Open up to Him and tell Him what you're feeling. He wants a relationship with you."

"Carolyn, I'm not sure that I've ever known God at all the way you speak of Him. But...for the first time in my life, I really want to. I need Him, and I'm desperate to know Him. I'm just afraid I never will."

Carolyn wrestled in her heart, searching for an answer. "Amy, who do you think Jesus is?"

"Well, He's God's Son—"

"Wait...stop. Don't just answer out of your head. Think about *Him* — as a person — and tell me who He is. No clichés." Carolyn smiled reassuringly.

Amy pulled her pillow tight against her. "I'm not sure I know. I know He's your Lord. I've seen the way you yield your heart to Him. But I want to know that for myself."

"Amy, is it possible that all your life you've learned about Jesus and His 'rules,' but you've never really met Him yourself?"

"Yes, that's it exactly," Amy responded with a note of certainty. Carolyn had put words on what she was already feeling. "But, how do I get to...meet Him?"

"Amy, have you asked Jesus to show Himself to you? To show you Who He is and how much you need Him and how much He loves *you* — really? Remember, He's a *person*, not just some 'higher power.'"

"No, I haven't. Not directly. But I will."

Carolyn left Amy in silence and went downstairs to wrestle with God on behalf of Amy.

Amy slid to the floor and soberly turned her face toward Heaven in a real, honest attempt to find the living Jesus and unveil her heart. She began to realize how often her prayers had been shallow and empty. Though it was subtle, she had chosen to stay on the surface of things to avoid having to face the darkness lurking inside her.

It had come to the point where the mounting pressure in her heart from the sin and guilt was too much to bear. With tears streaming down her face, she finally let go of herself. Pushing past her pride and fear, she spoke honestly with God about her sin and her deep need for Jesus. Through broken words, she agreed with God, "I didn't slip into sin accidentally. I chose it. There's no one and nothing to blame but me. And I'm so, so sorry, God. Please forgive me. I want You to live with me and to make Your home inside me. I want You to be the Ruler of my heart. Please help me not to hide behind my shallow personality anymore."

AMY GENTLY ROUSED Carolyn from the couch. "Carolyn, can we talk?"

"Oh...Amy. I must have fallen asleep. Yes, we can talk." She sat up and rubbed her eyes.

"Carolyn, I asked Jesus to show me how much I needed Him." She started to weep. "All I could think of after that was how awful I've been. All the unforgiveness toward the people at Pine Ridge. The anger with you. The whining attitudes with Mom and Dad. The pregnancy." She shook her head. "Carolyn, I've done some awful things. I've hurt Jesus a lot." She began crying even more. "So I told Him...to His face...I was sorry."

A smile held her face. She looked down at Carolyn. "Jesus is the Son of the Most High God — He is the King of the Universe — and He will forgive me of all my sin."

Carolyn, too, was crying, singing in her heart.

"I want to give my life to Jesus! I want to be His friend — and I want Him to be my Lord."

They talked for several more minutes before Carolyn went

to wake Ted. Though sleepy, Ted was elated to hear Amy wanted to give her life to God.

"She wants to be baptized tonight. Do you think we can find a place?"

"This late?" Ted asked.

"Yes! Amy said if people in the Bible were baptized in the middle of the night, she doesn't want to wait either."

"Well, I do still have a key to the pool at Washington High."

"Do you think it's okay to use it?"

"Sure. I still work there for another week."

"Okay. I'll go tell Amy."

"Great. I'll call Alan and Marsha and tell them the good news." He reached for the telephone on the nightstand. "I'm sure they'll want to meet us there."

This is what the Lord says,

"Do I bring to the moment of birth

and not give delivery?"

Isaiah 66:90

Birth Pains

47

"HEY, YOU!" The shout emerged from the large, burly man while smoke and saliva trailed from his cigar. "Get a move on! We don't have all day. This is a worksite, not a playground."

It was Wayne's third day on his latest temp job. He wasn't much of a construction worker. The sting in his palms after each new task made it clear that his white–collar hands were not accustomed to this kind of hard labor. *I've got to find another line of work.* He grimaced in his mind. *This is gonna kill me!*

Wayne finished filling the wheelbarrow with debris and hauled it over to the rented dumpster. Salt stung his eyes as sweat poured down from his forehead. The edge where his T–shirt met his sunburned neck provided an additional painful distraction.

Lord...I'm thankful for a job. I really am. But I'm not sure I'm cut out for this. A quick glance from his foreman jolted Wayne from his brief pause and brought him back to earth. *I know, I know, suffering produces character.* Wayne threw himself back into his work and knew in his heart that, for a time, this was exactly where he needed to be.

As a stream of sweat broke loose from his brow, channeling its way into his left eye, the thought struck him, "This is Adam and Eve's fault!" He chuckled to himself as he committed to persevere.

"WHAT WAS THAT?" Ted Stone peeked eagerly over the top of his book. "Sounds like someone just picked up the phone."

Amy laid down her cross–stitch and raced behind Ted into

the kitchen. Arriving on the scene within moments, they almost dog–piled Carolyn as she hung up the phone.

"Who were you calling?" they playfully demanded in unison.

"Why, no one." Carolyn took a step backward to regain her balance. "I was just checking to make sure there was still a dial tone. This phone's hardly rung in the two weeks we've lived here."

"I know." Ted opened the refrigerator and began to forage. "And we're paying good money for that phone. It had better start pulling its own weight around here."

Amy laughed. "I guess most people out in the real world aren't accustomed to getting a dozen calls a night, like we used to."

"I wonder what most people do with all this time on their hands," Carolyn mused. "They must be awfully lonely."

Ted stood up and shut the refrigerator door. "Well, I don't know about most people, but I'll tell you one thing: If I have to sit around this house one more night playing Scrabble, I'm gonna go nuts!"

Carolyn placed a hand on his shoulder. "I know how you feel. In fact, as much as I hate shopping malls, I've actually thought about going down to one just so we can see some people."

Ted grinned. "Now there's an idea!"

RRRRRRING!

All eyes were transfixed on the little phone by the toaster. It had rung. Yes, and it was ringing again.

RRRRRRING!

Three hands grabbed at the receiver, but only one was rewarded. Ted pressed the device against his face and cleared his throat.

"Hello? Yes, this is Ted Stone."

Amy and Carolyn watched his countenance fall. Ted sat down at the table and waited for a break in the monologue.

"I'm sorry," he said at last. "I just don't need another credit card right now."

Ted hung up and propped his elbows on the table. Carolyn and Amy sat down with him, half–resigned to another night of "bored" games. But something different was brewing inside of Ted, something he'd never given much thought until now.

"Why don't we spend some time asking God to help us meet some people who really care?"

"That sounds great." Carolyn perked up.

Ted looked up and pleaded, "Jesus, it was You who led us out here. You're the Good Shepherd. Please show us what to do next. We feel lost, not sure who to spend time with or even how to find them. Please, Father, bring people into our lives that we can care about. Please lead us out of this desert."

Silence followed as they each considered the implications of the request. Carolyn weighed her motives as she waited. She spoke up softly. "Jesus, we know You have a purpose for our lives. It was no accident that You led us to this place. Surely there are people out there who care — who want to *know* You. Please cause our paths to cross so we can share Your life together — for Your sake — not just because we're lonely."

48

GEORGE ARCHER PACED between the kitchen and the den with his cordless phone. As the phone rang on the other end, he reflected on his budding friendship with the Davidsons.

"Hello, is this Emily?"

"Hi, George. What's up?"

"I'm glad you're home!"

"Yeah, I...live here."

George chuckled at Emily's sarcasm. "There's someone I'd really like you to meet! She's a former student of mine." He walked to the window and watched a hummingbird at the feeder. "I've thought about getting in touch with her several times before, but — well, I didn't know any sisters for her to meet."

"Yes," Emily replied, "I know what you mean."

"So, that's where you come in." George sat down on a dark green sofa and propped his feet up on the coffee table. "What do you think about inviting her to dinner or something?"

Emily paused, considering. "I don't see why not. She might be a little uncomfortable eating with just Wayne and me, though. Maybe the four of us could go out somewhere."

"That could work." He hesitated. "But it still might be best if you called her. If you don't mind?"

"Sure, I can do that. Hold on while I find a pen."

He could hear her rummaging through a drawer while he waited. Finally, she returned. "Okay, I'm ready. What is her name?"

"Amy...Amy Hart."

"HI, I BELIEVE WE HAVE A RESERVATION, probably under the name Davidson."

Vito, a short, plump man with rosy–red cheeks and thinning black and gray hair — combed straight back — inspected a chart with a short, chubby finger. "Ah, here it is," he announced. He read the inscription off the paper as if to give it some kind of official honor. "Davidson. Party of six, for seven o'clock." He looked up and said, with Italian pride, "Welcome to Vito's *real* Italian Kitchen, Mr. Davidson."

"Thank you, but actually I'm not Mr. Davidson. I'm George Archer. But I assume Mr. Davidson will be here shortly."

"Ah, of course," the restaurant owner recovered. He removed six menus from a rack on the side of his podium and gestured for George, Ted, Carolyn and Amy to follow him. They were seated in a large, wooden booth and began absorbing their surroundings.

"So," Carolyn asked, "how did you find this place?"

"Oh...Wayne brought me here for the first time a few months ago. It's a great place." George laughed. "There's a waiter here you've got to meet. He's a real character."

They all browsed their menus as Italian Muzak softened the noise of the busy restaurant. "I like the manicotti here," George said.

"Now there's a man who knows his manicotti, let me tell ya." All eyes looked up, startled by the unexpected voice of the tall waiter looming over them with a warm smile. "Hi, I'm Tony. I'll be ya waida tonight." Ted, Amy and Carolyn looked at each another in amusement, then turned again to Tony. "What, is my hair stickin' up or somethin'?"

"No, your hair's fine. They've just never seen an Italian before." George introduced his three friends while Tony wiped his hand on his trousers.

"Pleased ta meetcha."

Just then, the host announced the arrival of Wayne and Emily.

"Hey, Wayne, is this the Mrs?" Tony gestured toward Emily

with feigned amazement. "Did he tell ya he's plannin' to buy my '71 Chevy Impala?" He surrendered a deep chuckle and looked at Wayne to be sure he hadn't offended him with his playfulness. Emily also looked at Wayne, conveying genuine concern.

"He's just kidding, Em. He's been trying to get me to buy that car for months."

"Da offer's still good." Tony winked, then moved out of the way. Wayne and Emily slid into the booth, while Tony began taking drink orders.

"Da usual for you, Wayne?" Tony raised an eyebrow, pleased with his personal service.

"Sure."

George promptly introduced the Davidsons to Amy, Carolyn and Ted.

Ted looked at Wayne and asked, "So, how do you and George know each other? Are you part of the same Church?"

"Well, no, not really." Wayne groped for words. "I guess we're just — brothers. We were both looking for some real life and a chance to grow closer. We only met a few months ago, though it seems like forever." Wayne ribbed George. "We've been learning some of the same things lately, and I think we're starting to rub off on each other."

"And what about you, Emily? Is that true for you?" Carolyn surprised herself with her forwardness.

Emily's face betrayed her struggle for words. "Well, I have been searching also. But I'm not sure...how..."

"Yeah, she's with us." Wayne interrupted. "Sometimes she just has trouble finding the right words." He laughed uncomfortably, and the lack of response from the others felt like a kick in the stomach. He sensed Emily's embarrassment.

Carolyn sat back in silence, wondering what would happen. She recalled how often tense moments like these had come up in the community — and how rarely anything was done.

Dodging the silence, they all began studying their menus. Behind his menu, George asked God for wisdom. *Father, please provide a way for me to talk to my brother without embarrassing him. I want to help. But I also want to cover over.*

Just then, Vito walked up to the table. "Mr. Davidson, you left the lights on in your mini-van."

"Thanks, Vito." Wayne scooted to the edge of the booth. "Excuse me for a minute, everyone."

George watched as Wayne walked toward the front doors. "Thanks, Father," he whispered, then stood up. "I think I'll join him."

George caught up with Wayne in the restaurant lobby. "Mind if I walk with you?"

"Not at all."

Once outside, they slowly made their way to the car. George forced himself to talk. "Wayne, I'm not used to getting involved in these kinds of things, and I feel a little awkward. But could I mention something to you?"

"About Emily?" Wayne cocked his head toward the restaurant, subtly referring to the incident that had just taken place.

"Yes," George agreed, nodding his head. "I think you hurt her feelings. Do you know what I'm talking about?"

Wayne nodded. "I sure do. I've been miserable ever since." He put his hands in his pockets and sighed. "I feel like such a jerk. I know it's wrong and I hate doing that to her."

Wayne looked through stinging eyes at his friend. "Please keep asking the Spirit of God to help me, and feel free to offer your input any time you sense something off in my life."

"Okay. Well, for starters, I think you ought to make things right with Emily." George waited as Wayne unlocked the van door and turned off the lights. "I think sometimes God is more interested in our willingness to be humble than in removing our weaknesses. It's unlikely God will change us unless we're willing to humble ourselves and ask for forgiveness when we've blown it."

"Should I apologize right now with everyone?"

"That's up to you." George initiated the walk back to the restaurant. "But everyone did hear you say it."

Butterflies churned in Wayne's stomach. A thousand sermons seemed easier than saying, "I'm sorry."

"Thanks, George." Wayne squeezed George's shoulder firmly. "Can we talk to Jesus for a minute?"

Wayne nodded. "I'd like that."

"Master Teacher, thank You for what You're doing in our lives. We don't want You to stop leading us. Help us to remain soft." George swallowed hard. "Jesus, we know that part of being soft is learning how to confess our sins and stay open with each other. Wayne needs Your help. Please help him make things right with his wife. Give him humility and courage. Also, Lord, please change his heart so that he will love his wife like You do."

As Wayne and George came through the entrance of Vito's, they could hear Tony's voice from across the room. To Wayne's chagrin, Tony was positioned in front of their booth talking with Emily. Wayne's stomach muscles tightened. *She's laughing now. Maybe this can wait.*

They closed in on the table. Seeing the women lock eyes on the approaching men, Tony turned and moved out of the way.

"But like I said, that's just the way Papa was. He didn't put up with that kinda stuff." Tony jerked his head in two swift motions toward a booth across the room where two young children were shoveling spaghetti into their soda glasses, disregarding their parents' idle threats. "He woulda takin' us out to the car and let us have it. But, I mean, it was for our own good, right?"

George caught Wayne's eye and lifted his eyebrows, noting the irony.

"Right," Ted agreed with a smile, amused by their waiter's transparency.

"So, anyway. You guys ready to orda yet?"

"I think we need a few more minutes, Tony," George answered.

"Okay. I'll be back in a few."

As Tony left, Wayne sat up straight. Appealing to Jesus for help, he spoke slowly. "I need to apologize to everyone here." Ted and Carolyn listened intently, their eyes fixed on Wayne. "I really blew it earlier by being rude to my wife and interrupting her. I want you all to know I was wrong." Wayne looked straight at Emily. "Will you forgive me? I'm sorry, Honey."

"I forgive you." Her eyes sparkled. "We're on the same team, right?" She beamed at Wayne.

"You bet." Wayne felt a ton of bricks lifting. *Why did I even hesitate? Satan, you're such a liar. It feels good to wash it all clean — not bad!*

The moment was packed with implications. Such simple words: "I was wrong. I'm sorry. Will you forgive me?" — but this was the threshold of the Kingdom.

It was a pivotal time for George, as well. It's always easier to let moments slip by, undealt with. It requires courage, wisdom, patience, and a love of righteousness to take responsibility.

"I'M STUFFED!" Ted exhaled as he started the mini–van. "I don't remember the last time I had lasagna that good." He peered at Carolyn. "Except when you make it, Honey."

Carolyn rolled her eyes. "It was good."

Amy leaned forward, resting her chin on the back of Carolyn's seat. "Isn't God awesome?"

"Yes!" the Stones answered in stereo.

"I mean…" Amy scooted between the two bucket seats. "We ask Him to let us meet some people who care…and the next thing you know, Emily calls me up and invites us to dinner!"

"You're right. It's incredible how God worked it out so we could see what kind of people they are — in just one dinner." Carolyn closed her eyes. "God is good."

Ted was quiet. He smiled as he considered the evening.

Carolyn stared out the window, watching the stream of cars pouring by. *Where are they all going, what are they doing with their lives?* "Don't forget to stop by Teresa Parker's house."

"Oh, I almost forgot about Marie." Ted blushed, moving quickly back into the right lane.

Amy shifted back into her seat, hunting for a comfortable position. "I hope we can see those guys again soon."

"Oh, we will," Ted assured her. "I got Wayne's phone number. They're gonna have a hard time getting rid of us now."

49

IT WAS FRIDAY NIGHT, and the Just Puttin' Around miniature golf center was packed as usual. The owners wanted to cultivate a "family atmosphere," with bright lighting, a safari theme for the children and frequent family discount specials.

Wayne swung into the parking lot, heading for the closest parking space he could find.

"I hope my directions were accurate enough," Emily said as she scanned a knot of people for any sign of Ted and Carolyn.

George eyed the two–story replica of a giraffe and an

elephant spewing water from its trunk atop a tiered fountain in the middle of the park. "Don't worry. I don't believe they could miss this place if they came within a mile of it."

"Come on, George! I gotta show you the hippos on the other side of that building!" Wayne's eight–year–old son, Blake, nearly climbed over George in the back seat trying to get to the door. "There's three big ones in a lake!" George made no attempt to hide the warmth of heart that had been growing for Blake. It was dawning on him that since God is building a family, not a compartmentalized organization, someone over fifty is free to build a relationship with someone under ten. Barriers of age, race and financial status need not exist in God's Kingdom. He smiled. *God truly sets the lonely in families.*

As they walked through the front gate, Wayne turned to Emily. "Hey, Em, did Virginia decide to come?"

"She said she would be a little late, but she'll be here."

"Great!"

"I called Eric," George added. "He may come as well."

Wayne and his crew rounded the corner of the clubhouse to find Carolyn and Amy sitting at a cluster of picnic tables. Ted, standing near the ticket window, was sorting through a pile of putters. Carolyn spotted them right away and rose to meet them.

"Hi, Emily, glad to see you."

"Good to see you, too. Have you been waiting long?"

"No. Don't worry, you're right on time. We were a little early."

Wayne and George pulled away from the ladies and slipped up quietly behind Ted.

Wayne whispered to Ted, "Choose your weapon carefully. My friend here is a pro."

Ted wheeled around to face them. "Hey, guys! Take your pick. They all look about the same, though. Besides, the trick is not in the putter but in he who swings it."

"That's what I'm afraid of," said George, "but I guess I can't do too much damage just putting, right?"

"Don't buy it," Wayne cut in. "I've never beaten him yet."

Wayne and Ted bought tickets while George outfitted everyone with clubs and colored balls.

Amy hit first. She gripped the club awkwardly, but managed a good shot. The ball banked off the left wall, just past the swinging monkey's tail, and rested a few inches from the hole. The other ladies nodded with approval as Amy, surprised, headed for the nearest bench to sit down.

"Are you pretty uncomfortable these days?" Emily asked as Amy sighed with relief.

"Not too bad. I just tire out faster than I used to. It feels like I'm carrying a fifty–pound sack of flour around my waist!"

"Be patient," Emily comforted. "It will happen before you know it."

"You're right. I can't believe I'm due in less than a month."

Carolyn and Emily went in turn, and the ladies moved on to the next hole, not bothering to keep score.

"So, Emily, how long were you and Wayne part of Hampton Street?" Carolyn asked as Amy finished up the next hole.

"A little over eight years."

"Were you close to anyone?"

"Oh, I had some friends. But no close ones."

"Why was that?" Carolyn asked as she positioned her ball for hole number three.

"I used to think it was all their fault...but I'm certain now that *how* we build His Church makes a huge difference as to how deep the relationships go." Emily sat down and pulled Ashley into her lap. "I was just telling Wayne last night that I'm starting to see more and more how shallow my own life has been." She stroked Ashley's hair. "And you can't have deep relationships if you're a shallow person."

Carolyn sent her orange ball rolling across the green astro turf. "I know what you mean." She walked toward Emily, forgetting to watch her ball. Five-year–old Amanda Davidson let out a squeal of laughter as she eyed Carolyn's ball returning to it's starting place.

"I guess I'd better hit it harder on the hills." Carolyn laughed with her young friend.

"There's something I've been wanting to mention to you," Emily began again. "I'm sorry for the awkwardness the other night at the restaurant. In reality, your question startled me."

Carolyn sat down on the bench beside Emily.

Emily took a deep breath. "I've spent so much of my life being a passive listener, and as a result, I never had to develop my own convictions. Don't get me wrong. I've been the dutiful 'pastor's wife' — teaching Sunday school classes and active in all the church programs. But spiritual things have never been the passion of my life. I fell into a role and I learned to play it well."

"Well, Emily, just the fact that you are able to see that shows me those things *are* changing." Carolyn's eyes sparkled with hope. "And I'm looking forward to getting to know you."

50

AMY LAY QUIETLY on the hospital bed, hoping to regain some of her strength before the others arrived. She closed her eyes and tried to rest. In the rocking chair next to her, Carolyn gently cuddled the baby girl sleeping in her arms. It was a special time for both women. They had worked hard today, but the joy of the moment overshadowed the pain.

They heard a knock at the door and Emily peeked inside. "Did we come at a bad time?" she asked. "Virginia's with me."

"No, this is perfect." Amy sat up slowly, offering a pain-filled smile. "I'm glad you're here."

Carolyn stood up and brought the baby closer.

"Oh, she's beautiful!" Virginia exclaimed. "So little." She put her finger in the baby's clenched fist. "Hi there, precious. Aren't you special?" Virginia looked over at Amy. "Does she have a name?"

"Did you decide yet?" Carolyn asked.

Amy beamed. "Well, it's taken me quite a while, but I think I've found a name that just seems to fit." She paused, letting anticipation mount. "Her name is Hope."

"Oh, that's a great name," Carolyn applauded. "Very fitting."

Hope was still gripping Virginia's index finger, digging in with her little nails. "You're a strong one, Hope." She gently pried herself free.

"Would you like to hold her?" Carolyn offered.

Virginia took the infant into her arms and sat down to rock.

Emily stood beside the bed. "Another August baby! You know you missed Amanda's birthday by one day?"

"Oh, that's right! August 16th. Is she excited?"

"You know she is." Emily looked at the clock on the wall. "Oh, I promised the guys I'd let them know when they could come in. Would that be okay?"

"Sure...that'd be fine," Amy said shyly as Emily headed for the door.

"Amy," Virginia whispered, rocking back and forth, "where's your mom?"

"She and Dad went down to the cafeteria for dinner." Amy looked over at her baby. "Could you pull that cap a little tighter over her head? I don't want her to get cold."

There was a rap at the door. Wayne, George and Ted came in, making the room seem much smaller. Emily had stayed with the children back in the waiting room. For the next several minutes, each of the men took a turn holding and cuddling Hope. George seemed captivated by the little bundle. He couldn't remember the last time he'd held a baby.

"All right! All right! The party's over. Let's all clear out of here and let this girl get some rest! She's been working hard." The authoritative announcement came from a nurse dressed in a surgical gown.

Her voice reminded Ted of his high school football coach. He snapped to his feet. "Yes, Ma'am!"

The nurse didn't miss a beat. "That's more like it." She walked over to Amy's bed and said over her shoulder, "Hospital policy: only two visitors at a time."

Carolyn smiled and whispered to Ted, "She's really not that bad."

The nurse focused her attention on Amy. "Now, how are you feeling, Dearie?"

Carolyn laid the baby back into the bassinet as they quietly left the room.

"Oh, I almost forgot." Wayne stopped in the hallway. "Carolyn, would you take this in to Amy for me?" He reached into his pocket and pulled out a white envelope. "It's a poem Emily wrote for Amy yesterday."

"Sure." Carolyn took the envelope and headed back into the room.

Amy pulled out the sheet of paper and felt her eyes tear up as she read the title: "A Promise of Hope."

51

The front door creaked open as Wayne dragged his tired body into the living room. With painstaking effort, he managed to remove his tool belt and work boots, leaving them on the mat beside the door. Then, with sincere gratitude, he sank his aching muscles into the inviting La–Z–Boy.

"Is that you, Wayne?" Emily called from the kitchen. "Carolyn and I need your thoughts on something."

"You'll have to come in here," Wayne groaned. "I can't move."

Emily strolled into the living room and kissed Wayne on the forehead. "Aren't you glad you don't do construction for a living anymore?"

"Yes," Wayne chortled. "In fact, I can't believe I let Ted talk me into reroofing that house, especially when it's this cold."

"Now, Honey, that was for George's sake."

"But," Wayne teased, "we should have helped him by paying someone else to do it."

Carolyn arrived from the kitchen, carrying two steaming mugs of coffee. "Can I get you anything, Wayne?"

He grinned. "No, I think I just want to lie here and die peacefully."

Emily knelt beside the recliner. "Wayne, I was wondering if you'd like to go to a concert next week."

Wayne managed a blank stare. "A what?"

"It's a Christian concert. Some guy named David Trueblood," Carolyn chimed in. "My old roommate from college, Teresa Parker, goes to Metro Chapel. She called today and invited us. I've wanted her to meet you guys, so I asked if I could bring some friends along."

"Did you say David Trueblood?" Wayne interrupted.

"Have you heard of him?" Emily perked up.

Wayne sat up straight in his chair. "Well, yeah, if we're talking about the same David Trueblood. He visited the school back when I was in seminary."

"So you've heard him before?" Carolyn was encouraged. "What are his concerts like?"

"You know, I wouldn't exactly call it a concert," Wayne recollected. "It was more like a devotional. It made quite an impression on me at the time."

Emily took a sip of her coffee. "What impressed you?"

"I remember he had a lot of energy, but it wasn't showmanship. It was more like Godly zeal!" Wayne stroked his chin. "And the songs he shared were about real things he was going through. Like, one of them was written just after God had exposed some things in his heart. It was about true repentance and being changed by God."

"Well," Emily prodded, "can we go?"

"Sounds great," Wayne consented, leaning back into his chair. "I'd like to see what he's up to these days."

52

AS THEY WALKED IN, they were struck by the sheer size of Metro Chapel. The concert atmosphere gave the place a stadium aura. It was big.

Ted and Carolyn cut their way through the crowd, leading their friends to the left wing in order to meet Steve and Teresa Parker. The foyer was buzzing with young adults and giddy teenage girls, many with too much makeup and sweet perfume. Wayne began to wonder if this was the same David Trueblood he'd seen when he was in college.

Teresa's exaggerated waves and large smiles guided the Stones and their friends to their destination. They spent the next several minutes in cordial conversation with the Parkers, leaning close in order to compensate for the roar of conversation around them.

"That's the lights," Steve Parker noted to Wayne. "I think it's time to start."

The noise level dropped as everyone scurried toward their seats.

Carolyn whispered to Amy, "I'm really looking forward to this."

The spotlight targeted the center stage. A tall, thin man in a dark sport coat emerged from a breach in the ruby curtain. He introduced himself as the music minister and welcomed everyone.

"We, of course, are very privileged tonight to have as our

special guest, David Trueblood." At this, deafening cheers and teenage screams erupted from various pockets of the auditorium. The music minister smiled broadly, proud to have this musical acquisition to his credit, then continued. "However, before we present to you this first class act, Metro Chapel is proud to present to you our very own budding young Christian artists, 'Altared Ego.'"

The spotlight disappeared and the sound of the stage curtain retracting could be heard as people shifted and folded programs, preparing to be entertained.

Light began flooding the stage, revealing a five–man rock band. A young man with shoulder length hair stepped up to the microphone and greeted the audience. "We just wanted to thank you all and God for giving us an opportunity to play on the same billing as David Trueblood. It's really a privilege."

Wayne surveyed the stage and found his eyes drawn again and again to a young man with a guitar. He had similar attire and a rock star haircut. Wayne could not place the face. As the band began to play, loud power chords and riffs crescendoed from the young guitarist. As he buried himself in his role, a sinister sneer flashed across his upper lip. *Where have I seen him before?* Wayne picked up a concert program and began searching for a familiar name. *"Lead Guitarist: Philip Malone, Jr."* Wayne remembered. *I don't believe it. That's the boy I gave a ride to. His dad must be one of the pastors here.*

WAYNE'S DISCOMFORT INCREASED as the evening unfolded. The shock of the opening act was now superceded by David Trueblood's polished presentation. *What happened to this brother?* Laser lights danced through clouds of manufactured fog, contributing to the carnival atmosphere.

George sat stone–faced, wishing for earplugs — unaccustomed to the decibel level of this cacophony.

Carolyn leaned over and whispered to Amy, "If you didn't speak English, would you know this was a Christian concert?"

Amy shrugged. "No, I don't think so...unfortunately."

During a much quieter song, Wayne was able to gather his thoughts. He tried to determine what was different from the David he'd seen a decade ago. Both appeared to have energy and enthusiasm. But this David seemed driven from without, motivated by the cheering crowd and enamored with his own stage production. Lyrics that had at one time brought tears of conviction to Wayne's eyes were now recited like an incantation used to exact devotion and homage — but not to Jesus. Even certain phrases in the thoughts he offered between songs and in his prayer were verbatim to those that had so touched Wayne's heart at seminary. *How could this be?*

SMOKE EVERYWHERE. Laser lights danced across the ceiling. In a flurry of dramatic chords, David Trueblood introduced his final song of the night.

"Where's George?" Wayne shouted into Ted's ear.

"I think he's in the lobby with Amy and the baby," Ted yelled in reply. "I say we find them and try to get out of here before the traffic jams up like it did on the way in."

The Stones and Davidsons stood up, waved goodbye to the Parkers, and tried in vain to slip past twenty teenagers without making a scene.

After they found Amy in the lobby, the sisters excused themselves to the ladies' room. George was standing next to one of the ministry tables, gazing in disbelief at a life–size cutout of tonight's star.

"There you are!" Wayne called as he approached the table. "Are you about ready to go?"

George fumbled through a stack of flyers depicting David in numerous poses. There was the two–day stubble look. The Hawaiian shirt and sunglasses motif. And a shot of David sitting on the hood of a red Corvette. "Well, I was hoping to talk with David," George said nervously. "Could we wait just a few minutes?"

"What *is* all this stuff?" Wayne picked up a CD and read the title aloud. "Greatest Hits, Volume 2?"

George put down the T–shirt he was inspecting and looked at Wayne. "What do you think it was?" George asked, the pain in his eyes obvious. "Did the money just get to him after awhile?"

"No…I think there's more to it than that. If we conform to the patterns of this world — the stage shows, the roadies, the contracts, the promos, the secular studio musicians — it's bound to have an effect on us. It's inevitable. You can't do business like the world system and not be slowly submerged into it — justified by the lyrics, condemned by the reality."

"Isn't there any way to avoid it?" Ted's question was swallowed by the sound of screaming fans as the doors to the auditorium burst open. The pastor who spoke earlier was back at the microphone.

Wayne cringed as he heard something about autographs. "Surely not," Wayne said with wide eyes. *How could a true man of God allow himself to be exalted in any way? How does singing songs make one follower of Jesus more worthy of signing autographs than any other saint of God?! Who dares to steal God's Glory or exalt himself above other saints?!*

Seconds later, the lobby was brimming with eager shoppers. All along the walls, the once–peaceful tables were transformed into vast centers of economic exchange. Ted tried not to be critical, though he couldn't help but think of the money changers at the temple.

Just then, David Trueblood emerged from a side door and took a chair behind a nearby table. Youthful admirers lined up in front of him, delighted at the prospect of having their purchases signed by the artist. George seized the opportunity to slip into line behind only a half dozen others.

Carolyn, Emily and Amy joined Wayne and Ted by the doors. "Where's George?"

Wayne pointed to the table nearest the auditorium. "I think he's gonna try to talk to David Trueblood. He seems pretty broken up by the whole extravaganza."

Crowds were beginning to retreat through the glass doorway, so the five friends decided to move outside.

It wasn't long before George reached the front of the line.

"Hey! One of my more mature fans." David Trueblood reached instinctively for something to sign. When he realized that George had nothing to give him, David's cheeks reddened. Catching himself, he pretended to straighten a stack of flyers lying on the table in front of George.

"Hi, Mr. Trueblood...my name's George Archer. I was wondering if I might ask you a question."

David glanced around the room, hoping his manager was close by. "Um...sure. Why not?"

George drew a deep breath and leaned over the table in an effort to speak privately. "All these CD's you have here...do you feel like they contain the Word of God?"

"You bet! People are always telling me how the Lord has used these songs to minister to them. Why? Is there something in a song you disagree with?"

George shook his head. "Oh, no. Not at all. I found most of your lyrics to be very encouraging. I just don't understand how selling the Word of God is even possible? I mean, can you imagine Peter selling 'sermon notes' to make a living? I promise you, I'm not trying to give you a hard time. I just want us both to serve God on the highest possible ground."

David Trueblood was becoming uncomfortable.

Meanwhile, the believers in the parking lot decided to make good use of their time. "Please, Lord. Don't let it just be words that George shares. Give him the ability to see the heart. Bring your *living* and *active* word into this situation and lay bare the motives and intents of the heart."

David scanned the room again. *Where is my manager?*

He could hear his manager's squeaky voice nearby: "Now, you know, it's common knowledge in the Christian music industry that if a song lasts more than two minutes and forty–two seconds, the audience tends to lose interest. So, that's why we felt as though..."

David abandoned his search and, forcing a smile, managed a civil reply. "Well, I don't really know exactly what it costs to put together a project, with the studio costs and the manufacturing and all. The label I record for handles all that. I suppose they would have to make some sort of profit in order to pay everybody."

"Maybe you've never thought about it this way, but there's a verse in Second Corinthians I'd like to share with you." George maintained eye contact as he spoke, trying desperately to care for David. "'Unlike so many, we do not peddle the Word of God for profit. On the contrary, in Christ we speak before God with sincerity, like men sent from God.'"

David was no longer able to conceal his irritation. "What *are* you getting at?"

"Well...it looks like this verse is saying that you either sell your gift to make a living or, on the contrary, you offer your gift freely as one sent from God. It's either for money or for God, not both. See what I mean? I'm *really* not trying to pester you. I care about you because of Jesus. Does any of this make sense?"

Hoards of impatient fans were pressing against the table. David snatched a poster from the hands of the girl next to George and signed it.

"I'm afraid not," he answered brusquely. "I've got a lot of people here I need to meet. Nice talking to you."

The conversation was over. George stood motionless for several seconds, pushed slowly away from the table by the surging tide of admirers.

"May I help you?"

Only now did George realize he was standing in front of one of the concert souvenir tables. Borrowing a pen from the friendly clerk, he scribbled a note on the back of a tour schedule.

Dear David,

I imagine no one has ever talked to you about these sorts of things before. The whole idea is probably new to your way of thinking. I believe you began writing and singing Christian music because you had a genuine desire to encourage the Body of Christ and honor Jesus. But I couldn't help noticing that it's your name and your photograph that are literally all over your stuff. I don't see much about Jesus. Yet you make your living selling His Word. Something just doesn't seem right about that. Is that what God wants His children to do with the gifts He's so freely given to them? "Each one of you should sell whatever gift he has received to others, faithfully marketing God's grace in its various forms." Could you really imagine 1 Peter 4:10 saying that? Please take the time to look it up. And would you please talk to Jesus about these things and find out what He thinks? If I can help in any way, please call.

George Archer, 335–4340

On the way to the van, all ears were attuned to George as he carefully related the story of his encounter. He gave his friends some specifics to pray about and learn from while avoiding, as best he could, anything that would grieve the Spirit as he spoke.

Carolyn detected remorse in George's voice. "Are you all right?" she asked, climbing into her seat.

Ted started the engine and turned around to listen.

George shook his head. "I think so. I...just hope he knows I said those things because I care, not because I have some axe to grind...Would it be okay if we prayed for him before we leave?"

Carolyn couldn't help smiling to herself. *This is so different. This is the way You meant it to be, Jesus. Isn't it?*

The Stone the builders rejected

has become the capstone.

Matthew 21:42

The Builder

53

STELLA COULD HEAR the sound of footsteps on the stairs. "Here comes Phil," she mentioned to one of the other secretaries.

"Yep, I'd recognize those steps anywhere."

Phil Malone let the door click shut behind him as he sailed toward her desk. "Stella, Hon, were you able to get that report on local demographics for me?"

"I was about to get on that today, but—"

"I told you I needed that for today's staff meeting."

"I'm sorry, Phil. I was trying to complete that report you asked for on last quarter's attendance stats." She looked fatigued.

He knew her limits. "That's okay," he conceded as he headed into his office. "Any messages?"

A few moments later, Stella came to his door and paused. Phil's dark eyebrows were furrowed. He was staring at a blue computer screen, waiting for the boot–up sequence to finish.

She ventured in. "Here are your phone messages, your mail, and your memos, all laid out in the format you requested. And I can get on that report right away, in time for your meeting if you want me to."

"I did want to give it to Pastor Reynolds at this afternoon's meeting." He looked back at the computer screen. "But if you don't finish it, I'll make it work — somehow."

"Oh, by the way, one of the messages is from Pastor Reynolds." She started toward the door. "He had to cancel tomorrow's lunch."

"Why?" Phil thumbed impatiently through the messages.

"I don't know." Stella kept walking.

Why is he cancelling? Phil sank in his chair. *First the report. Now Reynolds is cancelling lunch. Why did I come in?* He turned the computer off and stared at his wall, disgusted.

The paneled wall boasted of past success. He saw the picture of his college championship hockey team, surrounded by trophies. *Man, were we good.* He felt his chin, searching for the small scar — his trophy for making the winning goal. Below the hockey photo, another frame displayed an article he had written for *Church Builders Magazine*: "Small Group Innovation: The Key to Long–Term Growth." He nodded his approval and continued searching. The adjacent wall displayed his college diplomas: Undergraduate in Bible and Masters of Church Growth...

He shook free from the memories and stood up. *Today, Malone!* Steeling himself, he grabbed his Daytimer and bolted out the door.

A LIGHT SNOW WAS FALLING as Steve Parker drove anxiously to Metro Chapel. It had been another long day at the lab and now he was late for the home group leaders meeting.

Steve felt honored to be a part of all this. He had been converted only three years before, mostly due to the efforts of Teresa, the woman he married shortly after he found new life in Christ.

"Okay, everyone, we're ready to begin," Phil Malone announced as Steve slipped into the room. Phil's khakis were creased and his collar starched. His muscular frame and self–confident stance commanded the attention of the room full of newly appointed home group leaders.

"I'm glad you're all here. I'm not sure you realize just how important each of you is to the success of this new program." Phil spoke with authority, like a general addressing new recruits. "When people come to your homes on Thursday nights, they will feel awkward and out of place at first. Your job will be to make sure everyone feels comfortable and that everything goes smoothly."

Phil walked over toward the large–screened television situated in the corner. "I brought a video I think will help you see how best to deal with some of the practical situations that may come up." He turned it on and dimmed the lights. "This was done by one of the leading experts in home ministries. He has helped start many successful programs like the one we're beginning. Pay careful attention to the things he says."

The whole room was soon glued to the video screen as the speaker offered systematic, logical advice. Many of his points were backed up by short skits demonstrating proven methods.

"Now, let me recap the main points." Phil turned the television off and walked toward the light switch. "If there's ever a disagreement in a home group meeting, what should you do?"

Steve squinted as his eyes grew accustomed to the light. The man next to him spoke up. "You should nip it in the bud."

"Exactly. Defer the discussion until after the meeting is over, then talk with the person privately. While the meeting is in progress, be friendly, be polite, and don't ever let things get negative."

Steve raised his hand with a twinge of nervousness. Phil's tone made him uncertain as to whether or not questions were welcome. Phil nodded toward Steve.

"Couldn't there be other ways to handle a disagreement, Phil? Wouldn't everyone in the room benefit from hearing both sides of the subject and...isn't it possible someone else besides the leader could shed the most light on the subject?"

"What's your name, please?"

"Steve Parker."

"Steve, that sounds like it might work in an idealistic world, but it's too risky. You've got to think about the visitors and the young Christians. In the mind of a visitor, a disagreement is a negative, and they may never come back if they think home groups are negative. And, whatever you do, never disagree with a visitor. It might hurt his self–esteem and that may be the last time you ever see him.

"Now, how about a talkative person?" Phil paused for a second. "Same thing, right? Never let a talkative person dominate the meeting. If someone has been talking too much, you can tell them, 'I really appreciate what you are saying, but we have a lot of ground to cover tonight.' Then just continue where you left off."

Steve ran his hand through his hair, unsettled by what he was hearing. *Phil seems to know what he's talking about. I know we can't get bogged down in these meetings, but is this really how Christians should function together?*

"Now, I want you all to remember three rules for successful home groups." Phil held up three fingers. "Write these down. Rule number one: Keep things interesting and upbeat. I will prepare solid lessons and good discussion aides. It's up to you to lead the discussion in a positive way so that people will want to come back.

"Rule number two: Start on time and quit on time. We live in a TV culture and people are going to get restless after forty–five minutes. Also, if you start on time and quit on time, it will be easier for people to fit it into their schedule." Steve scribbled, reluctantly, on the pad of paper in front of him.

"Rule number three: Stick with the plan. The lessons I give you each week will be your game plan. It is very easy to get off on tangents. Don't let it happen." Phil stopped momentarily to em- phasize his point. "The whole concept falls apart if we're not all doing the same thing. Metro Chapel is a big place and one of the things that will unify us is having everyone in the home groups studying the same lessons on the same nights. Any questions?"

Steve hesitated momentarily, not wanting to be the only per- son asking questions. "Why are there so few home group lead- ers here. For a three thousand member Church, shouldn't there be twice as many of us at this meeting?"

"Well, not all the members will be a part of this program."

"Really? Why not?"

Phil responded matter–of–factly. "Statistically, a church is doing well that can get fifty percent of its members to be a part of home ministry for any extended amount of time. You'll espe- cially notice it this summer when people have so many other things to do. You know, vacationing, little league and things like that. So, we're right in line with the national averages."

"And you don't see a problem with that? Wouldn't every follower of Jesus crave being with God's people?" Steve cocked his head, genuinely baffled.

"Not necessarily. You don't want to demand too much from people. Some people need more time to grow. We don't want to scare anyone off. So we encourage everyone to participate, but we don't want to make anyone feel bad if they don't."

184

Phil noticed the look on Steve's face. "Besides, not everyone wants the closeness of relationships in a home group. For some, the Sunday celebration meets all their needs." He glanced at his watch. "One thing I almost forgot to tell you is you must have refreshments after these sessions. Pretzels, chips, soft drinks, cookies, coffee — that sort of thing. Refreshments are very important to the success of a home ministry."

54

STEVE STOOD AT THE ENTRANCE of their sunken living room. "Looks great, Teresa."

"Thanks. I almost have the refreshments finished. Are you ready?"

He took a deep breath and another glance at his watch. "Yeah, I think so. I've been studying all week, but I'm still a little nervous."

"Oh, relax. I'm sure you'll do great, Honey!" The corners of her mouth arched in a confident smile. "What lesson did Phil select for tonight?"

Steve walked toward the kitchen. "It's called: 'Rejoice in the Lord.' It's pretty good, actually."

She spun around onto her toes and touched his nose. "Well, I'm excited, too!" She then handed him a peanut–butter cookie.

He started to take a bite — but stopped. "Was that a car? I'll get the door."

SEVEN THIRTY–THREE. Looks like everyone's here but Mary Strickler. I know they told us to be punctual, but I'd sure like to wait for Mary. "Does anyone know if Mary Strickler is coming tonight?"

Everyone in the living room shook their head. Just then, the doorbell rang. It was Mary.

"Good to see you, Mary," Steve said warmly.

"Good to see you, too." She seemed tentative as she shook his hand.

Must have a lot on her mind. Maybe tonight's lesson will cheer her up. "Okay, everyone, we're a few minutes late and need to get started." Steve sat down on a white ottoman and opened his notes. Trustingly, he began as suggested: "Tonight's lesson is called 'Rejoice in the Lord.' So, in keeping with that theme, let's spend ten minutes in praise and worship to our King."

As the last song ended, he caught Mary's eye. She seemed worse now than when she came in.

"Please turn to the book of Philippians, chapter three and look at question one in the lesson guide." He waited until the rustling of pages ended. "Ready? Number one: Is it possible to rejoice in the Lord *always*?" He looked up from the lesson book and nodded toward a well–dressed man seated on the couch. "Ken?"

"If the Bible commands it, it must be possible."

"Okay." Steve looked down at his notes again. "Since that's true, then what are some of the reasons we don't?" As the words left his mouth, he caught another glimpse of Mary and felt a knot in his stomach. Her eyes betrayed pain and confusion. Her right hand was clenched, and she held it over her mouth as she stared out the window. *I wonder if we should be talking about this subject?* He remembered Phil's instructions — *stick with the lessons I give you. Okay...maybe something in the lesson will hit on her problem.*

"One of the reasons that we don't rejoice in the Lord the way we should is because we make mountains out of molehills." This came from the man sitting next to Mary. The hand over her mouth started shaking and her eyes welled up with tears.

Now what do I do? Indecision gripped him. The uncomfortable silence caused the knot in his stomach to tighten. *I don't know what to say. I don't know what to do. I'm not sure I'm cut out for this. Lord, please help.* He let out a deep breath. His discomfort intensified as the roomful of eyes stared at him. *Rejoice with those who rejoice. Mourn with those who mourn.* The Scripture interrupted his thoughts. *Maybe we need to drop this lesson and find out what's troubling her.* Mary started to sob. She stood up and walked to the bathroom.

The living room full of people exchanged nervous glances. Teresa got up and followed Mary to the bathroom. The discomfort was like a heavy blanket threatening to smother everyone.

I hope she's all right. Now what do I do? Steve shifted in his seat and looked furtively around the room. *I can't wait 'til tonight is over.* Now the sounds of weeping were heard coming through the bathroom door.

"Maybe we can pray for Mary," one of the women suggested.

"That's a great idea," Steve agreed with relief. Soon the roomful of people was praying, glad to escape the awful silence.

55

THE EVENTS OF THURSDAY NIGHT were still on Steve's mind as he arrived at Metro Chapel. It was Sunday morning, and he'd come forty–five minutes early in order to talk to Phil. He walked through the dark, three–thousand–seat auditorium and upstairs to the office area. Phil's office was dark, though he could hear Pastor Reynolds' voice coming from the open conference room door.

"At the end of my sermon, I'm going to say, "'It's about kindness. It's about love.' There will be seven 'It's abouts.' Count them as I go. That's your cue to play the soft chords on the keyboard. And please watch the volume on that. Last week it was a little too loud and almost ruined the whole effect. Got it? Okay, men, I think we're set. I'm going to review my sermon for the next forty minutes. I'll meet you back here just before we're ready to walk out."

I didn't know they planned the services like that. Steve kept his eyes on the door and sank into one of the couches in the waiting area. As the staff members filed out of the conference room, he caught Phil's eye.

"Morning, Steve." He glanced down at his watch. "You're sure early today."

"Well, I had a dilemma at my home group on Thursday night and I wanted to talk about it."

Phil sat on the arm of the couch. "I don't have much time, but what happened?"

"Well, the evening started off great. Everyone seemed eager, and I was excited about the lesson in the study guide. But after a little while, Mary Strickler started crying. Do you know her?"

"No."

"Well, she's recently divorced, and it turns out that an hour before the meeting she found out her daughter had decided to move in with her boyfriend."

Phil shook his head. "Hmmm. That's too bad."

"She didn't intend to bring it up," Steve continued. "But she looked awful from the moment she walked into the house. I wished that I could have talked with her before the meeting, but she came in after 7:30 and I was trying hard to be punctual like you taught us. So I thought I would just talk with her afterward."

"And did you?"

"Well, no. You see, we started the lesson about rejoicing in the Lord, but every time I looked, I could tell she was hurting inside." Steve winced. "There was so much turmoil inside of me. It seemed that talking about rejoicing was actually making things worse, not better. I even thought about stopping the lesson altogether just to find out what was on her mind."

"Well, you can't do that, Steve..." Phil stopped himself. "Why don't you finish telling me what happened."

"While all of this was happening, a Scripture kept coming to my mind: 'Rejoice with those who rejoice. Mourn with those who mourn.' She looked like she was mourning, and I thought maybe we should be mourning with her." He let out a deep breath. "Pretty soon she started sobbing and excused herself to the restroom. Everyone felt uncomfortable and nobody knew what to do. None of us really knows her very well." Steve looked down at his hands, then into Phil's face. "My wife, Teresa, followed her to the restroom to see if she was okay. She wasn't.

"I think we made things worse by sticking with the lesson. Aren't there times when the lesson should wait? Isn't serving the needs of the individual more important than the schedule?"

"I can sympathize with the position you found yourself in, Steve." Phil cocked his head. "But remember, statistically speaking, you are going to have a certain number of people who are emotional — especially women. It's our job to meet their needs without making everyone else suffer because of it. Remember, the material in the lesson is tied to the sermon topic, so it would be confusing to the sheep to jump around." He scratched his temple. "It's up to the home group leader to take charge and make sure things don't fall apart. If someone looks like they have problems, offer to talk with them after the meeting, but don't let them dominate. Remember? We talked about that at the training sessions."

"But isn't there any kind of flexibility? Isn't it our job to see the direction that God is leading with something and then follow Him?"

"Steve, of course we want to be led by the Spirit. But the Spirit led me to write those lesson plans. I know you care, but I have a degree in church growth and I have studied how home groups function for a long time. Flexibility is one thing, but flying by the seat of your pants — like you're suggesting — only leads to chaos. Believe me." Phil stood up. "If you're doing one thing at your home group and John Doe is doing something different at his home group, we lose our cohesion as a church and it can actually be divisive. Wolves rise up quickly in that kind of environment. So, resist the urge to do what seems right to you and stick with the program." His voice intensified. "Believe me, a lot of work goes in to preparing these lessons, and we'll end up with a lot of problems if the home group leaders think they have better ideas. So, please, stick with the plan I give you, okay? As I said, the Holy Spirit gave me the direction, so it *is* the Holy Spirit leading."

Phil stepped backward. "Look, I've got to run. But thanks for the questions. That's just the kind of input we're looking for."

"YOU SEEM KIND OF DOWN, Honey." Teresa Parker studied her husband's disposition. His eyes were fixed on the rear of the car in front of them as they waited in the long line of cars leaving Metro Chapel's parking lot.

"I'm still thinking about the conversation I had with Phil before the service." He didn't move his eyes. "I was hoping he would clear up some of my questions from Thursday night."

"Well, did he?"

"Not really. He basically said we should stick with the lessons no matter what happens." Steve still stared ahead, though the car wasn't moving at all.

Teresa tugged at his arm. "Even when someone is hurting as much as Mary Strickler?"

"That's what he said, in essence, and he had some convincing reasons." Steve finally turned toward his wife. "I don't know.

I mean, I understand Metro Chapel is really big and everyone can't be doing their own thing, but…" He hesitated. "There's got to be some way to respond to God in the middle of it all, even if it means changing our plans."

Teresa turned sideways in her seat. "It seems to me that after we took one look at Mary's face, we shouldn't have even started that lesson. We should've spent the whole evening trying to help her if we needed to. Or, at least, a couple of women could have gotten with her right away — rather than trying to go on like we did."

The line of cars started to move, and Steve turned back to the task of driving. "I kind of feel that way, too, but…" He winced. "We really do need to listen to Phil. He knows a lot about these things and…maybe he's right."

Suppose one of you wants to build a tower.

Will he not first sit down

and estimate the cost

to see if he has enough money to complete it?

For if he lays the foundation

and is not able to finish it,

everyone who sees it will ridicule him, saying,

"This fellow began to build

and was not able to finish."

Luke 14:28–30

Decisions

56

GEORGE ARCHER'S BLUE LINCOLN glided easily down the thoroughfare as he and Wayne talked, returning from a trip to the local supermarket. Spring weather had finally come and they were looking forward to a cookout at Wayne's home. Their ice–maker was on the blink, plus they couldn't eat barbecue with–out coleslaw — so the two men nobly volunteered to run up to Al's Food Emporium.

As they crested the next hill in their journey homeward, Wayne spotted a car stranded on the side of the road — jacked up, with two flat tires lying on the shoulder next to it. "Looks like Tony's car," Wayne mused.

"Sure does." They drove past slowly, scrutinizing the scene for signs of life. "Do you think we should go back and check it out?"

"No, look up there."

About 200 yards ahead, they recognized the familiar profile of Tony Veneziano, thumb out, walking backward. George pulled the car to the shoulder. As the car approached, Tony eyed it cau–tiously, hoping the occupants had good intentions. When the car stopped, Tony recognized them and ran to the passenger side with a broad grin.

Wayne rolled the window down and teased, "Now, is that the same Impala you've been trying to sell me?"

Tony released a stammered chuckle. "Really, there's nothin' wrong with it. It's just that my spare musta' lost its seal and wasn't no good, see."

"Sure, I understand," Wayne laughed. "Climb in."

Tony didn't hesitate. He opened the rear door and jumped in. George pulled back onto the highway and spoke first. "You have any plans tonight, Tony?"

"Well, I was gonna do some laundry 'til this happened. See, it's my night off and I got kind of a routine, ya know. Now, I'm not sure what I'm gonna do."

"Where do you live?" George asked.

"I live over behind the McDonald's on 18th and Spencer. My washa' is broke, so I've been takin' my stuff up to the Quick–Mat."

"You don't live too far from me," Wayne chimed in. "Hey, I've got an idea. We're on our way back to my house for a cookout with some friends. What if we swing by your place, pick up your laundry and bring it to my house? Then you can get your laundry done and we'll treat *you* to some great food and company."

Tony's expressive face curdled in concern. "Hey, listen, you don't hafta do all that. I can just—"

"Really, it's no trouble at all." Wayne turned to face him. "We'd like you to come."

"You sure?"

"Positive."

THE SWEET, PUNGENT SMELL of barbecue sauce filled the dining room as Emily placed a large pot of corn on the cob on the table to complete the buffet. Wayne gathered the children as everyone assembled around the table. Tony seemed to be enjoying himself and beamed as if he hadn't been with a family in a long time. His face displayed surprise as Ted began a song of thanksgiving to God.

"Give thanks with a grateful heart, give thanks to the Holy One..."

Tony looked around, smiling broadly as he noticed even the children joining this simple song of devotion. They repeated the chorus, and Emily's eyes lit up as she heard Tony's deep voice making an effort to join them.

When the song ended, there was a brief silence. Then Wayne spoke for the household of believers. "Jesus, we're very thankful for the way You treat us. You're really good to us, in spite of the fact that we frequently fall short of Your Glory. If You hadn't made provision for us, who knows where we'd be now. But You feed us. You clothe us. You shelter us. We live like kings, better than Solomon ever did. You're our God. We're Your children and Your servants. We want to bring You joy, Lord. We want to make You smile, to fill Your heart with joy the way You've filled ours. We love You, Jesus. We appreciate the feast You've laid before us and acknowledge that You are the Giver of all good things. Please join us as we share this meal together. Amen."

While those around him echoed Wayne's "amen," Tony reflexively reached for his left, then right shoulder with his hand. He stopped himself when he noticed no one else did...*These guys ain't Catholic.* He dropped his eyebrows. *I never heard anyone talk like that to God before. So real...and honest. Wayne talks like he knows Him.* He sensed a freshness he'd never associated with God and he kind of liked it.

"HEY, IT'S GETTIN' LATE. I'd betta' run."

"No problem, I'll give you a ride," George volunteered.

"Hey, Tony, before you go...should I pick you up at nine in the morning?" Wayne noted the puzzled expression on Tony's face and explained, "So we can get that tire fixed?"

"Oh...yeah. That'd be great. Thanks a lot!"

"No problem...Oh, don't forget your laundry."

"Wow, I can't believe I almost left that." Tony found his way to the kitchen where Eric was folding Tony's sheets and neatly placing them in his plastic laundry basket.

"Thanks. You didn't hafta do all that." Tony muscled the heavy, flimsy basket up onto his knee, then squeezed it against his chest.

"You're welcome, Tony." Eric waved as Tony and George made their way out the front door.

During the short trip to his house, Tony expressed curiosity in his usual frank manner, "So, what religion are you guys anyway?"

When George didn't answer right away, Tony spoke up again. "I hope that's okay to ask, I dunno."

"No, that's fine. We really aren't a part of any 'religion' in the sense of a denomination. We're just Christians." George parked the car in Tony's driveway, cut off the ignition, and turned toward him.

"Just Christians? Wha'd'ya mean?"

"We've come from different backgrounds and different

denominations. But we're trying to see past some of the man–made religious stuff we've taken for granted and just love God and each other."

"Sounds kinda simple. I mean, in a good way."

"It's what Jesus intended, though it got Him in a lot of trouble in His day. Things have really drifted a long way from simply loving God and caring about one another — to the mostly cash–register, plug–and–play religion we see around us today. We've really made a mess of things. As most people in the world are quick to point out — accurately, I'm afraid — there *is* way too much hypocrisy in religion today."

"Yeah, that stuff drives me nuts. It ain't right."

"You're right, it's not. And it was never meant to be that way." They sat for a minute in the dark. "Tony, can I ask you something?" Tony consented with a nod. "It's really easy for us to talk about the rest of the world, but how about you? Do you have a real relationship with Jesus?"

Tony thought for a long time, contrasting what he saw tonight and the void that existed inside. He was long in answering. Honesty was painful. "I'm not even sure I know what that means."

57

WAYNE PACED ACROSS his bedroom. *I don't want to speak at a meeting.* He shook his head. *But I don't want to pass up an opportunity you're giving me…What should I do, Lord?*

Wayne sat down on the bed as Emily walked in. "Are you still trying to decide what to do?"

"Yes. Any suggestions?"

"Why don't you call one of your friends in Miami?"

"Now, there's an idea." Wayne scooted to the edge of the bed and grabbed the phone on the night stand. He pulled Mark Wallace's card out of the top drawer and dialed the number.

"Hello."

"Hey, Mark, how's it going?"

"Wayne! It's good to hear from you again. I just got back from the marina, and Carlita's finishing up dinner. She's making some of her famous tortillas."

"Sound's great. Wish I could join you. I bet it's nice and warm there in Miami."

"Ah, you wouldn't like it. It's been eighty–five and sunny. I've had to drive around with the windows open. But I'll tell you what, we'll share it with you. Just take the next plane out. We'll hold dinner." They both laughed. "But bring your wife and some others this time."

"Sounds tempting."

"How's the job hunt going?"

"Oh, okay. Still working temp."

"George? The Stones?"

"They're all doing great. It's been a blast learning to walk together."

"Hey, did you guys ever hear back from David Trueblood?"

"No, but we didn't leave an address on the note, and he may not feel comfortable enough to call. We're just hoping he read it and took it to heart." Wayne hesitated. "Mark, let me get to the real reason I called. I've been asked to speak at a home group meeting. I haven't 'spoken' in a long time. And I kind of hate going back into that role, but we've been getting to know the leader of this home group, and he seems hungry and soft. So, I was hoping for some wisdom on how to view it."

"Well, something we've found helpful is bringing other trusted brothers along. So, maybe George and the Stones could go with you. And as brothers, not 'teachers,' you could share some of what God has been teaching you together. Then God could use each of you in the measure and way *He* wants."

"That's a great idea. I bet Steve would go for that."

"Let me know how it goes."

"You bet. Well, I won't keep you from your dinner. Talk to you soon, bro. Good night."

58

STEVE PARKER SWEPT the last of the cut grass off of the side-walk just as the long blue sedan parked against the curb. It was the first time he had cut the grass since before winter. He was glad to do it, but hated to ruin his reputation as the best dandelion

197

farmer in the neighborhood. He chuckled to himself, put the broom away, and walked toward his arriving guest. The tall, dark–suited Phil Malone walked briskly across the freshly–cut lawn, heading straight for Steve.

"Phil, you got my message. I'm glad you came."

"Parker, are you crazy?" Phil stopped right in front of Steve's face. "I've been trying to get in touch with you for the last hour to find out what in the world you think you're doing!"

"What do you mean, Phil?" Steve was puzzled at Phil's tone.

"You've invited someone from outside of Metro to speak to your home group."

"Well, that's why I chose Tuesday night." Steve was relieved as he thought he found the source of Phil's dismay. "This way, it won't disrupt the schedule."

"But Steve—" Phil's shoulders dropped as he explained, "it's not the schedule. It's bringing this guy in here at all. There are proper channels for doing this sort of thing. You've got to *think*! You've got to let those in positions of responsibility decide who should and should not be teaching the members. We need to stick to the curriculum we've laid out, so it will coincide with the Sunday celebration." His words were calmer than his thoughts as he acquiesced to Steve's naïveté. "Do you understand?"

Steve swallowed hard. "I think so. But I didn't think it through at the time. It just seemed like a good idea. Like I said on your voice mail, I met these guys a few weeks back and we've had some good time together." He gained some confidence. "Last week we were together over dinner for several hours and the time was excellent! I just wanted to share the good news with all the members of my home group and with you." Steve was beaming. "Maybe I acted impulsively, but I was excited."

"Good news? What are you talking about?"

Steve looked up across the lawn and saw a mini–van parking behind Phil's car. "Looks like they're here now. I'll let them explain it." Steve walked toward the mini–van as Ted, Carolyn, Wayne, Emily and George piled out.

Phil, still frustrated with the predicament, glanced at his watch. *Betsy's expecting me in thirty minutes.* He let out an exasperated breath. *I can't leave now.* He rolled his eyes. *Parker!*

He shook his head and followed Steve toward the small group now on the sidewalk.

Phil politely shook each hand as Steve generously introduced him. The sandy–haired Wayne Davidson looked Phil in the eye and set him oddly at ease. *Who is this guy?* Phil wondered. For a moment, he was taken off guard by the warmth of the new arrivals. He checked his emotions and squinted. *Be careful, Malone.*

Dusk was setting in and Steve led the way toward the house just as headlights announced the next arrivals.

The house smelled wonderful. The air was filled with the sweet aroma of fresh–baked cookies. "Smells great!" Steve kissed Teresa on the cheek and snagged a cookie from the pan while it was still soft and hot enough to sting. "Mmmm."

"I hope there's enough of those for everyone," Ted chuckled, accepting the cookie Teresa handed him. "Thanks."

Phil talked with Wayne, inclined to like his open manner and direct speech, but instinctively wary of the potential threat. *I still don't like this.* They found their way with the others into the living room and took seats on a long floral couch.

"So, you work for a book publisher?" Phil offered polite interest.

"It's a temporary job. I'm not sure what God has in store for me beyond that." Wayne felt at ease. "So, how about you? Do you find a minister's life fulfilling?"

"Yeah. I do." Phil nodded his head as he eyed the entrance, making careful note of each person who arrived. "It's just what I'm cut out for."

It was now 7:40 and, to Phil's disappointment, the living room was full. Steve, who was sitting across the room from Phil, announced a song he wanted to sing and the room swelled with thanksgiving and worship.

Finally, Steve looked toward Wayne and Ted. "Well, guys, I guess it's all yours."

The three men exchanged glances, then Ted spoke up. "Hey Wayne, why don't you mention the things we were talking about in the van?"

"Good idea," Wayne replied. "On the way over here we were talking about how essential it is that everyone, from the least to the greatest, have a living, vibrant relationship with Jesus. There is no substitute for that."

This is Steve's revelation!? Phil snorted to himself. *There's nothing special about that. It's elementary.*

"I know this sounds elementary," Wayne continued, grabbing Phil's attention. "But, you'd be surprised how many people agree with that and understand it — yet still spend none of their lives cultivating an honest, open, real relationship with God."

Phil felt a twinge, a spark — something inside of him he hadn't felt for a long time. He temporarily surrendered to an urge to look inward. *When was the last time I really did that?* He remembered being nineteen, a freshman at Bible college. There was something fresh and alive about that time. It was a time when he had talked to God...*Talked to God?* Phil closed his eyes. *This is strange. I haven't thought about that for a long time.*

His eyes shot open as he heard a deep voice nearby. He turned his face toward George, though his eyes darted around the room, making certain no one had thought him asleep.

"Something we've been learning," George was saying, "is that Christianity is two–fold. First, it means Jesus has made a way for us to have a real relationship with God, as Wayne was saying. But it also means that Jesus has provided the context for us to have real relationships with each other. And, that's the Church.

"In Acts 28:23, Paul made a clear distinction between the good news of the *King* and the good news of the *Kingdom*. Philip made that same distinction in Acts chapter eight." George cleared his throat. "Most people have very little understanding of what the Gospel of the Kingdom *is*. Or, perhaps, they've just assumed it has to do with something off in the future, rather than something 'now,' as Paul said in Ephesians 3:10 or 'at hand,' as Jesus said. To most of us, 'church' has always been a thing we do, not a family we are a part of. It's a meeting to 'attend,' not a *Holy Civilization* of people whose lives are intertwined with each other on a grass–roots level seven days a week."

Seven days a week? Come on! That's just in Acts two, and that was a temporary situation. Phil folded his arms and looked toward Steve.

"Listen to some of the descriptive phrases from the Scriptures," Ted interjected, opening a small New Testament. "It's all through the New Testament, not just in Acts two. Twenty years after Pentecost, the Church is described as:

'Publicly and from house to house...'

'Members of one another...'

'The hand cannot say to the eye I have no need of you...'

'Joined together by every supporting ligament...'

'When one part suffers, they all suffer; when one part rejoices, the whole body rejoices.'"

Ted closed the Bible and leaned forward. "That's not poetry. That's real connectedness!! As Jesus promised, if we'll lose our lives, we'll have a 'hundred mothers, brothers and sisters.'"

Bizarre! Phil relaxed his arms and stared intently at Ted. *Are they reading my mind?*

"How does the Hebrews writer instruct second–generation Christians to live?" Wayne asked. "Long after Pentecost, the writer commands believers to 'encourage one another every day' — which means that *every* single person should be engaged in heart level, side–by–side interaction *every* day! And the writer repeats himself to make sure we don't skip over it. He said that if we wouldn't live that way then we would be hardened and slowly tricked by sin.

"Try to catch the flavor of what I'm saying. It's who we are. It's not something we attend. The Redeemed are the Church. Fish live in schools, geese live in flocks, humans live in cities...and Christians — those who have truly been born from above — are meant to LIVE in real CHURCHES!! While 'attending Church' is common today, it is certainly not Biblical! How does one 'attend' family? How does one 'attend' life?

"Paul says that our lives are being built *together* to become a place where God comes to live. We are God's *House*. The place where he lives. *If* our lives are being joined together.

"You see, it's not about adding 'home groups' onto an existing structure of impersonal meetings, while our lives remain disconnected from one another. It's about setting aside our worldly, self–centered priorities and giving our lives to each other instead of to our jobs, clubs, little leagues..."

Phil churned on the couch in an internal stalemate. His heart was drawn by the message of a vibrant, committed Church. But his mind fought back, challenging the practicalities.

Wayne caught a glimpse of Phil's struggle as he scanned the room. "Oh, it's so much easier to just add an informal home group so we can all feel good because some optional percentage of the membership talk to each other a little more than we used to." He shook his head. "But please hear me. It falls so short of our God–given destiny." He pleaded with his hands. "Don't trade your birthright for a bowl of stew like Esau! Oh, what we could *share* together if we'd humble and empty ourselves!

"Picture in your minds what things *could* look like if we would only give our lives away. It's so much bigger than we have ever imagined!! Most of us have not seen the reality of a whole Church functioning in, and defined only by, relationship with God and each other. But it *is* God's Heart! We must not settle for less! God won't! The Church is the very reason the planet was built — so that God could demonstrate to Heaven, hell, and Earth His incredible wisdom. That's what Ephesians 3:10 says. Think about that for a minute. Think back on your Church experience of sitting in pews and listening to speeches. Could that really be all there is? Could *that*, really, be why the planet was made?! Certainly not. The Father wants to prepare a Bride for His Son!"

THE NEXT DAY, a maroon Toyota Celica cut a soggy trail down Grand Boulevard as Amy pulled a pink envelope from her coat pocket. Hope had already fallen asleep in the car seat next to her, thanks to the intermittent rhythm of the wipers and the constant *whooshhhhh* of the tires.

"Don't you worry now, Hope," she reassured the sleeping child. "God's gonna take care of us — just the way He always has."

Amy switched on the turn signal as she approached the subdivision. She looked down at the envelope again. *With love, Mom and Dad*. It was on time, as always. She couldn't help smiling as she imagined her mother stuffing twelve envelopes with twelve different cards, enough for the whole year, in advance.

Amy was relieved to find her fears of being observed unfounded. The streets were perfectly empty. Pulling up to the curb, she set the parking brake and took a deep breath. "For You, Jesus."

She reached into the card on her lap and drew out a $100 bill. Taking a plain white envelope from her purse, she quickly stuffed the money inside and sealed it. She swung open the car door, then turned back toward Hope.

"Stay there. Mommy will be right back." Amy kissed her daughter on the cheek and jumped out of the car. Her boots, squishing in the evening drizzle, seemed unforgivably loud as she climbed the steps to the kitchen door. The envelope slid effortlessly under the door, and in an instant she was back with Hope.

59

GEORGE AND WAYNE sat quietly at George's dining room table, waiting for Phil Malone's arrival.

"Lord," George said as he closed his eyes, "we don't know why Phil wants to talk with us. We're hoping some of the things shared last night have stirred his heart. Or perhaps...this will be an evening of heartache. Would You let that cup pass, Abba? Please give us Your wisdom and grace from heaven."

The dull thud of a car door lifted his bowed head. "I guess he's here."

George turned on the entry light and opened the door. "Come in. Come in." George shook Phil's hand firmly as he stepped inside. "Good to see you again."

"Thanks for agreeing to meet me on such short notice."

"No problem at all," Wayne said as the three converged in the brown–tiled entryway. He noted Phil's patterned country club shirt and "Ping" cap. "Did you watch Norman's win on Sunday?"

"At the Masters?" Phil answered as they walked toward the living room. "Yeah."

"I watched the last of it with Ted. He finally won the major he wanted most."

Phil gave a slight smile and shrugged. "He's top caliber. It had to happen sooner or later."

Seeing Phil's solemnity, Wayne asked, "So...what's on your mind?"

Phil took a seat on the fireplace hearth and wrestled inside, unaccustomed to vulnerability. "I guess...the reason I'm here is because of last night." Phil rubbed his neck. "I felt challenged in a way I haven't been for years. The things you said at Steve's house had a ring of truth." He wrinkled his forehead. "But I'm having trouble seeing how that approach could work at Metro. Maybe for you. Maybe for a living–room size group, but we have a few thousand members. How could we shut down the structure and just be a family? It doesn't seem realistic."

George and Wayne carefully considered their next words. The stakes were high. Metro was a large place, and they knew a lot of lives were on the line. Wayne began, "Phil, let me say how much I appreciate your heart in coming here. I know it was difficult.

"First of all, we weren't speaking of an optional way to 'have church' or an alternative system. Secondly, as far as 'shutting down the structure,' I don't think that's the next step. If a person hasn't walked in decades, you wouldn't just take his wheelchair and crutches away — at least not all at once." Wayne leaned forward and motioned with his hands. "If a man has become dependent on crutches, then he will need a time of 'physical therapy.' It's not healthy to rip the wheelchair out from underneath him, but it's even more unhealthy to just accept his wheelchair as part of life and do nothing about it. The goal is to make the man whole and not allow him to depend indefinitely on the crutches. There are some steps you can take right away that would please God and be a move in the right direction, but even the first steps of physical therapy can be painful."

Phil nodded as Wayne carefully studied his eyes for clues. "It was never God's intention that we, as His Body, become atrophied, dependent, and immobilized by the crutches we've invented. In most places, if you remove the structure, the congregation would disappear — because, in reality, it's just a loose connection of people held together by a scaffolding of programs and personalities. Or, perhaps, it's held together by convenience, comfort or habit. And sometimes, people are only there because of family ties and traditions."

George sat up to interject. "Phil, what would happen if you announced this Sunday that you had sold the building, eliminated the programs, the Sunday school, the scheduled meetings, home groups, etc. — all of the trappings, none of which are even mentioned in the New Testament? They're as unbiblical as rosary beads and purgatory." George spoke slowly. "If you removed all of it, whatever you would have left is *really* all you have *now*."

"I doubt there would be anything left if we did that at Metro," Phil conceded slowly, with agony and reluctance. He genuinely felt as if he'd done a pretty fair job and was as sincere and God-fearing as any minister in town. He leaned his head against the fireplace stones and considered the implications.

The gravity was evident in Phil's eyes. Wayne and George remembered that battle.

"We're not trying to be harsh at all," Wayne tempered. "We realize there are a lot of innocent lambs who are just caught in the machinery we inherited from our forefathers. But if we're going to move forward, toward God's true desire," Wayne's eyes pleaded, "then we must be firm in our convictions. If we view Sunday morning Christianity as an acceptable alternative — while we hope against hope that at least people are hearing the Word — we'll end up dragging our feet forever under the guise of 'being patient.'"

"Unfortunate but true," George admitted. "It's one thing to agree with a vision, but not know how to get there. It's quite another thing to justify using the man-made props, considering ourselves exempt from God's true plan and clear commandments. After 'beginning in the Spirit' in the church world, we have tried again and again to birth Isaac out of the womb of Hagar. All we'll ever get out of our slick oratory, flashy presentations, gimmicky small group and worship techniques...is *Ishmael* — 'the child born in the ordinary way' — just like IBM or Amway would bear a 'child.'" The look on Phil's face caused George to pause. He guessed he'd struck a nerve. "If our convictions are firm," he started again, "and based on the Word of God, then we might be able to temporarily *use* the present Sunday/Wednesday format as a means to reach people — without *accepting* it. But we'll have to fight to keep a clear understanding that it's not God's heart and mind at all, and in fact creates obstacles to God's Work. The same is true of male-bonding organizations, evangelistic organizations, music ministries, and other man-made institutions and professions. Good people, but the house is not the one God wants to build."

This was almost too much. Phil wrestled inside, half wanting to blow this discussion off as heretical and get back to his life. His years of 'ministry' success and position had given him a lot of momentum in the wrong direction. But something stronger urged him to listen, to consider. Something rang of truth. "Is it really as cut–and–dry as all that? I mean, it's a pretty heavy accusation to suggest that how all of the world practices Christianity is essentially wrong. How can you take such a clear–cut stand without coming across as arrogant and exclusive? Doesn't it seem 'holier–than–thou' to act like you have the corner on the market of truth?"

"To be honest," Wayne replied, "I don't have it all sorted out." He shook his head, half smiling. "I wake up some mornings and wonder if I'm crazy."

"So, how *do* you resolve it?" Phil's interest was piqued by Wayne's transparency.

"Well, again, I don't have *all* of it resolved, but I do have some touchstones I use for a sanity check. First, I go back to the inspired record of the first century Church and I ask myself: 'Is the kind of Christianity recorded in the Scriptures — under the leadership of Jesus Himself and those He trained in person — an accurate picture of what I see around me?' I don't mean wearing togas and the cultural food and dress. I mean what was their *priority* system? What was *life* to them? What were the components of their days, according to the Scriptures? That simple test clears up a lot for me." He looked to George, then back at Phil.

"Another test I use is one Jesus suggested when He said, 'A tree is known by it's fruit.' When I see the 'fruit' of rebellious teenagers in droves, worldly men and women, little real spiritual relationship, and leaven throughout the batch — which is forbidden by God in any Church He would claim — again, I'm forced to draw the same conclusion.

"And, lastly, I've seen it for myself. I've visited Churches that function as a family — some of them quite large. But still they have no hierarchy, programs, gimmicks, devices, or cracks that people just fall through. And once you've seen it, you no longer feel the need to justify the impossibilities."

Phil blew out a long breath. "What you're saying...makes sense." He sat up. "But how on earth can we turn the tide of all the centuries of...distortion?"

"Just like Luther did in his day," George replied. "One day at a time and one life at a time — but the standard must never be lowered. Never! For Jesus, and for the lambs, we've got to risk everything!"

PHIL MALONE SIPPED his first cup of coffee the next morning, anticipating it's needed help in beginning the day. Sleep had been hard to secure the night before. His thoughts had returned again and again to his conversation with Wayne and George. As was his morning routine, Phil isolated the sports section from the rest of the paper and began sifting through highlights and box scores.

He read the same opening sentence a third time: "NBA Western Division playoffs heat up as..." Finally he realized something was different this morning. The words he read seemed empty and hollow.

Has something changed? He felt a charge of excitement. *Maybe I'm being silly.* As he thought that, he eyed the bookshelf in the living room. He walked across the room, pulled his Bible from the shelf and returned to the breakfast nook. Setting the newspaper aside, he placed the Bible in front of him and opened it. It felt nostalgic, like driving through an old neighborhood he hadn't been in for years. Everything still where it always had been, aged, yet familiar.

"The steadfast love of the Lord never ceases. His mercies never come to an end. They are new every morning. Great is thy faithfulness, O Lord."

Is this a second chance? He stared through the window, taking mental inventory of his life. He now knew there had to be more than he was experiencing, though until two nights ago he had lost any sense that there was even something missing. Things had seemed pretty comfortable. He had a family, a good job, a big house with comfortable amenities. But now he'd been reawakened to that void.

Thundering footsteps descended the stairs, ending with a loud thud at the landing. Within seconds, Phil saw his oldest son foraging through the refrigerator in search of breakfast. Phil checked his watch, then addressed his son. "What time do you catch the bus?"

Startled, his son looked up, surprised to see his father home this late in the morning. "I don't," he responded with a hint of disrespect, then returned to his search.

"What do you mean you don't? How do you get to school?"

His son hastily threw what he'd gathered into a plastic grocery bag and moved toward the front door. Two short blasts from an irritating car horn beckoned from outside.

"I ride to school with Kenny, Ricky and Toast." He put his jacket on while holding his notebook between his knees and the plastic bag in his mouth.

"Toast? Who's Toast?"

His son smiled mischievously as he opened the door and looked at his father's concerned expression. "Eddie Sanchez. That's what we call Eddie Sanchez."

"Why?"

Two more horn blasts penetrated the house and sounded even more obnoxious through the open door. "Hurry up, Loner!"

Philip looked out the door and back to his father with a smile. "You don't want to know, Dad. I gotta go."

"No. Wait!" Phil stood up and reached out his arm. "Why do they…"

SLAM! The door closed with finality. As the tires gave a short screech, Phil walked over to the window. Blue–gray exhaust hovering in the air and two black tire marks on the white concrete driveway were the only evidence they had been there.

Phil tasted the other side of the bittersweet reality that had found him this morning. The investment he always intended to make in his son "someday" had been postponed for too many tomorrows. *Is it too late, God? No, this is the chance You're giving me to turn it around.* Hope flickered in his heart.

60

IT WAS SATURDAY AFTERNOON and the Stones' mini–van rounded the corner of the lot and pulled to a stop in one of the parking spots nearest the brightly lit sign: *Mid–City Fun Bowl.*

Ted cut the engine and looked over at Carolyn. "It looks like Steve and Teresa decided to come."

Carolyn nodded. "Yep, that's their car all right. I think that's the same one she drove when we were in college." She helped

Marie out of the car seat while Ted gathered the wooden puzzle pieces Marie had dropped during the drive.

"Bye–bye," Marie waved back into the open van as Carolyn set her down.

"No, Honey. Daddy's coming with us. He's getting your toys." Carolyn took her daughter's hand. Her little two–year–old was certainly growing up.

"Daddy go bye–bye." This time Marie giggled, hugging her daddy's leg as they made their way into the bowling alley.

Wayne saw them walk in and hurried over to the front door. "There you are. We just reserved three lanes side by side and it looks like they're ready."

The Stones rented their shoes and set out with the others for the lanes at the far end of the building. Carolyn had just sat down to change her shoes when Amy sat down beside her and pulled Marie into her lap. "Hi, Pebbles."

Marie laughed and pulled at Amy's cheek. "Hi, Maimee."

"Pebbles? Where did that come from?" Carolyn quizzed as she tied her shoe. Amy shrugged. "She's a little 'Stone,' right?"

Carolyn rolled her eyes and laughed. "Cute." She slid her tennis shoes under her seat. "How was your time with Emily?"

"Good." Amy tickled Marie under the arm. "I like talking with her."

"I'm glad you offered to help out. How did Hope do?"

"Oh, she was a little fussy in the grocery store. But we managed. Amanda was quite the little helper." She pointed to lane six where Amanda cuddled the squirmy Hope.

At lane seven, Wayne and his son, Blake, emerged from their ball hunt. As Blake deposited his spoil, Wayne walked up to his wife, who seemed entranced by the other bowlers.

"Hey, Em." He sat down beside her. "Virginia has her children with her today, so I'd like Blake to bowl with you. He still idolizes her Tim a bit much and I don't think he's a good role model...at least not yet. I know it's a little thing, but God's House is built with wisdom. So I think it's important we put some thought and prayer even into small things like that."

"Sounds great. Believe it or not, I was considering that on the way over." She paused. "I remember Carolyn showing me in the Scriptures that discernment is our inheritance."

Wayne looked in his wife's eyes. "Absolutely." He smiled. "So, how about you bowling with Virginia and her daughter this time around? Will that work for you?"

Emily returned his smile. "Sounds fun."

George was first in line on lane seven. He got up, hesitated to remember which foot to start with, then took three steps, sending the black and white ball down the center of the lane.

"Strike! Way to go, George!" Ted cheered from his post at the scoring table.

"That may be the only one," George said as he took a seat next to Eric.

Tim Ramsey was next. He positioned his lanky, fifteen–year–old frame behind the far line. Then, awkwardly, he sent the ball sailing into the gutter. He turned back, embarrassed, as Ted got up to give him pointers while the ball cycled back.

Wayne smiled as he watched Tim and Ted from his seat. Things were definitely changing. Two years before, Tim had grown tired of his role as an "elder's kid" and started looking elsewhere for his identity. Everything about him — his clothes, his language, his attitudes — betrayed a secret lifestyle away from home. It was something his parents, out of insecurity or perhaps pride, had chosen to ignore.

But things were different now. Tim was badly shaken when his dad was forced to resign and rumors began to circulate about the reasons. A new softness toward his mom spurred Virginia to seek help from Wayne and Emily. After many heart–to–heart conversations, as well as a few difficult situations, some good fruit was becoming evident. There were still reasons for being cautious, of course, but Wayne was glad for opportunities like today.

"You can be praying for him," Wayne leaned over and whispered to Steve Parker. "We're working hard to salvage his future."

Steve nodded thoughtfully and watched as Tim prepared to throw his second ball.

Tim measured his steps and mechanically swung his arm as he tried to follow Ted's advice. He unconsciously jumped as seven pins fell.

"Way to go, Tim," Wayne rewarded from his seat. Steve applauded while Ted gave Tim a high–five. Tim couldn't hold back his smile as he walked back to his seat.

"What do you say we young guys challenge these old fellows to some competition?" Eric slapped Tim on the back as he got up to take his own turn.

"Think you're up to it?" George raised his eyebrows, pretending to take the challenge seriously.

Eric's first ball sailed straight for the head–pin, but fell one pin short of a strike.

"They always glue that one down when I bowl," Eric complained. "But you watch. I'll get it. I've got a secret weapon." He winked at Tim and shot George a playful grimace.

He lined up carefully, holding the ball up to his eye. He then sent the ball sailing straight at the lone pin to clinch the spare. Tim jumped out of his seat and offered Eric a hand in the air.

"All right," George resigned. "Show them how it's done, Ted."

As the men battled it out, Teresa sat down in the seat that was back–to–back with Emily's. "How's Wayne's job search going?" she asked, sitting sideways to be able to see her.

Emily laughed. "After a year, it's kind of funny to still call it a job search." She turned to face Teresa. "He's still working temp jobs."

"Are you able to manage all right without a steady income?"

Emily spoke softly. "It's been hard at times. But God has been faithful to care for our needs. I've lost count of how many times we've been up against the wall, and then at the last minute a refund check would arrive in the mail or the temporary service would call with a job offer. Recently, we were past due on the car insurance. Wayne had forgotten about it until late that evening, and we were exactly $100 short. We decided we would have to call George or Ted the next day and see if they could help us out."

"What happened?"

"The next morning, without having said a word to anyone, we found an envelope that had been shoved under the kitchen door. Inside was a $100 bill."

Teresa gasped. "Where did it come from?"

"I'm sure it was one of these guys," Emily said, waving her arm toward the other two lanes.

Behind lane six, Amy was huddled on the floor with Amanda, Ashley and Marie, while Hope shared her smiles and babbles with the ladies waiting to bowl. The three girls giggled with delight as they pressed around Amy, each straining to see the brightly colored illustrations. This was one of Amy's favorite books, a collection of short stories given to her by Carolyn on her birthday. It had been written primarily for children, but the lessons behind the stories were good for adults as well.

The reading was interrupted by loud screams and ecstatic cheering. Amy looked up to see everyone crowd into lane seven, congratulating Emily. A glance at the scoring monitor revealed she had just scored a spare and a strike in the last frame.

As Amy looked into each of the faces, a very special thought occurred to her. *This is my family! It may not be "a hundred mothers, brothers, sisters" just yet, but Jesus' promise is definitely true!*

61

NO ONE ELSE is here yet. Good. Phil Malone felt a little awkward coming to Steve's house to talk. He peeked tentatively into the window that overlooked the Parkers' kitchen on his way to the front door. *Looks quiet. Hope they're home.*

Reaching for the doorbell, he was startled as the door swung open.

"Hi, Phil. I thought I heard a car pull up. Come on in." Steve pushed open the screen door and stood back to give Phil a clear path.

"Thanks. Did I interrupt your dinner?"

"Nope, we're finished. But we'd have made room at the table. I was back in the bedroom, if you want to come on back."

Steve led him back to a large bedroom, where several little piles of books were stacked on the floor.

"I was just cleaning out my bookcase. I'm almost finished. I didn't realize you were coming to our home group this week."

"Actually, I was hoping to talk with you before everyone got here." Steve noticed Phil was carrying himself differently. Quiet. More measured. "Here, Phil, you can help me with the books. What's on your mind?"

Phil bent down and grabbed a couple of textbooks. They were almost all on chemistry, Steve's major in college.

"I had lunch with your buddy, Wayne, today."

"Oh really?" Steve stopped putting books on the shelf and faced Phil.

"Yeah, we went to some Italian restaurant across town. It was a good time." "What did you guys talk about?" Steve sat down. The books could wait.

"We talked some more about the nature of the Church — eye opening. I've just been so conditioned to read the Bible as if it were a story of someone far, far away — rather than God's heart now."

"You're right," Steve agreed. "Imagine the potential of this home group if we'll apply the Word of God today and remain devoted to each other. Satan could be beaten up badly in a lot of lives! God could really use this home group in a big way!"

"Oh, it's even bigger than this home group." Phil was excited.

"What do you mean, Phil? What's bigger?"

"I...I'm beginning to see that what I've built, what I've trained for, what I've worked for...might be something less than God desires." Phil showed a hint of regret. "Maybe fixing and improving the organization we call 'church' isn't what God wants. I see it as a much bigger issue than this home group or even Metro. It encompasses all of Christianity." He laid down the books in his hand. "Has our whole way of thinking for the past nineteen hundred years been that far off track?"

"Wow, some lunch!"

"Some week!" Phil exclaimed. "I just hope I'm up for the task. It's not an easy thing, being a leader. You can lose sight along the way of who you're building for and what it is you're building. I'm not sure I even understand what a 'leader' *is* anymore! Or what a Christian is, for that matter."

"You're right," Steve responded. "But when we do see the standard, the high calling — we must respond. We must 'buy the truth and sell it not.'"

Phil nodded contemplatively.

The chime on the living room clock rang. "It's 7:30, we'd better get in there. Hey, Phil, would it be all right if, tonight, we leave the lesson plan...and try to let Jesus be in charge?"

Phil perked up. "Sounds great, Steve. I'm not sure what that will mean. But like your T–shirt says, 'I'd rather die trying than to have never lived.'" With that, he clapped Steve on the back and they walked out of the room.

THE TIME TOGETHER began comfortably and spontaneously, though a little slow at first. A song was started, followed by another, then another. Phil Malone, normally fearful of spontaneity, found himself enjoying it. *I don't know why I thought this was so dangerous.* He relaxed and joined in loudly.

As a song stopped, Steve Parker began to pray. "Father, we're grateful to be Your children. Thank You for leading us, not only as individuals, but as a people when we're gathered in Your name. Thank You for not leaving us as orphans. Please lead us now in the time we have together. Jesus, please be Lord of Your Church and Lord of each of our lives. Thank You so much! Amen."

"Amen!" Steve's prayer warmed the hearts of those present. Faith and expectancy filled the air.

"Phil and I were talking just a few minutes ago and thought we would leave the plan tonight and try to let Jesus lead us. We don't want to be so committed to a prearranged way of doing things that we become insensitive to the things on your hearts and Jesus' heart tonight. So, as Paul said in First Corinthians fourteen, if anyone has a song or a prayer or a word of instruction, feel free to speak up." Steve looked around the room, anticipating something good. "And hey, if it seems awkward, maybe we all just need to get to know the real Jesus a bit better — the 'meeting' is no biggie."

A man in his early forties, seated by the sliding glass door spoke up, looking only at Steve. "This morning I was reading ahead for what would have been tonight's lesson, and I read a verse that I have a question about."

"Okay, let's look at it," Steve responded eagerly. "Where is it?"

"Ephesians 2:10." Fred nervously looked for the Scripture in his hardbound Bible. It took a few seconds before he began to read, "For we are God's workmanship, created in Christ Jesus to do good works, which God prepared in advance for us to do."

Steve waited for a few seconds. "What's your question, Fred? Maybe someone here can help."

"Well, it's not so much the verse itself." He closed his Bible. "I started thinking about what it meant and I got excited. I'm glad God has prepared work for us because I really do want to live for Him." He hesitated again. "But I'm afraid, with all the junk in my life, I'll never be able to hear His voice or be useful to Him."

"What do you mean, Fred? What junk?"

"Well…" Fred swallowed hard. "I've been struggling for a long time with…anger. I blow up at the littlest things." He shook his head. "I know it gets in the way of being useful to God. I'm sick of it and I need help!"

"Fred, let me set your mind at rest," Phil began without hesitation. "The key to overcoming sin is simply appropriating the grace of God. Fred, you need to appropriate the grace of God. Don't focus on your difficulties or your weaknesses. Look at God's grace."

There was an uncomfortable silence as Fred slowly shook his head with disappointment. Phil felt awkward, knowing he had missed the mark. He wasn't sure what else to say. Words were unusually hard to find.

Fred's head was still down as he broke the silence. "I know about God's grace. I've thought of that again and again. Somehow, though, I'm still a slave. Paul said that sin won't be my master…so, why is it?"

Across the room, a timid hand went up. It was Judy — shy, quiet Judy.

Steve acknowledged her hand. "Judy, did you want to say something?"

"Yes." She opened her Bible, humbly but courageously looking Fred in the eye. "Fred, I don't know if this will help, but I noticed a verse the other day in Titus that I don't think I had ever read before. Would it be all right with everyone if I read it?"

Fred nodded his head. "Please."

She cleared her voice. "It's from Titus chapter two, verses eleven through fourteen.

For the grace of God that brings salvation has appeared to all men. It teaches us to say "No" to ungodliness and worldly passions, and to live self-controlled, upright and godly lives in this present age, while we wait for the blessed hope — the glorious appearing of our great God and Savior, Jesus Christ, who gave Himself for us to redeem us from all wickedness and to purify for Himself a people that are His very own, eager to do what is good."

She stopped, looked around for a minute, then started. "I

always thought the grace of God was something to turn to for comfort after we've fallen into sin. And that's true. But in this passage, it says the grace of God teaches us to say *no* to ungodliness. That means there's something wrong with our understanding of the grace of God if it doesn't teach us to say *no* to sin."

STEVE AND TERESA WERE CLEANING up the room after everyone left. Teresa gathered napkins and cups while Steve rearranged the furniture and put away the folding chairs.

She closed the dishwasher and stood at the entrance to the living room. "What was wrong with Phil tonight? He seemed awfully quiet most of the evening."

"Yeah." Steve bumped the couch with his thigh, settling it into the familiar carpet impressions. "He just had a lot on his mind." Steve straightened the cushions. "We had a wonderful conversation just before the meeting. With all the stuff God's been shaking up inside him lately, I'm not surprised that he seemed a little mellow."

"I don't know…" Teresa didn't move. "He still seemed… troubled."

62

VIRGINIA RAMSEY COULDN'T REMEMBER the last time she felt so alive spiritually. Because of the faithful encouragement of Wayne and Emily Davidson, she'd been able to persevere through one of the most difficult times of her life.

It was Saturday morning. Virginia was sitting down at the dining room table finishing a cup of coffee and a list of prayer concerns she'd been entering into her journal. Taking her last sip of coffee, she wrote:

Pray for Phil Malone — Metro Chapel. Seems soft. Critical time.

"Ginny, do you know where my blue shirt is?" Hal's voice came from the master bedroom.

"I'll be there in a minute!" She quickly finished her note and sandwiched her pen in her journal.

"Ginny!"

"Coming!"

As if she wasn't rushed enough, now the horn of Emily Davidson's mini–van announced she was in the driveway to pick Virginia up for their shopping trip. She ran to the bedroom and frantically searched for Hal's favorite blue shirt.

"BEEP–BEEP!"

Finding it, she handed it to Hal. "I'll be back around two! Okay, Dear?"

"BEEP–BEEP!"

She grabbed her purse and darted out the front door.

Hal stared out the window as the van pulled out of the driveway.

63

SENIOR PASTOR NELSON REYNOLDS stood at the front of the auditorium, talking with one of his members. Steve, distracted from the conversation he was involved in, watched as Reynolds placed his hand on the lady's forehead and prayed for her.

Steve turned back to his own conversation. He caught enough of the question to respond. "As I see it, that all depends on what the economy does. And I really don't think that's anything we'll have to face until election year." He glanced again in the direction of Reynolds, just in time to see the lady walk away.

Steve interrupted his fellow political theorist with a finger. "I...I really need to catch the pastor."

"Pastor...Pastor Reynolds!" Steve called, running toward him.

"Hello Steve. Good to see your glowing face. How's Teresa? I didn't see her this morning."

"She's here, somewhere." Steve scanned the large auditorium, then turned back to Reynolds. "I wanted to tell you about something exciting."

"Oh, what's that?" Reynolds glanced over Steve's shoulder to the clock on the back wall and shifted his weight.

"At our home group meeting Thursday, we were talking about grace and—"

"Good topic," Reynolds interrupted, then nodded for Steve to continue.

"Actually, it was the best meeting we've ever had. It was so different. It was like...Jesus was really there, teaching and guiding us — calling the shots Himself." He saw Phil Malone approaching out of the corner of his eye. "Hey Phil, you tell him about the great time we had the other night."

Oh no, Parker. What are you getting me into? "What night was that, Steve?" Phil asked politely.

"You know, the home group meeting at my house. I was just telling the pastor about it. Tell him what it's like to really let Jesus lead."

Phil Malone was unaccustomed to being caught off guard. He cloaked his emotions and was noticeably slow in answering. "Steve, I believe you're referring to what we called an experiment. Bear in mind: not every experiment is a success. That's the nature of experiments. They serve to test the waters and warn us of ways not to go." He emphasized the words *warn* and *not*.

Steve was confused. He looked at Reynolds, then at Phil. *Did I miss something?* He looked again in both men's faces, then directly at Phil. "Phil, don't you remember the time together before the home group meeting...?" He was trying to be sensitive and protect Phil's attempt to be vulnerable. "Do you remember...?"

Phil responded, "Oh, I remember. And I've considered the ideas you shared with me..."

Steve's thoughts interrupted: *I shared with you? I thought you shared with me!*

"...and I think the place for leadership, guidance and preplanned teaching is still obvious. I'll be the first to admit that ideas can come, at times, from the bottom up. And like I told you the other night, I'll give some serious thought to the things you suggested. But, change takes time. And realize that not all change is for the good. It can lead to anarchy and damaged emotions. We do need to watch out for the sheep. Don't you agree?"

Phil looked to Reynolds for a reaction. Steve creased his forehead and looked from one man to the other.

Reynolds saw his exit opportunity. "Gentlemen, it seems like you're on track to working this out. Steve, thanks for your ideas and hard work with the home groups. If you men will excuse me, I need to see some other people."

Phil watched Reynolds until he disappeared into the comforting crowd that lingered in the vestibule. He wished he could keep looking. He wished he could be lost in that same crowd. But he had to turn around. Seeing Steve's face, he felt an ice cold chill run down his back.

Steve was speechless and confused. He stared into Phil's face in disbelief. Phil stared back, trying to disguise his confusion and shame. "I've got to go." With that, Phil turned and walked toward the vestibule, leaving Steve to collapse in a nearby pew.

PHIL REELED. *What just happened?* He walked aimlessly, weaving his way through the sea of departing members. Their faces were a hazy fog. Undefined. The noise of conversation became a dull roar behind his screaming thoughts.

Steve, why did you have to do that?! You don't have to rattle off everything that's on your mind. And in front of Nelson Reynolds! Don't you realize there are consequences?

The effort of the stairs brought him back to his surroundings. His instincts had carried him to his office, to seek refuge from battle and to safely gather his thoughts.

On the way up the stairs, the thoughts hit again. None of this had been far from his mind since that meeting with Wayne and George. *Okay, so we both have seen some things — some **real** things — that God has in mind for His Church. And I know you mean well — but things are just more complicated than that. I just can't commit like that. I need more time!*

Phil slammed his office door behind him as he flicked on the light, surprised at the turmoil swirling inside him. He sensed a fondness for Steve and a kindling friendship he had been unaware of until now. The pained disbelief in Steve's eyes had brought it to light.

Steve, you've got to understand, you can't change everything in a day. You tell Reynolds we're changing everything...Do you know what it means? It means all my work...has been for nothing. You can't expect me to do that!

He buried his face in his hands. *There is more to it than sincerity and idealism. There's effort. Planning. Leadership.*

I want to do things God's way, too. Phil breathed easier, almost convinced it was true. *But does that mean I ignore seven years of Bible training? Turn my back on thousands of scholars and pastors and missionaries who've spent their lives for this? Am I supposed to pitch all of that so I can sit in a room and…and let Judy or Fred or whoever be in charge?!* The pent up energy and tension peaked. He sat in silence. Even his racing thoughts had stilled. No emotion. Nothing. He sat there, staring at the bright, early afternoon sky.

"NO!" he shouted, slapping his desk with a force that sent his pencil holder toppling. "I've worked too hard and too long! I've come too far to see all of this handed over to a bunch of housewives and untrained, emotional laymen who want to throw their ideas around in a living room!"

His ears were ringing. He sat back, spent, breathing a sigh of utter relief and release. It was over. The struggle was finally over.

RRRRRRNNNNNNG

"Phil, call on line one."

64

"WHAT ABOUT VIRGINIA?" Wayne called from the garage. "Did you call her?" Wayne tossed the remaining backpacks and the small beverage cooler into the back of the mini–van.

"Yes. She was thrilled." Emily sealed the rest of the sandwiches in a Ziploc bag. "She asked if we could pick her up on our way to the park."

The day was beautiful. The azure sky reminded Emily of the mountain lake where her family had vacationed when she was young. As they pulled out of the driveway, she handed sunglasses to the children, who tried them on in a flurry of giggling and teasing.

Wayne turned the air conditioning off and opened the windows. "Perfect day for a hike."

The car rolled into Virginia Ramsey's driveway, where she was waiting for them in a lawn chair. Emily got out and opened the van's sliding door.

"Hop out, Blake. You can sit up front with your dad. I'll stay back here and keep Virginia company."

It was a half–hour drive to the state park. While Wayne recounted his teenage wilderness hike for Blake, Emily focused on Virginia.

"You're sure quiet. Something on your mind?"

"It's Hal." Virginia wrinkled her face. "I get so frustrated."

"What happened?"

"Oh, nothing new. It's mostly my attitude about it all," she admitted. "He can be demanding, and I find myself complaining in my heart when he asks me to do things for him." She shook her head. "I just don't feel any respect for him at all."

Emily raised her eyebrows in concern. "I understand your situation and it is difficult...but, Virginia, there are many saints with unbelieving spouses. It's not impossible." She smiled. "You can treat your husband with respect, not necessarily because he's earned it, but because you love God — and because that's how God wants you to respond to Hal."

Virginia looked out the window for several minutes, working through the implications. "Thanks, Emily. That helps." She turned back. "I know that's what Jesus wants."

Passing through the gate, they found the Stones' mini–van parked in front of the entrance to the trail. Just beyond it, Ted was tossing a football with Eric, while Amy and Carolyn sprayed their girls and themselves with insect repellent.

"Where's George?" Wayne inquired.

"He went to find hiking sticks for the children." Ted lobbed a spiral to Blake as he made an eager exit from the van. "He should be back any minute."

Just then, George emerged from the woods carrying several long, stout rods. "What do you say we hit the trail now, and have lunch when we get back?" he suggested, handing Blake and Amanda their walking sticks.

"Sounds great," Eric agreed.

"Yea! Yea!" the children shouted.

"I am concerned about the trail," Wayne said. "It's pretty long according to the map. Do you think the children will be all right?"

"They'll be fine. If they get too tired, we could always carry them," Ted suggested. "It wouldn't hurt to make this a little more of a workout for us, you know."

"ARE WE GETTING ANY CLOSER?" Wayne puffed. "I'm starting to get a little out of breath."

"A little!" Ted chortled. "If your wheezing gets any louder, I'm gonna call 9–1–1."

"What about you, Ted?" George chimed in. "Is that perspiration, or did you fall into that last stream?"

"I'll tell you what: *you* carry Marie for the next mile. We'll see how you look."

"No, no. Looks like you're doing just fine."

"Don't forget, George," Wayne added, "I've seen you play racquetball."

George laughed. "Okay. Okay."

The ladies chuckled at the men's teasing.

"Amy—" Carolyn reached up to steady Hope in her backpack, "are you holding up all right? I'm sure one of the guys would be happy to carry this little load."

"Oh, thanks. I'm fine." Amy launched up a small rocky incline. "It feels great to get the exercise."

Emily watched Blake and Amanda skipping merrily ahead of the adults. Even Ashley, who was holding her hand, seemed undaunted by the rugged terrain. "Slow down, children. Wait up for your tired parents."

65

THE OFFICE SEEMED deathly quiet. His torturous thoughts were silenced. He sat staring at the blinking red light on his telephone. *Why don't they give up?* It continued to blink. *Oh, all right!*

He sat upright. "This is Phil Malone."

He had no energy for this conversation. *What is this guy talking about?* "Warn me...about what?"

"Divisive? Heretics? Well, uh..." Phil positioned his finger over the phone, preparing to disconnect. "I think you have the wrong number...Yes...I know that name." He relaxed his hand, letting it fall beside the phone. "You're kidding! That's a pretty serious accusation...you have what?" He leaned forward, listening intently. "No, actually, I'm not surprised. I'm very glad you told me."

He tapped a pen on his desktop as he considered the caller's request. "Get together? No, I can't see any reason to do that. You've helped enough already...Oh...yes...I see what you mean...okay, I'll see you then."

Blessed are you

when people insult you,

persecute you

and falsely say all kinds

of evil against you

because of me.

Matthew 5:11

Opposition

66

"GOOD MORNING. E.N.S. Pharmaceuticals! How may I help you?" The nasal voice was reminiscent of Hollywood's operator stereotype.

"Steve Parker, please."

"One moment."

Phil Malone waited as elevator music controlled the moment. His pulse quickened.

"Research, this is Steve."

"Hello, Steve...this is Phil Malone."

Steve was silent. He closed his eyes and swallowed hard, girding himself for whatever was next.

"The reason I called was to apologize...about yesterday. I was wondering if you could come by tomorrow afternoon so we can talk?"

Apologize! ? Steve was surprised. He breathed a prayer. *Thank You, Master!*

"Hello? Are you there?"

"Yeah...I'm here. Tomorrow would be fine." He was reflexively guarded, but hopeful. The wound still stung. "I get off around five. I can be there by 5:30. Will that work?"

"Perfect. See you then."

IT WAS THE KIND OF EVENING when the cool, soothing breeze seemed to carry in it the ambrosia of life. Tony breathed it in deeply as he walked from his car to the Davidson's front door. He eagerly anticipated the chance for another glimpse into this strange, new world. While he didn't understand everything George had said to him the other night, he knew he wanted to see more — though he wasn't sure why.

"Hey, Tony! Come on in!" Wayne answered the door with a hearty smile. "I'm glad you could come."

"Well, you said you needed some help polishin' off some ice cream." He shrugged. "Hey, what're friends for? Right?"

Tony was greeted warmly by the same people he'd met at the barbecue.

"Wayne, do ya have parties like this all the time, or did ya need a lot of help wit'da ice cream?" Tony said as he gestured animatedly at everyone. Children scurried past him from the kitchen, each carefully balancing an ice cream cone as they raced into the backyard.

"Hi, Tony." Carolyn emerged from the kitchen. "Do you want vanilla or butter pecan?"

"Do ya have any chocolate sauce?"

She smiled. "We sure do. And walnuts. And whipped cream."

"Sounds great. Vanilla wit' da works."

She disappeared back into the kitchen as Tony took a seat. "Hey, George, I really appreciate that Bible you dropped off at my place."

"Sure thing, Tony. I'm asking God to help you understand what He says in it."

"Well, I think He must be, 'cuz I feel like it makes a lot more sense to me now than it did when I was a kid."

"Here you are." Carolyn carefully placed a heaping bowl of ice cream in front of Tony. The whipped cream was swirled high above the lip of the bowl and it was topped with a long–stemmed maraschino cherry.

"Wow. Is this tag team or do I hafta eat this by myself?" He took the bowl and examined it from all sides until he found an entrance. Then he went to work.

Amy handed George and Ted bowls as they watched Tony skillfully devour his dessert.

"Looks like you've done that before," Ted teased as he scooped his first spoonful.

"Yeah." Tony looked up. The whipped cream on his nose was especially obvious against his dark complexion. "Like my fadda used to say, 'If you're gonna let your ice cream melt, ya might as well drink milk. It's cheapa, see.'"

"Here." Ted tossed a napkin into Tony's lap. "'Keep your nose clean' is what my father always told me." He laughed as Tony felt his nose, then wiped it with the napkin.

"Hey, at least I kept it off da furniture."

All three men laughed as they turned back to finish scraping their bowls.

Wayne sat down beside them as Ted finished up.

Ted turned to Wayne. "I've got a situation at the school that I'm not sure what to do about and I wanted to ask you what you think."

"Sure, go ahead."

"Well, there's another coach at school who claims to be a Christian. I'm with him a lot and there is a certain area in his life that, well, seems unlike Jesus. He's a great guy in a lot of ways. He'd give you the shirt off his back." Ted set his bowl on the coffee table. "But he tends to have a bad habit of complaining about his circumstances. Everything seems to be a rip–off to him. We buy some burgers at a restaurant and maybe they're too cold or burned. Or the coffee's too weak. Or the carpet he had installed last year isn't the quality he had been led to believe it was. Things like that."

Ted laid his spoon in the empty bowl. "I've mentioned it to him a couple of times and he just gets defensive. I want to help him, but I'm not sure how."

Wayne swallowed another bite of ice cream. "Well, Ted, it seems like, based on what you've said, the issue at stake isn't just the sin itself. It's also his attitude *about* the sin and his attitude about being confronted. Will he call it what it is — sin? If he won't even talk about it, humbly, then there really is reason, based on what Jesus said in John 3 and John 10, to wonder if he's really a true follower of Jesus. You have to 'love the light' to be a Christian! Does he want to make excuses and defend his right to live that way? Or does he know it's sin, will he call it sin, and does he really want to change? If so, then you've got a foundation from which to walk with him. If, on the other hand, he only makes excuses and even resents you bringing it up…then, according to Jesus, you can't even consider him a brother."

227

"So, what should I do?"

"Well," Wayne continued, "if he were in a Biblical environment — where all the members care for one another — you could ask a couple of brothers who know him to join you in talking with him about it, like Jesus commanded in Matthew 18. But chances are he's not in an environment where obedience to Jesus is expected, so there may not be two other brothers who are willing to hold up Jesus' standard with you. But you never know. Why don't you look into what sort of religious environment he is in? Maybe there will be some brothers there who can help him."

"So you're saying unless I find a couple others to help, I may have done all I can already?"

"Well, if it were me, I'd at least give it another shot by myself to see if he might be soft and willing to change. If he's not, then plead with him to not call himself a Christian if he doesn't plan to live like one. I know that may sound strong, but if a basic, gentle call to live like Jesus causes him to get defensive and stiff–arm you, then you don't have any Biblical ground to continue to walk with him as a brother." Wayne took a deep breath. "He's not a *brother* just because he answered an altar call or signed a card, or because he was simply immersed in water, or because he's willing to give you the shirt off his back. He's a *brother* if he loves the light and his life belongs to Jesus. As Paul said, a person won't be saved unless they 'agape' the truth. I'm not trying to be harsh. It's simply what the Bible teaches. Unfortunately, most don't view the teachings of Jesus as something to be obeyed. Instead, they view them as slogans to be admired, sermons to be preached, or songs to be sung."

Tony sat with his eyes fixed on Wayne, surprised by his directness. *Wow!* Despite his uncertainty, there was something comforting about what he'd witnessed. Though he felt ashamed and challenged, he also saw a peace and reality that were compelling.

67

"PHIL, YOU OWE it to your people to make sure they don't get mixed up with these guys."

KNOCK! KNOCK! KNOCK!

Phil looked at the door, then back at his guest. "Looks like he's here." He sat up in his chair. "Come in."

The door to Phil's office opened and Steve Parker entered. He looked around, his hesitancy obvious. "Am I...interrupting?"

"No, not at all. Good to see you, Steve." Phil stood up and extended his hand. Steve accepted firmly.

Phil motioned for Steve to have a seat in a chair near the wall. "I want you to meet a new friend of mine. Steve Parker, this is Hal Ramsey."

Steve reached over and shook the stranger's hand. "Good to meet you."

"Steve, I know you must be confused after Sunday, and I'd like to clear that up. I realize we were both excited about the things we've heard from Wayne Davidson and George Archer." Steve looked from man to man and shifted uncomfortably as Phil continued speaking.

"Recently, I learned some things which confirmed the concerns I was having." Phil paused. "I've called you here because I think it's *very* important that you hear these things as well."

Phil motioned toward Hal. "This gentleman is a local bank vice–president. He's also been an elder for fifteen years. So we're being advised by a very reputable, reliable man." Phil looked toward the distinguished man sitting beside Steve. "Hal..."

"Believe me, I understand what you guys are going through," Hal began. "I've known Wayne Davidson for a long, long time. I was one of his elders at the Hampton Street Bible Church. In fact, as chairman of the search committee, I was the one most responsible for getting him the job." Hal stared trance–like out the window. "For most of the time he was there, we were friends...best friends. He confided in me." Hal stopped, then continued in a slow, gloomy voice. "But he had new ideas, ideas he convinced me were for the good of the church. I believed, at the time, that they were. I thought his ideas would help breathe new life into Hampton Street. That's why I defended him."

"What happened?" Steve blurted, drawn in by the story.

"Well, somewhere along the way, he started to change. What started off as simple, fresh ideas aimed at helping the church...became rigid judgments." Hal finished with a sad, but firm tone. "I tried to reason with him from the Scriptures. One time, we spent all afternoon in a church classroom going over one of Jesus' parables. But he wouldn't hear me. He couldn't hear me! The deception had set in." Hal turned toward the wall as if to hide his emotion. "I could tell you a few things about his personal life that would shock you as well. But I'd rather do my best to protect him and be discreet."

This is terrible. Steve stared, unblinking, at Hal. *I can't believe this is happening!*

Phil glanced at Steve, comforted by his growing bewilderment.

Allowing the heavy silence to settle just long enough, Hal started again. "Did Wayne tell you why he left Hampton Street?"

"No...no, he didn't."

"I'm not surprised. Unfortunately, he finally concluded we were all lost and that he had to leave." He focused on the wall beside Steve. "He decided he couldn't associate anymore with people who were still struggling with weaknesses. Even his wife, a dear Christian woman, can barely live with him when he goes on his tirades."

Hal paused, glanced at Phil, then back to Steve. "When you have a man like that in leadership at a congregation, it creates all sorts of chaos. In fact, because of my closeness to the situation, I was swept up in his leaving and was forced to resign."

Hal watched for a reaction. Steve's eyes were closed, his face hard to read. Hal cleared his throat. "And as for George Archer. That's a sad situation, too. One of my colleagues here in town is a trustee on the board of that Bible college. They were shocked and dismayed when they learned from the students and faculty of this professor's behavior."

"Why don't you tell him some of the specifics, Hal," Phil encouraged. "I think that will help."

Steve reluctantly opened his eyes as Hal began to speak. "I'll give you one of many examples. One day he threw his diploma into a trash can in front of a classroom full of students." Hal drew a deep breath. "It's a total disrespect for authority. Just like Jude warned us about."

Hal raised his voice with energy. "It bothers me to think about the Godly missionaries who got their training at that institution. And, he...just throws his diploma in the trash can." His voice shook. "They're elitists who despise common Christians. They spend their time looking for people who will give ear to their ideas. It's dangerous!"

Hal's red face brightened as he continued. "As Paul warned in Galatians one, men who tamper with the *free* gift of God's grace are inviting eternal damnation."

Hal paused, regathered his emotions and started again. "It breaks my heart to have to mention all of this." He shook his head mournfully. "I wish it were different, but these aren't the kinds of characters you want influencing your wife and children. Believe me, I know what it's like to feel that responsibility. I'm a former elder. I don't take it lightly." Hal hung his head in a show of grief.

"I know it was difficult for you to share all of that, Hal." Phil's voice was peppered with sympathy and a hint of admiration. "Thanks."

He looked toward Steve. "Steve, as I see it, we owe a lot to Hal. He has saved us from finding these things out the hard way. As for the home group, we need to stick with the original plan. Of course, if someone is in tears, I realize we may need to make some alterations. I'm fine with that. But the thrust of what we do needs to stay on course. The lessons I have created should be the bedrock of the future." Hal nodded in agreement.

Phil stood. "I believe in you, Steve. Believe it or not, I wish all the other home groups in this church could go as far as yours has...and will!" He leaned onto his desk with both hands. "Are you with me...partner?"

"I...I think so."

68

STEVE STARED AT THE TABLE, mindlessly tracing rings around the mouth of a glass of milk, trying to unravel the conversation with Phil and Hal.

He stood, straining to push himself up from the table. Abandoning the uneaten sandwich he had made moments before, he wandered in the direction of the living room. The plush recliner offered no comfort as Steve grappled to make sense of the afternoon.

How could George and Wayne seem so real, yet not know God? Steve relived in his mind his last few interactions with them. *They didn't seem divisive or spiteful. They didn't seem like false teachers. I must be naïve!* He covered his eyes with the palms of his hands and leaned back in silence.

"What's wrong, Steve?" Teresa's voice was soft. He sat upright and tried to wipe the confusion from his eyes. *How long has she been there?*

She sat on her knees beside him.

"I thought, for the first time in my life, I was hearing God's voice," he said quietly. "How could I have been so completely off track? Was I just listening to my emotions?"

"What are you talking about?" Teresa's face showed concern. "Please...tell me what's happened."

Steve leaned back again and sighed. He had hoped to spare her the details. He hated to relive Hal's confident unveiling of Wayne's past and Phil's eager council. *But she needs to know.*

Teresa sat quietly as Steve spoke, but the frequent changes in her face reassured him she was following every word. He saw his own confusion mirrored in her eyes and it hurt. He longed to console her, but he couldn't even console himself.

"It seems incredible," Teresa broke the silence. "It's hard to believe Wayne and George have been through so much. And only a few months ago! They've been so encouraging, so helpful."

"Yeah, I'm still reeling from it, too. I couldn't have imagined yesterday that these things were true. But this guy has known Wayne for years."

"What did Wayne have to say about all this?"

Steve had no answer. Her simple question had caught him off guard.

"Well, I haven't talked to him."

"Steve!" She put her hand on his arm. "You haven't talked to him? How do you know any of this is even true? Maybe this Hal person has something to hide or is after revenge. People can be like that. Remember the forty men, referred to in the Bible, who were never going to eat again until Paul, the apostle, was dead?"

Steve ran his fingers through his hair and knotted them behind his head. He stared at Teresa for several moments, feeling the impact of her words. Hope, mingled with shame, prevented a response.

"I mean, don't you think it's important to get Wayne's side

of the story? Seriously, what do we *really* know about this Hal, anyway?"

Steve's countenance lightened and he moved to the front of the chair. Reaching over, he put his arm around Teresa. "You know," he said with a grin, "you're pretty smart for a college dropout." His face grew more serious as he looked into her eyes. "How will I know who to believe in all this?"

"Listen to your heart, Steve," she said quietly. "You'll know. The sheep know the Shepherd's voice."

STEVE PARKER'S CAR sliced through the thick summer rain, the wipers providing a hypnotic rhythm for his anxious thoughts. His gut told him there was Life in Wayne. But his head fought back. *I've only known him a short time — Hal said he was his best friend! Besides, I'm no Bible scholar...I'm a chemist.*

Traffic was slowing as drivers strained to see the contours of the road. Rather than cooling things off, the showers only served to raise the humidity and fill the interior of Steve's sedan with an uncomfortable muggy feeling.

Wayne did spend a lot of time talking about righteousness, but didn't Jesus and Paul and John and...Maybe I'm just gullible. Maybe Hal and Phil are right...or maybe I'm just tired of dealing with it. Does it have to be so hard?

Steve negotiated the final turn before reaching the Davidsons' driveway. He cut the ignition, hoping to secure a few more minutes of reflection before he went in. Unfortunately, the porch lit up almost instantly and he saw Wayne leaning out the screen door, trying to identify the late–night guest. As Wayne recognized the sedan, his face brightened and he waved. Steve took a deep breath and, in one fluid motion, opened the door, opened his umbrella and shot into the house.

"Hey, Steve, what's up? You sure picked a great night to be out!" Wayne teased, gesturing toward the blackened sky. Emily rushed off to make coffee, while her husband took the wet umbrella from their dripping guest.

Steve shifted nervously, anxious to get this over with. "Well, Wayne, there's something I need to—"

"Daddy, who's here?"

"It's Steve, Blake. Go on back to bed, Champ." Wayne

redirected the curious sleep evader with a rub to the head and smiled apologetically at Steve, gesturing toward the den.

"I'm sorry, Steve. What were you saying?" Wayne sat down on the piano bench while Steve found the end of the couch across from him. He sighed heavily, collecting his thoughts. Part of him wanted to yell, but part of him wanted to cry.

"Steve, what's wrong?" Wayne waited. "Can I help?"

"I hope so," Steve answered.

Wayne watched a dozen emotions wrestle on his guest's face as Steve chose his words slowly and deliberately. "I guess I've been wondering why you and George left the places where you were...Are there skeletons in the closet? It seems like you just float from one group of believers to another, and don't really seem to be accountable to anyone. You don't belong to any Church here locally, or any at all that I know of. Do you?" Wayne shook his head but sensed that Steve wasn't finished. "What about the need for leadership, or some kind of accountability to keep you from getting off track?"

Wayne raised his eyebrows. "Well, Steve, I'll get back to the skeleton question, but believe me, there's *nothing* that would please me more than to be totally immersed in a Biblical body of believers! If I knew of a body of believers locally who were embracing Jesus as their only standard, I would gladly make myself accountable to them. I'm not looking for perfect people, believe me. I just want the confidence of knowing that the Church I would give my life over to really wants to put into practice Jesus' teachings and commands — not just preach about them while the members live in the world as they please. That sort of place is harder to find than you'd think, unfortunately for Jesus and all of us.

"Currently, though, I walk in the light with the handful of believers that I know love Jesus. They would die for me — *any* of them. And I for them! And every day they give their input into my life. I love that and I want that!"

Steve refocused on Wayne. "Do you mean that you don't know of any Church in town obeying Jesus? That sounds elitist." His tone became terse as the borrowed accusation gained credibility in his own mind.

"Whoa. Slow down, Steve." Wayne slid forward. "Let's make sure we understand each other." Steve was surprised at Wayne's gentle composure. "Now, do *you* know of a Church anywhere in the city whose members are totally committed to each other — on a grass–roots level — seven days a week?" He paused for a second. "I mean all of them, *really* devoted to each other as Jesus commanded and demonstrated?"

Steve looked at the floor, considering his reply. "Well, no. I guess not." He raised his head. "But I wouldn't say they're not Christians!"

"Neither would I!! That's not the issue at all!"

"So, you don't think people should be instantly perfect…" Steve slowed down, donning a more puzzled look, "and that you shouldn't fellowship with people who are immature?"

"Steve, of course not!" Wayne locked eyes with Steve. "Who have you been talking to?"

Steve's eyes widened as he involuntarily pulled back. *How does he know?* Watching Wayne closely, he answered, "Hal Ramsey."

The name struck Wayne in the face like a brick. He was stunned for a moment, then asked softly, "Really? Hal Ramsey?" His eyes showed a painful battle with memories and questions. "How did you happen to meet Hal, if you don't mind me asking?"

Steve seemed calmer, relieved things were in the open. "Phil introduced me to him."

"Phil Malone?" Wayne shook his head. "Wow…that's too bad." He let out a sigh and stared quietly at the wall.

After a minute or two, he caught Steve with a sober gaze. "Just to illustrate the kind of obstacles we're up against in this pursuit to take Christianity seriously — if Hal and Phil had problems with me…why were they talking with you?"

"Hmmm." Steve rubbed his chin. "Good question. That's not the way Jesus said to handle things, is it?"

"Right." Wayne closed his eyes for a moment. "Steve—" he said, looking up, "I'm really not inclined to try and answer their questions with you caught in the middle. I'm not interested in trying to prove anything to anyone or make myself look good. There certainly were a number of things that were misrepresented, unfortunately. But, I'm not sure it would be productive to go into all those details."

Steve nodded.

"But," Wayne offered, "if there's anything unanswered for

you — I'd be happy to try and help."

"Oh," Steve nodded, "you already have."

STEVE SWALLOWED the last few spoonfuls of Captain Crunch as quickly as he could. He'd set his alarm clock later this morning to compensate for the lateness of last night's conversation with Wayne. Bowl rinsed and orange juice downed, Steve whistled a song of thanks as he slipped his shoes on and ducked into the family room to kiss Teresa.

"Bye, Honey," he said buoyantly. "Oh, did you ever find a repair shop that can fix the CD player?"

Teresa looked up from her Bible and smiled. "No, Dear, it wasn't necessary."

"What do you mean?"

She set her coffee mug on the table and threw both arms toward the entertainment center in mock showmanship. "Ta–da! A brand new ten–disc CD player with all the latest features."

Steve moved closer to the new stereo component and stared in disbelief.

"George Archer brought it by the day before yesterday. He said he thought it was a shame for us to be without one, and with all the trouble that old one kept giving us..."

"He brought it over the day *before* yesterday?" Steve stood gaping at the gift sitting in front of him. *What a heel I've been! But...maybe they're trying to buy my trust with fake acts of love. Wouldn't that be the ultimate deception...?* Steve's mind raced. *NO! I've SEEN their hearts!*

"I'm sorry, Steve. I meant to tell you, but so much was going on that it just slipped my mind."

Steve grabbed Teresa and gave her a bear hug. He looked straight into his wife's bright eyes. "Oh, Teresa, God has been so good to us!"

69

"THAT'S TWENTY–ONE. You win." Eric wiped his forehead with his sleeve and chased the ball Ted had just sent through the hoop. "I was close, though."

"Close?" Ted quizzed. "You call seven points close?"

Eric returned with the ball. "It's my strategy." He handed the ball to Wayne. "I gave you guys the advantage...to wear you out." He flashed a sly grin. "I'm sure you'll be taking it much easier next game. You wouldn't want to jostle your dentures loose or break one of those brittle bones."

They all turned their heads as a loud laugh erupted from the side of the backyard court. Wayne and Ted exchanged glances, then headed for the lawn chair in which the lounging George hid behind a large pair of sunglasses.

"What's so funny? Are you gonna let him talk about *us* that way?" Wayne hoped to lure George into a game of two–on–two.

George looked up at Wayne, dual suns dancing off his ridiculous black sunglasses. His face showed no expression. "I believe he was referring to you two, not me. Eric and I will run circles around you old codgers!"

Wayne and Ted looked at one another and laughed, nearly choking on the lemonade they had taken from the picnic table. Then George stood up, took the ball from Wayne and proceeded onto the court.

Now even Eric's jaw dropped as George dribbled fluidly to the three–point line, squared up, and sank a flawless basket. Nothing but net.

Ted shrugged. "Let's do it!" He put his drink down and soon the court brimmed with lay–ups, jump shots and passes as Eric and George took a quick lead. Eric fought hard for rebounds and sank two lay–ups. George seemed unstoppable from the three–point–line and surprisingly quick underneath. But in spite of George's closet basketball prowess, Wayne and Ted were too much. They overtook them and built a firm 37–29 lead.

Eric sank a six–foot jumper to make it 37–31. Wayne took the ball at the top of the key. George checked it and Wayne began dribbling, looking for a pass to Ted or a chance to drive to the goal. Then, out of the corner of his eye, he saw a medium–height man enter the Stones' gate. He held the ball and watched as the smiling Steve Parker made his way over to the court.

"I thought I'd join you guys." Steve kept his hands in his pockets as he stepped onto the court. The five men stood there, exchanging smiles.

George broke the silence. "Good, I need a replacement just about now." He pointed at Wayne. "You cover him."

70

HAL RAMSEY HARDLY NOTICED the television program in front of him as he savored in his mind the recent events. He relished the fact that Virginia had not been able to interfere with the work he thought God was calling him to do. He'd been able to slip into their elite circle, bring some justice, and slip out again. The feeling was reminiscent, in a way, of a time when he was a boy.

He and his brother had been given a small plot of ground by their father, where they both planted watermelon seeds. Each had two plants producing melons. The plants were difficult to grow, and halfway through the summer Hal was taking pride in the fact that he had three baseball–sized melons maturing on his vines. His older brother, Rex, had only two.

As the summer progressed, however, Rex's melons were visibly becoming larger than Hal's. To add insult to injury, one of Hal's largest melons succumbed to vine rot, and another was run over by his father's pick–up truck. One night, while his family was in bed, Hal snuck out to the garden with a hand spade and poked deep into the dirt around the base of Rex's plants, fatally severing many of the roots. During the next two weeks, Rex's plants slowly died a mysterious death — to Hal's pure enjoyment. After all, what had happened to his melons wasn't fair. No one had ever discovered the truth and Hal still congratulated himself on occasion — occasions like tonight. Now he was able to do the same thing to these elitist, self–righteous workers of iniquity. They would have been able to go on "masquerading as servants of righteousness"…if it weren't for him.

His déjà vu was interrupted by the telephone. He was home alone, so he placed his memory on its shelf and got up to retrieve the phone.

"Hello, this is Hal."

"Hal, this is Phil."

"Hi, Phil!" Hal said cheerfully, "What can I do for you?"

Phil leaned back in his leather chair, glad to catch Hal at home. "Well, Hal, I hate to bother you again, but I'm wondering if you would have time to come to my office again sometime this week and meet with Steve Parker and myself."

Hal paused for a moment, chewing on the proposition. "Why? What's up?"

Phil detected some hesitation in Hal's voice and sat up, giving the call his full attention. "Well, Steve called me this afternoon. He'd like to get together again and talk more about Wayne Davidson."

Phil paused, giving Hal a chance to volunteer his services, but continued when silence answered. "He stressed the need for you to be there."

"Do you think there's trouble?" Hal blurted.

"Trouble?" Phil echoed in surprise.

"I mean...do you think everything is all right with Steve?"

"Well, actually, he's talked with Wayne and has more questions on his mind. I'd really hate to lose Steve to these impostors. I think he could use another dose of the sober truth. If you could just..."

"Listen, Phil. I'd like to help you out, but I can only do so much. I told you guys everything I know. I don't want to get pulled into a 'he said–she said' sort of thing."

"Hal, you really don't have to—"

"I know I don't! And if Steve's going around talking to Wayne and my wife...I won't allow my name to be dragged through the mud anymore!"

"Your wife?" Phil was confused. "Well, I guess I..."

"Listen, I'll continue to pray for Steve, but I just don't think it would be wise at this point to get into all this again, okay?"

"Sure, Hal."

"Thanks, Phil. Listen, I've got some things going on here right now, so I'd better go."

"Okay." Phil slowly hung up the phone and sat perplexed. *This sounds fishy...Maybe Hal isn't credible after all. But he said he could produce dozens of other witnesses...But then, there were some "witnesses" at Jesus' trial, too...NO! I've considered this already. Stay on course, Malone!*

"TED AND CAROLYN are going to watch the children tonight," Wayne called to Emily, setting his briefcase on the table.

"Really? Why?"

"Oh, I was hoping we could go out."

"Are you asking me to dinner, Mr. Davidson?" Emily appeared from the kitchen.

"I'm only asking if you'll say yes." Wayne smiled as he kissed Emily on the forehead. Sometimes he was in awe of the changes he was seeing God work in her life. They were partners now in this journey.

Her face lit up. "So where are you taking me?"

"Oh, I was thinking Stewart's Steak House, if that's okay with you."

"Stewart's? Wow." She raised her eyebrows in jest. "You must have gotten a big paycheck."

"Actually, no. But a couple of mornings ago, as I was leaving for work, I found an envelope someone had slipped under our door with forty dollars in it and a note that said, 'Do something special with Emily.'"

"Are you serious?...How nice! And here I thought this was your idea."

"No, I think it was God's."

Wayne was close. God did have a hand in ordering tonight's events, as He often does for those living in the center of His will. But this time, steak was not on the menu.

"Sweetheart, I was wondering..." Emily started.

"Yes?" Wayne laid his tie across the back of the couch.

"I was wondering if we could go somewhere other than Stewart's."

"Sure. What did you have in mind?"

"Oh, maybe Chinese food."

"That'll work." He smiled, pulling back the curtain as the Stones' mini–van arrived. "China Garden or Peking Palace?"

"Peking Palace," she responded instantly. "I like their egg drop soup."

"Sounds great."

AFTER HIS UNCOMFORTABLE phone call with Phil Malone, Hal discovered he had an unusual hunger for some Chinese food.

It might have been more of an urge to leave his home out of fear that Phil might call again. However, Hal generally didn't like to look that closely in the mirror. He impulsively grabbed his coat and headed out to satisfy his appetite.

As Hal made his way to his booth at Peking Palace, he didn't notice the Davidsons tucked away in a small booth at the rear of the restaurant. It wasn't until after he ordered that he caught sight of them and quickly switched to the other side of his booth to cut off their angle. Periodically, he peeked nervously out at their booth, seeking solace in the fact that they appeared to be finishing their meal. *When the waiter brings them their check, I'll slip into the men's room until the coast is clear,* he mused, wiping his brow with a red cloth napkin.

His scheme worked, though his thoughts wouldn't allow him to enjoy his meal in peace. He vacillated between congratulating himself and justifying himself. *Guys like Wayne are dangerous.* Hal shook his head to clear his badgering thoughts. *I've got to get my mind off this stuff. Maybe I'll pick up a video on the way home.*

Hal hastily finished up his dinner and asked the waiter for his check. When the waiter returned, Hal looked at the check and then to the waiter in confusion. "What's this?" Hal inquired, pointing to the check. Written across it was the word: "PAID."

"Ah, a Mr. Davidson has paid your bill. He asked that you receive this." The waiter offered a folded paper napkin which Hal accepted reluctantly. Without smiling, Hal dismissed the waiter with a curt, "Thank you," and slowly sat back. He carefully unfolded the napkin:

Hal, we do care about you. For Jesus' sake, Wayne.

Hal felt nauseous.

71

THE STRIKING SCENT of lemon furniture polish filled the air. Stella was doing a little cleaning. She stood back, inspecting her work and admiring the large print that hung over the couch.

"Oh, a fingerprint." She turned to get a rag as the door to her office opened.

"Steve Parker! I didn't hear you on the stairs."

"Hi, Stella."

"Here to do some scheming with Phil?" She grinned, only half–covering her sarcasm.

Steve had been confident coming up the stairs, but seeing Stella brought him back to reality.

He swallowed hard. "Actually, I *am* here to see Phil. We have an appointment."

"Yes...yes, you are on the books for 5:15. Just in time." She pushed a button on her phone. "Phil, Steve Parker is here to see you."

"Send him in." Phil's voice rang over the speaker and through his closed door with authority.

Steve shuddered. *God, help me!*

He grabbed the door knob to Phil's office, hesitated, drew a deep breath and opened it. Phil was busy rearranging papers on his desk. He didn't even look up. "What can I do for you today?"

The knot in Steve's stomach tightened, his mustered courage waning. "Where's Hal?"

"He couldn't make it." Phil dropped the papers in his hands. "I tried to get him to come, but he...couldn't make it."

Phil placed his hands firmly on his desk. "Anyway..." He was again poised and in control. "I'm sure I can help you." He pointed at the chair behind Steve. "Have a seat."

Steve dropped into the high–backed chair. Phil loomed over him as he sank into the plush cushions. "I was wanting to talk about my last meeting with you and Hal. Maybe I shouldn't do it since...since Hal's not here?"

"No, why don't you go ahead. If it's important, it can happen now."

Steve felt more uncertain than ever. *This is not going well.*

His voice quivered as he began. "Phil...it seems to me that the last meeting we had was not God's way, if the Scriptures are the standard. It was, as far as I can tell, unbiblical and disobedient."

"Unbiblical?!" Phil looked down at Steve with raised eyebrows. "What could possibly have been unbiblical about that meeting?" The words came like nails, intended to permanently slam the door on Steve's courage.

"If one believer has a problem with another believer," he began, looking Phil in the eye, "didn't Jesus say you should go to him and him alone? As I see it, if you have a problem with Wayne, you should be talking with him about it. You shouldn't be inviting me into your office and talking with *me* about it."

Phil remained cool. "Steve, I have a lot of responsibility around here. I'm responsible for these home groups and I'm responsible for the people in them. I've been around a lot longer than you." He folded his hands on his desk. "Understand, there are a lot of religious nuts out there. My responsibility doesn't lie with them — to help them see their error. My responsibility lies with the people of *this* Church."

"But, still!" Steve pled. "Jesus just hasn't given us license to make exceptions. To put it simply, it's slander." He moved to the edge of his seat. "You just met Hal. Yet you're taking his word as the truth and using it to accuse and slander another brother. It's not right!"

"That's only if we know he's a brother." Phil scoffed. "Galatians one declares some very serious condemnations on a man advocating a gospel of perfectionism without room for God's grace."

Steve studied Phil. The change in him was stark. "Phil, I was with you the night you heard with your own ears...with your heart. That was no gospel of perfectionism. You're intentionally twisting their words, and you shouldn't do that! You knew then it was real and alive — it was Jesus. You were touched. I know you were."

Phil shifted in his chair. He felt the pulse in his neck quicken as his blood pressure raised. "Sure, it all *sounds* good. It does. Jesus as Head of His Church, the body of Christ...sounds great." His voice crescendoed. "But the only way Wayne Davidson knows how to get you there is through the bondage of perfectionism and policing one another, rather than letting the Holy Spirit do the work. All the focus is on what you do — not on grace. It's a sugar cube..." he paused for effect, "but it's laced with poison."

"Phil—" Steve scooted his chair closer to the desk, "you hardly know Wayne, yet you're speaking as if you're the expert on who he is and what he believes."

Phil shook his head, "Steve, you are—"

Steve cut him off. "You brought up grace. Let's talk about grace. You were there the night Judy talked about it."

Phil seethed and looked out the window.

Steve continued gently. "Please. Listen. There's a big difference between a weak person and a rebellious person. Although they both might commit the same exact sins, it doesn't mean much to the rebellious person. It might break their pride but it doesn't break their heart. Inside, they don't hunger and thirst for righteousness. They're not broken and contrite. They don't have 'Godly sorrow which works repentance,' but 'worldly sorrow.'" Steve looked into Phil's calloused eyes. "God's grace and His lovingkindness are extended to the weak, but He calls the rebellious to repent. Sure, God loves all people, even the rebellious. But He calls them to repent. He doesn't comfort them in their rebellion with sweet words of cheap grace." Steve was surprised at the sharpness of his own words.

"Remember the rich young ruler? The Scriptures say Jesus looked at him and loved him, but He didn't change the standard. No matter how many good things he had done, he still harbored rebellion and self–life in his heart. Jesus didn't offer him an installment plan of 'you're only human — hang around and you'll grow into it.' *Things* were more important to him than Jesus was." Steve didn't slow down. "Contrast that with the woman caught in adultery. She didn't have the same outward appearance of righteousness that the rich young ruler had. In fact, her sin was obvious. But Jesus treated her differently. He forgave her, told her to go her way and sin no more. He didn't soft–sell anything, but He saw the difference between rebellion and weakness." He enunciated clearly. "God loves everyone, but He can't work with rebellion or pride or stiff–necked defensiveness. That's why he didn't chase after the rich young ruler. He couldn't work with him or walk with him until he turned from his love of the world's stuff and his need to be in charge of his own life. You don't see Jesus comforting the rich young ruler with, 'Don't worry, God's grace will cover.'"

"That's where you are badly mistaken...or should I say deceived!" Phil's voice was raised. "You need to hear me carefully. Grace is not a doctrine to be toyed with. I've sat under some of the most learned scholars; I've done exhaustive Greek and Hebrew word studies — I know grace!" He glared intently at Steve. "And you've just demonstrated to me that you don't understand it in the slightest. In fact, if these are the kinds of views you espouse, I'm not sure I want you to be a home group leader!"

Steve didn't flinch. "Phil, I don't believe you have a doctrinal problem with me! I believe it's in your heart. We were both excited when we heard what the Church is really meant to look like. You yourself wanted to go back and talk with Wayne privately. Nobody prompted you to do that. *You* wanted to. Everything was fine until the night of the home group meeting at my house. It was a wonderful time together when we tried to let Jesus have control of the meeting, and you know that! Could it be that letting Jesus have control of our times together means that you can't count on being in charge anymore? Is that what really offended you? Is it your pride, your ambition, your paycheck...?

"I mean, here's what I know — I've only had two personal conversations with you in the past week. In the first one you bared your heart, questioning whether all you'd ever done was wrong. The next thing I know, I'm in your office with a man you barely know, listening to slander about Wayne Davidson. That doesn't sound like a doctrinal problem to me. It sounds like a price you're not willing to pay."

72

PHIL THUMBED THROUGH the latest issue of the management magazine to which he subscribed as he sat on the leather couch outside Reynolds' office. Frequent glances at his watch only added to the tension of the wait. *I wonder why he's running so late today. Tuesdays are his early mornings.*

Just then, Nelson Reynolds came walking through the door and stopped by his secretary's desk. "Good morning. Any crises so far today?"

"Good morning, Pastor. No trouble yet. I've booked all of your counseling slots this week, and there's a message from a young lady asking you to perform her wedding."

"Anyone I know?"

"I don't believe so. I think she just heard about how nice a job you did at that wedding two weeks ago. And I don't blame her. That was one of the most beautiful weddings I've ever seen." She looked for the phone number as her boss waited patiently. "Oh...and Phil Malone is here to see you."

"Oh, I didn't see you there, Phil. Good morning!"

"Good morning, Nelson." Phil followed Reynolds into his office and started to close the door behind them. "Do you mind?"

"No, go right ahead. What's on your mind?"

"I wanted to follow up with you on the incident with Steve Parker last week."

"What incident?" The Senior Pastor wrinkled his forehead. "Oh, that awkward conversation in the auditorium? What *was* that all about?"

"Well, Steve's been getting excited about some new ideas, and I'm concerned about the safety of the flock." Phil waited for the words to sink in. "I've grown increasingly alarmed at the way Steve Parker is running his home group. He is taking some dangerous liberties."

"Dangerous?" Reynolds took his glasses off and looked across the desk into Phil's face. "That's a serious accusation to level against someone for simply not using your curriculum."

That stung. "Nelson, this is not about my curriculum. Last week, Steve invited some nonmembers to speak to his home group."

"Without consulting anyone?"

"Yes!"

Reynolds raised an eyebrow. "Who are these people?"

"One of them is the former pastor of Hampton Street Bible Church, and the other used to be a Bible professor at the college. They've both left their positions, perhaps ousted by members or administration — there is some mystery about it all. And now they seem to have a vendetta against organized religion."

"Sounds like they're the problem, not Steve."

"That might have been true two weeks ago, but now he's bought into their whole idealistic, dangerous story."

"Have you tried talking with him?"

"Twice! He's not planning to stop and is aggressively pushing their views."

Reynolds rose to his feet and began pacing. "I had a lot of hope for Steve. He was so genuine, so full of energy."

"I hate it, too, but it's got to stop. He can't keep leading a home group!"

Reynolds stopped pacing, breathed a sigh, and looked out the window. "Agreed." He turned back to Phil. "I'll talk to him."

"WHAT IS IT, SWEETHEART? Is everything all right?" She took the telephone receiver from him and put her hand in his. Teresa hadn't seen Steve cry in a long time. Her heart began pounding as her mind raced with the possibilities. *One of his parents?!* Her fears were cut short by Steve's broken reply.

"I...I just can't believe it."

"Can't believe what?" she asked, almost frantic.

"That was Nelson Reynolds. He asked me to step down as home group leader and to not meet with that group anymore."

"What?" She cocked her head and squinted. "I don't understand. Why? I thought things were going well."

"Phil didn't think so."

"Did he say *anything* else?"

"He said..." Tears streamed down Steve's face. "He said he would pray for me and the people I may have influenced."

Steve rose, walked into his bedroom and closed the door.

73

TONY WIPED HIS HANDS on his white pants and looked at his watch. *11:05. Betta' hurry.* He quickly set the napkin–rolled silverware in place, straightened the salt and pepper shakers and moved on to the next table.

He pulled a cardboard table–tent out of his apron pocket and smoothly inserted it into the plastic display. He checked both sides, making certain it was straight. *That picture oughta sell 'em.* He studied the picture of Vito's new Lemon Cheesecake Supreme. *Mmmm.* He then flipped it to see a large slice of chocolate cake on display beside a generous scoop of vanilla ice cream. Tony involuntarily licked his lips.

As he finished wiping the table, the host seated an early

customer in the booth behind him. "I'll be right wit' ya," Tony promised over his shoulder as he walked toward the kitchen, carrying a gray plastic bus tray.

Tony returned to his patron, pulled a pen out from behind his ear and began, "Hi, my name's Tony. I'll be your waita'..." He caught himself. "Hey, I know you." He patted the dark-haired man on the arm. "You're..." He snapped his fingers, hoping to jar his memory. "You're Phil. Wayne's friend. Good to see ya!"

"Good to see you, too, Tony." Phil extended his hand. "How's business?"

"Can't complain." Tony accepted the offered hand and pumped it with a strength that displayed his pleasure. "Ya seen your buddy Wayne lately? How's he doin'?"

Phil lowered his eyes to the table. "Well, I'm afraid things aren't so good right now."

"What?" Tony's mouth dropped open. "He ain't sick or nothin' is he?"

"No, Tony." Phil sighed. "That's not it." Phil shook his head.

"Well, what then?" Tony raised his voice. "You and him havin' a fallin' out?"

"No, not really. I mean, I tried to help him...but..." Phil shook his head.

"Is he in trouble?" Tony sat down across from Phil. "C'mon. Ya gotta tell me. I like that guy."

"Well..." Phil seemed to consider. "Okay, I guess you ought to know." Phil's look became more serious. "I'm not sure you'll understand this, Tony, but Wayne's gotten himself in some hot water — spiritually."

"Hot watta?" Tony looked confused — as Phil intended him to.

"You know I'm a pastor at Metro Chapel, right?"

Tony nodded his head and Phil continued. "You see, that's the reason I was in here with Wayne the last time. I was trying to help him see the mistake he was making. Tony, you must understand I care about him and want the best, but I've got to tell it to you straight."

Tony was captivated, looking right into Phil's face. "Tell me straight."

Phil nodded. "Wayne and his friends are on a path that

is...well..." He looked from side to side. "I don't know how else to say this...sort of cultic." He paused to let the words find their mark. "They're very controlling of people and prone to use guilt to pressure and oppress each other." He shook his head again, carefully considering his next sentence. "They have a harsh view of God and strong legalistic tendencies. I've tried talking to them, but..." He let his sentence fall.

He looked at Tony, who seemed lost. "Most importantly, Tony...be careful!" Phil's voice was stern. "I'd hate for anyone else to fall prey."

Tony just stared through blurred eyes at Phil. "So, ya gonna eat?"

Phil sat up. "Yeah, sure. I've got a little bit of time. Let's see..."

Tony gave Phil a small nod of his head in deflated acknowledgement and turned to go back to work. His melancholy mood stood out in stark contrast to his nature. "What'll it be?"

74

THE AIR WAS THICK. The pit in Wayne's stomach matched the solemn faces in the room. They had shared many lighthearted evenings at the Davidsons' home since beginning this new adventure, but tonight was not one of them. The Stones, Amy, George, the Parkers, Eric, and Virginia were all there. The day had evolved spontaneously. The women had been together for lunch and ended up praying instead. Ted and George had been with Wayne since late afternoon. Now, this living room of friends searched each other for answers.

"How are we ever going to be able to win back his trust now?" Wayne disturbed the silent circle of faces by voicing his perplexity. "He seemed so close to the Kingdom... Ahhhhhh...What would motivate a man who claims to be a Christian leader to poison a young lamb trying to learn who Jesus is? As Jesus said, millstones were made for this!"

A long pause hung in the air.

"Did you get to talk to him?" Emily broke in. "To try and dispel the paranoia?"

"Yeah, we tried that, Emily," George answered. "Tony was polite but very brief and uncomfortable. It was obvious real damage has been done."

Wayne looked across at Ted. "The real battle is to help him clear his head so he can hear the gospel with the fresh perspective he had before — without it coming across like we're just trying to defend ourselves, or like we're trying to chase him."

"He thinks we view God as a harsh judge and said he doesn't want to get to know a God like that." Wayne slapped his knee, then continued, "What we need is for God to give us some kind of key, some kind of doorway back into Tony's heart. And I just can't find one." Wayne placed his face in his hands and rested his elbows on his knees.

A long gap of silence filled the air as everyone strained to see this puzzle from a different vantage point.

"I have a thought." Amy's voice caught everyone off guard, but her hopeful tone was refreshing.

"Please, go ahead," Ted and Carolyn encouraged simultaneously.

"Well, when we were at the restaurant that time," Amy began slowly, "it seemed like the thing that was the closest to Tony's heart was his father. Remember?" She looked around the room. "I was thinking that if you showed him that getting to know God was like his relationship with his father, he might be able to understand where you're coming from. His natural father believed in discipline, but Tony wouldn't view him as harsh. He disciplined out of need. It was for his children's own good. And that's how God is, isn't He?"

The dilemma, which before was a vapor and impossible to grasp, solidified. Her words — God's words — had given it form, as if it were now a child's puzzle, held simply in one's hand, with the last piece an obvious match.

"I think you're on to something, Amy." Wayne was already relieved.

The saints spent some time asking God to provide an opportunity to share these things with Tony and thanking Him for His provision.

As the last of his company piled out of the house, Wayne reflected to Emily, "Surely the hand cannot say to the eye, 'I have no need of you.' God really does use all the members of the body together and forces us all to need each other, doesn't He?"

"Yeah, and remember what else it says?" Emily replied. "The parts of the body that seem to be weaker are indispensable."

IT WAS TONY'S DAY OFF, and as Wayne had guessed, it was laundry day. Tony was busy preparing the week's wash when George and Wayne pulled up into the oil–stained driveway. Wayne's second guess was also right. The lawn was high as usual. For a bachelor who lives at work, the details of maintaining a home always seem to be one step behind.

George helped Wayne pull the lawn mower out of the back seat, and without being detected, they started the engine and began to battle the jungle in the front yard. George took the first shift as Wayne hoped the noise of the mower would rouse an opportunity to talk with Tony.

"Hey, what's going on here?" Tony's question was interrupted by the mischievous grin on Wayne's face.

"Oh, nothing," Wayne responded as he looked Tony in the eye.

Tony looked down to hide his softening uncomfortableness.

"Listen, Tony," Wayne continued, "I know you've been given some warnings about us. I know you've been told we have a harsh view of God and that we nitpick each other. I wish I knew some way to convey to you the reality of it all. While we do care about each other and the Words of God, we really are doing nothing more than what Jesus commanded: 'Teach them to obey everything I have commanded you.'"

Tony kept staring at the ground.

"Tony—" Wayne continued, "did your father ever discipline you when you were younger?"

Tony's eyes brightened at the mention of his father. "Ya betta believe it!" he replied. "Any time I was out of line, I knew I was going to get a good whelping from my fadda when he found out about it."

Wayne's heart burned within him as God's creative wisdom unfolded. "Well, do you think your father was a harsh man?"

"No! No way!" The response was instantaneous. "He was kind, real kind. But he just knew it would ruin a kid if he didn't have any discipline. You know, he'd be spoiled rot'n."

"Tony, that's the same way God is. He's not harsh and oppressive. He's not looking over our shoulders trying to find ways to stop our fun and make our lives difficult. That's not His nature." Wayne furrowed his eyebrows as he looked into Tony's face. "But, on the other hand, just like *your* father, He disciplines us for our good. He knows the things that will kill us, and He works real hard to keep us from trashing our lives."

A light bulb came on in Tony's eyes. It clicked — a revelation of God's nature, breaking down walls and uprooting suspicions. "Ya know, that makes a lotta sense. Like my fadda used to say...."

It was good to see the real Tony again.

75

"SURE YOU DON'T NEED anything while we're in here? My treat."

"Nope. All covered in the fishing, skiing and roller blade departments." Wayne chuckled as they passed a bass boat holding two mannequins, complete with rods, reels and the latest fashion in life jackets. "Thanks, anyway!" Wayne followed Ted to the checkout counter where Ted laid a shoe box and a pair of socks on the counter.

"Hey, I can't believe I forgot to tell you — our friends from Miami are passing through town and I asked if they could stay for a while," Wayne said, as Ted took the plastic bag from the cashier and thanked her with a smile.

"Really?! Are they going to?"

"Day after tomorrow. They're hoping to stay two or three days."

"Sounds great! I can't wait to meet them." Ted unlocked the doors to his car and they both climbed in. "I feel like I almost know them from what you've told me." Ted started the car. "Is Mark coming?"

"Yeah. He is!" Wayne's face lit up. "We're all looking forward to it. Blake's excited about giving his room up for a few days, and Emily's already started planning meals. She was digging through her cookbook for enchilada recipes last night after they called."

Ted joined Wayne in a laugh. "Maybe I should brush up on my high school Spanish."

"I think this will be a profitable time for all of us."

STEVE AND TERESA WALKED hand–in–hand up the driveway toward the Davidsons' front door. Looking over at his wife, Steve's sober expression gave way to a grin.

"I haven't seen that face in a while." Teresa returned her husband's smile and they both laughed.

"I'm glad we're here," he acknowledged.

As they walked through the entryway, the faces greeting them were a breath of fresh air. Wayne and Emily, Ted and Carolyn, George, Eric, Virginia, and Amy — they were all there, along with three men Steve didn't recognize. He instantly felt at home and let out a big sigh as he gave Wayne a bear hug.

"You certainly haven't lost any strength," Wayne gasped. Both men laughed as Steve loosened his grip.

"Let me introduce you to some of our friends from Miami." Wayne turned to his guests. "Steve Parker, this is Mark Wallace. I met him on the airplane."

"Good to meet you." Steve shook his hand firmly.

"And this is Luis Rodriguez and Richard Costa, a couple of the brothers who are also part of the Church there."

"What brings you guys to town?" Steve initiated, pushing past his own turmoil.

"We were out west visiting some saints," Mark volunteered, "and now we're passing through on our way back to Miami."

"Welcome to town," Steve smiled, shaking each hand. The warmth on their faces was striking.

"Well, Steve, is everything Okay with you?" Wayne asked. "I know it's been rough."

"Rough? Now that's an understatement!" Steve shook his head back and forth.

"Have you made a decision yet?" George asked as everyone ambled for a seat in the living room.

"Not yet." Steve took a seat on the floor next to the recliner Teresa had chosen. "I'm still trying to sort it all out. Half of me wants to stay and plow on, the other half just wants to quit. I'm not really sure what to do."

"Leave Metro?" Carolyn ventured. "Why?"

"Well, I'm not sure if Wayne told you, but I've been asked to step down as a home group leader."

"You're kidding?!" Carolyn stared at Steve incredulously.

"I wish I was."

"Did they say why?" Ted asked.

"They felt it was divisive for me to introduce unsanctioned persons to the home group."

"But Phil was there," Carolyn countered. "It wasn't a big secret."

"Phil told Nelson Reynolds he was there to 'protect' the flock, not to endorse the men." Steve shook his head. "I even told him I wouldn't bring anyone else to meet with the home group without their approval."

"What'd he say to that?" Ted asked.

"He said they feel my current views about the nature of the Church are not in keeping with the goals of Metro Chapel."

Teresa leaned forward and placed her hand on Steve's shoulder to console him as he continued. "I just wish it wasn't so complicated. All I really wanted to do was care about people." He shrugged with his hands. "I wasn't trying to start anything or be divisive."

The gathered friends sat in silence, wishing they could ease Steve's discomfort. Minutes passed. Steve scanned the room hoping to solicit a response.

"Would it be all right if I shared some thoughts?" came the quiet voice with a slight Spanish accent. All eyes turned toward Luis Rodriguez.

"Sure, that'd be great," Steve encouraged.

"I was just wondering if the solution might be easier than you think."

"What do you mean?" Steve asked hopefully.

"Well, we both know there's no such thing as a 'home group' anyway. Right?"

"Huh?" Steve looked perplexed.

"I mean, from God's vantage point. Keep in mind that home groups and home group leaders are man–made ideas. They don't

254

really exist in the Word of God, without doing some serious stretching. The Church was, in the Bible, a family — and simply had no 'Church building' for 250 years after Pentecost. Of course they met in homes — but there were no 'home groups.' Their lives were simply intertwined with each other *every day*."

"Okay, I think I follow you."

"Well, if all you want to do is to care about people — just do it! You don't need a title or a home group for that." Luis paused, studying Steve's face. "In a sense, they've done you a favor by lightening your load. The title and props are unneeded clutter. Now your schedule is free to be involved in the lives of hungry lambs seven days a week."

"Wow! That's a great idea! Why didn't I think of that?" Steve stared around the room, almost embarrassed by the simple wisdom.

"Just think about this get–together that we are having right now," Luis continued. "Who are we, after all? We're not a home group and this is not a worship service. We're just Christians who are devoted to God and trying to care for each other."

His expression grew more serious. "But keep in mind, not everyone welcomes others' investment in their lives. In fact, most would prefer not to have it. They would rather sit at home and watch TV. For those, there's reason to question whether or not they honestly consider the Word of God to be the measuring rod of who they really are spiritually." A chorus of nods confirmed Luis' reminder. "But there *are* others who, somewhere inside, have a longing for more. Focus on those people, pour your life out for them, and see if God blesses it. Depending on what happens, God can use all of that to teach and expand you, as well as to direct your future path."

The room was silent with everyone nodding agreement. Luis seemed to capture the heart of God and provide a way out of Steve's dilemma. Although he was a slight man and spoke humbly, his words seemed to carry an authority.

"That doesn't mean you've got to compromise and blend in." Luis leaned forward. "Stand up for Jesus' teachings," he said with energy. "Expect the saints and the leaders to conform their lives to the Word of God — with patience and kindness, of course. But don't just walk away. Continue trying to help until they flatout tell you they don't want it, and maybe ask you to leave. As Jesus said, 'I would have gathered you as a hen gathers her chicks, but you would not.' He tried until they *killed* Him."

Luis paused, closing his eyes momentarily. He seemed to be deciding if there was anything more to say. "Chew on it, Steve. Mark, Richard and I, and of course all of these guys, will pray for you about all of this."

Steve began to feel unburdened. *Maybe this WILL work together for good.*

VITO STUDIED HIS SPARSE RESERVATION LIST intently, as if the act alone would fill it up. *Light afternoon. Lightest I've seen in months. Hope it fills up soon.*

No sooner had the thought occurred to him, when he heard a multitude of voices in the outer entranceway. Vito looked up as Wayne pulled the inner glass door open and stood aside, letting a throng of friends pass through into the restaurant.

"Ahh, Mr. Davidson, I knew I could count on you to fill the place up. Our favorite customers are those who make a habit of bringing friends."

Wayne smiled broadly and yelled over the pack. "Hi, Vito. We're going to need the whole back section today. Think you can handle it?"

"For paying customers, we can always accommodate." The vertically challenged host smiled as he scanned the crowd. He recognized most of the faces.

"And who would you like to have as your server today, Mr. Davidson? Tony, perhaps?" Vito asked with a knowing glance.

Wayne smiled. "Yes, if possible. And Vito," he continued as he placed both hands around Vito's neck in mock strangulation, "call me 'Wayyyne!'"

Vito laughed. "Yes, Mr. Wayne, right this way."

The guests wove their way to the somewhat secluded back section. Teresa and Emily arranged the children into their own booth, careful to remove all the glass salt and pepper shakers — potential projectiles for little hands. Eric pulled the chairs away from the tables, and Ted and Steve began sliding them together into a long line.

Tony Veneziano's voice could be heard before he left the kitchen. He backed out the double doors with a pizza in both hands, and headed for the only other patrons in the restaurant. His jaw dropped as he saw the troop. He caught Wayne's eye and flashed a quick smile.

Wayne leaned toward Luis. "That's Tony, the guy I told you about."

Luis nodded. "Aha," he chuckled. "I'd like to meet him."

Moments later, Tony leaned over Wayne's end of the table. "Hey, Wayne." He looked around to make certain others were watching. "What'cha doin' here? The grass in my yard's getting a little long, ya know." He leaned closer. "Ya think you could come by this weekend?"

"Yeah, Tony, you bet. As a matter of fact, I could use the extra cash," Wayne taunted.

"Well, if you're looking for extra cash, we'a looking for a cook and a waita' here."

"Are you serious?"

"Sure. Got any experience with linguine?" Tony was surprised at Wayne's interest.

"Of course. I eat it all the time."

"Uh, maybe the waita' job." Tony winked.

"Excuse me, Tony." Eric was standing at the opposite end of the table holding a menu in his hand. "I can't seem to find your whole wheat pizza crusts on this menu."

Tony straightened up and answered, "Uh, all of the pizzas come on wheat crust. That's what flour's made of, right?"

Eric cleared his throat, preparing to launch into a subroutine. "Actually, if it isn't called 'whole wheat flour,' it's been stripped of the bran and the wheat germ and bleached so that all you really have left is wallpaper paste."

"So, did you want pepperoni or sausage on your wallpaper paste?" Tony asked sardonically.

Without flinching, Eric answered, "Neither. I'll stick with pineapple and jalapenos, thanks."

"Okay," Tony answered with a grimace, "one pineapple–jalapeno. Comin' up."

The pizzas came sooner than everyone expected and George offered a prayer of thanks. Then they continued their conversations and enjoyed the pizzas. Before long, they were the only customers left and had free reign of the restaurant and much of Tony's attention. He even provoked Wayne and Luis into a lively conversation about boxing and about life.

The evening ended with a simple song to Jesus, with Tony and Vito looking on.

76

"I HEAR YOU'VE BEEN quite busy this past week—" Phil said, making no attempt to hide his sarcasm, "visiting different members of Metro."

"Yes, it's been a really busy week, but it's been good." Steve repositioned the telephone to his other ear and sat down at his desk.

"Well, to tell you the truth, Steve, I'm not real comfortable with what I've been hearing."

Steve's neck tightened as he remembered the last conversation with Phil. "What do you mean?"

"Last night you were with the Smiths." Phil paused for effect. "The night before that, the Evans. Before that, it was the Woodells and the Cartrights."

"Yes, that's right and...those night's were all encouraging." Steve's words were deliberate as he tried to make sense of what seemed like accusations. "Is there a...problem?"

"You bet there's a problem! You were told to step down from leadership at Metro."

"And I've done that." Steve was surprised at Phil's tone.

"Ah, come on Steve. We know what you're up to. You're promoting Wayne Davidson's nonsense and trying to gain a following after yourself."

A following? He took a deep breath, hoping to ease his confusion. "Phil, wait a minute. All I've been doing is caring about the other members of the body of Christ and finding ways to serve them. That's all."

"Nonsense! You were asked, by your senior pastor, to step down because you are unfit to hold a position of responsibility! And the next thing we know, you're sneaking around making visitations, the very thing you were asked not to do."

"What?" he asked reflexively, unable to believe the accusation just leveled at him. "Phil, I'm trying to obey Jesus. You can't ask me to stop obeying Jesus. I'm *not* making visitations. And I'm obviously not trying very hard to be sneaky, based on the list of names you just gave me."

"I'm not asking you to stop obeying God. I'm asking you to obey the authority God has put over you!"

"I have made every effort to obey that authority." Steve spoke calmly. "You asked me to step down and I did. But caring about other believers is a direct command. I can't understand why you see that as a problem." He spoke with emphasis. "That's Christianity! Are you asking me to stop being a Christian?" He paused for a second. "I can't do that."

"What I'm asking you to do is to stop worming your way into people's homes and stirring up trouble!"

"That's not what I've been doing. I'm just trying to love people. And I have no interest in winning anyone over to anything except Jesus and His Ways. Why don't you come with us, so you can see? We'd love to have your company. Seriously."

"I'm asking you to stop your visits! If you can't stop yourself from talking about these heretical, divisive, and legalistic topics, then I don't want you to set foot in another Metro member's house. Is that clear?!"

Steve was stunned. *I can't believe he's saying this. God, what do I do now?*

"IS that clear?!" Phil was insistent.

Steve searched for words, his heart racing. "Phil, if I can't spend time with my brothers and sisters, then what does being a Christian mean?"

"Let me put it this way: if you can't submit to the leadership of this congregation and the decisions they make, then you are NO longer welcome."

"But Phil, it doesn't have to be this way. Please listen."

"Yes, Steve, it does have to be this way. Let me make it very clear: you are unwelcome at Metro! You are divisive, ambitious, and insubordinate. As a responsible leader of this Church, this is a step I have to take."

Steve's heart broke as his hand went limp. He could feel a

lump form in his throat. He knew the Great Shepherd of the sheep was heartbroken, too. Yet, he also knew that strange peace which comes from nearness to God — the nearness that comes from following through hard times and pain.

77

"HEY, WHO MADE THIS potato salad?"

"I made it," Virginia admitted from the kitchen. "Why? Is it okay?"

"Are you kidding? Don't worry. It's great!" Emily responded. "May I have the recipe?"

"Sure, it's nothing special."

After dinner, the children poured out the back door and onto the large, wooden swing set which rested in a fresh pile of sawdust. Ted had hung the final swing earlier that day. Emily and Wayne had both been surprised when Ted dropped by three days earlier as Wayne was leaving for work. He showed them a rough drawing of the swing set and asked if Blake could build it with him.

Blake was thrilled. He found Ted's investment in him fun and educational. He loved the trip to the hardware store, the adventure of driving nails and using the hand saw. And tonight, he was eager to show Amanda and Marie all the features of his masterpiece. Wayne was thankful to have another brother caring for his son, and Ted was glad for the opportunity to use his light summer schedule to help.

Once the dishes were washed, the ladies made their way into the living room where the circle of men were listening as Eric described a conversation he'd had.

After Eric was finished and the ladies were all seated, Wayne asked, "Hey guys, could I run something past everyone?" Taking the silence as consent, he continued. "I have a unique opportunity that's been thrown at me and I want to see what you guys think about it."

"Fire away," Ted invited.

"Tony has dropped a couple of hints about me being a waiter with him at Vito's." Wayne fiddled with the carpet he was sitting on. "I've never really taken him seriously. But it's been on my mind a lot since we've recovered some ground with him. I wonder if it might provide a great chance to continue sharing the gospel with him."

"How would it pay?" Ted inquired.

"With tips, it should come out about the same as I'm making now, which isn't quite enough. But it could work for awhile. Who knows, maybe I have a future in restaurant management?" Wayne chuckled to himself. "I really wouldn't be taking the job for the pay, but to spend more time with Tony."

"Well, I don't know why you shouldn't," Amy volunteered. "It sounds to me like a great idea."

"Me, too," Carolyn agreed.

After a brief pause George's face grew serious as he spoke up. "I only have one concern." George let his words trail slowly. "Are you sure you're qualified? I mean, you're not Italian."

Wayne maintained his poker face, despite the laughter around him, and replied, "Didn't you know, my mother's maiden name was Marciano?"

78

THE PAPERS ON NELSON REYNOLDS' desk were piled high. His hair was disheveled. His glasses were on the end of his nose.

"This is ridiculous. Everyone wants twice as much as we have."

It was budget time at Metro. He had been in his office all day long and was growing increasingly annoyed by this painstaking part of his job.

Outside his closed office door, Reynolds' secretary was busy preparing to leave for the day. She was exhausted, having spent her day preparing the bulletin and diverting the phone calls and visitors which threatened to interrupt her boss.

As she pulled her purse out of a desk drawer, she caught sight of Phil approaching, briefcase in hand. He was heading toward Reynolds' door.

"Don't go in there!" She was energetic. "He's not seeing anyone today."

"This is important!" He hesitated, looked at his watch, then continued on his path.

"Phil!" The tension in her voice was obvious. "Wait!...Don't!"

It was too late. Phil had the door open and was inside before she had time to leave her seat.

Reynolds looked up from the piles of paper in front of him, then threw himself back into his chair. "Not today, Phil. I'm up to my ears in this budget stuff. I have no time."

"I know. But this'll be quick. It's about Steve Parker."

"So, what's up with our friend, Mr. Parker?"

"He's leaving."

"Leaving Metro?"

"That's right."

"Oh, really." Reynolds took off his glasses, wiped his forehead and closed his eyes. "I was hoping it wouldn't come to this...Anything we can do to get him to stay?"

"I don't think so, Nelson. To be honest, I'm not sure we want him to. Ever since you asked him to step down as home group leader, he's been all over the place trying to propagate his Church fantasy nonsense."

"You're kidding." Reynolds sighed. "Do you think anyone else will go with him? He has a lot of friends at Metro."

"It's possible."

"Soooo," Nelson stared into space, "what you're telling me is we could lose that whole home group." He paused again. "That could be $25,000 a year."

Phil cringed. Although he thought in similar terms, he wasn't accustomed to hearing it spoken out loud.

"We can't have another contingent leaving us and going to Monument Street or Faith Christian." Reynolds shook his head.

Phil allowed several seconds to pass. "Well, Nelson, we haven't officially broken that home group apart. Maybe we should leave it intact. Some studies have shown that removing the support of a group atmosphere actually breeds discontentment. If we leave them together under strong leadership, we increase the odds that most of them will stay."

Reynolds rapped his fingers on his desk, then looked at Phil. "I like the idea. Let's keep them together. And how would you feel about stepping in as an interim home group leader — until the dust settles?"

Phil fought to keep the grin off his face. "Sure, Pastor, anything for the flock."

79

"HELLO." Catching the phone on its fourth ring, Steve hurriedly set his briefcase on the kitchen table and shut the door.

"They're not gonna get away with this!" Fred's voice roared on the other end of the line.

Steve sat down and collected his thoughts. "Fred, calm down. What's the matter?"

"They asked you to leave, didn't they?"

"Fred, that doesn't matter…"

"Didn't they?"

"Yes, but…"

"I thought so! I don't like it one bit," he snorted. "We're on your side, Steve. In fact," his voice raised, "some of us are thinking about leaving Metro Chapel and joining your group!"

"Fred, you've got to calm down."

"I'm going to stand up for you, Steve. I'm going to give them a piece of my mind!"

"Fred, please. Listen to me." Steve took off his tie and started pacing with the phone. "I appreciate what you're trying to do. You're a good friend. But to be honest, I don't have a 'group' for you to join. You and I are joined together by God's Spirit and by our commitment to each other. That's a gift from God. No one could have legislated it into happening, and no one can destroy it now by organizational structure."

Fred paused, collecting his thoughts. "That makes sense."

"Now, as for leaving the home group — you have close relationships with people there. Do you really think Jesus wants you to bail out now?"

"But *you* left," Fred objected.

"I was told to leave. That hasn't happened to you, Fred. At least, not yet."

"Well, I might be next after I talk with the pastors about how you were treated."

"Fred, stand up for truth — not me!" Steve's voice was firm, but gentle. "This needs to be about Jesus and His Word. Please, don't reduce it to a quarrel about me. Let your convictions be from the Words of Jesus and the Apostles. Stand up for what *Jesus'* Church must be — for *Jesus'* sake!"

Steve could hear Fred squirming on the other end as he listened to Steve's counsel. "Okay, okay. You're right," Fred relented. "So, do you think I should go to the home group meeting?"

"Yes. Give it a shot. Who is the new group leader? Do I know him?"

"You mean you haven't heard?"

"No. Why?"

"It's..." Fred hesitated for a second. "It's Phil Malone."

Ahhhhh. Steve's heart sank. *Now what?*

Fred couldn't stand the silence. "Hey, Steve, you all right?"

"I'm fine. I just had to look at Jesus for a second to get my balance. Sorry. Hey, Fred, be an ambassador of Christ tonight, as if God were making His appeal through you in whatever area of life that comes up tonight. Deal?"

"Okay. I'll do it. Will you still be up if I need to call you late tonight?"

"If you think you need to, I'll definitely be up."

"BOY, HE WAS sure upset!"

"What was that, Wayne?" Emily asked with surprise as she walked into the bedroom.

"My father."

"Did you just get off the phone with him?"

"Yeah, and he wasn't happy about my new career path." Wayne finished his sentence with sober thoughtfulness. Actually, his father's reaction didn't surprise him, though it did hurt. "He thinks I'm being financially irresponsible by deciding to be a waiter. I hate having him look down on me. I tried to explain my reasons from a Kingdom perspective, but he just didn't understand. I wish he would accept my decisions and trust me."

"Wayne, don't be upset with him," Emily pleaded. "He means well. He's just never quite understood your heart for God."

"I know, Em. But it's not just my heart he doesn't understand. It's God's heart. Dad's been a church–goer for years. Yet letting Jesus be the Lord of daily decisions is still a foreign idea. I reminded him that Jesus said to seek first the Kingdom...not security. But Dad just kept talking about 'stewardship' and really didn't want to consider the teachings of Jesus."

Emily paused and let a brief silence prepare Wayne for her answer. "I agree with what you just said, wholeheartedly. But I'm still concerned with how it's affecting you. You can't allow anyone's opinion of your honest desire to follow Jesus to cause you to become anxious. I know you want to uphold Jesus' ways, but make sure your jealousy is really for the truth and not for your reputation in your father's eyes. It's Jesus' opinion of you that matters."

Wayne's burden deflated as the simple truth sank in. "You're right...you're right, Em. Thanks."

STEVE LAID THE SMALL BOOK DOWN on the end table by the recliner and got up to silence the telephone. *Wow. 11:30.*

"Hey, Steve, it's Fred. Sorry I made you stay up so late."

"No problem. I was reading an Andrew Murray book. Had no idea it was even this late."

"Just wanted to let you know everything went okay tonight."

"Really? Good. I'm glad to hear it."

"Yeah, yeah. It went fine," Fred stated abruptly, anxious to end the conversation.

"Anything noteworthy?"

"Nothing really. We just had our devotional and went home."

"That was it?"

"Yep...Listen, Steve, I'd better go."

"Whoaa, Fred! Is there something you're not telling me?" Steve had known Fred for a long time. He knew something wasn't right. "Did something happen to upset you?"

"Look, Steve, I really don't want to get into all this." Fred's tone seemed curt.

"Fred, if you didn't think you should talk about it, why did you call?"

"Because *I* keep my word."

Lord, what is going on? Steve groped for words. "Fred, I don't know what happened, but we can work it out. We're friends, remember?"

"Friends! Well, that was before we heard the *whole* story."

"Fred, what are you talking about? *What* whole story?" Steve's heart sank again as the pieces began to fall into place. "What did Phil say tonight? Do you not love me enough to get a little more information before you shut me out and judge me guilty?"

"Listen! If you've got anything to say, you can take it up with the leadership at Metro Chapel."

There was a loud click, and Steve was left holding the receiver, unable to move. *Oh, God, help me!* He laid his head against the wall.

Do not be deceived:

God cannot be mocked.

A man reaps what he sows.

The one who sows to please his sinful nature,

from that nature will reap destruction;

the one who sows to please the Spirit,

from the Spirit will reap eternal life.

Galatians 6:7–8

Seeds and Fruit

80

THOUGH IT HAD BEEN THREE WEEKS since Steve Parker's last conversation with Fred, the wounds were still tender and Steve was still frequently tempted to hide inside himself. The choices he had made over those same weeks, however, demonstrated a Godly confidence and a desire to go on caring for others, regardless of his weakness and pain. Despite his wounds and temptations, he *was* pursuing the Life of the Body of Christ — the best he knew how. On this particular day, for example, he had eagerly embraced Teresa's suggestion to invite some saints over for dessert. He had been excited all afternoon by the prospects of his growing relationships, and was eagerly anticipating the evening.

And now, armed with a small plate of cheesecake and a soda, he made his way toward the hum of conversation coming from his living room.

He was barely out of the dining room when Ashley Davidson scurried past him, roughly brushing his leg. He caught his balance quickly, saved the teetering fork, then stepped against a kitchen cabinet just in time to clear the path for little Marie Stone. He laughed to himself as he watched after the dark–haired Marie, warmth filling his heart. *Precious freedom!*

At the entrance to the living room, he leaned against the wall and took his first bite. Though the room wasn't as full as it had often been on Thursday nights — it didn't matter. The atmosphere was warm and, to him, a breath of fresh air. *Thanks a lot, Jesus.*

"Hey, Steve, thanks for having us over."

Steve turned and smiled warmly at Eric, who stood beside him palming three peanut butter cookies in his left hand and holding a fourth, poised near his mouth, in his right.

"You're more than welcome, Eric. But be careful not to kill yourself with all that sugar," Steve lectured mockingly with his fork. "I'd hate for your first time at my house to make you sick. You might not want to come back."

"Not a chance of that. I'd come back." Eric took a bite of his cookie, then continued as he chewed, "Besides, I've got plenty of carbohydrates in me to dilute the sugar. Mom made spaghetti for dinner."

Steve laughed slightly at Eric's frankness as Wayne and Ted walked up.

"Hey, Steve," Wayne asked, "what do you think about heading to the backyard? It's a nice night, and I know my children could use a chance to burn some energy."

"That'd be great. We'll just have to keep an eye out. There's a creek about fifty yards beyond that big elm." Steve pointed to a distinctive moonlit, old tree looming forty–five feet into the air.

"We're going to take the children outside," Steve told Teresa, who was sitting on the couch beside Carolyn and Virginia. Emily and Amy were seated on the floor in front of her, talking. "Would you ladies like to join us?"

Teresa looked to the others for a hint, then back to her husband. "Would it be okay if we stayed in here?"

"Sure. I think the five of us can handle it." Steve winked at his wife and headed out the door.

"It is so good to see him enjoying himself," Teresa remarked to Carolyn as Ted slid the door shut. "These past few weeks have been hard for him."

"I really appreciate the attitude you've both had through all of this," Carolyn began. "Times of rejection and pain really make it clear who we are on the inside. You've encouraged me tremendously by the way you keep turning to Jesus and choosing to embrace His people and His ways. Thanks."

Teresa smiled, a little embarrassed, as she fought the urge to tear up. "Thanks. I don't think I could have done it without you guys."

Silence held the moment as the ladies each savored the supernatural fellowship Jesus had so graciously given them.

"Can I ask you all about something?" Teresa produced a neatly–opened envelope from the drawer in the end table. "It's a letter I got today."

"Sure," Emily said as Carolyn and Virginia nodded in agreement.

"Carolyn, I'm sure you remember Renee Clark?"

"From college? The leader of the campus women's Christian group?"

"Yeah, that's her." Teresa's face showed a hint of pain as she considered what to say. "Well, we've sort of kept in touch over the last ten years, and I hadn't heard from her in about six months until I got this letter yesterday. I'm not sure what to think about it." She pulled her legs up underneath herself. "So, I was hoping I could get your input." She scanned the four faces around her. "And see if you can help me find out what God might want me to do."

"What's the letter about?" Carolyn asked.

"Well...I normally wouldn't want to share a letter this personal with others, but she specifically asked me to. She's pretty desperate for a solution."

Teresa proceeded to read the lengthy letter, skipping over some parts that seemed the most personal. The letter explained that Renee had found out her husband, a deacon in the local church, had been unfaithful. Renee described her heartbreak and fury over the news. She said her husband had begged her for forgiveness and assured her he wanted the marriage to heal and grow stronger. But Renee wasn't sure she was ready to stay committed to their marriage. She told Teresa she had "scriptural grounds" for divorce and was leaning that way. The tone of the letter revealed some bitterness, but mostly the pain that accompanies a betrayal.

Teresa finished reading, and no one spoke for several moments.

"What's her marriage been like up until now?" Emily asked.

"It's been pretty rocky, lately," Teresa answered. "That's one of my concerns. I hope she's not just seeing divorce as a way out of what's already been a difficult situation."

Virginia felt tears stinging her eyes as she thought about

Renee. She knew what Renee was feeling. It hadn't been too many months since she'd faced very similar struggles herself. Tension, animosity, betrayal. The memories of Hal's sordid life were vivid...and painful.

Virginia clearly remembered the morning last fall when she faced Jesus about it all — honestly expressing her frustrations and her desire to abandon the marriage. As she faced Him that morning, a thought had pricked her. She knew in her heart it was from God — "While we were still sinners, Christ died for us." Through that verse, the true tenacity of God's love struck her deeply, and she knew God wanted her to lay her life down for her husband and trust Him in her circumstances. It hadn't been easy since then, but she had found peace and life as a result of her obedience.

She now cleared her throat and spoke in a soft voice. "I...don't know the answer for this exact situation, but I do know the answer won't be found until Renee faces Jesus. Whether or not she has technical grounds for divorce isn't the main issue. The main thing is, what does the Father want? Maybe He wants to teach her something through all of this. And she'll lose out if she runs away from it." Virginia fought back the tears. "I've been living for the past year in a marriage that hasn't seemed salvageable. But by sticking close to God and not giving up, He's using it to deepen me. It's been hard, but I wouldn't trade the Jesus–centered suffering I've been *given* for anything."

Teresa nodded, thoughtfully, thankful for this look inside Virginia's heart. Carolyn was also rejoicing and thanking Jesus. He had taken the pain — which normally crushes and embitters — and turned it into a tool to deepen her sister. He had also provided a unique situation for this quiet sister to express her heart. *God is good!*

"Well, I don't know about all of you," Carolyn said, "but that sounds like something Renee ought to hear."

"Maybe you and I could write a letter together," Teresa suggested to Carolyn. "I'm sure she remembers you."

Carolyn waited for a minute, considering Teresa's proposition. "I don't know," she mused. "I was thinking face to face might be good. There's nothing like being able to look someone in the eye and share Jesus' heart with them." She looked toward Emily and the others. "How's that sound to you?"

"Sounds good," Virginia responded.

"Do you think we could?" Teresa asked eagerly. "I'd like that."

"Well," Carolyn noted, "here come our husbands. Let's see what they think about the idea of taking a trip together."

"WHAT ARE YOU THINKING about, Steve?" Ted asked, sitting in the motel chair with his feet propped up on the bed.

Steve placed a pillow from the bed under his chest as he supported his weight on his elbows and shifted his body toward Ted. "Oh, I was just thinking about the look on Renee's face earlier when we dropped Teresa and Carolyn off at her house. She looked so empty, so despondent. It's hard to imagine she was once someone that both of our wives looked up to spiritually."

"I know exactly what you mean. I used to think things like this couldn't happen to Christians…"

"Hey, Ted, let's pray for them."

Both men lowered their heads and closed their eyes. Steve's clasped hands gave expression to the strong desire he felt to see Renee's life turn around. "Father, please breathe Your Life into Renee's house this afternoon and tonight. Enable Teresa and Carolyn to inspire hope and faith in Renee's heart. Please open her eyes so she can see that You are mighty to save, that You forgive sins and are willing to make all things new. Allow the choices in front of her to be very clear. We ask in the name of Your Son, Jesus. Amen."

Both men were silent for several moments as they considered the seriousness of the situation with their wives' friend.

"Hey, Steve—" Ted sat up, "you grew up here. Do you have any idea what we could do for the next few hours?"

"How would you like to go for a run? There's a hill I used to run up that has a great view of the city."

"Sounds great."

TED'S FACE STRAINED as he made his way around the bend in the road and saw the crest of the hill a hundred yards ahead. He surged forward, despite his heavy breathing and burning muscles. Glancing next to him, he noticed Steve running with relative ease — his breathing measured, not heavy, his gait bouncy and light.

At last they reached the top and both men stopped running. Ted bent over with his hands on his knees and his chest heaving as he tried to catch his breath. Steve walked to the lookout where he could see the city's skyline in the distance. The sun was low in the sky and cast a reddish hue on the faces of the buildings. He looked thoughtfully at the city for a long time while Ted caught his breath.

"Hey," Ted asked, his breathing still heavy, "where did you learn to run like that?"

"Oh, I ran cross–country in high school and in college. Since then, I've tried to get out a couple times a week, but I haven't had as much time lately.

Ted nodded.

Steve's eyes returned again to the view of the city before them. "You know, the first time I ran up this hill, I was a freshman in high school. I remember looking out at the city and dreaming of being famous one day." The city loomed before them, towering and impressive. Steve pointed to an especially tall skyscraper with copper–colored glass. "See the round structure on top of that building? That's supposed to be the finest restaurant in town. When I was in college, I used to look at that restaurant; I wanted to become rich and have a beautiful wife and eat in places like that all the time." Steve shook his head. "That seems like a distant memory now — like it's not even me."

"It's not you," Ted interjected. "You're a new creation. Remember? The old has gone, the new has come."

"You're right," Steve nodded, "this is the same hill I used to run up. It's the same road. It's the same city. But somehow, it's a different me."

"I used to feel the same way about football stadiums when I was growing up. No matter where I was, I couldn't pass a football stadium without dreaming of becoming a star and playing in the pros one day." Now Ted shook his head, marveling at the changes he had experienced in his life. "Compared to following God and knowing Him, all of my old dreams seem empty and meaningless."

"No kidding!" Steve exclaimed. "And this is only the beginning. God's going to continue to change us for the rest of our lives and show us more and more of what life's all about. All we have to do is stay close to Him."

Steve pointed back to the horizon, where the setting sun blazed like a fireball.

"Wow, that's beautiful!" Ted exclaimed. "A somewhat better destiny, don't you think? Eternally befriended, enlightened and empowered by the Creator of stars of fire! Not bad."

The two watched quietly as the sun continued it's journey.

"I'm looking forward to it."

"Me, too."

THE LATE AFTERNOON SUN shone brightly on Renee's house as Ted and Steve carried their wives' bags to the car. It was a large, attractive house with a well–kept yard — the type of place one usually assumes is the home of a happy family.

"Well, how'd it go, ladies?" Ted asked, as the last door was shut and he put the van into gear.

Carolyn and Teresa looked at each other, both uncertain how to characterize their last twenty–four hours with Renee.

"I think it went okay," Teresa began, "although it sure got off to a rough start. She feels very hurt, and at first a lot of pent–up resentment and anger came out. There were a lot of loud outbursts and tears. It was very ugly for awhile just after we got there."

"It was a delicate situation, for sure," Carolyn added. "On the one hand, we wanted to support someone who is going through a very traumatic time. But on the other hand, we had to help her see that many of her attitudes were unlike Jesus — and she needed to soften her heart and turn away from them. I found myself having to call out to God in the midst of it all. And He really came through, showing us His wisdom and providing keys to her heart that we might have otherwise missed."

"For example," Teresa said, "I think it was a turning point when you asked Renee what she thought Jesus wanted her to do, not just what He would allow. It seemed to stop her in her tracks. From then on, she stopped hiding behind 'her rights' and how she'd been hurt and whether or not she was justified in leaving Frank."

"Well, that really is the point of following Jesus, isn't it?" Carolyn asked. "Sometimes we forget He's alive and has an opinion about what we do. I know I've been guilty of forgetting that."

"So she softened?" Steve asked.

"It took some coaxing," Teresa explained, "but just before lunchtime today, she seemed to honestly face God on all of this. She was shaky and fragile, but I think something genuine transpired between her and God."

"I'm glad to hear that." Ted looked back to his wife. "So, it looks hopeful?"

"Yeah." Carolyn furrowed her eyebrows. "I'd say so. But she is very weak, and doesn't have much support close to her."

"What about some of the other women here?" Steve asked. "Aren't there other women in the church who are trying to help her?"

Teresa shrugged. "Maybe one or two. But they don't seem to know quite how to help. They encouraged her to talk to the counselor on staff."

"That's a shame!" Steve shook his head, grieved to again face how the normal, daily work of the priesthood of believers had been stolen and assigned to the "professionals." *Did Jesus promise to be with us where two or three are gathered...unless no one has a degree? No way! We've got to believe and trust Him for what He said.*

"You know, Steve, something really is wrong with the way Christianity is practiced today." Teresa was speaking with the energy of a first–time discovery. "It's been on my mind a lot this weekend. I was at Frank and Renee's wedding. Remember, they were planning to become missionaries? Now, they're separated and considering divorce. It's like things went backward, not forward. They should be busy changing other people's lives by now. Instead, their own lives have fallen apart. Renee was in better shape ten years ago. Something is very, very wrong when things like this can take place. And the shocking thing is that this is not an isolated case. There are thousands of Franks and Renees out there. It's tragic."

"That's not the only thing that's tragic," Carolyn said. "It's tragic for the children, too. I looked into their eyes several times while we were there. It was obvious they've been affected by all this. Their young eyes showed confusion and pain. My heart just wanted to break when I saw them. They deserve better than this. But even with the children, the posters on their bedroom walls gave subtle hints of a worldly upbringing. Nothing terrible by the world's standards — posters of athletes and singers — but still, it's holding up unbelievers as role models. And that stinks!"

"Right," Ted joined. "It's crazy to idolize someone because he's got great hand–eye coordination or a nice voice. Our children's only heroes need to be men and women who have a deep devotion to Jesus. When we give our affections to something besides Jesus, we are cultivating a love of the world which makes us enemies of God."

The car became silent as each of its passengers was struck deeply by the tragedy and pain that are so much a part of "modern christianity."

Carolyn looked out her window, deep in thought. "If the Body of Christ had truly been functioning as the Body of Christ," she began, "none of this would have needed to happen. But today's church can't function that way, often because too many people's priorities are all wrong. Most people in most churches lead independent lives that center around their own homes and families. It's ironic, but by focusing on the family rather than on Jesus, His commands, and His Body, they lose both — *not* a good idea! A healthy family is the *product* of focusing on Jesus and His life in the Church."

"That's what got Frank and Renee into this mess," Teresa added. "Renee said that Frank had been staying up late to watch movies on cable TV. But nobody in the church knew about it because they only saw each other once or twice a week at a church function. It's all so shallow! It falls so far short of what God wants and intends for His people. Frank was filling his mind with trash, so it's no wonder he got himself in trouble."

"But it doesn't have to be that way for us or *anyone!*" Ted reminded. "Our lives and our children's lives can be different!"

"That's true, Ted," Carolyn said. "There is something very special about walking it out together. This weekend alone has proved that to me." Carolyn turned and looked at Teresa. "You know, Teresa, it has really been special being with you this weekend. I'm sorry it had to be on an occasion like this, but I am grateful to God that He gave us the opportunity to do His work together. I'm looking forward to many more days of working side–by–side, being about our Father's business."

81

PHIL MALONE LOOKED UP from the home group attendance records as Nelson Reynolds walked into his office.

"Hello, Nelson. To what do I owe this pleasure?" Phil wasn't sure, but he thought it might have been the first time Reynolds had ever paid him a personal visit.

Reynolds closed the door behind him. "I've made a decision, Phil." He moved close to Phil and spoke quietly. "I wanted you to be the first to know."

"What is it?"

"Twenty–five years ago, I began to build Metro Chapel from the ground up." He raised his voice and gestured with both hands. "And here it is." He watched out the window, looking from the lawn to the parking lot and back to the building. "I've worked hard...it's paid off, and I'm glad I did it. But I'm ready to move on." He turned back around. "Phil, I've decided to retire early."

Phil remained expressionless.

"And you, Phil, are the man I want to see as Senior Pastor once I leave."

82

WAYNE WAS LEARNING the absolute reality of "the eye cannot say to the hand, 'I have no need of you.'" Although his spiritual life had grown tremendously over the last two years, he still realized that he needed the other gifts the Body of Christ had to offer — even when, as in the Bible, those gifts lived in other cities. This recognition prompted tonight's conference call.

"Luis, this is Wayne. Are you there?"

"Yeah, I'm here — but it sounds like you're in a tunnel."

"Nope, no tunnel. I'm here with George, Ted, Steve and Eric, and we've got you on the speaker phone. Is that okay?"

"Sure, no problem. That's fine. That's what modern technology's for, right? God's purposes."

"Righto. It's the next best thing to being with you there in Miami, though that would be great."

"So, how can I help you guys?"

"Well…we've got a situation here we've not quite been able to figure out what to do with. We were hoping you could help."

"I'll try."

"Well, there's a woman in her middle fifties we met recently. She's the next–door neighbor of Virginia Ramsey. She's been over a few times…but really, we hardly know her."

"So, what's the problem?"

"Well, last night while we were together, she told us she didn't have a 'church home' and that she wanted to be part of 'our group.' I didn't know what to say."

"That does sound like it might have been a little tricky. So what *did* you say?"

"For one thing," George interjected, "we tried to make it clear that we don't have a 'group' to join."

"Did she seem to understand that?"

"Not really," Wayne answered. "But I'm sure it will come up again. That's why we called. We don't want to be rude to her, but none of us is really comfortable with the thought of her just being around, thinking she's a part of something — just because she sat in our living room."

"I can understand your desire to be fair to her," Luis began. "But it would be even more unfair to her and to Jesus to prop up any shallowness by allowing her to 'attend' your living room. If it's not going to go any deeper than that, it shouldn't continue."

"We completely agree," Ted said. "But how do we communicate that in a way that's both clear and hopeful?"

"You might start," Luis said, "by letting her know that God's Kingdom isn't a *place* — nor is it a *group*! According to Jesus, the Kingdom isn't here or there but *within* you. It's found on the insides of people. You can attend a group but you can't 'attend' George or Wayne or Carolyn or Emily…get it?

"Yes, there is something that God views as a local Church, or *lampstand* — as Jesus would call it. But, according to Revelation chapter two, it is something that *God* grants or takes away. Gathering a number of people together for religious purposes does *not* make a group of people into a true Church, no matter how often they meet! Even mighty Ephesus was on the verge of losing its right to be called a true Church — from Heaven's perspective. If they didn't repent and return to their first love, it wouldn't matter if there were ten thousand people who considered themselves a 'part' or a 'member'. God wasn't going to call it a true Church any longer.

"So, not everything that calls itself a 'church' is one — though, no doubt, there are saved people there. Ephesus had more going for it than just about any place today, yet was just about to have the privilege of Jesus' Special Circulating Presence removed. They were saved perhaps, but no longer a Church.

"Secondly, people can't 'join' or 'place membership' even if it is a true Church, or Lampstand. In order to *find* the Kingdom, you must *lose* your life by melting it into the lives of those around you. It's like a mashed potato in a bowl of mashed potatoes instead of a whole potato in a bowl of potatoes. When you give your heart away to others and you receive their heart in return, then you can share in the Kingdom that's within them! But not before!

"You could attend meetings seven days a week until you were a hundred and three and still not be part of the richness of His Kingdom, because you had never melted your *life* into the lives of others. The hand doesn't *attend* the arm for meetings, does it? NO! It's vitally connected! Tissue, veins, bones — *life*. The body of Christ is no different. As Paul said, 'We are members of one another.'"

"We should have recorded this!" Eric blurted. "Then we could have just played it for her."

"The Teacher lives inside of you, too," Luis encouraged. "And the Spirit promises to remind us — so you'll be fine."

"O–K!" The men surrendered in unison.

"Hey, Luis, thanks a lot for your time," Wayne concluded.

"You're very welcome! Glad I was able to help."

83

DING! DING! DING! DING!

Eric looked up in dismay. "Uh, George? There's a train coming."

George looked down the track in both directions. "No, Eric. There's a bell ringing. That's all."

Eric sprang from the car and peered at George through the

open window. "That bell means there's a train coming, George. Get out and help me push."

"Do you see any trains, Eric?"

"No, not yet."

George smiled. "Well, trains don't just sneak up on you. Relax. The engine's just flooded. I'm sure it will start right up in a few seconds."

Reluctantly, Eric climbed back into the car. He sat fidgeting, his eyes darting back and forth between George and the horizon.

"Couldn't we just push the car off the tracks and *then* try to start it?" Eric swallowed hard as he spoke.

George looked at him and smiled again. "Who of you by worrying can add a single hour to his life?"

"It's not the adding I'm worried about," Eric muttered. "It's the taking away!"

A few seconds later, George turned the key again and the engine started. Eric watched until they were clear of the tracks, then sank into an exhausted heap. George peered at his watch. *Already 5:30.* Wayne would be wondering whether anyone was really coming to pick him up from work.

"How did I let myself get talked into taking the back way to Vito's, anyway?" George wondered playfully.

Eric shrugged. "Hey, did I tell you my sister called last night?"

"No. How did that go?"

"Oh...I don't know. Fine, I guess. I mean, it's not like we ever get into any arguments or anything. She thinks I'm a really great brother, and she's happy that I'm happy. But I wish there could be more to it than that."

George pulled up to a traffic light and turned to face Eric. "Like what?"

"Well...her life's a mess. And I don't think she really takes my life with Jesus all that seriously. She thinks it's good for *me*, but that's as far as it goes. And I can't say I blame her. Why should I expect her to take me seriously when I'm always cracking jokes about everything? She probably just thinks this is one more kick I'm on. Know what I mean?"

"I think so."

Eric's eyes narrowed as he sat up. "You know, I always have

something to say. A quick comeback for everything. Ahhhhk! It bugs me!"

George pulled the old Continental up to the curb across from Vito's. He nodded slowly, collecting his thoughts. "There's a certain amount of risk in making wisecracks because it does make you the center of attention," he began.

"But," Eric cut in, "it's not the kind of attention you get because God is overflowing in your life. It's a safer kind of attention. One that's not meant to be taken seriously. I don't want God's life inside of me to be hidden behind my personality." Eric pounded the dashboard with his fist. "Maybe I just need to practice being more sober!"

George shook his head. "You need to *practice* being more real — with yourself and everybody else. How do I become more like Jesus? By acting stoic and serious? No. While it's true that Jesus was a man of sorrows and familiar with grief, He was also full of joy in the Holy Spirit. So how do you know which way to act? By current fellowship — communion with Him. By not doing anything you don't see the Father currently doing — exactly the way Jesus said He functioned. The most serious side effect to joking around all the time is the loss of fellowship with God, not how you're perceived by others. Stay *connected* to the Head, and as John three says, you're guaranteed to be like the wind. Not predictably comical or serious."

Eric ran both hands through his disheveled locks. "You're a good friend, George. You know, I'm gonna need some help learning how to listen to Jesus' voice over the noise of my loud personality. This is uncharted territory for me."

George laid a hand on Eric's shoulder. "God designed your personality; it's not the enemy. It just has to be brought under His government, or it becomes twisted into something that was never His idea."

Eric swallowed hard, then smiled. "That's what I want then, for sure!"

VITO LOOKED UP from behind his cash register as the two men entered the restaurant. With a warm smile and a friendly nod he gestured toward the kitchen.

George and Eric spotted Wayne in the far corner of the large room loading the dishwasher, while Tony scurried from station to station, lending a hand wherever it was needed.

"Now mosta *my* customas really prefer their Alfredo a little creamier," George heard Tony say to one of the new cooks. "Maybe if ya wouldn't mind addin' just a little more parmesan."

Wayne looked up from the pan of baked–on lasagna he was scrubbing and smiled broadly at George and Eric. He noticed a distant look on George's face — something in his eyes. *Hmmm.* Wayne made a mental note of it as he quickly shoved the pan into the dishwasher and untied his apron.

"I was beginning to wonder if you guys forgot about me," he said with a smile.

"We ran into a bit of car trouble," George apologized.

Eric grinned and resisted the temptation to chide George about the car. *Thanks, Father! I want to learn to walk with You — and to encourage my brothers with lightheartedness as YOU see fit, not as I see fit.*

Wayne noted Eric's grin and raised an eyebrow.

"Inside joke," George explained.

Tony looked up and spotted the friends in the corner. He came bounding across the room and stood next to Wayne, beaming from ear to ear. "Hey, thanks for lettin' our star dishwasha stay late taday."

"No problem," George returned with a pat on the back. "Glad we could help."

Just then, Vito poked his head into the kitchen. "You might as well take off, Wayne. I think we've got the rest under control." He started to leave, but stepped fully inside instead. "Besides, if you are still here when the dinner rush pours in—" he raised his eyebrows in mock seriousness, "you're mine again!"

Wayne smiled and put the last of the dishes in the washer. Then grabbing a wad of steel wool, he quickly scoured a spot on the stainless steel sink. Wayne caught one last look from Vito, then raised his hands in surrender. "All right. I'm outta here." He waved to Tony, then threw the steel wool onto the counter.

GEORGE SLID BEHIND THE WHEEL and forced the key into the ignition. Eric scrambled into the back seat and leaned forward on the large, middle armrest.

"I know a shortcut to your house, Wayne," Eric offered.

"*I'll* do the driving, thank you," George scolded playfully. "Remember, we want to keep Wayne alive. Right?"

Wayne fought back the urge to pry this joke out of them, thinking it would be safer not to know.

The three rode in silence for several minutes. Then Eric, leaning over the seat to catch Wayne's attention, asked, "So how's it going with Tony?"

"To be honest, it's hard to tell at times. He's so easy–going, and with his quick wit, I'm not always sure how deep things go."

Eric nodded slowly, reminded again of his own need. "Do you guys have much time to talk while you're working?"

"Well, not so much during the lunch and dinner rushes. I hardly even see him while we're both serving tables. But we do get to be together a decent amount when we're getting things ready. And at night, sometimes, when we're both closing."

"Anything we can be asking Jesus to help with?" George inquired.

Wayne turned in his seat in order to see Eric and George better. "Actually, something that's been on my mind is that I really don't want to see Tony or anyone else after the flesh. If I walk away from a conversation feeling good about it, I don't want it to be because he made me laugh or because I enjoy being around him. I want it to be because I see God's thumbprint there. I want to see the Spirit at work in his life, convicting him and drawing him into a love relationship with Jesus."

George eased the large vehicle into Wayne's driveway. "Well, let's make every minute we have with him count."

"Don't get me wrong," Wayne said. "There have been some good signs along the way. Like the other day, Tony came up and told me that he's been treating one of the cooks pretty bad for over a year. You know, lots of sarcastic remarks here and there. He wanted to make things right, and it seemed like he was actually broken about it. Anyway, he was asking me what I thought God would want him to do."

Wayne unfastened his seat belt and breathed a sigh. "I don't want him to just start becoming 'moral.' He still needs a revelation, a seeing, an experiencing of the person of Jesus in his inner man, just like the Scripture says. I'd really appreciate your pleadings with the Father, guys."

"Can we do that now?" Eric suggested.

"Sounds good," Wayne said as they moved closer together.

"HELLO?"

"Hi, George, this is Wayne. I hope I'm not calling too late."

"Oh, not at all. I was just staying up late to do a little reading."

"Well, the reason I'm calling is because I noticed an unusual expression on your face when you walked into Vito's tonight. I wanted to make sure everything was all right with you."

"Oh, everything's fine. Eric and I had just finished a pretty important conversation in the car right before we walked in. It was good. I'm really glad we got to talk."

"So what did the look mean, if it's okay to ask?"

"When I walked into the restaurant, it was occurring to me that I never could have had that conversation with Eric if I had stayed behind my rostrum and behind my desk at the university. The verse that came to my mind was from First Thessalonians chapter two: 'We loved you so much that we were delighted to share with you not only the gospel of God but our lives as well, because you had become so dear to us.'"

"That's the bottom line, isn't it? Jesus said He came to be *with* them that He might send them out. It was the *'life* that became the light of men' — not *ideas* that became the light of men."

"Exactly! Isn't it so much different than just sharing truths in a classroom or a sermon? It's the way Jesus lived. He shared his life with the disciples day in and day out. And it's the way Paul lived, too. He always seemed to have a group of people with him wherever he traveled. And when he spent some time in a city, he shared his life, not just ideas, with the people. He wasn't a religious expert who dispensed truth at assigned times and places. No pulpit. No speeches or sermons. No titles. No religious garb or lingo. He simply loved people and gave his life away to them."

"I've felt the same way since I started working at Vito's," Wayne added. "It isn't glamorous to do ordinary things with ordinary people. But I'm convinced that daily, real life, countertop–level interaction — and not distant teacher–student information exchanging — is the way God wants us to build into each other. That's the way lives change. *That's* the Kingdom being enlarged — not so much the glamorous, untestable stuff, but hearts being enlarged for Jesus! 'In the pains of childbirth until Christ is formed.'"

"Absolutely," George nodded. "Anyway, those were some of the thoughts flooding my mind when I walked into Vito's tonight. I felt like God was confirming to me that I had made the right decision in leaving the Bible department. I felt awed by God's Goodness and Majesty."

"It makes me think of the verse, 'For the foolishness of God is wiser than man's wisdom, and the weakness of God is stronger than man's strength.'"

"Amen, Wayne. Exactly."

84

PHIL STEPPED DOWN from the stage, confident his delivery was crisp and engaging and the message sound. On this, his first Sunday as Senior Pastor of Metro Chapel, everything was going like clockwork. The audience had received him with applause as he stepped on stage. They had given rapt attention to his sermon, "Blueprint for the Future," in which he had laid out his plans for taking Metro Chapel into the next decade.

"Wonderful sermon, Pastor Malone." This first compliment came from one of the members seated on the front row. "It's comforting to know we've got a visionary like you at the helm now that Pastor Reynolds has retired."

Phil beamed. "Thank you very much." He made his way to the lobby to greet his members on their way out. After the last of them had left, he went upstairs to get his things.

Walking into his office, something new caught his eye. He took two steps back and stared at the wall by his door. *Philip J. Malone, Senior Pastor.* "Hmmm. Looks good in gold."

He only planned to grab his briefcase but was drawn to sit and think before joining his family downstairs. He picked up a pencil and began tapping it on the desk. *This is **my** office.* He liked it...although, somehow, it just didn't seem as large from this side of the desk.

He sat in his chair, soaking up his new surroundings. "Malone, you've done well." *The people love me. This is what I've always wanted. For God's Glory.* Even before he finished his thought, he was stung by an almost unconscious discontentment, as if he were talking himself into rejoicing rather than just letting it out.

He quickly suppressed those thoughts and continued the inventory. Trophies...his diploma...*summa cum laude*...an aerial photo of the property. He felt a swell of pride, but that sense of dissatisfaction remained. *Isn't this what I've always wanted?*

On his desk sat a new computer, the latest and the fastest. Beside it was a photo of his family, framed in mahogany. His wife and children were all smiling. As he stared at it, he again felt...regret. *Oh, it'll all turn out okay. He's just a teenager. He'll come around.*

He shook the thoughts, or tried to, as he continued to scan the room.

SNAP!

He jumped in his seat as the pencil broke in his hand. *What's bugging me?!* He ran through the possibilities in his mind. *I have all I ever wanted. This is the pinnacle I've been living to reach.*

He sat for a few moments in silence, then felt his heart stop as he heard a loud rap at the door.

"Who is it?" Phil snapped, perturbed by the interruption.

"Sergeant O'Donnell with the State Police Department. Could I have a word with you, Mr. Malone?"

Phil's stomach tightened but he maintained control and answered evenly, "Come in."

The solemn face of the state trooper only tightened the knot. His heart rate accelerated and his palms became instantly moist.

"Are you Philip J. Malone?" the blue–uniformed officer asked in an official tone.

Phil swallowed hard, fighting to sound unaffected by this still mysterious visitor. "I am."

"Sir, do you have any idea where your son, Philip, Jr., is right now?"

Phil relaxed a bit, wondering what trouble his son might have caused. "Yes, I believe he's in his room." Phil shuffled, slightly embarrassed. "He usually sleeps in on Sunday mornings."

The officer took a deep breath. "Sir, it is my duty to inform you that there was a single–car, drunk driving accident at four this morning." The man took off his hat. "We believe one of the young men killed in that accident was your son."

The broken pencil slipped from Phil's hand and landed on the carpet.

85

"PIZZA!" DECLARED a young girl full of blonde curls, barely able to balance the pizza box in her hand.

"How much do I owe you, Miss?" Wayne Davidson asked.

"Four hundred seventy–three dollars," the girl said without flinching. She smiled broadly as her father repeated the number incredulously and then opened his hand in her palm, filling it with imaginary money.

"There you go," Wayne said, carefully receiving the box from his youngest daughter, Ashley. "This better be good," he warned with mock seriousness. Ashley, full of delight, carefully placed the imaginary tender into her little pink purse covered with a thousand shiny beads. She looked up and was about to leave when her dad, seeking to enhance the role–playing that she was so obviously enjoying, startled her. "Hey, what about my change?"

Ashley looked wide–eyed, taken back by the question. But she resumed her fantasy with a smile when her father's grin and sparkling eyes revealed he was still playing.

"Hey, Dad, it's your turn," Blake entreated eagerly. They were sitting opposite each other in the living room with a ripe back-gammon game on the table between them.

"Hold your horses, Champ. I'll be with you in a sec." Wayne slowly pivoted in his chair as he watched his little girl skip off to her room to prepare another pizza with her sister Amanda. He savored the moment, reflecting on the changes in his children.

"I think you're just trying to stall, Dad—" Blake said with a playful grin, "because you know the outcome is in–evable."

"That's *inevitable*," Wayne said as he poured the dice from his shaker onto the board.

"In–ev–i–ta–ble," Blake enunciated slowly. "Two and a three," Blake observed. "With rolls like that, I may be right no matter how you say it." Wayne looked up and smiled at his son's quick wit, then resumed his study of how to maximize his unfortunate lot.

Wayne moved his piece, then gathered his dice, internally sifting thoughts triggered by Blake's new vocabulary word. His musing was interrupted when his son announced his own good fortune. "Double sixes, Dad. Sor–ry." He quickly moved various pieces around the board, and as he finished, announced his father's current condition. "Doesn't look good, Dad. Now you have two on the bar, and the only way you can get out is with a five."

Wayne surveyed the situation, conceding his son's analysis with a slow and heavy nod. And that word once again invaded his thoughts.

"Inevitable, Dad."

Wayne rolled a two and a six, neither number able to help him.

"See?" Blake said, rolling his dice. He quickly positioned his pieces as the numbers allowed, grimacing as he debated whether it was wise to have left one of his tokens vulnerable in the fifth position of his home row.

"Do you know what *inevitable* means, Blake?" Wayne asked, tasting an opportunity.

"Sure," Blake answered robotically. "It means: not able to be prevented or avoided." He smiled proudly. "I'm home–schooled."

"I know what Mr. Webster thinks. Now, can you put that in *your* words?"

Blake thought for a minute. "Um…It means that something has to happen, that it can't be stopped. That there is no way out of it. That it's a sure thing."

Wayne smiled and tilted his tumbler, and to Blake's dismay, when the white cubes rested, they reported double fives. Wayne moved his pieces deliberately around the board, noting Blake's expression as the tide of the game turned.

"You know, some things are inevitable, Blake, but many things aren't. God's law of sowing and reaping *is* inevitable. We *will* reap what we sow. But *what* we sow is not inevitable. We have choices." Wayne could see Blake was trying to understand but wasn't quite connecting.

"In this game, for instance, I rolled, by chance, certain numbers and I had to make choices about what to do with those numbers. Some pieces move forward and are given safety; others, I had to leave vulnerable. You also made those kinds of choices. You see, the outcome was never inevitable. You had choices to make within the rules of the game." Wayne pointed at Blake's piece. "You took a risk and left that guy open on the five position, and it may have cost you the game.

"The rules of the game, like God's law of sowing and reaping, don't change — though our choices can affect our outcome. And of course, in backgammon and in all of life, there's God's Sovereignty involved as well — to keep us from ever getting too smug in our thinking."

Wayne hoped some of what he said was making sense. However, it was as much for his own benefit as it was for his son's that he was verbalizing these thoughts.

Blake rolled his dice. "Double sixes again, Dad! You're going to have some tough choices to make." Blake beamed as he moved his pieces around the board with zeal.

Wayne smiled in his heart, and sighed, "That's true, son. That's true."

"Pizza!" Both of his girls now stood in front of Wayne and Blake, boxes in hand, ready to engage in imaginary barter.

"Decisions, decisions," Wayne said playfully, shooting a smile at Blake. "Now who has the peanut butter pizza?"

The girls twisted with giggles. "Daaad."

86

"TONY VENEZIANO, who do you say Jesus is?" Wayne and Tony were standing knee–deep in a stream. On the bank were the disciples Tony had come to know and love.

"He's LORD. Lord of heav'n and earth. He is the Son of the Living God. And today, I'm makin' a vow with Him that I will make him my Lord and follow Him for the rest of my life!"

A series of "Amens" and "All rights" exploded from the bank.

"Tony, are you ready to die?"

"Ready ta die and ta *live*!"

More cheers.

"Tony Veneziano, based on your choice to surrender your life to Jesus and be washed in His blood, and by the authority of our Brother and Lord Jesus Christ, I bury you in the name of the Father, the Son, and the Holy Spirit. Enjoy, for a billion years, the forgiveness of your sins and the deposit of the Holy Spirit to protect and guide and teach you."

SPLASH! Claps! Cheers!

As Tony came up out of the water, he threw his arms around Wayne and gave him a big bear hug. Tears of joy escaped from Tony's eyes as he whispered to Wayne, "Thanks, man. Thanks." Then Tony tackled Wayne.

"What are you doing?"

"Well, I read in my Bible that they *both* went down into the water! Right?" Wayne succumbed and went under.

Songs filled the air as various saints welcomed Tony into the family of God. "I'm so glad I'm free, I'm so glad I'm free..." swelled the musical chorus.

The flock of believers made their way up the hill into Steve Parker's backyard. "Isn't God great?" George said to Steve.

Steve smiled broadly at George. His whole countenance said, "Amen!"

"Hey, George," Amy called from across the lawn, "I got a letter today that I think you might like to take a look at." George was taken back at Amy's excitement. She was bubbling.

"It must have been quite a letter. Who was it from?" George asked.

"Rick!" Amy reached into her pocket and pulled out an opened envelope. "I sent him a short note with some pictures of Hope over a month ago, and he has finally broken the silence."

"You're kidding! Can I read it?"

"That's why I brought it," she teased.

George's hands almost trembled as he quickly glanced at the beginning of the letter. It had been so long since they had heard from Rick, he had given up on hearing from him again.

Dear Amy,

I am very, very sorry I haven't written or called. I don't know why you and George have continued to send me letters

291

of encouragement when I have been so rude and cold to both of you. Thank you so much for sending the pictures of Hope! She's beautiful! I thought my heart was going to melt, and I really regretted not being there.

I've been doing a lot of thinking lately and have begun to try to pray again. I've planted a lot of bad seeds and lost a lot of ground. I hope it's not too late for me. Please ask everyone to pray for me every day, if they'd be willing. I hope we can all talk more soon...

As George continued reading, the emotion of the moment surged. The small circle of saints embraced and offered a heartfelt prayer of thanksgiving for this window back into Rick's life. They were grateful because it seemed his heart was drawn to the Father, rather than to some worldly sense of guilt or chivalry. There was a hearty and tearful, "Amen."

The solemn moment was interrupted once again as Carolyn let out a cry from her edge of the circle. "Look, Amy, she's walking!"

All heads turned to see. Little Hope tottered off balance, pressing on toward the sound of her mother's voice. Amy called to her daughter who was struggling against the contours of the lawn, trying to make her way across the circle.

"You can do it, Hope. Hang in there. Walk to me, walk to Mommy." Amy's eager tone was echoed by the rest of the backyard onlookers as little Hope made her first trip on foot toward her mother's outstretched arms.

"One, two, three..." Ted and Carolyn led the count, the excitement building with each step.

An eager round of applause punctuated Hope's arrival into her mother's arms. Amy beamed at the unexpected surprise.

"I can't believe how much she has grown," Carolyn cooed. "She will be running soon."

"Oh, don't grow her up so quickly, now," Amy chastised playfully. "I want to enjoy her."

"I have a song that's been on my mind all day," Teresa offered. "Can we sing *Sovereign King*?"

A chorus of deep, genuine gratitude erupted from the small band of happy saints and echoed through the neighborhood. It was clearly a day of Sovereign beginnings.

THIS BOOK ENDS HERE, but like the book of Acts, this writing is intended as a plea for YOU to continue this journey. You write the chapters that are to come. Add your life and Church experience to this book — for the Glory of God and the advance of His life's work in the Church.

"Go ye therefore..."

PLEASE READ

Epilogue

THERE ARE TWO THINGS about our story that we feel compelled to mention. If we did not mention these things, then on the surface this novel could be somewhat misleading.

It was our aim in this story to paint a picture. We wanted to "whet your appetite" by giving you a taste of what the Holy Journey **toward** Christianity was supposed to be like. And *can* be like — and *will* be like again.

We also wanted you to see, and to feel, that it is worth it! We don't need to live like Esau — satisfied with a measly bowl of stew — when we've been promised the Blessings of living in the New Covenant. We wanted to inspire your faith and urge you to GO FOR IT!

But in the process of telling this story, we had to take some poetic license.

FIRST: The spiritual growth of the main characters.

In our experience, the quality and depth of growth depicted in this story does not usually happen this fast. The last chapter of Galatians teaches that in order to reap a harvest of spiritual life, we must sow bountifully to please the Spirit.

Unless our God were to stretch out his hand and speed up the process (which He has done before and could do again), the growth depicted in this book would need to come the "hard way": through time, fire, equipping, and planting lots and lots of good seeds. But to depict all of that would take another seven thousand pages. And while the Wisdom from Heaven that certain characters seem to instantly possess usually comes the hard way (over some time, with "constant use," "equipping," pain, prayer and experience)...the **lifestyle** of consecration to Jesus should happen **immediately.** This is a product of true conversion (Acts 2:36–47) when proper, gifted leadership is available to help "compact" (Ephesians 4:11–16 KJV). This brings us to our next point.

SECOND: The necessity for gifted leadership.

The quality of relationships depicted between the main characters of our story is almost extinct today. And the level depicted is far short of what God is really after. We have portrayed a group of sincere, devoted disciples who are just starting down the road of learning how to be a family, with Jesus as their King.

It would be unfair to whet your appetite for the life of God's Church without telling you that what we have described is not enough! Sincerity, courage, commitment, and even true regeneracy (though rare) is not enough for the body of Christ to be "joined and knitted together by every supporting ligament" as Ephesians four says we can be.

These kinds of close, light–walking, fun, free, deep, committed, satan-threatening, Jesus–centered relationships only come about when there is true, heaven–sent leadership to establish them! And believe me, we are NOT speaking of clergy when we say leadership! The idea of a "leader" with a title of "the Pastor" or "the Minister" or "Reverend" or "Father" or even "Brother so–and–so" is not only foreign to the New Testament — it is forbidden by Jesus Himself! We speak of an organic ("in the midst," "among") gifting from Heaven, that God bestows amongst the Saints — NOT an "official" anything! That would be unbiblical and obviously far less fruitful than God's plan about where leadership comes from.

The same section in Ephesians chapter four that talks about the maturity and depth of relationship possible in the Body of Christ, also mentions the tools necessary to reach those ends: *Gifted leadership.* Without gifted leadership, we will continue to be "tossed to and fro" and we will never fully experience true "joined and knittedness."

So please don't treat this as just a "story." Instead, join together with us in crying out to the Lord of the harvest for Heaven–sent workers (as Jesus asked us to do in Luke 10). We need them desperately. Join with us and others in every country that desire love–obedience to Jesus in our everyday lives and relationships. This is **NOT** about "a different way to have Church". This **IS** about a radical call to allow Jesus to rule and reign over every person, every home, every Church, every gathering...every moment. And it's a call for all of us to take responsibility as a "Kingdom of priests" to wrestle to help everyone else do that too! (Gal 4:19, etc.)

In the meantime — even though the gifts that the Body of Christ needs to fulfill her destiny may not be fully in place — Please, Please, Please, Please, Please — never settle for less!

King David found out that God was not going to allow him to "build" the House of God (the Temple). Instead, he could only gather the materials for construction. The task of "building" would fall to his descendants. Nevertheless, he remained faithful and never lowered the Standard by pretending the Temple wasn't important anyway. God's House and Work remained precious to him — despite the Sovereign limitations. He was, as he said himself, content to be a "doorkeeper" in God's House. God's House and God's Presence were everything to him — as they were to Jesus. How about you?

May you continue to look to Jesus, the Starter and Finisher of our faith.